Edith Pargeter was a distinguished author of historical fiction. Her work includes the *Brothers of Gwynedd* quartet and *A Bloody Field by Shrewsbury* as well as the *Heaven Tree* trilogy. Under the pseudonym Ellis Peters she wrote the best-selling medieval whodunnits featuring George Felse detective series. She lived in Shropshire, until her death in October 1995.

Also by Ellis Peters:

EDITH PARGETER

The Scarlet Seed

WARNER FUTURA

A *Warner Futura* Book

First published in Great Britain in 1963
by William Heinemann Ltd

Published in 1987 by Futura
Reprinted 1987, 1989

This edition published by Warner Futura in 1992
Reprinted in 1994, 1995, 1996, 1997

Copyright © Edith Pargeter 1963

The moral right of the author has been asserted.

A CIP catalogue record for this book
is available from the British Library

ISBN 0 7515 0475 0

Printed and bound in Great Britain by Clays Ltd, St Ives plc

Warner Futura
A Division of
Little, Brown and Company (UK)
Brettenham House
Lancaster Place
London WC2E 7EN

In January 1234 Richard and he (Llewelyn) devastated the border far and wide,
making their power felt as far as Shrewsbury.

> Sir J. E. Lloyd: *A History of
> Wales from the Earliest Times
> to the Edwardian Conquest*

Wendover, B.T. and Ann.C.MS.B. mention the burning of Clun, Oswestry and
the Teme valley, and the capture of an unknown 'castell hithoet'. The last-named
appears as 'Castell Coch' in B.T., but his castle was in Llewelyn's own territory of
Powys Wenwynwyn.

> Footnote to the above

CHAPTER ONE

Parfois, Shrewsbury: *August* 1232

The blunted tourney swords clanged in mid-air, shivering the sunlight in sullen blue splinters. The shock jarred Harry from wrist to shoulder, but he held his grip doggedly, and slid his opponent's blade clear of his head by all the inches he could gain. If that stroke had got home he would have been stunned at the least, even if he had escaped being carried from the exercise-ground with a broken head. Old Nicholas Stury never played gently. Sometimes Harry had suspected that he enjoyed bruising and battering the young gentlemen-at-arms who came under his tuition, and certainly there were several among them who were afraid of him.

They circled with the impetus of the swing and the parry, changing ground in two quick steps. The ring of intent faces swung with them, the hushed voices muttered in speculation and excitement. Harry knew them too well to suppose that he had their good will in this bout. They used him tolerantly enough, some among them had even grown to like him in the long months he had spent in their company, but when it came to a passage of arms they could not wish success to the Welshman and the prisoner, not even against Stury whom they heartily detested. Let old Nicholas be what he would, he was of Parfois, and one of them, and they were for him against the stranger.

He was fond of that full, swinging stroke at the head, was Nicholas, perhaps he liked to see it terrify before it got home or was desperately parried. Give him time, and he'd try it again, and Harry knew more than one way of dealing with it. He wove warily to the right, clashed aside a couple of probing strokes that were meant only to mislead, and essayed a few of his own no less guilefully; and then it came, fast and hard, intended to club him into senselessness through the padded exercise helm. Instead of flinching away from it and flinging up his blade to slide it from his head, this time Harry crouched and sprang in under it, and as he darted past his opponent, right side to right side, swung his sword back-handed and thumped Stury in the ribs so heartily that he fetched a great grunt out of him, and then, for good measure, dug his rounded point into the stretched armpit in token that he could have pierced him there at will had this play been earnest.

The young men roared honest acknowledgement. One of the pages perched astride the sill of the nearest armoury window shrilled: 'A hit!' with an ungrudging glee that warmed Harry's heart; it seemed he had at least one partisan among them. Walter Langholme, my lord's own body-squire, echoed the cry with authority and, when Stury pressed in again, advanced a tilting spear between them and prodded him in the breast with the three nodules of its blunted end.

'Let be, that's enough. Talvace had the better of you, Nick, you may as well own it.'

A hard enough thing for a seasoned master-of-arms to do at any time; harder still when his too apt pupil is an alien prisoner, and a mere stripling of seventeen at that, kept kicking his heels in the household at its lord's whim, and allowed his share in the games of the young men as an act of grace.

'He barely touched me,' protested Stury, pushing down the tilting spear from his broad chest with a hand like a projection of the sandstone that held up Parfois. 'Call that a hit? If my foot hadn't slipped he'd never have got below my stroke.'

Harry turned away into the shadow of the armoury and dropped his sword on the stone ledge that ran beneath the high windows. He unlaced his padded helm, as squat and plain as the ceremonial tourney helms were lofty and elaborate, and emerged flushed and panting into the air. The page in the window dropped a napkin down to him and he wiped the sweat from his face and neck gratefully, and flung over his shoulder:

'Give me another bout, then, if you dispute my point. It's all one to me, I can do as much again.'

That was no wise thing to say in the circumstances; it roused the local loyalty even of those who liked him best, and brought a howl of aggressive acceptance of his offer. And to tell the truth, he was by no means sure that he could make good his boast. To turn the tables once might be all very well, it was merely a matter of patience and caution; but when Stury was forewarned, as now, and his blood well up after one setback, he was no man to be meddled with. But it was too late to think better of it now; he'd said it and he must stand to it. He picked up the pitcher of water that stood on the stone ledge and drank thirstily, while they wrangled loudly over the issue, and Langholme thumped the tilting spear against the ground and bellowed for order.

From the shade of the archway which led into the inner ward of the castle a loud, clear voice said: 'It was Talvace's win, no question. Who disputes it?'

The clamour died instantly. How he had made himself heard through the babel of voices Harry could not guess. Perhaps the first words were felt rather than heard, cutting their way to the stretched nerves of awe as a small, sharp sound can set the teeth on edge; but by the end of even so brief an utterance he had created a silence about himself, and every man in the group before the armoury was respectfully on his feet. When their lord came among them they looked only at him, with an attentive anxiety to which Harry had long become accustomed.

He thought now: I am the only man here who is not afraid of him. And then, correcting a too hasty estimate: No, perhaps Langholme has no fear of him any longer, though I'm sure he had once. He's been close about his body so long now that he's outlived his fear, and they've come by a sort of understanding of each other that puts it out of mind. Walter has no ambitions towards knighthood, and wants nothing from him more than he has, and my lord Isambard knows there's no self-seeking in him, and puts a value on him I

7

doubt if he sets on any of these others.

He watched the tall, lean figure of the lord of Parfois walk towards them at leisure from the shadow of the archway, through the silence he himself had made. He did not hurry for them, as he had never yet checked or hurried for kings. He had cast off surcoat and cotte in the August heat, and unlaced the collar of his loose linen shirt from the gaunt but erect throat in which the cords stood taut as bowstrings from the brown flesh. He loved the sun; he had torn deep lancet windows through his grandsire's tower walls to let it in to his chosen apartments; and it seemed that the sun was a good friend to him in return, for yearly the summer burned him into a dark recollection of beauty, stripping from him with his Flemish brocades fifteen at least of his sixty-eight years. It could not put back the black into his iron-grey hair, that coiled thick as a boy's on his head, but it gilded and polished the shapely, dominant bones of cheek and jaw, and the weathered cliff of his forehead, and warmed the winter stiffness out of him, so that it seemed right he should move like a yearling roe, and glare like the sun in the zenith in a red August.

'As clean a hit as ever I saw,' he said. 'Man, he could have cut the heart out of you. You've taught him too well, he knows your every move.'

'He'd never have touched me, my lord, had we been out on the grass. But the hit I don't dispute.'

He could not, thought Harry grimly, with Isambard staring him in the eye and laying down so absolutely what was truth. His own obstinacy stiffened in him against all of them; for essentially they were all his enemies, and he was damned if he'd conciliate any one of them.

'My lord, I've offered him a new match if he's not satisfied. I'll not stand on what he claims to be no more than a stroke of luck. If I can repeat it we may come by a just name for it.'

He stood passing the pitcher from hand to hand, pouring a little cold water over his wrists and letting them steam dry in the hot air of mid-morning. He knew he was being foolish, but he was sick and tired of being wise after seven months of going patiently and abiding without offence the constrictions of his isolated position among them. If Stury could prove on his body that he was the better man, then let him do it. Harry would not go back a step for him until he was felled by force. Nor for Isambard himself. If all his household were afraid of him, Harry was not of his household. Let them see that being the alien and the prisoner gave him a stature greater and not less than theirs. He looked steadily back into the hollow dark eyes that studied him unsmiling across the circle, and wiped his hands slowly, flexing the tingling fingers ready for the hilt again, though the shock of that one harsh impact had not yet passed out of them.

'With your leave, my lord? I'm ready when he is.'

Isambard had taken the tourney sword from Stury and gripped its hilt with a long, emaciated hand, pressing the rounded point into the ground and leaning his weight upon it in an experimental thrust.

'Not my length, but it will serve. If you're so ready and fain, Harry, you may give me the benefit of a few minutes' exercise.'

So he won't have old Nicholas made a fool of, thought Harry, without surprise or any great resentment, and I'm to get a thrashing for it by another way. Well, let's take it further, since he offers me the first such meeting he's ever condescended to put in my way. He braced his sturdy feet squarely into the ground and lifted a bright, inimical stare to Isambard's face, a naked challenge that might well escape reading by any other present, but would surely speak clearly enough to him.

'But, my lord, there's nothing at issue between you and me; it was Master Stury who wanted satisfaction.'

He felt all the young squires of Parfois shift and grin at that, understandably gratified at hearing him back out so hastily. Someone close at Isambard's elbow sniggered. Harry let them enjoy the taste of it, and never lowered his eyes. Isambard himself had neither moved nor smiled; he balanced the heavy sword and watched Harry across the runnels of splintered light, waiting without impatience. He

9

knew there was more to come.

'But if you please to try me with unblunted swords, my lord, I'll gladly give you a bout as best I can.'

They gasped at that, aghast at his insolence and bristling against him for the dignity of Parfois; marvelling, too, at his hardihood, and sparing him a grudging morsel of pity for his folly. His own heart contracted a little at the stark sound of it, but he kept a stony front and waited. Only Isambard gave no sign of having heard more than a current remark any one of them there present might have made. His long fingers, handling the clumsy hilt with absent delicacy, never started or tightened; the movement of his head as he looked up over the blade was smooth and slow, even the long, thoughtful stare he bent upon Harry's face gave nothing away to those who watched him so narrowly, and waited for him to crush the impudent boy or kill him, according as his humour led him.

Harry expected a curt refusal, and a part of his mind, honest in sensible physical fear, would have welcomed it. But the great eyes, burning tranquilly in their clear pits of polished bone, smiled at him faintly and held no anger or impatience. Not that that made it any safer to have meddled with him; he could kill just as well without either.

'Bring a pair of combat swords, Walter.'

His voice was placid. No one dared so much as look consternation while he denied it. Langholme went without a word, tramping heavily into the armoury.

'No haste, Harry,' said Isambard, seeing the boy reach for his discarded helm. 'You're hardly breathed yet, take your time.'

'You'll put on harness, my lord?' said Harry, quick to anticipate a slight and take offence at it.

'Oh, be content, I'll match you piece for piece.' He turned over the pile of leather hauberks with a casual foot and, discarding them as short of his measure, strode after Langholme into the dim coolness of the armoury.

When he was out of earshot they let out their pent breath in a gust of hushed abuse and advice at Harry, those who had some liking for him cursing him roundly for a fool to tempt death so wantonly and urging him to back out even now, however abjectly, those who had none promising him with satisfaction more than he had bargained for, at least a humiliating lesson in swordsmanship, at worst a maiming. None of them thought of death. They took it for granted that Isambard wanted him alive, since he had kept him so for nearly two years when he might very well have ended him; and they were no less sure that, since death was no part of his plans for the boy, the boy himself could not invoke it. Isambard could play with him as he pleased, beat him into repentance of his presumption, let him a little blood, mark him for life if the fancy took him, and then let him go.

Harry shut his ears, hunched his shoulders against abuse and advice together, and waited dourly, scrubbing the sense back into his tingling hand. What did they know of the good reasons he had for being afraid of what he had done? They could not even recognize what had happened before their very eyes. Only he knew how far in earnest was this apparent and dangerous game, and so far from shrinking from it, he felt his bowels burn in him for desire. There was fear in him, too, the fear of falling short as well as the sane man's fear of death; but these he would not acknowledge, and before Isambard came back from the armoury they had burned out of his body, and left only the molten lust of hatred and pride in possession of him.

Langholme flattened the length of a tilting spear against the crowding breasts that hemmed the ground, and enlarged the clear, trodden space for them. They were both long in the reach, the boy by five or six inches taller than his father before him, though still short by some three or four of Isambard's commanding height, and his young flesh built upon lighter, slenderer bones. At least let him have room to give back, if my lord was bent on punishing. Langholme swung the spear, none too gently, and was not happy. Who could have foreseen this in a little play no rougher than usual?

'Yes, give us room,' said Isambard, flicking round him

11

from under the open visor of the exercise helm a sharp glance that moved them back more effectively than Walter's spear. 'And take this trash from under our feet, Nick.' He kicked aside the pile of leather and cloth hauberks, and watched them hurried away out of his sight. 'Walter, you'll stand marshal for us. So, Harry, are you ready to guard your head?'

'To the first hit, my lord?' ventured Langholme hopefully, eyeing his master's face before the visor closed.

'As Harry will have it, I'm content.' Shadow covered the brilliant eyes, and in the easy voice there was nothing to be read.

'To the mastery,' said Harry, carefully holding back the word 'death', that was like a secret between the two of them there, and not to be shown to any other.

It was on them now, no way out but one, and wide enough only for one. Langholme dropped the truncheon of a lance for the onset, and they moved in with a double, weaving, essaying swiftness, like one man before a mirror. The ring of staring faces, the girdle of avid eyes, went out like quenched lights, the taut murmur of voices that dared not speak aloud lurched away into silence; and they were left alone in the world, as in a sense they had always been alone in it, confronting each other in arms, from the moment of their first meeting, the boy with his long score to settle for his father's sake, the man with his heavy toll of debts to be paid.

Watching the balanced motions of the long arm that probed his defences, Harry rehearsed within his mind the heads of his hatred, and steadied his heart against the hope of vengeance. You are he who brought my father here, with his foster-brother Adam Boteler, to be your master-mason and build you a great church. Did he fail of giving you what you asked? Did he default in his service? You know he did not! It was in the church I first met with you, I saw you stare upon my father's work, and you knew its perfection. You yourself have owned it to me. In what particular did he play you false, then? How did he offend? He took a captured

Welsh princeling, a child of nine, out of your hands when you would have done him to death at King John's orders, and sent him in charge of Adam back to Prince Llewelyn his foster-father. That was all! Cheated King John of Owen ap Ivor's little body, and you of a morsel of your ghastly fealty that you loathed and yet would not forego. And came back and delivered himself into your power, because he had sworn not to forsake you until his master-work was finished. And finish it he did, in chains, and when the last pile and hurdle of the scaffolding came down you brought him out before his own church to a traitor's death, a fearful death. 'That heart of yours,' you said, 'I'll have living out of your body – ' And so you would have done, but that Madonna Benedetta whom you brought from Paris with you, Madonna Benedetta whom you loved, went about secretly to find him a better end, quick and clean, at the hands of her archer, John the Fletcher. And even then, even then you could not let him be! Nor her, because she loved him and saved him. You stripped her living and him dead, and bound them fast and sent them down the Severn in flood, to rot in each other's arms for ever, if John the Fletcher had not drawn them ashore and given the one life and the other quiet burial at Strata Marcella. You can never have done, short of your devil's will. You picked up her traces again, with my poor little mother still feeble from bearing me, where Benedetta had hidden us, and hunted the three of us over the border into Gwynedd, to a refuge you never foresaw, to Prince Llewelyn's maenol and Prince Llewelyn's fostering.

And did you think I would not come back? Did you think you were clear of the last Talvace? That the story could end so?

Yet he had made the assay too soon, climbing the escarpment of sandstone at fifteen to hide himself in the church, until he could break into Parfois by stealth in search of his vengeance. And in the church they had met, and in the church he had done his best to kill, to kill at all costs, even if he himself must die to achieve it. He remembered that bitter struggle in the triforium, the desperate leap to take his

13

enemy with him over the edge, thirty feet down to the flagstones below. He felt the gaunt hand twisting mercilessly in
his collar, gripping cotte and shirt and flesh and all, dragging him back to fling him down against the wall, beneath
the corbels his father had carved. He remembered, with a
ferocity that brought the blood stinging now in his smitten
cheek, three brisk, deliberate blows, from that same hard
palm that gripped the hilt before him now, and sent the point
flickering low to test his guard. He heard the cool voice say:
'That's for despising your own life, fool.' And then the cell
below the tower, and the long captivity, the long baiting
that was not over yet.

They had never fought but that once; never until this
day had Isambard consented to meet him so again.

All the accumulated grudges of the years gathered into
Harry's sword hand and flowed into the steel. If he squan-
dered this hour there would be no second such hour for him.
The enormous weight of the occasion made his arm tremble
and ache for a moment, and then fused hand and weapon
and arm into one intelligent lightning.

The swords touched and slid away, hissing, whirled and
clanged again head-high, and parted again harmlessly. How
often he had watched Isambard at sword-play, and seen the
formidable face graver and stiller than at other times,
measuring as it were another man's efforts, not his own.
Now he glimpsed the eyes that held him fixed through the
grille of the visor, and saw them smiling. This stroke he
knew, he had seen it a hundred times and admired its cunning, studying in his own mind how to deal with it. Now he
dealt, and his eye was sure and his arm competent. And the
eyes confronting him burned to deep red, and laughed. They
laughed still as Harry lunged and swung, following the
parry closer than the echo of the steel, and his point grazed
Isambard's shoulder as he leaped away from the stroke.

The ring of faces, dizzily reappearing for an instant out of
the void that circled them, breathed amazement and wonder
in a great, shivering sigh, and again vanished.

There was blood in Harry's mouth, he swallowed it and

14

sickened; but he had only bitten his tongue in the stress of his lust. And he had lost the opportunity to follow up that unexpected success. Never wait to see the result of your stroke, drive in another one after it, and another, before he can believe in the first. He's old, sixty-eight, an old man, you can tire him out and wear him down until his hand sags or his foot falters. He knows you mean to do it. He consented. He said: 'I am content.' To the mastery, you said, but he heard the word you did not say, and he said: 'I am content.'

Isambard's long arm swung fast and hard at his head. He was late in parrying, but he reached it. The flat of the blade bruised his shoulder as he hurled the blow away from him. The stunned muscles shrieked, and he swallowed his heart and leaped back to draw one breath at least out of range. The spurt of panic burned out instantly into steely coldness. The flurry of blows that drove hard after him were put off as solidly as though a rock covered him, and he would not withdraw another step from his enemy. His eye was as quick as the old man's, his arm as steady, and surely he could out-last him. All he lacked was the long experience, the recession of battlefields shadowy behind him, the terrible wit that could bring new strokes from the very revulsion of the ones freshly parried, the invention that was never lost for a surprise. Watch and be ready, no other way. Remember all you have seen of him, these two years. And if he wavers for an instant, wrest the bout from him then, for it will never happen but once.

Even on that once he did not rely, and it was well, for Isambard did not release him for a moment from the intensity of his concentration. Hand and eye and light-ranging foot, he gave him the best that was in him; and the critical glance that directed the sword laughed and approved the mirrored intensity that glared back at him and clashed steel so imperturbably against steel, waiting with such ferocious patience for the single chance.

Sweat running on them both now, the arm muscles groaning at the weight and the exertion, the arched thighs straining, even the vaults of the braced feet a stretched articulation of pain; but neither of them would show any sign. The jarring shocks of sword against sword shivered through the nerves of shoulder and side, but still eye crossed eye warily, following every insinuating stroke without pause.

The ring of faces had swung back into vision, the murmur had grown feverish, almost fearful. Langholme shifted uneasily, stretched senses tingling, in agony whether to meddle or leave ill alone. At the edge of his consciousness Harry was aware of these things, but he had no attention to spare for them. It was Isambard who felt the disquiet at his back, and for one instant flashed a glance aside to warn them off from touching what they did not understand.

Harry caught the infinitesimal shift of the head, the momentary release from the eyes that fixed him. He was in like a fury, his sword flashing cross-wise, and lunging beneath the startled blade that leaped with recovering skill to beat him off. There was no parry left within Isambard's reach, fast as he was, he could do no more than leap back once and again before the onslaught to get arm-room to stand the boy away from him. And Harry pressed after, fierce on his advantage, driving them both by the weight of his attack into the ring of appalled spectators that broke and gave them place.

And suddenly he was down, Isambard was down! A long pace back, close to the wall now, and the trailing cord of a laced helm rolled under his foot, and he was down, on knee and hip along the beaten earth, the sword half-torn from his hand. He fell with the expert lightness of a cat, he gathered his lean legs under him with a cat's startling speed, but Harry's rush had flung the boy astride him before he could rise, and Harry's point was at his throat.

A moment they hung thus arrested, and the world froze round them into such a stillness and silence that they heard the creeping of the sweat in their eyebrows, and the tightening of their sinews as the boy gripped and braced his blade, and the man took fast hold of the ground and held still for the blow.

Then every held breath had broken in a gusty cry, and Langholme was lunging to come at them, with Nicholas Stury hot on his heels; but there was no need for them, the thing was over. Harry had swung away and walked back on tremulous legs to the extreme of the ground, and was waiting there with his point in the earth for his enemy to rise. A clamour of voices rushed to protest that the vantage was no vantage, that but for the cord my lord would not have fallen. A dozen arms were offered eagerly to help him to rise. As though he needed any help from them! He was on his feet before they could touch him, stamping the earth experimentally and putting off solicitude with contempt and impatience.

Young Thomas Blount, foremost as ever in courting favour, cried in his high, provocative voice: 'You'd do better to keep him to hammer and punch, my lord. He even fights like a stone-mason.'

Harry heard that, but distantly, and it added nothing considerable to the score he had marked up long ago against Thomas. It was doubtful if Isambard heard it at all. He stood with the recovered sword dangling from one hand, staring across the circle of stamped ground at the boy who waited with head stubbornly lowered.

'It was no vantage,' said Langholme, in a voice that shook with the reverberations of an excitement already ebbing into unreality. Give them time, they'd come to think they had dreamed the point steady at their lord's throat, the tightening fingers and the tensed bodies. He'd overrun, and could not halt short of his fallen opponent, that was all.

'I've claimed none,' said Harry shortly.

'Then, my lord, if you're content – '

Walter wanted it over: from the first he'd had no liking for it. He alone, perhaps, of all those watchful hangers-on, felt something of the tearing current that moved beneath the quiet surface, dragging those two antagonists, bound by hatred as close as lovers, headlong downstream and out of reach.

'Are you content, Harry?' said Isambard. The voice had

no implications; he would not prompt him.

'My lord, neither of us has yet had the mastery.'

Fool, fool, he thought, furious with his own quaking body, feeble now with bewilderment and reaction, you can hardly hold the hilt. What use is it to invite him to kill you? But he shut his teeth on the words, and stiffened his legs under him, and would not withdraw. He owed his enemy a death for a death, nobody should say he grudged him his due.

'As you will,' said Isambard, and the shadow of a smile flared in his eyes for a moment, as he marked in the level of the stubborn voice the tremor that did not show in the braced legs. 'Guard your head!'

Harry did his best. His body obeyed him, but with less conviction than he would have liked, as though it no longer believed in the bitterness of his intent. Three times he fought off the probing blade, late and anxiously, contending with the quivering of his own wrist no less than the hard certainty of his opponent's. Then he got his second wind, and trod the ground more vigorously. It should not be all for nothing. It must not. The old man was surely tiring. He failed to press home, his movements were slowing, he held off from too close an engagement.

Harry drew breath hard, and closed. Isambard gave ground by one measured pace, and the boy followed, encouraged, and putting aside a tentative stroke that felt for his left side, swung suddenly with all his weight. Isambard sprang in beneath the blade, locked hilt under hilt, and wrenched the boy off-balance across his braced thigh. There was no haste about the final execution. He stepped back coolly, swung a measured round blow at the blade as Harry lurched to keep his legs under him, and struck it dispassionately and with no wasted force out of the boy's hand. It clattered three yards away upon the ground, and the blade sang aloud like a broken bow-string.

For the second time a huge, concerted sigh shuddered away after the snapped tension. Content, this time, with the right ending. And young Thomas Blount laughed. High and

18

clear and deliberate, a peal of laughter as nicely calculated as a girl's. It sent the echoes flying, and rang gallingly in Harry's ears as he tramped wearily across to pick up his sword from the ground. He lifted a closed and shuttered face; Thomas should get no satisfaction from him.

Isambard swung on his heel, the sword still in his hand.

'Ah, Thomas! You found this a poor showing?' Voice and movement had the suddenness of a whip-lash, but his face was amiable and smiling. 'Then come and show him his errors. Come, give him a lesson in swordsmanship, it would please me to see you matched.' He reversed the sword in his hand and held it out by the blade. 'Harry'll not refuse to learn from a master.'

Between the shoulders of the men-at-arms Harry saw Thomas's face fallen into pale consternation. He essayed a smile that sat badly askew upon his smooth features, and faded blankly when Isambard gave no sign of withdrawing the proffered hilt. All heads had turned; a good many of the men-at-arms were grinning. One should be very careful with laughter; it so easily shifts to the other side of one's face.

'My lord,' protested Thomas, mustering what remained of his assurance, 'he's in no condition to fight another bout. Look at him! It would be no fair match.'

'He'll waive the point. Harry, have you yet the breath for another encounter?'

'Gladly, my lord!' said Harry, his face bright and grim.

'There, my bold heart, you hear that? Come, let me see you school him.'

'My lord,' said Thomas, backing away from the hilt with a nervous grin fixed on his pale face, 'he must needs consent if you order. He can lose no glory by such a match, and I can get none. My lord, you would not ask me to fight a tired and bruised man?'

His eyes were uneasy, but his voice was bold in its indignant innocence. Thomas would always find a way to slide gracefully out of every situation that was not to his liking, and never yet had his master failed to laugh and let him make good his escape. Why should it be different this time?

19

'Well said, my noble Thomas, my pattern of chivalry. I could not ask you to do so rude an injury to your honour.' He stood smiling a little, not kindly, and tossed the sword from hand to hand. 'Then we'll see you matched at a more suitable time,' he said, the smile twisting suddenly into an oblique and devilish grin. 'Tomorrow, when Harry is as fresh as you, and you both have glory to gain or lose.'

A moment he looked his most indulged page in the eye to drive home the threat, and then turned and held out the sword imperiously for Walter to take from him. 'Remind me, Thomas,' he said, and flung away towards the archway of the inner ward. The short bark of his laughter, hard and clear, was blown back to them over his shoulder.

His withdrawal had sent the blood back into Thomas's cheeks in a wave of relief, but that laugh ripened the rising wave into a crimson surge of mortification. The heavy breath that hissed round him as the tension broke resolved itself unmistakably into a quiet titter at his expense, and the broad grins of the men-at-arms bit like acid at his sore dignity.

'Ah, be easy, lad,' said Langholme, shouldering the combat swords resignedly, 'he won't hold you to it. You keep your mouth shut and keep out of his way tomorrow, and he'll be pleased to forget. He never meant to drive it to the issue.'

More galling comfort never was uttered. Thomas bit at lips suddenly quivering with temper and spite, and looked round wildly at his grinning compeers. He had enjoyed a favourite's ascendancy among them, was he to let it slip out of his fingers now without a struggle? He struck out recklessly to reassert himself, before the urgent moment could escape him and leave him discredited for ever.

'And well he did not! He may lower himself to play with labourers and stone-hewers if he pleases, but it's not for him to ask it of others.'

His voice was high and hard with rage; it carried to Harry's indifferent ears, and swung him round in a momentary hesitation whether to resent it. Did Thomas Blount matter enough, that a man should do him the honour of quarrelling with him? Sometimes Harry had suspected that not affection but tolerant disdain accounted for Isambard's attitude to Thomas, and the long rein on which he let him run. And what Isambard could shrug off from his consciousness, that Harry could let pass, too. Why should he dissipate on frivolities like Thomas the concentration of hatred that belonged only to his master? He turned on his heel dourly to tramp away.

'Stone-hewers, and rank even at their craft,' said Thomas rashly, seeing the brown homespun back turned squarely on him, and misreading the signs. 'Stone-butchers, like father like son!'

That brought Harry back, without haste but with head formidably lowered. Thomas did not give back before him. Langholme was there, and a dozen more of the elders, they would not let the affair come to anything.

'You were pleased to mention my father,' said Harry civilly. 'The exact matter I think I did not hear well. Be good enough to say it over again for me.'

There were three yards of space between them, and Langholme already had a shoulder thrust forward warningly, and an eye commanding the master-of-arms to be ready on the other side. Thomas weighed chances, and made his bid.

'I called him a stone-butcher, like his son after him.'

He had miscalculated the degree of protection to be expected from the elders. Langholme, fended off by a lunging elbow, reeled several yards across the exercise ground, and Thomas Blount was on his back in the dust with Harry on top of him. They rolled and snarled like fighting dogs, and before Nicholas Stury and a dozen more had got a grip on them and torn them bodily apart, Isambard was back among them like a thunder-cloud, red-eyed and stormy-browed.

'How's this? Will you be at each other's throats as soon as my back is turned? You were not so fain a moment since. Am I to have my wards turned into a schoolboys' brawling-ground? You, Walter, who began this? How did it fall out?'

Langholme told the tale fairly enough, and half a dozen voices joined in, retailing word for word what had passed.

'So that was the way of it,' said Isambard grimly. 'You must trust me, Thomas, there are men in the world who will not have their sires abused. I know well you have little love for yours.'

'My lord, if I said what I thought too openly, is that cause for falling on me by surprise?'

'My lord,' said Harry contemptuously, 'he was staring me in the eye when I fell upon him. Where's the surprise there?'

'You may save your breath, both of you, you have need of it. This shall be fought out and finished here and now.'

'With whatever weapons he pleases,' grunted Harry scornfully.

'With what weapons *I* please,' said Isambard, the deep fires burning tall in his eyes. 'And I please you shall fight it out with none. I'll have no killing, and no mortal damage, but you may teach each other what lessons you can with your own good arms. Three falls, and I'll see fair play.' He swept an imperious arm round the circle. 'Stand back there, and give them place. And, Walter, set them on.'

Against that voice and that face there was no possible appeal. Harry stripped off his cotte gleefully, and went to his place grinning. Thomas crept mute and reluctant to his, and shed his brocade with trembling hands. He was a year older than his opponent, and heavier, well matched with him in height and reach, but no wrestler. It took Harry no more than two minutes to down him heavily and pin him by the shoulders at Isambard's very feet.

With the first fall he forgot his own aches and exertions, with the second he outlived his anger. In the third bout he put Thomas down almost as gently as he would have dumped the youngest of his antagonists on his back at practice.

'For a stone-butcher,' said Isambard critically, 'that was very prettily done. Well, Thomas, you have what you would have. And I rede you both, let that be an ending.'

Thomas picked himself up from the ground slowly, and

slowly limped to reclaim his cotte. He was not greatly hurt, even the limp was largely for his own comfort and justification; he kept his eyes lowered from them all as he wiped the dust from his face.

A few of his fellows, some in obstinate allegiance and some in rough compassion, encircled him and made good-natured efforts to pass off his defeat with commonplaces, but he did not give them a word or a look. Only once did he look up, and that was when Isambard passed him without a glance and walked away into the inner ward; then indeed the dishevelled head lifted, the blue eyes flashed one long, half-veiled stare after the erect figure, and again were hooded. But Harry had caught the gleam beneath the large, fair eyelids, bleak and bitter as winter. This was no ending. For Thomas Blount's humiliation and loss of status no one would ever be forgiven, least of all the lord of Parfois.

Isambard came into the tracing-house at sundown, when the light lay level and long across the corner bench by the window, and lit small golden fires on every rounded brown knuckle on Harry's hands as he worked. The stone burned into a gold not so far different from that burnished skin, drawn so supply and closely over the bone, moving so rhythmically and faintly over the smoothly gloved joints. Golden hands and golden stone glowed in a single radiant focus of light, as though they had fused into one life. There was a hawk, with arched wings and stretched throat, prisoned within the stone, half-frantic to burst from its captivity; the patient hands laboured delicately at its liberation. Isambard came to his shoulder, and the boy paid him no heed. Not one light, loving stroke of the mallet on the punch rang a wry note or broke the easy rhythm.

The stone was a fragment of the last ashlars left after the church of Parfois had reached its wonderful and terrible completion, and its builder his strange and awful end. The boy handled it with love and respect, and infinite and uncharacteristic patience, for it had hardened with the years of exposure, and carving it now challenged all his half-

23

tested powers. He smoothed a thumb along the braced pinion, and blew off fine dust that settled again in a thousand glittering points of light.

'Well?' said Isambard at his shoulder. 'Were you content with your victory?'

'No, my lord.' He exchanged his punch for a finer one, and began to hollow out the stretched feathers of the hawk's wing.

'Faith, you're hard to please. Why not? You did what you would with him.'

'The bout favoured me. Thomas is too lofty to think wrestling a fit sport for a gentleman. And I could have beaten him with whatever weapons you might have allowed us.'

Isambard laughed, pushing aside the litter of tools to make room for himself on the bench. 'I take that to be a truthful word, if not a modest one.'

'You should have given us blunted tourney swords. He prides himself on his swordsmanship.'

'And you could still have beaten him black and blue? So you could, but he would have suffered all the more to satisfy your vanity. What kind of mercy is that on your enemy?' said Isambard, grinning.

Harry frowned down at his work and stood off for a moment to look at it more critically. He did not lift his eyes as he said abruptly: 'You'd best be careful of him.'

'Careful of him? Of Thomas?'

'If we had not an enemy in him before,' said Harry seriously, 'we have one now, you as well as I.'

'That gives us at least one thing in common, then, if the only one.'

He had taken up one of the fine chisels, and was playing with it absently, testing its edge with a lean brown thumb, but his eyes were steady and measuring upon Harry's face.

'Boy,' he said abruptly, 'let me understand you. As I read it, you came looking for me here, two years ago, to pay off a score you owed me for your father's death. And no fault of yours if you did not pay it at our first meeting. By

God, you did your best. All through these two years you've been waiting and hoping for as good a chance again, now that you have your growth. Have I the right of it? Did I indeed bring Master Harry to his death? Did you truly come looking for me dagger in hand, there in his church? Have I had my pleasure all these months in keeping you at heel here, and tormenting you with glimpses of liberty? Did I play you all manner of tricks to get out of you the secret of his burial place?'

'And tore him out of it,' said Harry, the mallet abruptly silent in his hand, 'like a scavenging wolf as you are.'

A cruel trick indeed Isambard had played on him that time, leading him to believe, when all persuasions and threats failed, that he had blurted out the secret in his sleep, and then setting Thomas on to him, Thomas with his candid, deceitful face and his hypocritical sympathy, to promise him escape and lead him out of Parfois by night. And he in his desperate anxiety had fallen headlong into the trap, and led them straight as a homing bird to the nameless grave under the walls of Strata Marcella. He remembered Isambard's smiling face in the moonlight, his fingers tracing the shape of the carved leaf in the stone, his assuaged voice saying: 'Take him back, he's told me what I wanted to know.'

'Ah, good! I begin to think you had clean forgotten. I see you have it as fresh in mind as the day it happened – when you swore to kill me for it. Do you remember?'

'I well remember,' said the boy grimly, and set his hands again to his work, turning a shoulder on his questioner. Piercingly clear he heard his own voice crying: 'There's no name vile enough, my lord, for creatures like you who vent their spite even on the dead.'

'And have not changed your mind?' The tapping of the mallet spaced out the silence evenly. 'Then why did you not kill me when you had the chance, like a sensible man?'

The rhythm lurched, faltered, was taken up again stubbornly.

'Do you think God is going to throw me on my knees at

your feet every day? It was ungrateful to toss his gift back in his teeth. Why am I still alive? Tell me!'

'I could not take advantage of an old man,' said Harry viciously.

'It will do you no good with me to try to offend. In the pursuit of knowledge I do not take offence easily. I *am* old. Say it over a hundred times to yourself, and still it will not make you my master with a sword, and you know it. Not yet! Why am I still here to plague you? I will know.'

'It was mere chance that you fell,' said Harry, goaded. 'I would not have your life on those terms.'

Isambard threw back his head in a short, harsh bark of laughter. 'There's a true Talvace word, at least. That I believe. In his time he would not take favours from man nor God, and you're as like him in that as one oak is to another. And yet,' he said, sharp as a lance and abruptly grave again, 'that's not the whole truth, neither. What, would you hold your hand on a battlefield, because your enemy's girth broke?'

'We were not on a battlefield,' said Harry, taking his hands from the stone with reluctance, for the light had dulled into dusk, and the gold was faded to dun. He put down his tools gently, as though too sharp a sound might have set the tranquil surface of the everyday world quaking, and let the demons of disruption through at him. Behind him the silence gathered intense and still.

'We were not?' said Isambard, low-voiced through the hush. 'Where else have you and I been since the day we met, Harry? When you looked me in the eye and invited me to something more than play do you think I did not know it was a challenge to the death? God knows you had waited for it long enough. Why did you refuse it when it fell ripe into your hand?'

The fading of the day had veiled his face, he was a gaunt shadow against the clear pallor of the window. By the utter stillness of his body, by the level and muted voice. Harry knew that he had reached the thing he had come here to say.

'You need not hold your hand,' he said deliberately,

'from any fear of consequences. I have already given orders, and bound de Guichet and Walter by oath to see them respected, that if you should kill me in fair fight there shall be no revenges. You will be held to have won your liberty fairly.'

Harry rolled down his sleeves in dogged composure, and fell to putting his tools away. 'You should have told me that before,' he said grimly.

'I'll give you another chance tomorrow.'

The moment was past, the voice already lifting to astringent mockery; in a minute more he would be flinging words again in the old fashion, every one with a sting like a whip.

'Do you not want your freedom? With the princess of Aberffraw and David your prince-brother already bedded at the abbot's town house in Shrewsbury? Not more than two hours' ride away, Harry, and only this old body between you and their arms.'

He had learned to keep his hands steady and his face mute, under whatsoever goadings; there were no sparks to be struck from him now by these means, even though his heart ached in him to think of the Princess Joan and David so close, and he helpless to go to them, or even send them a word of his love and loyalty. Did he not want his freedom! By day he could tire out his body and cloak up his mind well enough, but at night in his bed the anguish of his longing to be at liberty gripped him by the vitals and wrung him until he clenched his teeth in his forearm to solace himself with a more bearable pain.

He was seventeen, and had been mewed up here nearly two years; and the uneasy truce between England and Wales, the year's truce that bound Llewelyn's hands from reaching out to loose his foster-son, still held intact, for all the long memoranda of accusations filed by either side, and all the listed infringements, and bade fair to be extended for another year when the first was out. The envoys of King Henry and Prince Llewelyn were off-loading their pack-horses in their Shrewsbury lodgings at this very moment, and scanning their briefs ready for the meeting in Shrewsbury castle three days hence. Their business this time was merely to agree upon arrangements for the sitting of a papal court later in the year, to adjudicate upon the many allegations of border infringements. But agree they would, and come to the winter court bent on agreement, too, for King Henry had things on his mind that made it necessary to him that Wales should remain pacified, and the Prince of Aberffraw had his son's inheritance to secure in full, and must not put it in danger by a premature act of war. Yes, the truce would continue, and with it his captivity. Isambard saw to it that he was well-informed; he knew how little to expect from man.

But God, it seemed, had presented him Isambard's throat bared to his point, and he had refused the gift. And why? Did he even know? For fear of being hanged for it? He strained back to recapture the truth of that moment, but it did not seem to him that anything would have been changed, even if he had known what Isambard had just told him. And Isambard, whose every word and deed had a purpose behind it, was deploying before him still dearer enticements than merely his freedom. Only this old body between you and their arms! Harry looked for the oblique intent. He had been tempted to break faith; was he now being tempted to do murder?

'You may carry them my respectful duty and service,' he said steadily, 'when you go to the king's court tomorrow. I could not have a more punctilious messenger.'

'For the price of a word you might carry your own message,' said Isambard softly. 'Give me your parole to return with me afterwards, and you shall go to Shrewsbury in my train.'

'No, my lord. I give you no more paroles, now or ever. When the time and the means serve me to escape you, I shall go, and there'll be no word of mine tying my feet then.'

'Harry, Harry, when will you learn to bend with the wind? How many times already have you essayed to leave me?'

'As I make the count, five. But there will be other such

28

essays yet to come.'

'And five times been brought back before ever you reached the rock outside the walls. And main glad you were, once at least, to be hoisted back to solid ground with all your bones unbroken. And how long is it now since you found foot-room even to begin on such another enterprise? With two archers at your heels at every step? Give up, Harry, there's no escape from Parfois for you. Take the chance to ride out at the gate when it's offered you.'

'No,' said Harry, rolling up the much-used parchments that carried his drawings. He had learned not to waste energy in shouting; the refusal was as absolute as death, but also as still.

Isambard sighed elaborately. 'As you please. I cannot give if you will not take. But remember what I have told you. Next time, if you can bring me to a next time after the fright you've given me, strike home. No one in Parfois will slit your throat for slitting mine. There may well be some,' he said, sliding from the bench and beating the stone-dust from his crimson cotte with a vigorous hand, 'who would thank you for it.'

He was turning towards the door when they both heard, hollow and deep, the thudding of hoofs on the timbers of the bridge, coming fast. The deep cleft in the sandstone, that severed the castle of Parfois on its cliff from the grassy headland where the great church stood, took the sound and sent it rolling in cavernous echoes between the walls of rock. As soon as the riders reached the cobbles under the archway of the gatehouse, the hoofbeats ceased to be audible; only the dying reverberations, like distant thunder, quaked away into stillness slowly and left a quivering on the air.

Isambard had halted, ears pricked. Riders at night and in haste were few at Parfois, but at such a time, when the court was trundling its ponderous way into Shrewsbury, this might mean no more than a visit from one or another of the nobility of the march, on his way to join the king. Harry had reared his head no less intently. From anything unwonted he could still hope.

29

Blown horses stamping in the outer ward, the creak of stirrup-leathers, boots tramping the cobbles, words passing urgent and low. Isambard's wild-beast senses caught the known voice first.

'Walter!' he said, head up, like a stag nosing aliens on the air. But it could not be. Why should Langholme ride back all this way, when he had but set out for Shrewsbury in the early afternoon, to make ready the town house in the Wyle for his lord's coming, and see his bed-linen aired and his plate burnished? And why, if for some unknown errand come he must, should he come riding hard, and with at least one stranger in his train? There was a voice Isambard did not recognize for a man of his own: hoarse and low, choked with the dust of riding and creaky with long fatigue.

He was at the door in three long strides, and came breast to breast with them on the threshold. Langholme knew where to look for his master at this hour.

'My lord,' he said, gusty with haste, 'there's news you should hear at once. I left all in train in Shrewsbury, and made bold to bring the messenger back with me.' The man was at his elbow, grey in the face with weariness, hollow eyes fevered. Isambard looked upon him and knew him: a minor knight of the earl of Kent's following, and trustworthy. He had run errands more than once between de Burgh's three castles in Gwent and this outpost above the Severn on the borders of Wales. But then he had worn the red and green mascles of the justiciar's livery, and now he came cloaked and anonymous.

Isambard's deep eyes flamed redly. He caught the man by the arm and drew him within.

'Here, in here! And, Harry, do you close the door.'

'Shall I go, my lord?' said Harry, springing to obey.

'No, stay. No need to cry the alarm too soon. Now speak out, man, quickly. Yes, before the boy you may, he's in my worst secrets already. What brings you north in such haste? And in this case?' The absent device cried aloud.

'My lord, the earl of Kent – no man who can shed his livery is wearing it today. Safer so! My Lord, he's down –

30

he's out of grace and out of office. Six days ago, before the whole council, the king turned on him and accused him of monstrous acts, and put him from his side and from all authority. He's impeached for his very life. And Stephen Segrave who helped to bring him down is justiciar of England in his room.'

So it was come. Hubert de Burgh, the great earl, the king's master, was fallen, down and out of office, and the ground shaky under many another foot. His Poitevin rivals had their day and their way. Peter des Roches, bishop of Winchester, no question, had been the prop at Henry's elbow that gave him the courage to turn on his best servant. Let de Burgh be what else he would – not even this cataclysm could make of him saint or martyr – yet he had certainly been the ablest, the most devoted, the most honest administrator in the land of England, and the one who best grasped what England was, and what she could be. In the past Isambard had forgiven him much for the sake of that quality in him, the vision of England that passed beyond the bounds of a feudal honour, and looked towards a nation, an indisseverable unity fenced within an impregnable sea.

And did not this flagged floor underfoot quiver a little upon the bedrock of Parfois?

'I came to warn you, my lord,' said the messenger, coughing dust out of his lungs. 'Look to yourself, for any who have held with him in the past may be in danger now. Look well to yourself!'

'Ay, so I will,' said Isambard, and the oblique smile came and went upon his mouth like a sudden wry lightning. He stood for a moment with head reared and black brows drawn together, staring ruefully back upon a heyday that was gone, comet-like, into perpetual eclipse. 'Sit down here, man, and tell me. I must hear all. And, Harry, do you go and fetch wine for him.'

'Am I to bring it myself?' asked Harry doubtfully.

'Fool, do you think I want some ninny like Thomas? And make haste.'

31

Why should he, on that brusque word, take to his heels and run to do Isambard's errand? He crossed the outer ward full gallop, his heart in a turmoil of excitement and confusion, caught up against his will into the troubled affairs of this England which his mind and upbringing insisted was no country of his, but to which his blood leaned irresistibly in an unwilling alliance. And because he was curious he ran back again with the wine hardly less precipitately, greedy even for the few words he had missed.

The three heads turned sharply as he entered the tracing-house, and turned back again, satisfied, at sight of him. Why should that give him so unmistakable a tremor of pleasure? They were none of his people, not one of them; why should he take pride in being trusted by his enemies? None the less, he poured and offered the wine with a conscious delight in his own quiet, adroit movements, that never broke the thread of the narration.

' – honour for honour, these last weeks, for every new grant to des Rivaulx the like to my master. And then they were all together, early last month, at my lord's manor of Burgh in Norfolk, and there at Bromholm priory the king pledged himself to maintain all his grants and charters to them all, my master no less than the Poitevins. By the most solemn oaths he bound himself, and his heirs after him, and took God for his surety.'

'So he would,' said Isambard grimly, 'when most he purposes to undo both the oath and the man to whom he binds himself.'

'But to all – he bound himself to all. Why should the earl have doubted him? We thought the danger was past, and the contention between them resolved. And even if he had foreseen this then, how could he have warded it off? What could he have done but run, and empty-handed at that? And the Lady Margaret, and his daughter? Would he ever have got them out of the king's hands? But hear what followed! Come the end of July there was to have been a great round table held, and London would have been full. But what does the king do but issue a letter prohibiting it, and ordering all those who purposed to attend it to make ready instead to escort him to Shrewsbury here for this meeting with the Welsh. All's been done in good haste, the safe-conducts issued for the Welsh princess and her train, all to empty London and turn men's eyes away from what else he intended, at least until it was done.'

'And there was no want of a bishop ready to his hand, to preach against the sinfulness of tournaments, and prop up his decree,' said Isambard, tramping the floor with long, light paces, bright and fierce in the gathering dark. 'This came from Winchester's brain, not from the king's.'

'True, my lord, he did speak against the round table, and before the king acted.'

'Well, and having set his stage? Six days ago, you say, in council – Who first opened against the justiciar? Des Roches, or Rivaulx?'

'I was not there, my lord, but Gilbert Basset was, and I had it from him. The bishop of Winchester was at the king's elbow throughout, but the storm arose out of a seemingly clear sky, and it was the king himself who brewed it. He turned on my lord the earl in a burst of rage, like a frantic man, and God knows as though he verily believed what he said – '

'He does believe,' said Isambard, wrenched into stillness in the middle of his furious walking by a violent spurt of laughter. 'It's his secret. He can produce such a sacred rage at will, and believe in it as in the gospel. I've seen him do it to suit his purpose, over no more than the getting of a jewel he fancied.'

' – and accused him of I know not what crimes and enormities, and called on any who willed to confirm, or had any complaints to urge against my lord, to speak out fearlessly. And speak they did, not des Roches and Rivaulx only, but many another. Why not? They had the signal, they knew how to please the king and get a foot on the ladder at the same time – over the earl's trampled face. He was the mounting-block for many an ambitious office-seeker that day, I tell you. And then the king declared him solemnly deprived of all his offices, and named Segrave justiciar in his stead.'

'But in God's name, man, did he not speak out in his own defence?'

'The king would not hear him. Speak he did, swearing he was as true a man to his lord as any ever lived, and had done nothing to affront his duty or his conscience. But they shouted him down. And they say the king was loudest in the shouting.'

'The divine outburst had him well into his stride then, and out of reach of fear. It must have cost des Roches a deal of cunning and persuasion to launch him, but once his sails were well filled he'd drive. Have I not seen it? What then? He has not dared clap him in hold? Not the Tower? Even in his holy exultation he would not dare!'

'No, my lord, he's yet at liberty, but for how long only God knows. King Henry ordered him from his presence and bade him hold himself at his disposal to answer the charges. But even so they could not let him rest. Within two days they were after him to demand an accounting of all treasury receipts and all his official holdings, back to the late king's time. The bear-pit they made of England then, and to demand an exact accounting!'

'He had a charter of quittance from King John, exempting him from any such accounting. That I know.'

'He pleaded it, but my lord bishop of Winchester nudged the king's elbow again and prompted him that King John's death rendered his charter null and void. And the upshot of it is they've formulated a list of charges against him, and summoned him to appear before the council at Lambeth on the fourteenth of September coming, to answer them. And having so contrived his ruin, the king took up the court by the roots and dragged it with him here to Shrewsbury, out of the way of the Poitevins until they close the trap on him past escaping. What use to defend himself, when his judges are his accusers?'

'And where is he now? Is he free to move?'

'No, my lord, he's watched day and night, he can't stir abroad. But they let him retire to Merton priory by Wimbledon to prepare his answer, and while he's there he's safe at least from violence. The lady's at Bury St Edmunds, and no one's troubled her there yet, thank God. It's my hope they'll scruple to touch the sister of the king of Scots.'

'So that's how it stands! And des Rivaulx holds custody of the household accounts, with boundless authority, and the treasury filled with his friends. I tell you, this is to be a country run from the wardrobe unless we stir ourselves. I counted over the number of his county sheriffdoms lately, and made the tale twenty-one. We shall see the great offices of state withering away to fatten the privy chamber, and baronage and commons left without voices or rights. One pillar of the house is down, it seems, and no man to lift a hand to prop it. What, did no one speak for him? Was there not *one* to give them the lie?'

'Not one. Chester was not there, or he might have opened his great throat. He hates the earl, but with an honest hate. And he hates conspiracy and injustice even more. But he's old, and sick, they say. He was not there.'

'And the charges?' said Isambard, halting abruptly before the drained messenger.

Harry stood watching with held breath, appalled by the calm, even the cheerfulness, of the leaning face; only devils, surely, can devour trouble and distress and smile over them thus serenely. The shock of the news, the reeling shock of seeing his England jarred shivering off her course, these were already accepted and mastered. Whatever he meant to do now to cover his own traces he would do with resolution and precision, nothing in agitation, nothing without thought. It had seemed to Harry sometimes that the lord of Parfois truly loved his England, yet here he assembled his powers to his own defence, and left her lying adrift to dangerous currents without a scruple.

'Let me know the charges, and then I have done, then I can deal. All the charges.'

De Burgh's knight – no one had named him, perhaps no

one remembered his name – propped his sagging eyelids and held his forehead, dredging out the last details.

'All his household were watched. I got away by night and joined myself to a company of the advance party for Shrewsbury, where I had friends to give me cover, and so I've ridden the news to three or four others who may be attainted like you, having been of his way of thinking. The charges – but there'll be more by now, for they're beating them out of the bushes like conies – they accuse him of writing to the duke of Austria, when the king was of a mind to marry his daughter, and putting him off the match so that the suit failed.'

'God's life!' said Isambard, laughing through his teeth. 'They must think we have all short memories. That suit foundered of its own weight, and the king was never better than lukewarm in it at that.'

'And of hampering the king in his campaign for the recovery of Normandy.'

'Ah, that's another matter. So we did, and well for him we did, or he'd have left his kingdom of England there, too. Go on!'

'Of seducing the Lady Margaret, when she was in his wardship in King John's day, and seeking to make his heirs kings of Scotland by marrying her.'

'Faith, it's Alexander should complain of that, not Henry. Even if it were true! This will never hit, and they know it.'

'But it adds one to the list, and every straw counts. Then there's a tale that he stole from the treasury a stone, one that makes its wearer invincible and puts him out of reach of wounds, and sent it privily to the prince of Aberffraw.'

'Ah, that's ingenious – some soured soldier thought of that. A master-stroke to find an apology for Llewelyn's prowess, as well as an arrow to loose at Hubert.'

'There are those who believe it, my lord. As they'll believe also the next count, that my lord of Kent sent letters to Prince Llewelyn condoning the execution of William de Breos, after he was taken with the Princess Joan.'

36

At mention of that discovery, long past and half-healed in his memory but still quick in anguish at the first touch, Harry's flesh shrank and burned. It came so unexpectedly, he dreaded that Isambard might have seen him flinch. But the musing voice said only: 'That he owned the prince's right I doubt not. I know none who denied it. But that he wrote such letters is a wild shot. Well, is that all?'

'Yet one more, my lord, but the most dangerous and the hardest to disprove. And it was the bishop of Winchester first laid it. That the earl has feathered his own nest these many years by dealing dishonestly with the treasury.'

'Which of them that ever held office has not?' said Isambard with a curl of his lip. 'And I won't deny the possibility even where Hubert's concerned. There's no blinking his inordinate appetite for castles. But on balance I take it to be likely he stole less than most, and gave better value for it. And that at least,' he added reasonably, 'can't be levelled at me. I've never handled treasury funds, I've held no office that could be plundered. Well, so we have it. And not one man among them to say a word in his defence!'

'My lord, the thing was sprung so suddenly, and most went with the tide. And then, there were many quick to pay off old grudges, never thinking what worse grievances they might come to carry against the Poitevins. It's my hope that some will take thought later, with cooler heads, and in time their doubts will speak out.'

'I pray you may be right. I owe you thanks for bringing me word, friend. I might have ridden down into Shrewsbury tomorrow with no thought for the game before me, and been taken on the hip.' He turned to Langholme, who waited with an anxious face, eyes straining upon his lord's darkened countenance. 'See him well lodged and cared for, Walter. Go or stay, friend, at your desire, and choose what you need from my stable. I am in your debt. And, Walter, I have changed thoughts about my ride to Shrewsbury.'

'You will not go, my lord?' said Langholme almost eagerly.

'But I will go, Walter, and with double the retinue I proposed, and thrice the splendour. But first house our guest, he has need of sleep. Then come to me, and let's see what provision is needful.'

They departed, and a great quietness fell upon the two who were left alone in the tracing-house. Suddenly they saw how dark it had grown while their minds were on other things. Night folded the shapes of bench and tracing-tables and chests, and pale, mellow stone.

'My lord,' said Harry, hollow and small with wariness and wonder, 'what will you do?'

'Do, Harry? I will go down, attended like a prince, and myself attend on my king, as is my duty. And I will have dutiful speech with him,' said the low, light voice out of the gathering dark, 'whether he will or no, Harry, whether he will or no.'

King Henry held audience before supper in the great guest chamber of Shrewsbury abbey, in a gilded chair set up on a dais draped with gold and red brocades and velvets, and against a backcloth of tapestries unrolled not two hours earlier from the pack-saddles of his unwieldy train. He was in high spirits, and even for him inordinately fine, with jewels in his ears and on his long, fastidious fingers. The nobility of the march bruised their loyal lips on his gold-set rubies, and trod delicately about the skirts of his glittering gown. The air still quivered faintly with the reverberations of a resounding fall; they breathed the dust from it, and held their breath. He felt the tension of awe that held them poised against him, and a sweet excitement filled him. It was done, it was truth, and no longer an aching wish, an unsatisfied appetite; they were the proof of it. He had made the great, the effortful beginning; the second step and the third would be easy, and who would dare try to halt him now?

He was twenty-five years old, and out of tutelage. The release of power ran in his blood like wine, and he felt a gust of triumphant hatred against the old men, with their experience and their assurance and their iron determination to cramp and fetter him from all action of his own. Old men, spent, cautious, slow to venture but absolute to instruct and hector him, and hem him about with prohibitions and warnings. He thought of the shedding of his shackles, and his heart leaped with angry joy, remembering the broken, bleak, foolish astonishment in the justiciar's ageing eyes. He could not believe that his world was shattered, that his fledgeling had taken flight, that his day was over. A long day, a golden day, gone down at last in a clap of thunder.

Thanks be to God, said the king devoutly in his heart, savouring the joy of his freedom, and to my sweet saint who stood by me and put the words of justice into my mouth. O blessed Saint Edward, sweet Confessor, this year on your day there shall be more new knights than ever before, and the clerks in my chapel shall chant the *'Christus vincit'*. Only be with me still, and show me how to confound my enemies. Breathe in the faces of those who set themselves up against me, like the fiery wind of God, and let them be blown out of my path even as the earl of Kent, to their destruction. To their ruin!

Now my house shall be set in order, he thought, exulting, and I shall be the master in it. Not de Burgh with his stifling cage of law and custom and civil right, not these old men walled up in their feudal honours, not my turbulent barons of the march, but I the head and my household officers the instrument, and a sound order under us. O sweet Saint Edward, be with me and I shall show them the truth of kingship.

He closed his eyes momentarily upon the ecstasy of his heart's prayer, shutting out the gaudily-coloured throng that filled his audience chamber. He opened them again, smiling with the pleasure of his thoughts, upon a face like a death's-head, beautiful and dreadful, that advanced towards him between the ranks of his clerks and courtiers, and night-mare-like smiled upon him.

He called soundlessly upon his unfailing patron, and the dazzle of light that swam towards him and bore the terrible reminder ever closer dimmed at the saint's touch, and resolved itself into a surcoat stiff and glittering with gold

39

thread, over a golden-brown cotte, covering a veritable human body and no shape of dreams. A lean body and tall, and erect as a larch, bearing aloft that formidable head that smiled faintly and grimly as it drew near and leaned over his hand. He had extended it to ward off a terror, but the gesture was easily turned to regal account as he surrendered his long, jewelled fingers for the kiss of the lord of Parfois.

An old man. Always old men; there was no easy escape from them, they pressed in on him wherever he turned. Ralf Isambard of Mormesnil, Erington, Fleace and Parfois, and some fifty other lordships and manors scattered over England. What did he want with this resplendent attire, what right had he to that arrogant and wonderful walk of his, with death looking out of his head through the two deep, restless, insatiable eyes, that burned red in the heart of their blackness? The great forehead, once as sheer as a cliff, showed now the polished ivory of the skull within, the cheekbones stood gaunt from the fleshless face, and the iron jaw, clean-shaven in the old Norman manner still, thrust pale against the drawn brown skin. A death's-head. But who would have thought that the stark lines of bones could be so beautiful?

'You are welcome to our court, my lord,' said the king; but his fingers shrank from the touch of the dry lips. They barely brushed his rings and were away, as though they sensed his revulsion, and willed indifferently to indulge him. He remembered with a kind of rage that this was yet another of the elders from whom he had taken advice too tamely all these years. On all matters appertaining to the Welsh marches Isambard's word had run like a royal writ. Had he not urged the removal of the de Breos wardship from Richard of Cornwall, only last year, and its handing over to de Burgh? Henry stiffened, remembering. He was ready to find treason in all old men. All, perhaps, but the bishop of Winchester, who had helped him to cut himself free from their leading strings at last.

'I am at your Grace's bidding and service at all times,' said Isambard, and straightened up from the sensitive, irresolute hand to look into the pale, comely face, a little melancholy in repose, a little petulant in speech. The short brown beard carefully curled as always, the rich hair meticulously dressed and perfumed. He was of no more than medium height, and slender, but give him his due, he could pass for a king.

A pity, though, that his one drooping eyelid should give a look of worldly cunning to a countenance and a creature so transparent. An unchancy flibbertigibbet of a young man, always blowing hot or ice-cold, with no happy mean, for ever with his head laid in your bosom or his dagger in your back; and yet there was still a kind of innocence that clung about him, like an outworn garment from his childhood, not always very becoming to the grown man, but treacherously disarming to those who might otherwise have been tempted to treat him like a man, and demand a man's measure from him.

'I trust your Grace had pleasant riding by the way,' said Isambard amiably. His eyes, in ambush like momentarily peaceable wolves in their deep caverns, passed at leisure over the faces of the assembled court, and lingered longest on those nearest the king. 'And sweet company,' he said, and his voice was honey.

They must have left des Rivaulx in London, no doubt to keep close watch on the game in progress and stop every bolthole the quarry might try. And Winchester was too subtle to appear always at the king's elbow. But Brian de Lisle was there in his stead, to give weight and reverence as an old adherent of King John among the new, young, ambitious faces. De Craucombe, Henry's steward of the household, hovered close to the king's chair, Passelewe hung discreetly behind it, the royal clerk *par excellence*, the new man of affairs, propertyless as yet but already hungry, birthless but already quietly treading out about him the competence that should keep his descendants in coat-armour.

The old baronies were being silently dismembered to make new for such men as these. The great council of the land, if they did not stand to and defend its rights, would be

41

left to moulder harmlessly, high and dry of the life-stream of government, while the diverted flood turned the mills of this little clique in the king's wardrobe, and every source of the king's revenue converged into their hands. Already des Rivaulx had the exchequer, as well as the purse of the household, and he who held the purse held the power. And the thing had been done so well, never a move against de Burgh until all was ready and the king primed and brought to the pitch of ecstasy necessary for action.

There were honest men there, too, in plenty, Isambard's peers and contemporaries. He turned to salute three or four of them, turned again to look round the room with a long, raking stare, and back to the king.

'But where is the earl of Kent?' he said, in a voice pitched to carry without over-emphasis to the farthest corner of the great room. 'I did not see his livery in the courtyard.'

The silence fell like a stone, crushing and cold. Heads turned almost stealthily in the hush. The bright assembly held its breath.

King Henry's face had paled with apprehension and shock, and the timid beginning of a defensive rage. He gripped the arms of his chair nervously, looked aside quickly at de Lisle for prompting, and as furiously wrenched his gaze back to Isambard's face, aware of the desperate need he had to lean for once on no one but himself.

'I cannot believe, my lord,' he said, 'that you are ignorant of what has passed concerning the earl of Kent.'

'Why, certain rumours have come to my ears, but I paid them no heed. Unless I hear it from your Grace's own lips that you have so used your best and most faithful servant, I should be loath to believe it. It would not be the first time rumour has slandered my king. Shall I be quick to think your Grace unjust and ungrateful? And so ready a gull for the spites of place-seekers who grudge the best his eminence?'

After the white of consternation the red of mortification surged in the king's too eloquent face. He felt the hue of

42

shame, and willed it with all his strength to become the hot red of anger, for shame he could not afford and must not acknowledge.

'I have in good earnest been gulled by place-seekers,' he said, his voice thin and high, 'and for all too long a time. But that is over, and I am awake to my error. The earl of Kent suffers no wrong from us. He has his due and no more. His due, did I say? He has a measure of mercy more than his due; he has his freedom yet, and a grant of time to answer his accusers.'

'And is it your Grace who tells me so? Then am I to accept that what else was told me is true? The justiciar is put from his office? And charged with I know not what treasons?'

'He is, my lord, and justly. And justly!'

'And stripped of the honours your Grace lately heaped upon him? Those royal castles and manors you delighted to bestow, all snatched back from him? Is that true, too? And the office pledged him lifelong, by oath, so short a time ago?'

He saw the king's face blanch at that, and wondered for a moment if superstitious dread could get any foothold in that rich soil of self-persuasion; and for a moment he abated the hardness of his tone to give the seed time to grow.

'Your Grace, I stand as true a man to you as any in this land, against you I will no offence. But for your soul's sake, take care you yourself do not offend. You are being betrayed into a wrong which time to come will hold against you. Think better of it now, and take back what has been done, while there is still time.'

He had been too generous, it seemed, to what was after all but the beginning of the holy rage. The burning pallor, white as pure flame, seared the colour even from the king's eyes and left them staring grey as glass. Better so, thought Isambard, warming into a strong, perverse content. I am too old to change now, I could not stomach this without the knife-edge and the drop below.

'My lord, do you defend him?' The king breathed thickly.

43

'A felon who has robbed our treasury to provide himself, and that for many years? One who stood in our way when we willed to take back our province of Normandy? One who has been rather in the French king's service than in mine? The earl of Kent shall answer for all. Think better of it? Well I may think better of the clemency I have showed him, and consider to take back from him full payment where I might have pardoned him the half. He has done me greater wrong than plundering my revenues. He has plundered my reputation and my spirit, gaining ascendancy over me by sorcery. I have drunk with him, trusted him – Do you doubt me? You shall see the charge brought home, you shall see it proven on him.'

So that was to be the excuse and the vindication of his long tolerance. Since someone must carry the burden of the king's changefulness and weakness, as well lay it all on one pair of shoulders. Sorcery! That blunt, practical, self-made man, that collector of castles, that tireless, devoted, grasping, generous administrator! And was there still more to come? It seemed they had indeed been busy beating the bushes for charges to lay against him.

'He has killed privily, with poison. Do you defend that? Old William of Salisbury he made away with thus, and Pembroke, too – and our good archbishop –'

What, even Grant in Italy? These were wilder and wilder flights, and Henry was whipping himself deliberately into a frenzy that might well give birth to still more fantastic images. Isambard stood before him and watched without passion how the young body jerked and writhed, as though tethered by the clinging hands to the arms of the chair. His patron, he thought, got his visions in quietness, as simply as a child. This one sends his demon out to drag them down to him unwilling.

' – besides the horrible impiety committed against Holy Church in the person of those Italian priests it pleased us to advance to livings here in our country. For it was he, and that's been shown, who suborned this William Wither, this Yorkshire blasphemer, to his acts of violence. And he who

44

dealt so rigorously and cruelly after those troubles in our city of London, and killed wantonly when he might have shown mercy –'

'At the peril of your realm he might,' said Isambard dryly, 'but in my view you have need to be glad, your Grace, that he had the hardihood to deal as he dealt. And all that can possibly be urged against him on that score your Grace has known since the event; it is late to turn it against him now.'

'It is never too late to do justice. The arm of law should be long enough to reach through time, and so it shall prove. I will have the full penalties loosed upon him. And there are others, I say there are others, my lord, who will do well to consider their steps and put a guard on their tongues.'

The gentlemen of the retinue had drawn in a little about them, stepping delicately, watching the king's face as the mirror of their own conduct. Isambard looked round them calmly and without haste, and saw in their closed visages the measure of the reserve de Burgh had failed to estimate with any accuracy. Dislike would not have shut their mouths so firmly from saying one word in his defence. What sealed off their compassion from him was his alien nature. He was not of them, and never had been. Their lands had come to them by right, and been worn as easily as their clothes. Their birth was such that they had no need to assert it. The earl of Kent had come landless and ambitious, climbing into their hitherto unviolated stronghold, anxious, assertive, jealous of ceremony, himself the first of the new men, and the loneliest. In their midst and richer in establishment than they, he had never been accepted. They neither envied nor acknowledged him; nor would they reach a hand to him now that he was down. He was nothing to them. And to me? thought Isambard, marvelling a little at being thus confronted with his own impregnable fortress of birth and blood. In the name of God, what is he to me?

'I am grateful, your Grace, for that word of warning, for so I read it. Nevertheless, will you hear me a word more? I have somewhat to say for the earl of Kent, before you come

45

to judgement.'

He waited for no permission; better to take what might otherwise be denied, and he was speaking now not for the king only. Before the half of it was said Henry was out of his chair, his face congested with so violent a flush of blood that Isambard spared one detached and measuring glance for the hilt of the royal dress-sword, and the elegant hand working in fury so close to it. There was no Ranulf of Chester here now to drag him from Henry's point at need, as once he had dragged his enemy de Burgh. That outburst of spleen at the unreadiness of the fleet Henry had meant to use to invade Normandy – the dearest ambition of his dreams – showed now as a prophetic glimpse of a deep and formidable hatred, not the childish tantrum they had thought it.

Who knows, thought Isambard, but I may die a royal death yet? And he swept aside the gilded folds of his surcoat with a disdainful hand, to show that he had not so much as an ornamental dagger in his belt.

' – and I charge your Grace, take thought how this will look to those who watch you closely from Europe, and what they will say of you where kings meet together. Do you think you can make them believe that the earl of Kent was ever less than loyal to you, them who have known his works as well as you, and understood them better? I tell you, he has held you firm in your place when none other could, and lent you his heart's blood many a time. If he has maintained himself, God witness he has also maintained you, and set you up ever more firmly in your kingdom, and you have good need to thank him and remember him in your prayers. He is a man, and faulty. But I think you, of all men, have no right to complain of him, for he has not spared himself in your service. And look you how this will be read. You lay yourself open to the charge that the king of England is without gratitude or humanity, if this is how he uses his friends. Unless,' said Isambard, loud and grim over the rising scream he saw contorting the king's throat, 'they say of you more charitably that you have not the wit to know who your friends are.'

The hand on the sword-hilt was twisting and trembling. A velvet-shod foot stamped impotently at the hollow dais, and the voice that came out of the congested throat was husky and laboured with fury.

'My lord,' whispered the king, gulping air, 'I told you beware lest you stir my memory too well. You, too, I remember – you, too – in Normandy when I was hedged about from every venture that might have won me back a lost kingdom. Kept fretting in camp, and my men wasting their hearts and their harness in play – inglorious, inglorious! Well I remember! You, you were hand in glove with him then. You were his man always. Take heed that you do not pay a like price for it.'

'Under you,' said Isambard, blunt and clear, 'I have been nobody's man but my own since your father died. I have done as I judged right, for you and for England, and if it marched often with the judgement of the earl of Kent, do you marvel that I speak up for his sound services now? Well for you that we made shift in Normandy to keep you from any act that would have brought the king of France into the field, or you would have left your kingdom of England there, and likely your life with it. You would have your folly, but at least we saw to it that it cost you no more than it need. Be grateful!'

The scream came then, a blazing outcry almost void of words. The king lunged forward with a contorted face, and Passelewe, leaning from behind his chair, caught him insinuatingly by the arm and whispered in his ear. A flurry of voices murmured in agitation, a few of the elders closed in about the throne, but the king waved them furiously away. Isambard stood impassive, watching him with the crooked smile dragging his long lips out of line.

'My lord Isambard – '

He trembled still, but he had his voice in control; those frenzies of his knew always how far to go, and where to stop.

'My lord Isambard, you charge yourself with treason and think no shame. And if I use towards you a mercy I could not show towards the earl of Kent, take it thankfully and make no further presumption upon my grace, for I shall not so withhold my justice a second time. I will not have suspect traitors about me.' His voice was rising again, shrill as a woman's with injury. 'You are dismissed, my lord. Go back to your castle of Parfois, and there remain until I call you back to my presence. When I return to Shrewsbury for the papal court I may send for you to attend on me. Till then, think in your retirement what words you have used to me, and marvel that you are left at liberty. Go!' he said, translated and exalted in his rage like a man invulnerable within his strongest castle. 'Get out of my sight! Get to your hermitage!'

'At your pleasure, your Grace, to stay or go!'

Isambard swept him a deep bow, and withdrew from him half the length of the hall without turning his face away. They saw the oblique smile curl into something between disdain and honest amusement. The dark cheeks did not flush; the highlights over the jutting bones, the stark shadows beneath, were as fixed as stone. The skirts of his resplendent surcoat whirled about him in a coruscation of gold embroidery as he turned deliberately and walked to the door, between the silent ranks that parted to let him through. He did not look back; and his knights, who had waited upon him in watchful quietness all this time, fell in at his back and followed him from the king's presence. In the courtyard their grooms sprang to attend them, and the young squires held their stirrups and mounted after them, a princely company, orderly and proud and splendidly appointed. It was like the departure of an army.

The king heard them go, and shook with an anguish of detestation. How dared they, how dared they withdraw from his censure with the discipline and assurance of conquerors? How dared that man, that gilded *memento mori*, gather up the honours from between them with a sweep of his bony hand, and leave his lord here thus bereft and disparaged?

Isambard rode easily, the reins loose over his wrist, the smile still touching his mouth. They were out of sight of the wall of Shrewsbury, and pacing the broad grassy verge of the

48

Roman road, when he suddenly put back his iron-grey head and laughed aloud. All this for de Burgh!

'God's wounds!' said Isambard to the green dusk that hung like a silver-sewn web over his head. 'You would think I loved the man!'

CHAPTER TWO

Parfois, Shrewsbury: *December* 1232

The snow came early but grudgingly that year, filming over the meadows by Severn so thinly that the dormant grasses showed through in pale and frosty green. Harry stood on the leaded roof of the King's Tower, huddled in his felt cloak against the biting wind, and looked down into the distant valley, from the crowded roofs of Pool, upstream, to the grey walls of Strata Marcella downstream. His abbreviated world went no farther; the murk of snow crept in and folded the hills from him, and all he could see of Wales was the cold shore glittering with frost, and the first darker heaving of trees on the slope behind. The shallow by-channels of the river were frozen, and shone sullenly with a lambent light in their hollows; only the main stream, edged with ice, still flowed darkly down towards Breidden, rolling its sombre brown waters along the foot of the Long Mountain, far below the turrets of Parfois.

He looked long at the Welsh shore, and it seemed to him like the countryside of a dream, for ever beyond his reach. Under those grey abbey walls he had embraced his father's unviolated grave, and unwittingly betrayed it to violation. What had Isambard done with the poor, hunted bones? Ripped them limb-meal and sent them down the Severn again, to complete his thwarted vengeance? By that ford, pale beneath its broken brown water, he had crossed the river to ride after his foster-brother and prince, when Isambard had let him out on his long leash of temptation to his bounden duty in last year's war, and by the same ford he had returned according to his promise when the war was over and his freedom again forfeit. Now in the icy stillness of winter the desired land withdrew from him, hiding in leaden cloud, and he could hardly believe that he would ever set foot on its summer hills again. A mere ribbon of river between them, but he could not cross. The birds that came back at night to the warmer roosting-grounds of Parfois from their Welsh pastures made nothing of their incredible journey. He watched them come and go, and envied them their wings; and the unceasing ache of longing knotted itself a little more tightly into his vitals.

From this eyrie there was no way down for him without wings, not even into England, not even to the invisible assart below there in the woods, where Aelis waited for word of him, and no word ever came.

He owed so much to Aelis and her father. When he had run from Aber and come prowling about Parfois in search of his vengeance they had taken him in and given him house-room without question, thinking him some runaway from justice or from a hard master. Many a fugitive had passed through their hands; they had no fear of outlaws. Aelis had helped him in everything, fed him, mended his clothes, showed him the paths that scaled the cliffs below the castle. When he was known to be prisoner, she had sent word to Castell Coch, that the news might reach Llewelyn at Aber. And while he was with her, while there was time, he had not even been very kind to her! Thus from his eyrie he saw himself below, infinitely small, ungrateful and inadequate. Even when he was loosed out to his war, and slept that last night under her father's roof, he had used her like a child and told her but half the truth, saving the worse half for his return; and pride, conscience, whatever it was that drove him, had cheated him in the end, and left Aelis uncomforted.

So she did not even know, she did not even know that he was so near! She thought him free, and by this time must be sure he had forgotten her. Perhaps she had even ceased to care, and thought no more of him. His heart turned in him, furious to deny it, fighting off the pain, but the fear clung to him and would not be driven away. What better had he deserved of her?

'What, still bent on leaving me, Harry?' said Isambard,

51

sweet and rueful at his shoulder. He could move more softly than a cat when he willed; but he could not startle Harry now, they had played this bitter game too often. There was his place, leaning at his favourite prisoner's back, whispering like a prompting devil in his ear. 'Ah, but put off your flight until more clement weather. I should nót like to have to hack you out of the Severn ice.'

'Why not?' said Harry. 'You cast my father into it, why stick at sending me after him?'

'I'm not done with you, Harry. You do not cease to please me. Not yet!' And that must be true, or he could easily have killed him, that day in the summer, instead of merely bludgeoning the sword out of his hand. 'But should you not be looking rather towards England?' said Isambard, leaning his cloaked elbows on the weathered stone at Harry's side. 'Prince David and his mother are in Shrewsbury again. In two days' time the papal commission meets at Saint Mary's. Would you not like to be there to see it?'

'Would not you, my lord? King Henry lies at Wenlock priory, so I've heard. Won't you put on your cloth of gold and go and attend on him?'

'Well struck, Harry!' said Isambard with a crow of laughter. 'Lay about you and give as good as you get. I am as like to be called back to favour with my king as you are to be loosed to your prince. But I doubt you suffer from the banishment more than I.'

'As yet, my lord, as yet.'

Harry slid one curious glance along his shoulder at the hawk profile that gazed down so tranquilly into the river valley, and could find no tremor of regret or uneasiness anywhere in its fierce, fine lines. Was it true that he cared so little? That he felt neither shame nor fear in his disgrace?

Parfois had quaked to its rocky foundations when he rode in from Shrewsbury late at night in his banished splendour. Harry well remembered the running and whispering, the agitated speculations, the torches flaring, Langholme white and stunned into silence attending his lord to bed; and in the heart of the turmoil, brisk and calm and as if unaware of the storm he had raised, that barbaric golden figure stripping its rings and yawning, and calling the first neglectful servant sharply to heel, to demonstrate beyond question that nothing here was changed. His hand had been as heavy as formerly, but no heavier. No one paid for his disgrace, no one took advantage of it; he saw to that.

And gradually, the passing days easing the awe that gripped them all, the story of the king's audience had come out, as the knights who had attended him there opened their bewildered minds to those who had not seen. Wantonly, deliberately, he had invited his own fall, out of pride, out of spleen, out of that vendetta he had against life, that kept him always walking the edge of the precipice and defying death to come and take him. Or perhaps coolly, for a purpose, to frighten King Henry – they said he was easily frightened by men of authority – into reconsidering his courses, and relaxing a little the rigour of his grip on the earl of Kent.

If that was it, had he struck as far astray as it had seemed? De Burgh had fared ill enough, in all conscience, hounded, stripped, plucked out of sanctuary, driven from pillar to post, robbed, imprisoned, and shut up now under guard in exhausted retirement at Devizes. Was that failure? Or was it a success that he was still alive? They said the London mob had been loosed on him once by the king's order, and only old Ranulf of Chester had stood up and forced Henry to call off his pack. Five weeks later old Ranulf himself was dead; and de Burgh in his extremity, they said, had wept and prayed earnestly for his ancient enemy's soul. But how if Isambard had played the same part earlier, and stood off a more private death?

'Don't build too hopefully on my fall, Harry,' counselled Isambard, grinning at him along a lean shoulder. 'Oh, I doubt not he would like to move against me, but what he dare do he's done already and, as you see, it was feeble enough. I am no de Burgh, to be lopped like a tree. I have no manors of his gift to be snatched back from me whenever he loses his temper. I hold no royal castles, nor never coveted any; he cannot strip me of one furlong of land. My line is older than his, and all I have is mine by inheritance. Nor have I ever held or sought office, or handled royal monies, or the funds of the realm, either, which is the chief hold they have on poor, harried Hubert. I am unassailable. I have nothing he can take from me but his countenance, and that I can spare as willingly as he denies it.'

'You have a life,' said Harry.

'You are more likely by far to be the death of me, Harry, than ever King Henry is.'

'You comfort me, my lord. Consider on that promise, and have some care for yourself.' He hesitated a moment, hugging the folds of frieze more closely about him, but whether to shut out the icy wind or to shadow his face he did not know. The toe of his shoe kicked moodily at the stones of the merlon against which he leaned. 'There are some,' he blurted, 'who are licking their lips.'

'Because I have put myself into temporary eclipse? I doubt not. Do you think there was ever a man whose disgrace did not give comfort and pleasure to somebody? I am as well hated as any and better than most. That's no news to me.'

Harry would willingly have left it at that, but it seemed his tongue had more to say. It came out of him grudgingly enough, but it came.

'Some close about you,' he said, 'turned very thoughtful after you came home from Shrewsbury. There's those in your household are none too stable in their allegiance. As soon as they're sure you've had your day they'll be off to meet the coming men.'

Isambard looked up from his musing on the steel-grey river below. He was smiling.

'The coming men,' he said, pondering the phrase, and the soft, contemplative note of his voice said plainly that he had understood. Those who most pretended indignant devotion to him were already casting speculative glances out of the corners of their eyes at the rising fortunes of des Rivaulx's new men, those competent clerks and function-

54

aries of the household who had climbed into office with their leader. One of the closest at his elbow, so they said, was William Isambard, the old man's younger son, the same whose boyhood clothes had been refashioned for Harry to wear, when first he was a prisoner in Parfois. William had waited a long time for his inheritance. And the old man showed no disposition as yet to die, or even to grow senile; to be honest, it had not even dawned on him yet that he was old. The king's displeasure might be useful; it might even be fed with new fuel if it threatened to cool.

Was it a new thought to Isambard? There was no telling; he had that formidable face of his in such control that no man could read the mind behind it, unless he pleased to lay it open, and it was his pleasure always to confuse and confound. Harry wished he had not spoken. Why should he warn him? What was it to him if they betrayed him?

'And who are they, these snakes in my bosom?' invited the soft voice gently. 'Name them, Harry, name them. I can be grateful, like other men, when I see cause.'

'No!' said Harry, jerking indignantly away from the too close scrutiny of the illusionless eyes. 'I'm not your spy.'

'Child, child, not for your freedom? Their names, and you can turn the key in the lock and let yourself out. The princess will feast you in Shrewsbury tonight, and you'll ride home at David's side. What more could I offer you?'

Sweet, unbearably sweet, the voice and the promise, and even the close, caressing regard of the deep eyes, smiling at him so temptingly and tenderly. Praise be to God, he knew the way of it now, he had mastered it, he was not even shaken.

'You waste your time, my lord. You know you'll get no names from me.' Once he would have raged and hurled abuse, like stones fending off an advancing enemy. For a moment he was consciously proud of his growth. Something, at least, he owed to Isambard. What use would there be in lesser tempters trying him, after this?

'No, Harry? Then listen if I am so far astray.' And he named them, one by one with terrible accuracy, down to

Thomas Blount who was no more than an afterthought, a trivial note at the end. 'And de Guichet, of course,' said Isambard without bitterness, and he laughed to see how the boy, who had accepted all with a stony face, turned and gaped at him on hearing the name of the seneschal of Parfois.

'Did you not have him in your list? Then you lacked the chief.' He stood up from the chilly stone and stretched himself. 'I am too old to learn caution at my age, Harry; I must play the cards as they fall. But never think I am in error about the love men bear me. I have lived with them a long time; I can read passably well by now.'

'I see you need no help from me,' said the boy, smarting. 'Neither with your master nor your servants.'

'My master? Ah, King Henry! To be plain with you, child, though I am his man, whether he believes it or no, he is no man's master, not even his own. His father, let him be what he would and as faulty as he would, was a man. This one is a reliquary of spites and prejudices. Even the virtues he has, even his piety and his charity, he uses as counters for bargaining with God.'

Harry turned his head in quick alarm to look for his two guards, who would surely be lounging somewhere in the most sheltered corner above the staircase. 'My lord, keep your voice down!'

'Ah, they're out of earshot, Harry. Why should they follow you out into this wind? They know you'll not jump to your death; you're absolute for life.'

'My lord, no one will say as much of you. Think, have you not exposed yourself enough?' Harry shrank in amazement from the note of his own illogical anger. 'You'd best not speak so of the king before everyone.'

'Nor do I,' said Isambard, smiling, and took him by the arm and turned him towards the dark hollow of the staircase where the archers waited, 'Only to my enemies, Harry,' he said softly into his ear. 'A man's safe with his honest enemies. Do I not know you? You'd no more deliver me over to the king's justice than you'd exempt me from your own.'

The splendid assembly gathered in Saint Mary's church on the sixth of December dispersed towards nightfall, and all the people of Shrewsbury jostled about the college close to see them go.

First the papal legates, grave gentlemen and reverend, swathed to the eyes in gowns and cloaks, for their Italian blood ran thin and chill in this inhospitable climate. Their liveried servants were more gorgeous than they, and made a stately procession, but for the caution and irregularity of their gait on the frozen cobbles of the close. Then the king with his retinue, and the crowded street rang with illustrious names as the horses paced by: Ralf Neville, bishop of Chichester and chancellor of England, Segrave, the new justiciar, de Lacy, earl of Lincoln and constable of Chester since old Ranulf's death. And that tall lord with the open face and the austere smile was Richard, earl marshal, the new earl of Pembroke, more than a year established now in his unexpected honour. He was the second of five fine brothers, and had never looked to inherit, but the eldest had died childless, and Richard, long settled on his French estates, had been called home in haste to fill his place. More foreigner than Englishman as he might be, it was already being rumoured about the court that he was no lover of King Henry's Poitevin officers, and had a good English respect for the established order and custom of the realm, which these bade fair to dismember.

Baron and earl and functionary, bishop and prelate, knight banneret and knight simple, the noble cavalcade swept down the Wyle, young King Henry in the midst in his glory and dignity, of which he was always tender and aware.

There had not been so many great personages in Shrewsbury since the days of King John, from whom the town had extorted so many useful charters and liberties in return for its cash and loyalty. Flourishing business followed the crown; the burghesses of the borough shouted their acclaims

57

very contentedly, stamping their cold feet on the frozen, rutted ground and breathing fanfares of silver vapour into the sparkling air. Even the Welsh, when they came, got no black looks, only the same craning curiosity. Many a time they had terrorised the borders, and once within living memory ravaged Frankwell and occupied the town; but where was the sense of looking on them as enemies, when hardly a native-born family in the borough was without kin on the western side of Severn? Boundaries were recognised and jealously guarded by kings, but common folk could not carry on their daily business without crossing them freely, and leaving their footprints impartially on either side, and now and again their accidental children, into the bargain.

The Welsh came afoot, for the abbot's town house, where they were lodged, was but a short walk from the king's free chapel of Saint Mary's. The princess of Aberffraw and lady of Snowdon, Llewelyn's consort and King John's daughter, swept out of the close on her son's arm, out of the shadow of the squat sandstone tower into the torchlit gateway, and there paused for a moment to catch up her long skirt and drape it over her arm. A tall, grave woman, vigorous of movement and calm of face. She walked with assurance, unsmiling, untroubled, and there was no telling from her countenance whether she was carrying triumph or disaster back to her husband in Aber. She had lived all her life exposed to the torchlight and the craning stares, holding her own in a world of statesmen and princes for Llewelyn's sake; she knew how to contain and protect both her mind and her heart. And yet hardly more than a year ago, as every man in England and Wales knew, she had lain in her husband's prison for faithlessness, and her lover de Breos had hanged on the salt marshes of Aber, a dear price to pay for any woman, even a princess.

They stretched their necks to view her as she passed, and thought her hardly worth the risk: her hair greying under the gold circlet, her cheeks pale and her eyes sombre. She would never see forty again. And he so young and gallant! What had he seen in her, that they could not see?

Joan sustained the burden of their eyes, and felt nothing now of the anguish of her first re-entry into the light. When she was on Llewelyn's business she was Llewelyn; her voice took on the authority of his voice, the words she chose were the words he would have chosen, even in her gestures she caught the ardour and magnificence of his large and generous movements. While he had no occasion for timidity or shame, she could not be put out of countenance. She had risen before the legates at the chancel steps and spoken for more than an hour in bold and reasoned terms, detailing without heat the many infringements of the border, the many infractions of the terms of truce, with which Llewelyn charged his English neighbours. And she had sat with an unmoved face to listen to the counter-charges, and been the first to urge concessions and a new good will upon both parties, offering redress where it might be adjudged due from Wales, and claiming it with formal courtesy where it was due from England. Could any man among them have done better? Llewelyn was in her blood and in her spirit, an eagle from the crags of Snowdon looking through her face from his nest within her mind.

On her right hand walked her son, David, Llewelyn's heir acknowledged; tall and slender and fair like his mother, and grave almost to sadness like her, but with a quick, flashing smile, rare and brief, that was his father's gift. On her left, the older man must be Ednyfed Fychan, Llewelyn's chief agent and confidant for many years. And the thickset, dark young man who followed hard on their heels, reported the more knowing among the crowd, was Prince David's foster-brother, Owen ap Ivor ap Madoc, no mean princeling himself in the cantrefs of Arfon and Ardudwy.

They paced the frozen ruts of the street, the sergeants clearing a way for them; they came and passed, their retinue of dark, stocky, wild tribal princelings behind them. At the corner of the Wyle the watching crowd was shaken by a convulsion that suddenly cast out a slight, cloaked figure into their path; one of the sergeants stretched his staff to block the way, but she darted round him, quick as a squirrel,

59

and had Owen ap Ivor by the arm before anyone could thrust between.

'Master, wait! Master Owen!'

He looked down, startled, into a bright oval face, rosy with cold in the frame of the brown hood. Blue eyes, fringed with long, childish lashes, stared up imploringly into his. 'Master Owen, you remember me, Aelis?'

The sergeant had her by the arm, and would have hustled her away, but Owen held her by the wrist and put him off with a reassuring hand.

'Let her be, she does no harm. Let her speak.'

The momentary flurry of movement had reached Joan's ears, she turned to look back.

'What is it? If the child would ask something of us, let her not be denied.'

The day had gone well for Wales, they owed alms to whoever sued for them. She came back with her long, impetuous step, and looked gravely into the girl's face. A young creature, not more than sixteen, her slight body shrouded and shapeless within the coarse cloak all the country people wore. She was frightened now, she tried to draw back, but Owen held her, his arm about her shoulders for fear she should slip out of his grasp and be off into the crowd.

'Madam, this is that child I told you of, she that sent us word once of one we'd lost.'

It was only habit to hold back names from his tongue. Who in this self-confident border borough would have heard of Harry Talvace?

'Shall I bid her to the house?' he said quickly, seeing the bright flame of understanding flare in Joan's face.

'Yes, do so. Yes, come, child, follow us to our lodgings, and you shall have your asking, whatever it may be.'

The creature was wild as a forest doe, and might run from her if Owen relaxed his hold. Joan turned and went on her way with a hastened step, to leave them alone together. Owen she knew and would trust; and if her wanting was sharp enough, she would come in search of it. The fierce and innocent face moved her; it was quick with desire, and so agonizingly young. She would come! Even if he loosed her now, even if she cowered and hid like a deer in the covert, yet she would come.

'Follow us home,' said Owen quickly into the tangle of corn-coloured hair that burst in soft strands from under the rough hood. 'In the courtyard I'll wait for you; come to me there.'

She gave him one wild, wary glance of her great eyes, and her mouth shaped a silent assent. Then she darted back from him and was lost among the throng; but when he looked back at the gate of the abbot's house he saw her slipping silently along the wall after them, shadowy and quick and shy, like a city cat hunting by dusk. She was close on the heels of the youngest pages as they entered the courtyard, and her step so light that no one heard and challenged her. The gate closed after her. She turned at that, and it seemed that she would have clawed her way out again in a panic if she could, but by then it was too late.

He ran and caught her by the shoulder, holding her hard when she would have drawn back from him. 'Aelis, why? This is foolishness. You knew me, you called me. Come in to us, come and say what you have to say. What have I done to frighten you?'

'I didn't know,' she said incoherently. 'I never thought you'd be so close to the lady. All I meant was a word alone with you; I never wanted this.' But her body had softened and calmed between his hands, and she went unresisting where he led her.

'Are you afraid of the princess? No need. Even if she were not kindness born, she owes you kindness, as we all do.'

'I'm not afraid,' said Aelis with indignation, and thrust him off stiffly and walked before him into the hall.

The torches were burning already, hissing and resin-scented in their sconces on the walls. The log fire in the hearth cast leaping lights and shadows over the smoky brown panelling, and over the princess as she put off her cloak and held out a cold foot to the blaze. Two or three of her women were about her, busy with unlacing her shoes and

61

bringing her her house gown, but when she heard the latch of the door, and saw the girl quivering, curious and shy on the threshold, she put them off with an uplifted hand and sent them away.

'Madam,' said Owen, when the door had closed after their rustling skirts, 'this is Aelis, Robert's daughter, who first sent us word last year, when Harry was lost, that he was carried prisoner into Parfois. She and her father had him in their care some weeks, not knowing who he was, and were good to him. And but for her we should not have learned so soon what had befallen him.'

Aelis bent her knee and averted her eyes, casting quick glances from under her long gold lashes first at the lady, and then at the young prince, who had come forward out of the shadows and stood behind his mother's chair. They were richly but sombrely dressed; they wore jewels and velvets and brocades, for they came from a ceremonious occasion of state, where splendour was a formidable weapon in every party's armoury. Aelis was a little afraid that Owen had made her sound like a beggar come to be rewarded, and the lady might strip off one of her rings and pay her off for her services accordingly. Not that she would not have liked to hold that shining red stone in her hand and put it on her finger; but not as quittance for her share in Harry Talvace.

But Joan said only: 'Then we are deep in your debt, Aelis. And it seems to me we may in some sort be able to repay, for you had something to ask of us. Ask it now, and if it's in our gift you shall have it.'

'I only wanted to ask Master Owen,' said Aelis, slipping back the rusty folds of her cloak upon her shoulders, 'if he could give me word of Harry.'

Word of him for word of him: that was a fair and dignified exchange.

'When he got free from Parfois,' she said, warming now into ardour and anxiety, 'he came to our cottage for his horse, and slept the dark hours with us, and promised to come back when he could. And since then I've had no word of him. I came here to Shrewsbury thinking he might come

62

in attendance on your lordship, and I might at least see him and be sure he was well. Maybe speak with him,' she said, and flushed suddenly and angrily at háving exposed her need and her longing before them. 'Not that he owes me anything. or that I have anything to ask of him, except only to know that all's well with him. But when he didn't come, and I saw Master Owen pass so close, I made bold to call to him, only to ask for news.'

She saw the look they exchanged, and wondered at the shadow that passed from eye to eye; and she held her breath for fear that there was none but bad news to tell. In a year and a half how much could happen! And she with no way of knowing whether he lived or died.

'And you did not know, then?' said Owen wonderingly. 'He was with you, and told you nothing?'

Joan saw the young face chill with apprehension, and the great eyes, bluer than speedwells, widen and darken in a terror she could well comprehend. Fear for oneself can be mastered, there comes a time when it is pointless; but for fear for another dearer than oneself there's no cure, however gallant the spirit, however lofty the mind.

'He's alive,' she said, reaching for the largest and readiest comfort she could find in words, 'and please God he's well. And if he did not keep his promise yet, it's because the time's not yet come, and not because he's forsworn. I never knew him break his word, child, and he'll not begin now.'

She saw the soft, rich colour flood the girl's smooth cheeks again, and the smiling light of joy quicken in the assuaged eyes, and shrank from what more there was to tell; but she had begun it, and she would not leave it to Owen to add the bad to the good.

'He should have told you the truth,' she said, 'about his freedom. It was no more than conditional, until the war should end. And when it ended he was pledged to go back into captivity. He'd given his word. And he kept it.'

Aelis lifted her head, staring from great eyes that did not know whether to be grateful or grieved. The cloak slipped from her shoulders unnoticed, and left her standing slender and still in her rough, dun-coloured gown of homespun, her hair disordered by the heavy hood and falling out of its coils. The uncurling strands had a dark-gold lustre, clothing her with a splendour of her own.

'He's back in Parfois!' she said in a bitter whisper, and let out her breath in a long sigh.

'A year ago and more.'

'He should have come to me when he returned,' said Aelis faintly in her pain. 'He could have trusted me.'

'Surely he trusted you, child. He did not come to us at Aber, either, before he went back. When he was newly let out and came running to you, I doubt it seemed to him he had all the time in the world. Only when his parole fell due did he come to see to what hard terms he had bound himself. To return to his prison as soon as peace was made, that was the pledge he'd given. And he held to it, to every word and scruple of it. Even you were a mile out of his way, I doubt, and his honour was too proud and too sore to bend and take you in. It's how men treat us,' said Joan with a wry smile. 'If we would have them at all we must take them as they are.'

The girl stood mute, quivering a little, unaware how eloquent her eyes were. Back in Parfois, they lamented, prisoner again and nothing gained for all this year of waiting. And so near, and I felt nothing, and so wretched, and I sometimes blaming him. But he hadn't forgotten, they exulted. If he didn't come it was because he could not.

'Madam, what can we do?' she said appealingly.

'Little enough, except wait and hope.' At sixteen there could be nothing harder to do; at sixteen there is so little time. 'Go back to Parfois,' said Joan gently, 'and keep watch as best you can on all that happens there. If there is anything strange, anything we should know, send word to the castellan at Castell Coch, as you did once before, and we shall hear of it. And believe that Harry has not forgotten his word to you. He'll keep it when he can.'

She looked at the bright face, the vulnerable mouth, the radiant eyes, at the beginning of beauty not yet awakened, and her heart ached for the tyranny of time, of which she, having relinquished youth, had enough and to spare. No, she thought, he will not have forgotten!

'And this place, this assart of yours by the Severn, it is a long way from here. How did you come?'

'I walked.' She smiled a little at that. What other way did they suppose poor people had of getting about?

'Alone?' said Owen. 'Or is your father here in the town with you?'

'How could we both leave the cow and the hens? No, I came alone. I'm not afraid,' she said. 'Footpads pay no heed to people like me; what have I got they could covet?'

'You must not go back alone. Owen, have Madoc make ready a horse for her, and send two safe men to bring her home. And David, bid Margaret prepare supper for her before she goes.'

They went upon their errands obediently, and the two women, left together in the warm room pulsating with firelight and torchlight, looked long and covertly at each other, and said no word for a while.

'And do you love him so much?' said Joan at length, sharp and sudden across the silence.

'I want nothing from him,' said Aelis haughtily, 'but what he freely wills to give me.'

'That I believe. But that is not what I asked you.'

In the shadow of the dark-gold hair the blue eyes lifted fiercely to her face. 'Yes,' said Aelis, 'I love him.'

The legates departed, the brilliant assembly of nobles and bishops and princes began to disperse, and Shrewsbury's winter heyday was over. They parted in amity and good order. The king had already approved and ratified the agreement reached before the court, earnestly affirming the good will to peace of both parties, and setting up an arbitration commission to adjust all the issues which might arise between them. Both sides had bound themselves to accept whatever rulings the commission might make, and agreed without difficulty to the names put forward; and the legates had solemnly handed over their powers to the bench thus filled, and set out for London, leaving their blessing upon the continued peace.

Would Henry have been so amenable if his mind had not been on other matters? Wales was almost invisible to him now, he saw only what he and his new order meant to make of England. He had never room for more than one passion at a time.

Having thus taken every advantage of his preoccupation, and doubtless thanked God for it, the Welsh party left the abbot's town house, and took the winter road for Aber.

Harry worked late at his bench that day, and would not leave it to go in for his supper even after the light failed. The hall would be full, the torches there too revealing, and he was not ready yet to show his face. However he might cover his hurts from sight, that did not keep them from aching.

They had been so near to him, and it might as well have been the width of the world. He sat curled on his dark bench in the cold, fingering his unfinished work desperately to fill his mind and give his courage ground, but he could not get the princess out of his eyes. He saw her now always as he had last seen her, in Llewelyn's chair, frowning over Llewelyn's dispatches, so changed and still for the lost year, grey and ageing and in need of every creature who loved her. Now she would be riding away from him mile by mile with David and Owen beside her, lighting down somewhere to spend the night, perhaps at Valle Crucis, and tomorrow setting out on another day's journey, dragging out the stretched cords of his heart with her. They were going home to his mother, to the great prince who had been one more father to him, and to Adam, who had supplied Master Harry's place lovingly and patiently ever since his son came into the world. And he must lie here kicking his heels and fretting his heart out; and no end to it, never a sign that it might some day end. The peace was sacred, and David's inheritance must not be imperilled. And here was he, the price of it, suddenly in tears of frustration and misery and loneliness, and scrubbing his cheeks angrily with a coarse sleeve to wipe the shame hurriedly away. He must have his hour in the dark, even if it cost him his supper. He could not face them yet.

So it happened that he was still crouched among his tools, and stroking the half-cut stone for comfort, when the rolling, distant thunder of hoofs crossing the bridge from the plateau of the great church brought his head up alertly and froze his sad senses into instant attention. Apart from the guard there would be few people abroad in the outer ward at this hour. He mustered enough curiosity to slide down from his bench and feel his way out of the dark tracing-house to see who these riders might be. The court was still in Shrewsbury abbey. More than one pair of ears in Parfois would be stretched anxiously for any sign of Isambard's being taken back into favour. If this was a summons from the king there would be some scurrying to get back into the old alignment.

Half a dozen riders were dismounting by the stable-yard; he saw them fitfully by torchlight, and as silhouettes against the faint glitter of frost on the thin snow. Well-muffled, well-mounted men, with large voices and confident gait; they could well be from court. The grooms were running to take their horses, and two or three pages to hold their stirrups; and the officer of the guard was being exceedingly respectful and attentive to their leader, who had lighted down and was stamping his chilled feet. Harry drew near, his ears pricked for names, since he could not hope to recognize faces; but in the issue it was the stranger's face that identified him.

A tall, well-made man, this visitor, with a rich beard and lavish clothes. For all the beard, for all the flickering light and darkness that showed him only by glimpses, there was likeness enough to put a name to him. He carried more flesh, he had not the malice or the glitter or the beauty; nevertheless, at sight he owned his sire.

So this was William Isambard, whose clothes Harry had worn; the younger son, the courtier, the new man, des Rivaulx's man. Careful though he might be to go with the running tide, it seemed his blood was thick enough to bring

67

him visiting to the father who could not go to him.

And then one of the torches flared, with a hissing of resinous wood, and cast a stronger light for a full minute upon the visitor's face. Hot eyes, quick and resolute, looked round upon Parfois in a sweeping stare, weighing and measuring and assessing the very harness and mounting-blocks of the stable-yard. He was smiling, the kind of smile which is not meant to be shared. The few steps he took across the cobbles had the large assurance of a proprietor.

And suddenly de Guichet was coming to meet him out of the archway of the inner ward. What was he doing out of hall at this hour? No one had run with a message yet, no one had called him. The seneschal should have been close at his lord's side.

Close at his lord's side! And perhaps he was. He came hastening with lavish surprise, his bow was no more obsequious than was reasonable to his master's son; but his voice, loud and clear in the first astonished greeting, fell very readily into a confidential undertone as they drew together. It was nothing, only a pricking of the thumbs, a tremor of the imagination; and yet it bit into Harry's mind like acid, and left a mark there was no erasing. No commitment yet, it was too soon; nothing, only a small, cautious reconnaissance, to make sure how the land lay. But very surely this was no embassage from the king; William was here on William's own business.

Suddenly Harry thought of Isambard at his high table in the crowded hall, of the thousand or so knights and squires and retainers and men-at-arms of his household gathered below him, of the inescapable light that would show them every motion, every change in his face. He claimed to care nothing for his banishment, did he, to set no store by the hope of his recall to the king's favour? They should see, they should see whether he cared! They should see his hopes raised, if secretly he cherished hopes, and see them dashed; and if he came unscathed through that test let him devise what punishment he would for Harry in return.

Harry ran, his heart beating up hot and vengeful into his

throat, and slid through the shadowy archway ahead of them, and came first to the steps of the great hall. The din and the smoke and the warmth came out to meet him. He edged between the hurrying scullions and began to thread his way in haste towards the high table.

He could very well have gone round and whispered his message into Isambard's ear, but that was not what he wanted. He came to the steps of the dais and mounted them boldly, taking his stand at the end of the high table, where he could command a view of the hall and leave Isambard exposed to the eyes of every man present.

'My lord – !'

He waited a moment for the expectant hush; he wanted them all to hear, not merely the knights, but the last pot-boy at the end of the room.

'My lord, there are messengers come from Shrewsbury to wait on you, from the court.'

There was so little time, he could hope for no more than two minutes before they made their entry and shattered the grand illusion. But two minutes was enough. The babel of voices, stilled to hear him, broke out again on a lower, warier note, wondering, excited, waiting for the proof. Isambard's lounging body did not stiffen in his chair, his hands did not tighten on the tapestried arms; only his eyes widened a little and his eyebrows rose, and he sat looking speculatively at Harry across the loaded table, not as though he disbelieved, rather as though he wondered at the reason behind the announcement. If he was glad and relieved, if he felt any small, thankful surge of triumph and exultation, he dissembled them uncommonly well. He kept, you would have said, an open mind, and waited the event with a certain amount of illusionless interest, but without any great concern.

No, it was not he who rose to the bait. If Harry had wanted a revelation, he had it. He looked round the high table in one wild glance, and saw how many faces closed like shuttered windows, how many pairs of eyes, flaring for one instant into uneasiness and consternation, glazed over next moment in the sealed countenances, and cloaked up the motions of the minds within. In haste and disquiet they made their reassessments, and composed their faces woodenly to cover the agony. All the waverers eased their coats on their shoulders, ready to turn them again according to the way the wind blew. Harry stood dumb with dismay to see how many they were.

'Well, bid them in,' said Isambard, and the dryness of his voice brought the blood to the messenger's cheeks. 'They are welcome.'

'They are here, my lord.'

It was done now; he could not undo it if he would. He stepped aside into the hangings of the dais as de Guichet came in by the high door, bright and dutiful as became the bearer of tidings, with William Isambard at his back.

Every eye in the room flashed to them, and settled upon the newcomer. A vast sigh shuddered through the air and quaked into absolute silence, as William walked to meet his father, bowed above the extended hand, and kissed the fleshless cheek. The two faces leaned together a moment, and their likeness and their violent differences shocked Harry like a blow. It was done so tenderly, with such filial devotion. He heard the affectionate greeting, the air between was so still.

'My dear lord and father, I grieve to see you unhappy.'

'Do you see me so, William?' said Isambard with his crooked grin. 'I had thought I looked in very fair spirits. You, I see, are in good heart enough. Do you stay with us for a while, now that you are here?'

'I would I might, but the king leaves Shrewsbury tomorrow, and I must ride back in good time. I have no leave of absence for more than a few hours.'

'I could spare you the half of mine. I have leave of absence without limit. Sit down with me here, then, while you have licence, and let me hear your news.' He made room for his son on his right hand, and the pages ran to cover for him and pour the wine. Across the table Isambard lifted his sardonic glance to Harry Talvace, frozen and mute against the wall.

'Go to your place, Harry,' he said mildly. 'You did your errand well. I could hardly have bettered it myself.'

That was praise he could well have done without, but he could not complain that he had not earned it. He went on trembling legs, burningly aware of de Guichet's eyes boring into his back. The seneschal could not well ask his lord which errand, but he could reason and connect sharply enough. Maybe he was wondering now on whose side this lonely alien was playing, and whether the mocking intimacy Isambard affected with him did not cover his private employment as a spy about the castle wards. Harry felt the complications of intrigue sticking to his fingers, and the sensation outraged him, as though he had found himself physically soiled by some filth he could not wipe off. And even when he had taken his seat at a lower table among the young gentlemen-at-arms of birth comparable with his own, he was not delivered from having to hear the voices from the dais. It seemed that Isambard was bent on pitching the tone of the conversation so high and clear that it should carry a fair way down the hall and reach hundreds of witnesses; and in the presence of the noble and unexpected guest the young men of the retinue hushed their own talk into whispers, so that he had no defence from hearing.

'And how did you leave his Grace?' asked Isambard serenely, tilting his wine-cup to catch the captive ruby in the light of the candles on the table. 'Is he content with his prolonged truce?'

'Very well content, and in excellent spirits. He goes to keep Christmas at Worcester.'

'And you with him, William?'

'I have that honour. As an officer of his household now –'

'Ah, yes, I had not forgotten. But put *my* household out of its pain, man: he did not send you to call me back to court?'

'Alas, no, Father, not yet. Give him time, and he'll cool. His Grace was cruelly hurt by your censure, but I know it came from your loyal heart, and your concern for him. Only wait, and he'll forgive. I shall be there at his right hand to see that you're not forgotten.'

'Ah, that I never doubted,' said Isambard, smiling like a happy devil. 'And you will be my advocate and speak for me, will you not, my son? For the honesty of my intent and the unquestionable faithfulness of my attachment to him?'

'You know I will, my lord. Assiduously.'

'Assiduously!' He uttered it slowly, rolling it on his tongue as if it had a flavour stronger and more to his taste than the wine. 'I marvel, William, that he spared you to me even for an hour, you whom he values so highly. Let me see, is it three sheriffdoms you hold now, or four? I have forgotten.'

'Four, my lord.'

'And his Grace has been pleased to confer another manor upon you for your services, so I heard.'

'Yes, my lord – Burhythe, in Suffolk. I have not seen it yet. When the court moves south I must ride over and view it.'

'On my word, I'm glad one of us is in the ascendant. I never doubted your vigour and efficiency. If you stand my friend how can I fail to speed in the end?'

'In good earnest, Father, I've done my best, but the time is not ripe yet. He's very bitter against de Burgh, as I for one can well understand. Bide here and wait and trust me, and I won't fail you.'

'I call that more than generous in you,' said Isambard, 'seeing you do not hold with me over the issue of the earl of Kent.'

Was it deliberate or merely habit in him, that he still insisted on using the old style and title, now ripped from the fallen statesman's name?

'I do not. But I know the honesty with which you hold your views, and I know you are the king's true man, and that's enough.'

'And how was it with the earl of Kent when you left London? What was the news of him?'

Twice in a row could not be accident; this was perversity.

He was declaring his contempt for the judgement and his continued respect for the victim, publicly and provocatively.

William told more than he was asked, and elaborated the whole sorry tale so willingly that Harry could not but read something of a threat and a warning into the narration. Why else should he dwell on the malice and viciousness of the long persecution, that shrieked out the king's meanness of spirit even while the narrator found excuses for his venom? No man had ever been more mercilessly hounded than de Burgh. By the time he should have appeared before the king's council at Lambeth in September they had amassed so long and gross a farrago of charges against him, and so many were pressing for his blood, that it was no wonder he feared for his life to come.

And then to tear him out of sanctuary and, when the bishops in holy indignation forced his restoration to the altar, to lay siege to him there for the forty days' respite needed before he could be declared outlaw, to deny access even to his priest, to forbid the very servants who took his food to speak a word to him, to have his personal seal ceremoniously destroyed and his prayer-book taken away from him, and at the end of the forty days triumphantly and righteously to withdraw food and attendants from him, so that he must needs surrender himself or starve. Was that the behaviour of a king, or of a vindictive child sick with his own spleen? The Tower must have seemed like a gentle hermitage after such usage.

All the same, Henry had not killed him. Why not? Because Isambard first and Ranulf of Chester afterwards had spoken for too large and formidable a body of opinion to be quite ignored? At least when Hubert came before the commission of earls and the justiciar at Cornhill the issue had been pressed less rigorously than might have been expected, considering what had gone before. Surely sick to the heart of the whole business of living and struggling by then, de Burgh, it seemed, had refused steadily to submit to a judgement or make a defence, and simply thrown himself on the king's mercy, to use as he would. The lands of his inheritance or purchase had been left to him, but all those held of the crown stripped from him with his earldom; and the four earls of the commission, Richard of Pembroke, Lacy of Lincoln, Richard of Cornwall and the earl of Surrey, held the broken man in protective custody at Devizes. Held him, thought Harry, watching William Isambard's face as he deployed the wretched details of the long harrying, more gently far than the king would have wished could he have had his way.

'I take it very kindly, dear son,' said Isambard, spreading his velvet sleeves at ease over the board, 'that you go to such pains to acquaint me with every circumstance. I take the warning as it is meant. I am a tamed man, William, I grow old.'

The glow of his secret amusement had ripped ten years from him, or else the wine was flowing more freely than usual up there at the high table; and the wolf had never roved more happily at liberty than now in his mildly smiling eyes.

'It is my fixed intent to do it at leisure and in liberty,' he said with gentle emphasis, and pledged his son with an infinitely private parody of the affection and deference William was lavishing on him.

Rather ill-matched at first sight, those two; but by the time he had watched them to the end of the long supper Harry was not so sure the son favoured the father as little as he had thought. His was a different subtlety, yet he was subtle. In his way he went as directly and dauntingly for what he wanted as the old man had always done, and would tread down whoever stood in his way with as little compunction. But his wants were comprehensible things, land, office, money, power, and therefore his ways could be guessed at with some accuracy; and he would not care that they were known provided they could not be blocked. He must know that his father was laughing at him now, and it mattered to him not at all, and certainly would not deter him from his purpose. But who knew what the old wolf wanted, and who could guess by what devious ways he pursued his ends?

Land, status, money, power, all had fallen early into his hands. These were not what tormented him, and it was not for these he tormented others.

'I am sorry from my heart,' said William when he rose at last from the table, 'that I cannot offer you better comfort, or stay with you longer. I ride with the advance party tomorrow, to make all ready for the king. But when next I visit you I pray it may be with better news.' He seemed to hesitate for a moment, and lowered his voice a little when he proceeded, but so little that those at the knights' tables and some below could not choose but hear. 'If you wish to have some message carried, I'll gladly be your courier.'

Harry heard that, and his senses tightened in silent resistance, as though by straining his flesh he could cry a warning. But Isambard, rising and stretching lazily beside his son, and by some two or three inches the taller of the two, let the invitation rebound stonily from his eroded cliff of a forehead, and smiled.

'Why, since you are so kind, you may carry my respectful greetings and service – to the king.'

They went out together, and the irony of their going was almost more than Harry could bear. For William offered his arm tenderly to his hard, athletic sire, and the old man in pure mischief took it, and leaned heavily upon it all the way out into the inner ward, and across the frosty parclose to the archway and the stable-yard.

For the life of him Harry did not know why he followed. It was nothing to him which of them destroyed the other, he wished all their house under the sod; and yet he was drawn after them wretchedly, raging at himself but still following, with pricked ears and anxious heart, to see the party from Shrewsbury mount and ride. He saw William Isambard stoop to the old man's hand, and then, rising, lean to his gaunt cheek once again with the deferential kiss of a loving and faithful son.

The stab of prophetic anguish pinned Harry to the wall, and set him writhing in the shadows where he stood. He dug his nails into the stones, suddenly overwhelmed with shame, as though he had seen and abetted a terrible twilight betrayal. Smoke of torches and murmur of voices, and one coming all affection and loyalty, with a kiss and an acknowledgement.

They were gone. The bridge creaked before them and thundered distantly under them, and for a few minutes crisp, frosty echoes of hoofbeats clanged hollowly back from the plateau of the church, before the cavalcade swept away into silence down the ramp to the lower guard.

Isambard, straightening with a cat's fluid grace from his parody of an old man's careful walk, shrugged off his attendants and stalked back alone through the dark archway. He all but flattened Harry into the wall, and stretched an arm good-humouredly enough to steady him on his legs again.

'What, Harry, have you not been busy enough for one night?'

There was no displeasure in his voice, only the faint, distant echo of laughter, though he was not laughing now. He held him a moment between his hands, peering narrowly through the frosty starlight that showed them to each other silvery and strange, more transparent than by day.

'Never look so shamefaced, child,' he said, clapping him hard on the shoulder. 'What have you to hang your head about? It was I bred him, not you.'

He had gone but a couple of steps more when he halted abruptly and looked back. He was himself again, his eyes quick with demons, his mouth wry.

'The dispensations of God are always just,' he said. 'We get the sons we deserve.'

CHAPTER THREE

Aber, Strata Marcella: *August* 1233

Above the last dry-stone sheepfold, above the russet flanks
of the heather, where the tussocky upland grass bleached in
the sun mile upon rolling mile, there was an old wooden
calvary under a penthouse-roof of shingles, and beside it the
two anchorite huts: Saint Clydog's, of withies and daub,
on the left, a beehive with a lancet doorway facing east, and
on the right the stone cell of the holy woman of Aber, with a
carved lintel and an arched window to southward. All
round from sky to sky there was nothing to see but the seeding grasses and the grazing sheep, and in the occasional
hollow the clustering, low bushes above the coney-runs. But
in the still of the August day the sound of the sea came floating on the hushed air, the long, slow heave and fall of the
rising tide along the salt marshes of Aber, far below and
out of sight; and sometimes in the evening they could hear,
infinitely faint and far, all the little bells ringing in all the
little oratories on Ynys Lanog of the saints, across the silver
strait.

Saint Clydog and the holy woman were under the direct
protection of Prince Llewelyn, and could have commanded
whatever comforts they would from him; but they never
asked for anything. What he sent up to them by his regular
monthly messenger he sent of his own will, before they
could so much as feel want; and much of it they gave again,
to the birds and the small, shy beasts of the hills, and the rare
travellers who passed by on the upland pathways. The saint
had all but forgotten that he had a body, and took thought
only to give it what would keep it from crying out on him
from hunger, and disturbing his prayers. And the woman,
who had once been broad and bold and sturdy as a tower,

77

had fined away these last years into pure, steely flame, wearing away her flesh from within and without. Her eyes were full and calm, and fixed always a little beyond the rim of what other men could see. They had a deep, clear colour like purple irises, that the full light of noon paled to lustrous grey. The country people said that Saint Clydog saw into the future, but what Madonna Benedetta saw nobody knew, except that it was not in this world. And yet the rest of her face was not made for repose, not for a life withdrawn and a blessed death. It had such breadth and challenge in its bones, such a curled, bright, resolute flower of a mouth. The queens in the old stories had such faces, and the great sorrows of them, and their loves, came to mind in beholding Benedetta, and put a new awe and a new meaning into the name they had for her; for great sorrow and great love are awful and holy.

Of the past she never spoke. In the solitude and silence of the hills there was no need, and among the herdsmen who brought milk and eggs to her door there was no curiosity. She had been there for sixteen years, and might have been there always, like the heather on Moel Wnion or the outcrop rocks above the brook, so unquestioningly did they accept her. If she had drifted from Italy to France with a Parisian merchant grown fat on the pickings of the Crusades, from France to England in the loftier company of the lord of Parfois, and from England to Wales as a fugitive at last from that same formidable lover, what was that to them? Why ask whence the seed had blown that rooted and flowered to stillness and holiness among their native grasses?

There were things they did know concerning her. She had brought with her in her flight a lady, a servant and a child, and placed them all under Prince Llewelyn's powerful protection. The lady had married the prince's English mason, who was foster-brother to her first husband, so they said, and had long been close and kind with her; and her son had grown up well fathered by craftsman and monarch alike, and well loved and more than a little over-indulged by his princely foster-brothers. But a good boy for all that. There had been the devil to pay when he ran away from his privileged place at Aber on some mad quest after his father's murderer; the cloud of his loss still hung upon the court, and rescue still delayed.

But the holy woman of Aber, though she had taken no vows, kept her place constant as the crown of the mountain in her fixed station, abiding by her silent bargain with God, never looked reproach, never uttered complaint, never gave house-room to desire. Only when the boy's mother paid her rare visits, bringing back the old world in her fresh, fierce voice and brilliant, grieving eyes, did the blood quicken in Benedetta's cheeks to the stirring of God knew what memories.

She sat in the grass of the hollow hillside above the huts, with Gilleis beside her, watching the men cut fresh withies in the fold of the brook below. Adam Boteler, master-mason to the prince, was big and comely and fair, and at this distance there was no telling which of his thick locks were flaxen and which were white. Gilleis, as often as her eyes chanced to rest upon him, softened and smiled secretly, heavy with the weight of her tenderness. Second husbands find a place of their own in generous hearts, where they have room and to spare without ever infringing the rights of the first. And in any case, the two had been all but inseparable, when both were living, and lain in the same bed long before they had ever set eyes on Gilleis Otley. It was a question whether she always knew which of them she held in her arms, or made any distinction between them.

'Adam misses him as sorely as I do,' said Gilleis. 'Would ever you think that I could almost hope for a war? I never wished ill to any poor creature, English or Welsh, but now it shames me to feel my blood quicken when I hear of these disorders in the south, and of the earl of Pembroke collecting his malcontents together in Gwent. How else are we ever to get Harry back? The prince made a vow to go and fetch him in arms, but while there's truce how can he move?'

'And how will civil war in England help him?' said Benedetta, looking up over the embroidery she held in her
79

lap. 'He cannot take sides for earl or king unless someone first offers offence to his territories.'

'Ah, but here are Pembroke's holdings so tangled into Wales that the king can hardly move against him without infringing land that's Welsh. That's cause enough to bring us in, if once these brawls turn into warfare. And let his hands be once loosed, and the prince will keep his word. That I know! But oh, Benedetta, it curdles my blood to find myself wishing for it. There are other women have sons, as dear to them as mine to me; how can I wish them sorrow to bring mine home?'

'God forbid,' said Benedetta, 'that ever I should preach patience to any man. But God may have other ways of bringing him home.'

'What other ways? He'll take no ransom for him, he'll neither give nor sell. "How can I put a price on a Talvace?" he says. Philip told us how he smiled as he said it. My child's growing a man,' said Gilleis, grieving, 'and I have not seen him for two years.'

It was nearer four since Benedetta had seen him, but that she kept unsaid. What use was there in measuring love by days and months? One hour, one night, could contain so much of it that even if no second such miracle came before death, life would still have been filled to the brim.

'Ah, but I remember he did not visit you at all, that time,' said Gilleis, reaching a remorseful hand to touch her sleeve. 'He meant to, but then he pressed his promise so hard it would not bear any indulgence. The proud wretch! The poor lamb! "If it were anyone else," he said, "but to that man not one scruple, not one farthing short of my debts."'

'I know,' said Benedetta, very still. 'I had the prince to be his messenger to me. I know!'

'"There is no price he has at his command," says Isambard when Rhys went to him on the prince's errand, that last time, "no price in money or aught else I would take for Harry Talvace. I'll name none and I'll consider none he may name, not in land, nor falcons, nor flesh." And to think how he delights in using him! Oh, Benedetta, when he told me how he came there to him in his cell, and took away food and drink and light from him one by one, how he had him dragged to the rack – '

'But he never used it,' said Benedetta suddenly and strangely, and raised the clear grey glance of her eyes to the rim of the grassland, where the hawks wheeled in great, languid circles.

' – and always tempting and trying him, to get out of him where Harry was laid, until he tricked him into betraying the place. And then to tear my dear out of his grave . . . And to think the man who used the father so has the son in his hands, and can't be forced to give him up.'

'Tell me,' said Benedetta abruptly, folding her hands on her work, 'what Harry told you of his captivity. Tell me the whole of it. The prince brought his message faithfully and delivered it well, but these things he never told me. I'm hungry for every crumb of him; give me to eat.'

Gilleis drew close and poured out the long, strange story. The boy had stamped his own smouldering distrust and hatred into his mother's mind and found a ready soil there. Every test and temptation imposed on him she recounted. All had been done in malice and mockery, all, even that astonishing act of releasing him to his prince's side for the duration of the bitter war of two years ago. He had surely willed him to break parole and never come back. To demoralise the boy would be to have the better of his race and his blood, and to destroy sire and son together at last.

'And where's it to end?' lamented Gilleis. 'If he cannot break him to dishonour, how much longer will he keep his hands from worse? If he had not sent such a message back by Rhys I should have been afraid for Harry's very life, and even with his pledge to keep the child safe, how can I be content he'll do him no injury? I know he never yet broke faith, if he had no other virtures, but there's a first time for every recreant – '

'But he did so swear? To keep him safe?'

' "Come when you will," he said, "fetch him away if you can. Till then I'll hold him safe for you." But how can we

81

know he'll keep his oath?'

'It would be late to change,' said Benedetta, and turned again to her work. Her hands were steady, but her eyes looked far away, and into a sudden brightness that dazzled and blinded them.

The men were coming up from the brook, John the Fletcher shouldering the cut withies, Adam swinging the brushing-hooks. Every year there were repairs to be made to Saint Clydog's modest cell, but he would not have them build him a hut of stone. He, too, was too old for changes. Benedetta turned her head and looked along the hillside to where he sat nursing his beads and revolving his interminable thoughts, hardly more than a tussock of bleached grass himself in the tangled head of Moel Wnion. He looked as if he had been there since the beginning of time; and he would be there still when she was gone. Had he not told her so once, when the inner sight opened within him, and a voice cried out of him in the night and brought her running?

Llewelyn's messenger was re-saddling the horses, below at the cross. Adam came and dropped into the grass beside the women, sunburned and gentle and flushed with the work.

'We'd best be moving soon, lass. The sun's dropping lower. If you've had your women's talk out?' He knew what the subject would be, it had them all by the heart; they were bled pale from living with it. He slipped his arm round his wife's shoulders and drew her close; she leaned to him gladly and gratefully, but he felt the ache in her for the boy whose place he could not supply.

'Women's talk, is it?' said Benedetta. 'We were on matters of state. I hear the earl marshal has withdrawn himself from the king's council, and taken a great number of other lords with him, out of discontent with the new order. Is it true there's even some fighting in the south?'

'Why, since de Burgh fell, and in such fashion,' said Adam, 'there's no man in England trusts the law to keep him from a like fate. If it could happen to Kent it can happen to Pembroke; small blame to him for placing himself

82

out of the king's reach. Since he made himself the voice for all those who dared not speak out against the Poitevins themselves, the king may well be planning to clap him in hold and beat up charges against him as busily as he did with the other. They could lean on custom and feudal law once to preserve them from summary usage, but custom and law are being thrust out of court now. If the charters are to count for nothing, then a man must preserve his rights himself as best he can.'

'But how did this dissension grow into violence? It seems they've gone past complaining, if the king has summoned the host to assemble at Gloucester, as Gilleis tells me. That looks like war in good earnest. What does he mean to do with his host from Gloucester?'

'Take it into Ireland, so they're saying, and strike at Marshall through his lands in Leinster. There was some talk that de Burgh's nephew there might be disaffected, too, for his uncle's sake, but there's no love lost between Marshall and de Burgh over there, and it seems likely Richard de Burgh will hold with the king. So Henry may find work for his muster nearer home, after all. The whole flare-up came from a small spark, but it's well ablaze now. And the issue's not so small, neither, if there's to be any law left. There was a manor belonging to Gilbert Basset of Wycombe that the king wanted to give to one of his own servants, and he disseised Basset of it without any proper process. "By the king's will" is law enough, nowadays. Richard Marshall stood up for Basset, and before you could turn he was being warned Henry meant to seize and ruin him when next he came to attend the great council. So he never came. It might not be true, but there's de Burgh to show the way it's done, and even an earl has only one life to lose. He took himself into Pembroke, and mustered his confederacy after him. And now the king's going to all lengths to have extra watch kept everywhere, and calling in hostages from the barons of the march, like his father before him. And what with Basset having served once as constable at Devizes, and knowing the castle too well for comfort, there's an alarm that he means to take Hubert de Burgh out of captivity and have him away to join the earl marshal's allies in Wales. The king has his own guards in Devizes now, and I doubt the poor wretch will find his bed grow harder again, even if they leave him out of irons. They say the bishop of Winchester is busy persuading the king to make him Hubert's gaoler. Some say he's even urging his execution. I doubt the one would be as effective as the other. They ran to him for help when the mob was after Hubert, that first time. The bishop reproved them for interrupting his prayers, and closed the door on them.'

'What if the king marches on the earl marshal's Welsh lands, what then? What will the prince do?'

Adam shook his head. 'If he can forbear, I think he'd liefer. This government has never threatened him, and the peace, if it can hold, serves his turn well. But if the king breaks it, and the prince is pressed hard to take sides, he'll surely side with the earl marshal.'

'Then the matter of Harry may solve itself,' said Benedetta, 'for surely Isambard will hold with the king. He has always been the king's true man, even when his heart and his judgement went the opposite way. John went far to sicken him, but he held by John to the death, and if John's son calls him on his fealty, he'll come in arms. He'll be on his way to Gloucester now.'

'He would,' said Adam ruefully, 'if the king had summoned him. But with things the way they were there, I stake my head that's one place where the writ won't be served.' He saw the pale, bright face quicken with wonder, and the grey eyes flare wide. 'Did you not know he's out of grace? The king has forbidden him his presence and ordered him to remain at Parfois until he sees fit to recall him. A year ago, about this time, it befell. And no one ever thought to tell you?'

It was not so surprising, after all. They rode up here but two or three times a year, and there were other things to talk about when they came. Isambard had cost them grief enough in the old days to banish his name for ever between them, if young Harry had not renewed the ancient pain and called him back into their minds only too nearly and dearly.

Benedetta rose from the grass, gathering her thoughts like mustering armies behind the deep grey of her eyes.

'How did he come to this case?'

'As we heard it, it was just after de Burgh's fall, when King Henry came to Shrewsbury. Isambard went down in his state, and told the king in open audience he did very foully and ungratefully, and the earl of Kent was a loyal servant to him, not deserving of such usage. Gave it to him in his teeth, and would not abate one word for the king's anger.'

'That rings true,' said Benedetta, frowning back into her own memories. 'That he would, and all the more for threatening. And he's down, is he? Disgraced and banished the court?'

'Till the king recalls him. But there are those who think he never will. And sure I am,' said Adam, as they went three abreast down the hill to the waiting horses, 'he'll hardly call him to the muster against Earl Richard, if he reckons him to be of de Burgh's party, for what with their common enmity against the Poitevins, though God knows it's almost all they have in common, Pembroke's party and de Burgh's are being lumped together as one. No, Isambard will sleep undisturbed in Parfois. The king daren't call on him to fulfil his dues, and daren't move against him.'

'And Harry'll still lie and rot under close guard,' said Gilleis bitterly. She heard Benedetta draw breath upon a stab of pain, and turned remorsefully to embrace her. 'Ah, it's wicked in me to complain, when you love him, too, and miss him as I do. All his best years taken from us! Who will help him to his manhood there? Who'll delight in him and measure the strides he makes? And forgive him his mistakes, and love him for what he does well?'

'God will,' said Benedetta, staring great-eyed against the far pallor of the sky, 'if there's none other. And God can provide him another if he chooses.'

All night she lay awake, and the dead came into her bed and lay with her. She held him in her arms, and he was both father and son, and doubly dear. She smoothed her cheek against his head, covering him with her cloak of crimson hair, silvered over now with the dust of time; and the turmoil within her and the calm without fought out the long hours of the dark with words that had no voice but silence. My heart, my love, my little one, my sweet friend. Is it time? Has the world a use for me, after all? Has the child a use for me? Has God a use for me? Have I been keeping faith with him all this time that I lay here still, or have I been breaking faith? My soul, my darling, what must I do? Once I kneeled to him, kissed his feet, prayed him for your life, and was denied. There was no price I had to offer him that could buy you back, no way but to take you by force, and so I took you. But how if I am richer now? How if I can offer him a ransom for the child that even he will not refuse? And how if I pray him this once more, and how if I am heard? Will you lend me your countenance and approval, or will you turn from me? My love, my heart, I am in darkness. Light me! I know no other lantern but you.

She had held him but once in life like this, on the night before he died. It had taken so little prompting to induce the old chaplain to remind his lord how it had always been his custom to allow condemned men their chosen indulgence before they died, and Isambard in open hall had pledged himself to grant anything short of liberty. Still she could see that stricken, dreadful mask with which he had received the trembling answer: 'My lord, he asks – May God forgive him! – he asks for Madonna Benedetta to be his bedfellow.' He had pledged himself and he could not withdraw; and smiling, smiling she had gone from him, slowly, careful that he should know how she gloried in his anguish and impotence. 'It touches your honour. What am I beside the sacredness of your word?'

Eye to eye with him now above her darling's sleep, she stood him off unsmiling. When did I ever deceive you until then? I told you from the first, when you would have me come with you to Parfois, that my love was given once for all, though he that had it neither loved nor desired me, nor ever would. But still you would have me, all that was left of me, even on those terms. And I came, and I kept my bargain with you. 'Until death or he call me from you,' I said, 'or you discard me.' And death and Harry called me from you with one voice, and then you thought you understood all. Fool, could you but have heard the first word I had for him when he reached his hands to me! 'She's safe, she's well, she sends you her heart's love.' Could you but have seen in what manner of fellowship we passed that night, the only night ever I had my love in my arms! How I talked to him of Gilleis and of his child that would be born, and promised him that he should not be broken, that death was in God's gift, not in yours.

Then, as now, Harry had slept while she watched out the hours, loving and sinless; and in the morning she had kissed him awake to make himself fine for death. What did Gilleis know, or Adam, or any other living creature, of that inexpressible union? But God knew, and God could rip time apart and give the hour back to her, to hold her heart steady while she found her way. Where were the slender, nimble bones now, the intrepid hands, the swart, stubborn face? Ravished from the secret grave, tumbled, perhaps, down the Severn a second time to end that vengeance, as Adam bitterly believed. Yet not lost; even this lesser part of him God might yet restore her.

When the first softening of the darkness came before dawn she rose from her sleepless bed and went up to the crest of the hill, where the wind was waking and the moan of the sea came up to her, the heave and fall of the incoming tide, like great sighs from a long-remembered grief, grown still and tranquil at last after great anguish. She loosed her long hair about her, and paced out the remaining hours of the night like a questing hound in the colourless grass, silent and intent and charged, waiting for the sign. And in the dawn she came down from the hill, with a calm upon her like the finished stone, which is shaped and perfected and must not be touched again, for awe of its absolute integrity.

John the Fletcher, squat and bowed and brown as an oak, was rolling up his bedding from across her threshold. She had stepped over him in the night and he had never stirred, and for that he was angry with himself and her. What was the use of a watchdog, if she could evade his guard so easily?

'So you're there, are you?' he said gruffly, stepping out of the doorway to let her go by. 'What ailed you to go gallivanting about in the night? If you wanted aught you should have sent me on your errand. What else am I for?'

'For comfort and company to me, and much more besides. I wanted nothing but air and quiet, and what was there to harm me there on the hill?'

'And no shoes on your feet against the chill of the dew,' he said crossly, and brought the thonged leather shoes and made her put them on, warming her feet in his calloused palms before he shut their whiteness up from sight. 'Do you want to be laid sick, and only me for nurse?'

'I could well do worse, John.'

He had nursed her once, long ago, how tenderly and constantly, drawing her back half-unwilling from the doorsill of death. She remembered the hard hands cradling her head, and wiping away the apprentice tears of this second birth. And a pitcher of milk warm from the cow, she remembered that, and a countrywoman with dark gold hair and gentle eyes; dead now, so they said, having first stamped a child in her own true image. Benedetta felt the old years gathering about her like close acquaintances, unchanged and unforgotten. This new day in which she moved was all the days of her life, like the instant of death in a heart at peace.

'But I have an errand for you now,' she said, putting out her hand and touching his grey, bushy hair as he latched her shoes. 'There's a letter I must write and send. Will you ride with it, when you've broken your fast?'

'I never yet knew you to remember everything you had to tell Mistress Boteler when she came up,' he said tolerantly. 'I suppose there's threads you should have asked for, and had so much else to say you never called it to mind. Yes, I'll ride. You write your letter.'

'It's not to Gilleis this time, John, it's a longer ride I had in mind for you. But leave me write it first, and I'll tell you.'

He gave her a long, sharp look for that, but asked her nothing more then. There was nothing she could ask of him he would not give her, even his silence and absence if she willed it so. He left her alone with the newly-pointed pen he kept fine for her, and a cleaned parchment from the chest, and she wrote with deliberation, pondering the words. By the time she had finished, and sealed the roll closely and carefully, he was waiting for her with milk and new bread, and honey from the heather bees. He had three hives in a sheltered place in a hollow below, and nursed his swarms through the winter lovingly so that Benedetta should not want for sweets.

'Am I to saddle up now? I see you've done your writing.'

'You'll need food with you,' she said, coming gently to the heart of it. 'And money for your lodging on the way. I told you it's a long ride.'

He was stiffening already with doubt and wariness. 'Where is it you'd have me go?'

'To Parfois, John, to my lord Isambard.'

It was out. She saw the knotty hands shut into fists at his sides, and the gleam of old remembrance spring like flame in his sharp eyes. He had forgotten nothing and forgiven nothing. Whoever forgave, John never would. Once his life had been wantonly threatened, and she had retrieved it, but it was not that he saw, sharp and clear after years, at the mention of Isambard's name. He saw the Severn in turgid brown flood below the Long Mountain, and the dead man and the living woman, bound together breast to naked breast, rolled under in the deep currents and dragged down towards Breidden, wound in the streaming weed of her long red hair.

'Have you no errand I can do for you in hell?' he said. 'There's cleaner company there.'

89

'But Harry's in Parfois, John,' she said mildly. 'Will you go?'

'Ah, I thought that was what you had in your mind. You know well I'll go wherever you send me, but not gladly, not there,' said John grimly. 'For you'll get nothing for your pleading. Wait and let the prince fetch him away with the sword. I'd liefer not see you stoop to beg and be refused.'

'But how if I am not refused? What right have I, John, to hold back from trying, when it may be he'll give me the boy, for all you say?'

'Others have asked. Others have pleaded and offered ransom, and I know not what, and never a word back but mockery. Why should you submit yourself to the same usage?'

'Why should I spare myself the same usage? Who am I, that I should go free? Ah, John,' she said in a sudden soft cry, 'bear with me. I do only what I must.'

'I'll go,' he said resignedly. At worst she would not have to see Ralf Isambard's triumph. If he could bring her back nothing but a refusal, at least he could spare her the cruellest of it. 'God he knows I'd rather cut his throat than speak him fair, but what you bid me do I'll do, and God spare you from any pain of my giving. Let me have your letter then. What am I to do when I get to Parfois?'

'Tell them at the lower guard that you ask admittance to my lord Isambard, with a message from Benedetta Foscari. And to prove that you do truly come from me,' she said, 'you will take him this.'

She stripped the ring from the little finger of her left hand. Often she had wondered why she had kept it, that single opal in its circlet of gold. It was the only thing he had left on her, when he stripped her and had her flung into the river, so small a thing neither she nor he had thought of it, or she would surely have tossed it at his feet. He had given it to her in Paris, before ever they crossed the sea together on their way to Parfois, he with his heart set on her, she with hers full of Harry Talvace.

'He'll know that,' she said, 'past doubting.'

He took it in his brown, horny palm, and held it gingerly, as though it might burn him, or break in his grasp.

'And if he have me killed on sight?' he said reasonably.

'If he receives you as a messenger he'll not harm you. For good or evil, he was always punctilious. Once he lets you in your life will be sacred. He'd kill anyone who touched you or offered you offence.'

'And if I speed?' he said.

'Then give him my letter and bring me back his reply, whether he write it or speak it. And God go with you, John, and prosper my intent.'

'Amen!' growled John, but without much faith.

When he had made his preparations, she followed him out and watched him buckle on saddlebags and cloak. Saint Clydog beneath the crucifix never turned his ancient head, but she felt that he knew already what was afoot, and would speak his mind about it when it suited him.

'John – !' She held him by the stirrup-leather when he would have drawn away. 'You're not angry with me?'

He looked down at her, and through the bushy beard she saw the smile tremulous on his mouth for love of her.

'Never be angry with me,' she said like a child. 'If I had not you, what should I do?'

'God love you!' said John, shaken, and his hand pushed back her hood and stroked clumsily over the mane of her hair. 'My little lass!' he said, and pulled away from her and set spurs to his horse down the hill.

When the prior of Strata Marcella came back from Prime, somewhat after seven in the morning, it was to find one of the hospitaller's assistants waiting anxiously at the door of his chamber, to ask audience for an importunate guest.

'He slept here the night, Father, and had nothing further then to ask of us. But this morning he came to me and begged that you would see him on a grave matter. He says there's life and death in it.'

'What manner of man is he?' asked the prior, frowning.

'A manservant, Father, and trusty. We have provided

him a roof before. He is servant of that lady who brought the body of Master Talvace to rest here. They call him John the Fletcher.'

'Bid him come,' said the prior. For what touched the affairs of Madonna Benedetta, however she chose to hide herself from sight and memory in a cranny of the north Welsh hills, touched Llewelyn's great princedom and was knotted close with his generous patronage of the Cistercian order on this side of Severn. He could not afford to turn away any man of hers.

John the Fletcher came into the cool, stony cell, and went on his knees to kiss the prior's hand. The thin fingers blessed him.

'My son, you have something to ask of me. I am listening.'

John got to his feet, square and knotty and brown like the bole of a tree, a growth out of the soil of Flintshire. He held Benedetta's letter before him in both hands, his fingers tight on the coil of parchment.

'Father, this is a story I must tell my own way, for I need your help, and I need that you should know the whole of it. Three days ago my mistress wrote this letter, and bade me take it, with her ring to be my warrant, to Ralf Isambard of Parfois, and there to deliver it into his own hands, and bring back his answer. Father, it is well known to you that this man holds prisoner young Harry Talvace, who is foster-son to Prince Llewelyn, and dear, more than dear, to my mistress. It was she brought him safe out of England when he was but a child new-born, and his mother with him. I know, for I was her man on that journey as I've been her man ever since, and shall be as long as I live. Father, what was I to think when she sent me with a letter to Isambard?'

The prior pondered for a moment what seemed to him a plain question, and hardly likely to account for the darkness in the weathered face before him.

'I suppose that Madonna Benedetta desired to make her own plea for the release of the boy, trusting to move a heart that once set a high value on any wish of hers. I suppose that she hoped to win him where others with ransoms had failed.'

'And that seems to you a reasonable hope, Father?'

'It is not *likely*. But it is not unreasonable. There is nothing to be lost by the attempt.'

'Then I am justified so far,' said John grimly, 'for so I thought also, and I took the letter and rode, thinking no ill though I expected little good. Sure I was she would be refused, and in some cruel fashion as the devil lent him wit, who has always lent him more than enough. And yet there was still the small corner of hope that he might be moved. All these years he's had no word of her, I doubt he knows certainly whether she's living or dead. To hold her ring in his hand again, suddenly, without warning, I thought it might shake even a stone. Yet consider, Father, how he used her before. What, give her what she wanted, he who cast her living into Severn there and sent her down with Master Harry bound in her arms, to rot with him unburied? No! Rather if he knew of a thing she still wanted, of a thing she would plead for, it would be joy to him to use it for her hurt and shame. Why did I ever trust her? Why did I believe it? Yet she never lied to me. Take the letter, she said, and bring me the answer. It was I who took the text as read, and never asked her what I was carrying.'

'It was your duty so to do,' said the prior sternly. 'It is still your duty.'

'My duty as a servant. But I am a man, too. I was a man first. I do my duty by her, being her servant, as well as I may. But I love her, being a man, more than my life or my duty. She covered me with her cloak and kept me man alive – man, not servant! Shall I let her go to her death to keep my own record virgin?'

'You have read the letter!' said the prior, rising in indignation.

'Father, if I could read I should have no need of you. I am not asking you to tell me what to do.' He came a step closer, holding the parchment before him. 'Father, in the night I dreamed of her. I was by the Severn in flood, brown and full and fast it was, and the timbers of the stage creaking and straining in the run of it. Many a night I've seen it in my sleep, but never so clear. And like that day, she came down the current pale and naked, with a man in her arms, and like that day I went in and drew them ashore. But this time the man stood up from between my hands as I unbound him, and went from us alive and hale, and I saw it was the young one, the boy she wills to set free. And this time she lay in my arms, and I breathed my breath into her mouth, and warmed her in my bosom, and she never moved again. I held her on my heart dead, Father. And when I woke I knew it was God sent me the dream, and it was her death I was carrying, under her own seal.'

The hoarse voice had stilled and stilled to a husky whisper; the words came slowly, too laden with his dread and faith for passion to find any room in them. At the end of it he lifted his shaggy head and looked the prior in the face, advancing the rolled parchment on his hands like an offering.

'Father, read it to me. I must know what she does, that I may know what I am to do.'

The prior drew back a step in haste to avoid the touch. 'I cannot violate your lady's seal, man. What is it you are asking me to do?'

'There is no need. I have parted the seal. I can mend it again. A fine knife and a candle-flame is all I need.'

'You have opened it? What treason is this towards your mistress? What have you done?'

He knew that he cast his breath into the wind; as well ask a tree knotted into the roots of the mountains to suffer a sense of guilt for growing after its urgent and laborious nature. And who was he, in the face of such an intensity of love and fear, to herd all issues into the compartments of social usage? It was the unlettered man who had the eloquence now; it might be he who saw the truth plainest.

'I have done what I must. I would not ask it of you. For what I've done I'll answer to God in the day of judgement, and if he wills to damn my soul for it I'll never murmur, so long as hers stays in her dear body until God please to come to her quietly and take it to himself. Should I come to you,

Father, with anything that made me ashamed? What do I matter? What's honour to me? My honour is to keep her from harm and from grief. I have no other; I want none.'

The prior had half-stretched out his hand towards the letter, only to hesitate and draw back again.

'Father, read it to me. I could have gone to one of your novices with it, but I came to you because I want the blessing of God on my unfaithfulness that I see as faithfulness. I have not concealed anything. I want no forgiveness. Only tell me what she has written to him.'

'In the name of God,' said the prior, and laid hold of it strongly and unrolled it between his hands.

The silence was long and heavy, weighted with the unbearable burden of the man's waiting, agonised eyes. By the silence he knew all but the words she had used, and knowing her as he knew her, he could guess even at those. Nevertheless, the prior began to read, in a low and level voice:

    ' "To the most noble and puissant Ralf Isambard, lord of Mormesnil, Erington, Fleace and Parfois, these:

    "My lord, you are in possession of the person of Harry Talvace, son of that Harry Talvace whom doubtless you remember all the better for having the print of him constantly before you. I am in possession of the body and life of Benedetta Foscari, sometime well known to you. As to the body, it is not now so rare a property that I should think it of any great value to you. As to the life, if you do set any value on it, as once you gave me dear cause to suppose you did, it is still intact to be disposed of at my will. If you are pleased to consider the exchange of your prisoner for mine, I will close with you on those terms. And on the exchange I place no conditions, except that all debts and grudges whatsoever you may hold against Harry Talvace shall be held to be perpetually discharged, and he set at liberty, with horse and habit and all that is his. Of my person and my life, if you accept them, you may dispose as you please. Send me back your word, aye or no, and if it be aye, I will come at once to Parfois.

"In the hope and expectation, therefore, that I shall shortly see you face to face, I spare to use many compliments, adding to these only the prayer that your lordship may live long enough and be of a gentle enough mind to open your gates to me again after many years.

"By the hand of my beloved and trusted John the Fletcher, this tenth day of August, 1233.

"Benedetta Foscari." '

The thread ran on unbroken to the end, though the low voice thinned with realisation at 'As to the life', and when he reached the 'beloved and trusted' John put up his gnarled hands helplessly in an aimless gesture of hurt and longing, and twisted his fingers in his beard. When it was done, and the silence had lasted a moment unbroken, the sounds of the world came in faintly, the chanting of the first mass, a scattered bawling of sheep from the river meadows, a shrill arguing of birds.

'Did I not tell you?' said John thickly, through the knotted anguish in his throat. 'She is giving her life away, to one that used her as he used her, giving herself back to him to be stripped and shamed and drowned again, to get the boy free. Ah, mistress, was it right to use me so! Was it fair?'

'God sort all!' said the prior in a shaken whisper, and the parchment trembled in his hands. 'You will not deliver the letter? Such a bargain must not be made.'

'God sort all, but under him I'll do what I can.' He held out his hand, stonily calm now that he knew the worst of it. For a moment his heart had drawn him to turn his horse and ride back in anger and horror, to confront her and reproach her for using him so ill. But that was already past. There were other ways of dealing, now that he knew. 'Give it back to me, Father. You've done your part, and I thank you. The rest is for me to do.'

'But you will not deliver it?' The prior watched him roll it up carefully, handling with bitter delicacy the slit seal he had yet to repair.

To that he answered nothing, only hid the letter in the

96

breast of his cotte, and drew back with soft, sidelong steps towards the door. His eyes were bright and hard over the pain; he had no more need of anyone here.

'Pray for us, Father,' he said from the doorway. 'Pray for us all, that we come out of this without scathe.'

CHAPTER FOUR

Parfois: *August* 1233

Isambard came down from the crest of the Long Mountain refreshed and in good humour after his ride, his iron-grey hair uncovered to the sun and the wind, half a dozen of the young gentlemen of his retinue cantering gaily at his back. At the foot of the rising road that climbed the ramp to Parfois the chestnut horse, eased and happy and in no hurry to go back to his stall, dropped into a gentle amble; and Isambard loosed the rein low on his neck and let him have his way. They were in high content with each other; it galled Harry, no doubt, to see his Barbarossa go so blithely under his enemy, but he contrived to contain his chagrin, and even to utter an occasional formal word of thanks for the beast's excellent condition and the care that had been taken of him. Stiff-lipped and stiff-necked, but roundly and steadily, as became a man, and looking his captor straight in the eye as he paid his disagreeable dues.

They came to the place where the track narrowed and the trees closed in, hiding the rocky drop on the left side, the rising slope of broken grass on the right. The one completed tower of the lower guard came into sight, and the piled building materials stacked about it, undressed stone, timbers, laths, scaffolding, cords and hurdles and the glaring white of lime, lining the path for twenty yards down the ramp. The second of the old towers had already been pulled down, and the rubble and stone of its falling waited to be cleared away. The foundation plan of the new one which was to replace it was staked out with thin white cords opposite its finished fellow. They had had to cut down to the bedrock to make a firm enough base for such a weight so near the edge of the steep slope. The light of mid-morning danced and glared from the stripped, pale sandstone.

Isambard remembered another site cleared and pegged out for building, and beside the great open scar the first cartloads of stone from the distant quarry in Bryn, fresh from their voyage up the Severn, dove-grey with overtones of gold, with all that splendour of beauty sealed-up and safe within it, all those shapes of worship and wonder. He never saw dressed stone lying ready but he thought of the great leaves uncurling in Master Harry's church, upholding on their taut, triumphant fronds the vault of heaven and all the world to come.

'My lord,' said young Thomas Blount, assiduous at his elbow, 'here's the warden watching for you. I think there's some messenger come; that horse is surely none of ours. It looks like a mountain pony.'

Isambard withdrew his eyes from the inward vision that beckoned him so often since the boy's coming, and looked ahead to see the guard at the tower holding a shaggy cob, brown and short and powerful, and in the act of alighting from it a brown, short, powerful man, even a little like his beast in the thickness of his bristly, greying beard and curly hair. Bright, alert eyes, narrowed against the sun, stared at him from under bushy brows. A stab of recollection pierced and eluded him; he could not recall that this stocky country-man had or could have anything to do with him, and yet the prick at his heart set him staring back into the past, and would not be discounted.

'My lord,' said the warden, respectful at his stirrup, 'here's a fellow says he comes with a letter for you from one you used to know well. But he'll give no name, and he'll hand over the letter to no one but you. He says he has a token will satisfy you. Will you be pleased to speak with him?'

Isambard walked the chestnut horse slowly forward, and looked down long and thoughtfully at the man who stood before him waiting without reverence or speech. The nar-rowed eyes stared back at him impenetrably, and gave no sign.

'Do I not know you, fellow?'

'That's not for me to say, my lord. But I know you,' said John the Fletcher.

The voice did its part. Twin flames kindled in Isambard's eyes and burned up into red. There was no recognition yet, only the knowledge that time had turned, and sent the past to meet him at his own gate. He freed his right foot from the stirrup, and in a rush of dutiful zeal Thomas was down from the saddle and holding the other one for him as he dismounted. He was even more devoted in his services of late, always present, always ready, always near, so near that hardly a word escaped his pricked ears if he had his way.

Isambard brushed him off with a quick frown, never taking his eyes from the messenger's lined face.

'Were you not my man once?'

'Body and soul, my lord. More yours than the horse you're riding.'

That brought a more perceptible smile. Isambard let his lean fingers caress the chestnut's burnished neck, but his eyes went on searching behind the surly face and the opaque stare for the lost image. He was a long step nearer; the fellow knew Harry Talvace's horse, and did not fear to declare his knowledge.

'You say you have a token I shall know. Let me see it.'

John reached into his breast and brought out the ring. The small gold circlet, so small that even she had had to wear it on her little finger, rocked gently in the seamed hand, and the heavy opal took the light and devoured it, burning into a sullen, blue-veiled glow.

Isambard had put out his hand to take it up before he saw it clearly enough for recognition, and the shiver that passed through the extended fingers and checked them on the air was visible to them all, and sent a convulsion of wonder and wariness through them no less. All eyes flashed from the token to Isambard's face, dreading his lightnings and sharp with anxiety to avoid them in time. He was always incalculable, and here they were lost. He hung in such a stillness that they did not know what might blaze out of it. They held

100

their breath, shifting uneasily in the agony of waiting, and he was no more aware of them than he was of the breeze that ruffled his hair. Even his face was still as death, but without the tranquillity of death, still with the potentialities of pain and rage and love and hatred quick in the charged lines of it, and only God knew what in ambush under the great arched eyelids.

'Do you know your own gifts again, my lord?' said John the Fletcher.

Yes, he knew them now, both gifts, the ring and the man. Eighteen years is a long time; it lowers a man's stature, hobbles his gait, whitens his hair, corrodes his face, but leaves him still that look in the eye that spells his hatred plain, and that acid in the heart that burns through into the tongue.

Isambard looked back into a well of memories. This was the fellow she had snatched from the dog's jaws and asked of him in Paris, the same who vanished with her into Wales at the end of it, and helped her to get Gilleis and the child safe to Llewelyn's care. And he it was who had loosed the shot that robbed the Gascon executioner of his prey. Strange how the images came back, those that mattered least springing to life most readily and clearly, with every line and colour restored. The Gascon he could recall now perfectly, a thin, elegant fellow who looked like a well-born prelate, and prided himself on knowing how to disembowel a man and still leave him a voice to lament. The very warders who had kept Master Harry in his last captivity had left their images not far beneath the surface of memory, ready to quicken at a touch. Only she withdrew herself, shadowy and remote. He knew every line of her, yet the eyes of his mind peered and strained after her in vain; she would not show herself.

The arrested hand continued its broken gesture, took up the ring and held it delicately.

'I am satisfied,' he said, and his voice was low and mild.

'Then give me audience in private to deliver my lady's letter.'

101

'You may follow us up to the church.'

Not into the wards, not yet. Harry Talvace might be abroad at this hour, at exercise with the youngsters, or out in the sun before the tracing-house with his tools and his stone. Whatever this trespasser from the past might be bringing, it would be folly to let the boy see him too soon.

'Let him come after us,' said Isambard to the warden, and turned to remount Barbarossa; and there was Thomas in devoted haste at the stirrup, his fresh blue eyes, that could muster so blankly innocent a stare, still a little too bright with the curiosity the unknown lady of the ring had roused in him. Let him look sidelong under his lashes as attentively as he would, he'd get no more now; his lord's face was closed and calm. He had broken the tension with finger and thumb as he took up the ring, and flicked the shards of the incident away from him with authority; none the less, Thomas saw him stow away the ring in the breast of his cotte, and found a certain interest in the manner in which he did it.

They trotted up the ramp, and out on to the grassy plateau where the church stood; and there Isambard dismissed his companions.

The sun was high, the shadows raven and thin beneath the crenellated wall of Parfois, the roofs that seemed dull black under cloud were now glowing copper. In the church, when Isambard thrust open the wicket in the great west door and led the way into the porch, the direct rays of the sun lay almost vertically through the windows, and spilled jewels down the walls beneath; and all the great inverted ship of the nave, to the remotest boss at the end of the roof-rib, was full of reflected light. The air quivered with it, like the last almost soundless echo of a note of music. Radiance and space seemed to lift their steps from the stones and set them afloat towards the vault.

'Give me her letter,' said Isambard.

He took the roll and broke the seal without hesitation, and John breathed again, the first leap already safely passed. He watched the dark face for a moment, until the

102

rainbow light beyond the motionless head shimmered with the intensity of his stare, and the haggard's profile stark against it grew black by contrast.

Isambard had read but a few lines when he swung abruptly on his heel and walked with the parchment the length of the nave. There he stood with his back turned, and read to the end in silence, and even then remained still for a long time. There was no sound at all, only the trembling of the living light, that seemed to sing although it was voiceless. Once John heard the heavy iron latch of the wicket relax and shift in its socket, as though the door had been moved by the touch of a hand or the weight of a leaning body; but it was a sound so small that he would not have heard it at all but for the intense hush within, and he paid no heed to it then, and forgot it afterwards.

Even if Isambard had not known the hand so well, the broad, bold hand as resolute as a man's, the very wording would have been enough to call her back to him. The unendurable memories crowded in after her; her face burned clear to him at last, wide-set eyes and noble bones, the passionate and adventurous mouth, the great cloak of dark-red hair. Eighteen years! What had time made of her now?

He turned and came back, his long, soft tread quiet on the stones. No triumph in his face, no shame, no grief, nothing; only the faint curl of the long lips, and the windows of the hollow eyes shuttered.

'Say to your lady that her offer is accepted. Say to her: Yes, come.'

'That's all your answer, my lord?'

'She'll need no more. And in exchange for her token, take her this.' It was the ruby from his own finger, so seldom disturbed from its place that he had some ado to get it over the knuckle, and it left a pale band about the lean brown flesh when he had succeeded in removing it. 'She'll know it,' he said, looking down at his hand with a dark smile. 'She'll need no more words.'

'My lord, since you accept her terms —'

His head came up sharply at that, fire looked out of his

103

eyes again for a moment. 'You know the content, do you?'

'She trusted me,' said John, abrupt and harsh, twisting the knife in his own wound.

'Aye, so she might. I remember she had good reason. Well?'

'Since you accept her terms, I am bold to ask you a favour she did not ask for herself. You know you can trust her word as she trusts yours. If you mean to give her the boy, give him now. Let him come back with me, and give her the joy of seeing him alive and well before she yields herself up to you in this place.'

'No,' said Isambard at once, 'That I can't do.'

'You know well she'll keep her bargain.'

'I do know it. But the boy is another matter. Do you think he would let such a bargain stand, between her and me, and he with no say in it? You would find he would have the last and the loudest say,' said Isambard dryly. 'I know him. He has but to set eyes on you here, and to be told: Go, go with him, you're free. Do you think he would not know who had bought him out of hold? And do you think he'd ever rest until he knew on what terms?'

John stood open-mouthed, knocked out of words. It was no more than the truth, and he should have known it for himself. There would be no getting Harry safe out of Parfois that way. If this failed, all failed, and he was left without excuse or recourse but to let her surrender herself or to lie to her and leave Harry undelivered. If once he could have got the boy away to Llewelyn's care he had trusted to the prince's power to prevent Benedetta from keeping so bad a bargain. There would have been argument enough and accusations of bad faith. What did that matter? It was he, and he only, who could be contemned as the faith-breaker, equally treacherous to them all; and the rest would have been compounded somehow by ransom, by arbitration, by reference to the truce commission, by any means short of giving up the recovered fosterling. He had foreseen every difficulty but this simplest difficulty of all. Harry would never suffer it.

'He's but a boy,' he said, arguing strenuously against his own heart. 'He need not be told the truth, however hard he may question.'

'And do you think, fool, you would ever get him over the bridge until he had an answer that satisfied him? Or stir him a step afterwards? He would not budge. No, he stays here until she comes to set him free. Go, deliver my answer to her.'

The audience was over; no king could have made it more royally clear.

'Will you enter Parfois and refresh yourself and your beast before you ride?' he asked. 'I could not bid you in until Harry was put well out of your way, but he'll be safe out of sight before now.'

'I ate my last at your table many years gone, my lord. I want no roof of yours over me, and no bread of yours in my mouth.'

'As you will,' said Isambard with a shrug and a sigh. 'Then I forbear from offering you other rewards I see you would cast back in my teeth. And my thanks, I fear, you will regard too lightly to make them worth tendering. Nevertheless, I thank you.'

It was over. There was no more to be gained here. John withdrew from him into the shadow of the porch, and left the lord of Parfois standing tall and still and black in the nave of his church with the singing air bright about him, a carillon of colours tremulous as sunlit water, or the vibration of wings in flight. The figure in the midst might have been of stone. The same head in stone held up the voussoirs of the doorway beside him as he emerged into the warmth of the noonday meadow. Of the two images the one Master Harry had made was the more eloquent; and even after eighteen years of weathering it was questionable if it could match the man within for hardness.

Fifty yards away in the meadow Thomas Blount strolled with an arm over the saddle of the grazing cob, his girlish face as serene and blank as the summer sky.

Aelis flew to meet him as he came in through the little gate of the paddock. She had been milking, and had her skirt kilted up to her knees, and her hair coiled on her head to be out of her way.

'Did you see him? Is he well?' She caught at the cob's bridle and led him towards the undercroft; better not to show him in the open field or about the clearing, for fear somebody should see and recognise him. Travellers were few along their riverside path, but Parfois was near and perilous.

John shook his head glumly. 'No, not a glimpse. Leave me go in to your father, lass, I must talk to him. No, I got nothing. He isn't let out of the wards, and I wasn't let in. Or not until they'd smoothed him away out of reach somewhere.'

'But you did talk of him? John,' she said, clutching at his arm, 'it's true he's alive, isn't it? That's something we can cling to?'

Was he even sure of that? Could a man be sure of anything he had not seen and touched and heard with his own good senses? But he soothed her quickly: 'He's alive. And well, too, by all accounts.'

'But you could not get him free,' she said with conviction, and bit fiercely on what could hardly be called a disappointment, since she had expected little else.

'No, we've still to wait a little while, my lass.'

What could he tell her? He did not even know himself what was to be done next. The one thing certain was that he would not go back to Benedetta at Aber and deliver the ring and the message, and let her keep her terms. Whatever happened, she should never fall into Isambard's hands again. He could go back and lie to her, tell her her offer had been refused, but that would be to leave Harry unransomed and uncomforted still. And besides, he found himself afraid of facing her with the lie. She had known him so long that he was crystal to her; she might see the falsehood rising black and alien in his throat, and reject it as he uttered it. She might even see from the hang-dog look of him that he

106

had betrayed her, violated her letter and done everything counter to her will. A life without her trust was no life. He could not go back to her empty-handed. If there was another way he must find it. If he prayed for it, would God hear prayers from one so lost in treasons and disloyalties? He might hear the girl, might even speak through her. She at least was clean of all stain.

'But what happened?' she persisted, blue eyes brilliant in her roused and resolute face. 'What did they say to you?'

'Come in to your father, girl, and I'll tell you.'

They stabled the cob, and went in to Robert in the house, and John told them the whole of it.

'You'll not go back with that for a word,' said Robert.

'I'd die first. There's no one else but the handful of us here knows she's even tried to buy him. I would have turned back and told her what I'd done, and refused her errand, if I had not thought I might win him to let the boy go on trust. She would have wanted to pay the score when she knew, but I meant to make sure the prince had the ordering of it before then. But I was the world's fool to think it could be done so. He was right: Harry would never have let any of us take his load from him. Even if I'd tricked him into coming home with me, he'd have been off back as soon as he heard the truth. And I doubt now whether the prince would have stood in his way. I doubt he'd have kissed him and sent him off with his blessing. So we're back where we were before. I've played her false,' he said bitterly, 'that's the only change. And for nothing! For nothing gained!'

'What will you do?' asked Robert, low-voiced.

'Do I know? If God would but nudge my elbow and show me a way. There must be one, if we could but find it.'

The girl sat crouched on the floor with her chin in her palms and her eyes flaring wide, and who could tell what she was thinking? Maybe she would have sold Madonna Benedetta ten times over to win Harry out of captivity. Maybe she had the contempt of most women for the fooleries of honour, that would yield up a man's life for a scruple, and compel an obstinate boy to return to durance voluntarily rather than enjoy his freedom and accept the slur of faith-breaking with it. But she had taken the boy to her heart, and his values and his virtues with him, and more than likely his faults, too. No, she would never blame him. She accepted that he had done what he must. Her mind was moving upon other paths.

'If the old lord died,' she said suddenly, 'we should have no need to trouble any more.'

She did not know what she had said. The silence, that was like the silence after a thunderclap to John, had no terrible significance for her. She went wistfully along the same path.

'No one else there would care to keep him; your prince could buy him out of prison with no more sweat than a little bargaining. It's the old man keeps him just to plague him. If the son had the disposing of him, you'd see he'd let him go lightly enough. He never knew Master Harry, and he knows nothing of Harry, either. What's a Talvace to him? He'd sell him gladly, for the sake of good will.'

She lifted her head and looked up at John with wide eyes innocent of any dark intent, seeing no distortion in the reflected understanding which stared back at her.

'You told us the king wants no more enemies; he has enough. And the king's new men have no call to go looking for any, now so many lords are up in arms against them. The lord Isambard's son is one of the king's men. He stands to lose much if his enemies gain allies in Wales. He'd *give* Harry to Prince Llewelyn, to keep him content and this border quiet.'

Out of the mouths of maids and little children the oracles come. He sat with face half-turned away from her, to hide the unbearable spark of hope and intent that burned up behind his eyes and made a core of molten heat in his mind. She was right; she had put her finger on the only pathway, and pointed where it led. William Isambard held office now, was hand in glove with des Rivaulx, and close, close in his counsels; he stood to fall with the Poitevins if they fell. He had favour and power and place to lose. If he inherited here, his interest would be to keep the prince of Aberffraw from entering into the earl marshal's confederacy, and so greatly strengthening des Rivaulx's enemies. Llewelyn would only have to ask, and he would get his foster-son back unharmed. At a price or as a gift, what did it matter? William would be glad to find he had such a gift in his power to make, and if he put a price on him for form's sake it would be a nominal one, the better to engage Llewelyn's gratitude and stay his hand from any inimical action.

From all accounts there was no love lost between father and son, either. William had waited a long time for his inheritance. He might be only too happy if the old man could be hurried out of the world.

'That's very like,' said Robert ruefully, 'but he won't die just for our asking. He owes a death to a good many folks, besides the death he owes to God. But I doubt we must wait for it to come in its own good time.'

But need they? Need they? These hands had loosed the shaft that took Master Harry out of the world before the hangman could touch him. They had said in the villages that it was God who took him, and the arrow had come from somewhere far higher than the top of the church tower. Might not God have another use yet for the same hands and the same skill? It would take him a few days to make ready, to work out place and time. And Robert and Aelis must know nothing. What need was there for them to be involved? If the thing went well, the secret was safer with one than with three; and if it went awry, better only one should suffer the consequences.

And he had been alone with him in the church that day, and had not recognised the opportunity when it leaned to his hand. The erect back turned, the attendants all dismissed, the way open to him to leave after the act; and yet the dagger in his belt had not started and loosened to summon his hand, or pricked the blind flesh that stood inert and let the hour go by. It would never again be so easy to do the deed and withdraw alive. What did that matter? He had relinquished his claim on life, if she needed his death.

'Ah, I know,' said Aelis, sighing. 'It's mortal sin even to

think of such things. I was just seeing, all in a moment, how simple everything would be if he died.'

He was waiting for another utterance that would light his way, but God spoke no more by her. The burden came down upon his own shoulders, and he let it lie, knowing it was not more than he could bear. Mortal sin, she said, to think of it. Much worse to do it. He had let go the charge of his own life, he sent his own soul after it, not in defiance, but in resignation and humility. Well that one man should be damned, if that was God's price for setting Benedetta's heart at rest.

'You'll bide over the night?' said Robert gently, seeing him withdrawn and lost so far within the always solitary reaches of his mind.

'Gratefully, Robert, gratefully. But tomorrow I must ride.' He did not say where, he did not say it would not be far, and Robert asked him nothing. They were of one mind. It was well not to know.

He was three days about his preparations. The bow he borrowed from the armoury of Castell Coch, and used Owen ap Ivor's name to get it, though the manservant of the holy woman of Aber had good enough credit wherever the prince's writ ran. He made use of the butts there, also, to loosen the cords of his ageing arms, and get his eye in at a target, for he had had little practice of late with a long-bow. To justify the loan and the earnestness of his trials he told some tale of a contest and a wager against an Englishman in Shrewsbury who fancied his arm, and they would have given him anything he asked, and their ready and varied advice into the bargain, to down an Englishman. John had been so long on their side of the border that they had forgotten his birth; almost he had forgotten it himself.

The skill came back readily into his hands, and the power into his shoulders. His eye had never lost its keenness and judgement. When he was satisfied with his weapon he recrossed Severn by the ford at Pool, hid bow and shafts in a copse of bushes close beneath the steep escarpment of the ramp to Parfois, and pastured his cob on a long line in a clearing nearer the river. He kept away from Robert's usual pathways, and avoided the places where he knew his snares would be. Once or twice during those two days he caught glimpses of him slipping unobtrusively through the trees, and once he saw Aelis in the dawn taking night-lines out of the river. By then he did not miss them; his sense of loneliness was so deeply accepted that it seemed to be his natural and eternal condition, and it was as if he did not look to see the silence broken again. He went back no more to the companionable butts of Castell Coch; he was not drawn to the assart above the mill. Beyond the act he contemplated there was nothing. If he survived it he would be coming as a stranger into a strange world, with everything to learn again, even speech.

The first night in the woods under the mountain he slept rolled in his cloak in the bushes. After that he did not sleep at all. He spent the hours of daylight watching the approaches to Parfois, and searching for the best and most commanding spot he could find from which to cover the lower guard. He could go no higher except by climbing, and he had not the native-born Welshman's agility or head for heights, and wanted, besides, to remain where he had at least a reasonable chance of retreating rapidly after the thing was done. He had no will to throw his life away; if it must be offered, let it be offered as something of value, and prized accordingly. God should not be able to complain that his creature had despised his gift.

Twice a day Isambard rode, at least while the summer weather invited. Sometimes he went in company, with his young men about him in a riot of colours, and his falconers in attendance, to hawk across the open heath by the old earth fort. Sometimes he rode almost alone, Langholme keeping his distance behind him, and perhaps two favoured youngsters suffered to take exercise with him provided they did not intrude on his solitary mood. Once John was in a fair way to draw on him as he rode so, upright and sombre and alone, but held his hand because the distance was too great for certainty. On the third day he would be in his chosen station, and there would be no haste about loosing the shaft, and no fear of a miss or a mere flesh-wound.

The trees clustered close and thickly at the edge of the ramp below the lower guard, on the valley side where the foundation of the new tower was scored deep through turf and soil to the rock. Piled stone for building, and the old masonry and rubble waiting to be carted away, made a ragged rampart between the road and the downward slope. A man could drop from one of the trees there and go running and leaping from bush to bush down the raw slope towards the river, while his pursuers were climbing over the barrier of stone to be after him, and ploughing through the lesser hazards of cords and timber and hurdles. And the greater of the trees commanded a clear view of the space between the towers, and the road beyond, down which all riders from Parfois must approach and pass. It was full summer, the screen of leafage thick enough to hide an army. John chose an elm that spread its branches clear across the road, overhanging the pale grey stacks of stone. There was room enough in the crotch for him to sit out the night in very fair comfort, and with the first light of dawn he shifted outward to the branches, and found himself a firm station facing the descending ramp.

The early evening would have given him better prospects of shaking off pursuit in the woods and by the river; but the morning ride offered him the better light for what he had to do. Yesterday they had stayed a while to watch the masons, while Isambard conferred with his master of the works. It could have been done then, if John had been better placed, but he had been on the ground, among bushes that marred his view and his aim, and would have betrayed him by their rustling before he could draw. This time there should be no such wasted moment. If God offered, John was ready to take.

The light grew and brightened; the labourers came, and the masons, and the guard yawned in the sun and watched them matching and measuring. Two or three young journeymen sat by the roadside dressing stone, spattering the pale grass of August with glittering grey chips of granite, fine as frost. A creaking cart came up the slope and unloaded butt after butt of fresh, unslaked lime, tipped out in a grey-white mountain beside the road. Master Edmund came down from the castle with his clerk at his back when the sun was already climbing, and stood by to see the laying of the first courses of stone on the stripped rock. The daily business of Parfois went forward briskly, and the watcher in the elm waited without impatience. On so fine a morning Isambard could not fail to ride.

It was past eight when he came, late for him; but at last the shimmer of bright colours quaked through the trees and hung among the branches like flowers, as the morning caval-cade poured down the path from the plateau of the church. The soft thudding of hoofs quivered along the ground; to-day he went handsomely attended, with half a dozen knights at his back, besides the squires and the pages and the gentle-men-at-arms, ambitious younger sons of knightly families getting their training for a hard life in which only the fittest would survive, and the weak would be elbowed aside and trampled underfoot. They took their strenuous apprentice-ship lightly and gaily enough, perfected their courtly skills and their ability in arms, and hoped to be advanced to a manor somewhere in return for their services.

They had not yet begun to desert their lord, it seemed; his position was held to be unassailable, and the king's present troubles had made even the waverers draw in their horns again and reflect on Isambard's prospects of regaining his ascendancy. If de Burgh could fall so suddenly and re-soundingly, so could Winchester in his turn when the wind changed. There was no telling yet which way this present contention would go. Tomorrow Isambard might be up again, or the Poitevins might have the better of the struggle, and he go down finally and utterly with the broken men. But for the moment the place-seekers and land-hungry were holding their hands. If ever he fell beyond recovery, the signs would show early. The landless knights would be the first

113

to go, the younger sons with a career to make the second. And Langholme, it might well be, the last. Why should a man feel loyalty to one far out of reach of love?

The man in the elm tree steadied his knee cautiously against the branch on which it rested, and reached over his shoulder for a shaft, never taking his eyes from the lofty head that rode so high and easily above the lean, black-clad shoulders of the lord of Parfois. The summer glow was on him, burnishing all the sharp edges of bone into bronze and gold. He looked no more than fifty. The chestnut he had between his knees was Harry Talvace's Barbarossa. For the last time, thought John, moving softly among the leaves that they might not stir.

Softly he fitted the shaft to the string, and softly drew it back a little, and waited. The point nosed gently between the leaves, and reached hungrily towards Isambard's breast, there where the black cloth cotte was opened and the white shirt loosed over the heart.

There was no haste. The cavalcade came winding its way down at a dancing walk. He had still time to count the heads of the young and agile who would have to be reckoned with in flight, and to offer thanks that they came without hounds. He circled experimentally with the elbow of his drawing arm, and there was space and freedom enough for all the movement he would need.

Nearer now. Langholme was at his lord's heels, several of the younger men jostling to left and right, but no one rode close beside him. At the head of every cortège he would always be alone. Gay with voices and glowing with colours his court followed him down to the tower of the lower guard; and there he halted to speak with Master Edmund and walk his horse the length of the newly-begun foundation. He dismounted, and tossed Barbarossa's bridle to Langholme. That was well, that made him a better target, if the workmen would keep from standing too near him; and the awe in which they held him moved with him like an invisible wall, thrusting them back before him, so that but for Master Edmund he stood alone.

Some of his retinue had dismounted, too, used to his halts and guessing at the length of this one. That would hamper the movements of those still mounted, at least for a moment. But there were a few archers among the company. He must do it now, quickly, while the ranks were still closing at leisure, before they were fully assembled beside the tower. The range was short and certain, the light perfect. If only the old man would stand aside!

Master Edmund, eager and proud, darted from his lord's side at that moment, pacing out the shape of the proposed outer wall, and marked its thickness with a stamp of his foot. Isambard stood alone, his head turned to follow the old man's movements, his uncovered breast fronting the pathway, bared to the shaft that strained to his flesh like a living thing.

'Christ aid!' whispered John from dry lips, and with all the weight and passion and skill of his body he drew the bow.

It was the force of his hatred that undid him. Under the ultimate strain of his thrusting knee the branch cracked and gave, and the sped shaft, splitting the radiant air with a whining cry, lurched downward out of true. The group below heard the vibration, felt it in their flesh and looked up aghast, before ever the shaft struck and sang, quivering, in the earth at Isambard's feet. Not six inches from his long stirrup-shoe it bristled and quaked, whining still with an angry sound. He had jerked round and stood staring, for once slow to react to danger. How far must his mind have been from this place and these affairs of every day, to keep him there entranced and exposed, open to assault.

John had recovered his balance with a convulsive heave, reeling back against the main crotch of the tree from the downward lurch which had all but displaced him. His hand was at his shoulder, plucking out the second arrow in frantic haste, when the archers found him by the threshing of the branches.

A boy's voice shrilled: 'There! In the elm!'

Langholme had leaped to catch his lord by the arm, and

115

drag him into cover. They were locked immovably together for a moment, and John hung in agony on his bow-string, willing them to part. His fingers were tightening on the shaft, gripping for the steady pull, foot braced, knee braced, when the archers below drew and loosed. There was not a second between the shots, but it was John who was late. He could have transfixed the pair of them where they stood clasped and inseparable, but what had Langholme ever done to him or his?

The burning bolt took him in the breast in an explosion of shock and pain, driving him backwards with a rending of leaves. There was air rushing past his face, stopping his breath, and, at the end of an instant that seemed a year long, a burst of pain and terror and darkness that enveloped him body and spirit like a gust of flame.

They saw him fall, and gasped aloud, shuddering to the awful, shattering sound of his bones smashing on the stacked stone. Turning in mid-air, he struck the barrier of granite with a sickening shock, and was flung off like a jointless doll into the heap of lime.

Isambard stood stricken into stillness and silence, staring uncomprehendingly from wide, blank eyes. But those about him tore their feet from the grass and ran, baying like hounds, upon the spot where the intruder had fallen. Before Isambard could drag himself back to the scene they were on their victim with stones, staves, swords, whatever they had that could maim and bludgeon and kill.

He heard the dreadful, wordless crying, and thrust Langholme off with a sweep of his long arm. The flames rekindled, surging in his stunned eyes. He ran, shouting aloud at the last pitch of his voice, raging, slashing at the nearest with his short riding-whip to drive them off.

'Let be! Off, I say, off! Let him alone!'

Those who were not too far gone in frenzy to hear and understand fell back from him dismayed, dropping their weapons and shrinking out of his reach. He hurled himself between, swinging the whip about him like a flail, calling them off ferociously, like hounds at fault, until they gave

116

before him and ran, cowering, and so let him through to the broken thing that heaved and jerked and moaned in the smoking lime.

Blood steamed and boiled about it, and heat struck him in the face as he leaned and stared. The bronze mask hung motionless for a moment, the eyes fixed and veiled. At his feet the torn remnant of a man writhed and stiffened in spasmodic contortions, half hacked to pieces, and out of it came a low, continuous, lamentable sound. It had still two eyes unmarked in the ruin of a face, light blue eyes, bright to frenzy, that fixed upon Isambard's countenance in an intolerable stare, and knew him, and were known.

The designers of slow death could not have done worse to him, and yet the eyes lived, with a tenacious, burning intelligence that would keep him chained for interminable hours yet to this nightmare of pain.

Isambard set hand to the dagger at his belt, and dropped smoothly and surely as a hawk for the stretched and palpitating throat.

The last convulsion of passion shook the dying man, the last blaze of defiance heaved him from the ground. Clawing on either side his maimed body, he filled both hands with lime and flung it into the plunging, haggard's face. Too late Isambard threw up his arm. The charge took him heavily, filling and searing eyes and nostrils and lips. Blindly, gasping, he fell and rolled upon John the Fletcher's floundering body. Running feet shook the ground; he felt hands reaching out to him, and even in that extreme bellowed at them, spitting out scalding foam and corroding pain:

'Stand back! Let us alone!'

It seemed his voice still had authority. Blind, his mouth burning, his eyes a furnace of agony, he lay panting over his enemy, jerking his head from side to side to shake off pain that clung to him and clawed him; and yet they obeyed him. They hung over him in an appalled circle, but they kept their distance, afraid to trespass where he had forbidden it.

Close in his ear shallow, rustling breath strained and laboured, and a dreadful, desolate, animal sound that made

117

his flesh shrink with terror that it might be coming from his own mouth. He shut his teeth upon the furnace within, and still the keening tore at his senses. He felt towards it with his left hand, touched cloth, climbed a heaving shoulder to a crushed breast, blood hot under his palm. The cords of the old throat were taut, the battered head strained back. He laid his fingers along the jerking flesh, and the dagger slid in between them quick and cleanly.

A rush of blood gushed over his hands. The awful lament broke upon a bubbling cough, and sighed into silence. The broken body ceased to heave under him, quivered faintly for a long minute, and then relaxed and lay blessedly still.

Isambard took his hands from the dagger, and rolled away from his kill with his arms clenched hard over his face. He came to his knees, and still the hush and stillness about him held. They were afraid even to go to him until he commanded, and he could not unclench his teeth for fear of howling aloud. He could see nothing through the rush of water in his eyes, that boiled as it flowed, and ran scalding through his closed eyelids and down the hollows of his golden mask. He dragged one arm down from his eyes and dug his nails into the hard flesh of his breast inside the open bosom of his shirt, to provide himself with an easier pain, and croaked through his teeth:

'My eyes – water – My eyes burn –'

They stirred then, and a horrified murmur broke like bees in swarm; some ran, some cried to others up the slope to ride for Master Hilliard the physician. From a confusion of sounds he found none of any comfort, and groped round him with a lame hand, turning up his contorted face with tight-shut, streaming eyes and strained lips to the light.

'Walter – !'

'Here, my lord!' Langholme was on his knees beside him with a rush, his arms supporting him.

'Help me rise, Walter. Get me home – out of their sight.' The burned lips whispered clumsily and slowly, but the words were clear. He gripped his squire's steadying arm and set one foot to ground, and drove himself upright.

118

'Rest here, my lord, wait – lie in the shade till Master Hilliard comes. You cannot go. We'll bring a litter.' Langholme's teeth were chattering with shock and distress.

'No, get me home. I am not sick, I can ride. Bring me to Barbarossa, and mount me. I will go. I will not be a spectacle here. . . .'

Trembling and appalled, Langholme brought him on his arm the few yards to where the horse grazed quietly, calmed now after the brief turmoil. Isambard walked like a drunken man, the pain twisting his head ceaselessly after the ease that was nowhere to be found, and the coolness that turned to fire as it touched. The bony fingers gripped ever tighter in Langholme's arm, until he could not choose but wince at the pressure; then they released him quickly and lay almost lightly on his sleeve, but he felt them rigid, like a dead man's.

'I am hurting you, Walter. Forgive me!'

'No,' he said, shaking, 'no!' and wished the grip back again. 'Here's the bridle, my lord.' The groping left hand reached for it, gathered it steadily, pressed hard knuckles into the glossy neck for an instant in a laboured caress. 'And here the stirrup. Your foot . . . so.' He was up; he gripped with muscular knees and drew the first longer, steadier breath.

'Give me a kerchief, Walter. And stay by me!'

He held the kerchief to his eyes as they went, his head down, like a mourning woman, and halfway up the ramp. Langholme, anxious and attentive at his elbow, saw that his lord's teeth were locked tightly in the folds of linen, and the bone of his jaw stood pale and rigid from the brown flesh.

The young men of the retinue, shocked into silence, drew aside from the path to let them pass, and fell in close behind them subdued and orderly, their only speech agitated whispers. Falconers and pages and knights and grooms filed after them across the plateau of the church, and over the bridge into Parfois. They brought him in procession through the wards to his own apartments in the Lady's Tower, the physician running before, de Guichet coming in solicitous haste to embrace his lord and all but carry him up the stone staircase.

The door closed and shut the crowd out from him. They could bubble and marvel and shout as much as they would now, and exult if they would; he was out of their reach. He could uncover his marred face, and let go the iron grip he must keep on something or someone in order to be silent. He could groan and curse and do whatever he would, except weep; if he wept, the brine of his eyes would burn like boiling pitch.

He let them bed him, and bathe away the blood and dust with water, and the lime with milk. He could not eat, but they made him take raw eggs to ease his burning mouth and throat. They closed to the shutters to protect him from the light. He lay on his pillows and surrendered all care for himself, turning submissively under the physician's hands and obedient to every order. All his own energies were engaged with containing and coming to terms with his pain, for it would not be a short acquaintance; that he knew. There was but one thing that needed his attention besides, and that could wait for an hour at least, until they had had their will of him and left him alone.

They even discussed him across his great bed, the old leech and de Guichet, as though he were asleep or dead, or a child, or a beast that was sick. His swollen lips smiled a little at that, and never grudged the pain.

'Is he gravely burned, Master Hilliard? Will he be marked?'

Did it matter? That old mask had had a long day, it could live out the evening without beauty.

'Very little, I think, very little. He's strong, he has no fever. He'll do well if he'll only be ruled and lie quiet. The eyes, of course – ' Do him justice, he did hesitate there, and sink his voice a little when he resumed. 'The eyes are a more serious matter. We cannot tell as yet. We must hope.'

The eyes are a more serious matter! To a man who uses them as one weapon of his authority, much more serious.

From beneath the steeped linen that covered his mouth he

said: 'Leave me now, I should like to rest. But let Walter stay.'

'He shall, my lord, he shall. Someone must be with you, to keep these cloths moistened with milk. Master Langholme, bathe my lord's eyes and see the pads kept damp over them, and send for me at once if there's any show of fever.'

He was gone; they were all gone but Langholme, hushed and still beside the bed. Quietness and pain wrapped him, and he lay and let them possess him, ungrudging. What was done was done; no one could take him back to the beginning of the day and let him have the living of it over again. He must make what he could of what remained.

'Walter!'

'Here, my lord.'

'Walter, I have work for you more testing than moistening my dressings with milk. That poor wretch below there – him I killed – he brought me a letter a few days gone, and I gave him my answer to take back again, but it seems he thought to win a more acceptable trophy than I sent by him. Somewhere about him you'll find my ring, the ruby. Will you go deliver it in his stead?'

'My lord, whatever you bid me,' said Langholme earnestly.

'To a lady you may remember. To Madonna Benedetta Foscari. I killed her, but she would not die, Walter. She's turned Welshwoman, and hidden herself, I judge, somewhere not far from Llewelyn's maenol at Aber. More's the pity, I never asked him where she lived or what she did, but if you ask for her round Aber I think you'll find her.'

'And what am I to say to her with the ring, my lord?'

'Say to her that I say: Yes, come, your offer is accepted.' The words brought him a certain evening content; it was time that it should be ended, he could not keep the borrowed joy for ever. 'Only that. She will know. And tell her what befell her servant. Tell it truly, and she will understand. She knows him better than I, and I know him now well enough. God rest him!'

121

'He tried to kill you,' said Langholme, sombre and wondering.

'I owed him that twice over. What he has given me may be part payment of my debts, who knows? Only tell her.'

Langholme hesitated, loathe to leave the bedside. 'Am I to ride now, my lord?'

'Now, Walter. Send up one of the pages to me if you will, but bid him stay outside the door. If I want him I can call.'

He heard the reluctant footsteps turn to the door, and called him back for a moment: 'And, Walter . . . when you have taken back the ring from him . . . see his body cared for. Tell de Guichet he is to have proper burial.'

Harry had barely crossed from the stables to the tracing-house and moved his work into the sun when he heard them riding in, so numerous a company that they could hardly be other than the hawking party returning. He peered out for a moment to see them pass on their way to the stables and the mews, astonished that they should have come back so soon. Isambard, whatever he might be, was not capricious. But he was in time to see only a handful of the young men, riding in rather subdued order, and unusually circumspectly, but with nothing about them to indicate disaster. He turned back to his work, but could not settle to it for the thought of Barbarossa cheated of his outing; and presently he laid down his chisel sullenly but resignedly, and went back to the stables, at least to groom and pet his favourite, and if possible to beg another rider for him. He was as well with Isambard as any, no blinking it, and went under him joyfully; but someone else would do at a pinch. There must be errands to be done out of Parfois, at some time during the day, and Walter would lend an understanding ear to his request.

The stable-yard was full of returned riders, and some were silent and pale and some feverishly voluble, and all out of their usual selves. Harry stood at a loss, staring from one group to another.

'What is it? What's happened?'

Three or four turned and began telling him together, so variously that he was little wiser, but much shaken.

'What, my lord shot at? From a tree? And *hurt*?' There could be no other reason for this return, Isambard would never turn back merely for a stray shaft loosed at his life. Harry looked round wildly for Barbarossa. 'And his horse? *My* horse!'

Barbarossa was there, pawing discontentedly outside his stall in the hold of a groom. Harry took the glowing head to his heart, and breathed again; not a scratch, nor a stain of sweat on him. He turned a doubtful face.

'There was no damage? My lord was not hit?'

'Not by the arrow, no. The fellow who shot at him was brought down, though, and what was left of him *he* finished with his own hands. But he got a fistful of lime in his eyes, doing it. We brought him home streaming like a widow at a funeral, and they've closed the shutters on him and fetched in his physician.'

'Is he bad?' asked Harry uncertainly.

'Who's to know yet? Bad enough to quieten him for a while.'

'And the man who loosed at him is dead, you say? Who was he?'

That none of them knew. There were plenty of desperate fellows about the borders who had grudges enough against Isambard, who could tell which of them had staked his life on so crazy a throw?

'But dead – dead is one way of saying it! If you'd seen him! Some of the archers got to him in a hurry, till *he* whipped them off and cut the poor devil's throat. He wouldn't have them touch their master's meat!'

'And he's taken to his bed?'

That knocked him hard, it was so unlikely. When had Isambard ever spared himself or entertained so much as the thought of sickness and weakness? Harry groomed his darling, and thought of it over and over, and listened to the confusion of whispers and rumours and comments that buzzed round him, with a curious trouble in his heart.

123

There was no Isambard in hall at dinner, and no de Guichet or Langholme, either. Harry went looking for someone
who might know the truth of it and be willing to tell it.
Walter was still with Isambard in his bedchamber. Harry
sat down at the foot of the staircase and waited, and presently de Guichet and the physician came down from the sick
man's room with sombre faces and hushed voices, and went
away across the inner ward. He did not ask them for news;
they were no friends of his. But in a little while he heard
footsteps descending, and looked up to see Langholme coming down towards him.

He scrambled up and confronted him in haste. 'Walter,
how is it with him? I heard from some of the others what
happened. Is he bad?'

'Bad enough,' said Walter shortly. 'Burned and in pain.
But he's still his own master and ours, for all that, and I'm
on his errand, so don't keep me.'

He would not stay, but Harry ran after him and walked
beside him, questioning still. 'The man who shot at him –
Walter, who was he? Roger said a Welshman by his bow
and his clothes. Was he a Welshman?' Langholme halted
abruptly, seeing the anxiety in the blue-green eyes; the boy
had it in his mind and on his heart that this death somehow
lay at his door.

'Welsh he may be, but he's no concern of yours, as far as I
can see. He came as a messenger to my lord from a lady,
and was to have taken a message back again. But for some
reason best known to himself he chose rather to stay and
attempt my lord's life. There were old grudges. No fault
of yours,' he said kindly enough. 'Go and chip your stone,
boy, and let be. He's alive, and will be, even if it's no joy
just now.'

Harry kept his place, clinging to the arm that would have
put him gently by. There were too many echoes here that
struck true in his heart – a Welshman, a lady, old grudges.
'What lady?' he said. 'You know, Walter, you must tell me.'

'One that you probably know well enough, but I tell you
this is nothing to do with your case. It's old history, before

124

you were born.'

'Walter, what lady? I must know her name.'

'Madonna Benedetta, if you must know.'

The colour ebbed from Harry's face and left him pale as the wall. He took his hand from Langholme's arm to feel at his own blanched cheek, and stood staring with wide, sick, green eyes.

'Madonna Benedetta,' he said in a whisper. 'John the Fletcher! Oh God, oh God, *John*! And he killed him – he cut his throat – '

Langholme turned and took him by the arms, holding him before him. There was no leaving him like this. If he had every detail he might make sense of it, and come to his own senses.

'He killed him, yes. Dear God, boy, listen to me. I saw it. He was blind and burned, with his eyes and his mouth full of lime, and he felt his way to his throat and killed him. Did they never tell you? He'd fallen from a tree on the piled stone – if he had a whole bone in him it was wonder – and the men-at-arms had run at him, besides, with stones and staves and whatever they found to hand. He beat them off from him to keep the man alive, if you ask me what I think, but it was gone long past that by the time he got to him. And he killed him. I tell you, I saw it. It was more like a mercy to a broken-backed beast, and one he valued at that, than the dispatching of an enemy. And do you know what was his last charge to me now? See his body cared for, he says. Tell de Guichet he's to have proper buriel. And I'm off to do it.'

He plucked his hands from him, and went about the first of his errands; and Harry, trembling and amazed, refuged in his corner of the deserted tracing-house and was seen no more that afternoon. But when he came out it was to march straight to the Lady's Tower, and ask with humility and some constraint if Isambard would be pleased to receive him.

The bedchamber was a room he had never seen before, large and rich, hung with tapestries and summer branches that gave a green, warm scent of the woods to it. The scent of sickness was there, too, acrid and faint and daunting; and the man in the great bed lay so still beneath the single linen cover that he might almost have been composed ready for his coffin. The wonderful head stared at the ceiling from two round white eyes of linen that steamed faintly. The cloth that covered his mouth had been removed, and the mis-shapen lips, swollen and scarlet, were fast closed on any utterance. Harry watched the great bony breast rise and fall, and shook to the shallow irregularities and broken rhythm of pain.

He did not know why he had come at all, he had nothing to say; the coming was everything, but it seemed to him now an incomprehensible folly that it should be expected to speak for itself. He closed the door behind him very softly, though the man in the bed was not asleep; and slowly, on dragging feet, he approached the bedside.

'Is it you indeed, Harry?' said Isambard, fumbling out the words through stiff lips. 'This is an honour I never looked for.'

'You did not come to me or send for me, my lord,' said Harry, in self-defence playing the prisoner still, 'So I came to you.'

'Ah, you thought I should want my daily report on you?' Even thus distorted, the voice kept the honeyed sweetness he could use when he would, caressing and tormenting; and even on the marred lips the half-smile could still play its shadowy game. 'And did the day go well without me, Harry?'

'My lord,' he said hardily, 'I think it did not go well *with* you.'

He had not meant to keep that tone; it was so deeply engrained a habit with them now that it was hard to leave it, and the dismaying words came out of themselves, before he was aware. But he would not soften them now they were sped. He watched the deepening of the shadows in the hollow cheeks, the brief contortion of the mouth that told him Isambard was smiling.

'The more reason it should go well with my best enemy.'

He remembered then that the boy must have known Benedetta's man from his childhood, closely enough to have some affection for him. 'But that it served another even worse than me,' he said with compunction, 'and he a friend of yours. Have they told you?'

The small, constrained voice out of the darkness above him said: 'Yes.' The face he could see clearly in his mind's eye, wary and grave, even a little sullen and ungracious, solemn eyes lowered to the pillowed head of his enemy brought low. No joy in them, but somewhere a shadow of baffled doubt that there should have been joy. He was still enough of a child for that, though the child was passing.

'And told you who he was? But that I think they could not, for none of them knew it. It was Benedetta's man, that archer of hers she had from me. I have forgotten his name –'

'John the Fletcher,' said Harry in a very low voice.

'Ah, John was it?' He drew breath painfully, and raised himself a little upon his pillows. 'I see you do know.' Silence between them a moment. 'Did they tell you also that I killed him?'

The careful voice, articulating so laboriously, probed its way through to the heart. It was as though that death and loss had lodged somewhere in the borders of Harry's consciousness until now, known but not yet fully realized, and Isambard had suddenly reached into the middle of his being and laid his affirmation there. He opened his lips to answer and could not, he was so full of tears, and must carry himself with aching care for fear they spilled over.

'Faith, I am sorry, child,' said Isambard.

'And I, my lord.'

It was hard to breathe, harder to speak, and worst was the dread in him that the man in the bed could follow every vibration of the struggle that convulsed him. His head was turned a little on the pillow, to bring the shrouded eyes to bear on his visitor, as though he strained after another kind of sight. Wanting one sense, he still saw too far into other

127

men for comfort, and without eyes he could still out-stare his opponents.

'That he missed his aim, Harry?'

In answer to that, nothing. The young mouth drawn down a little now, no doubt, dourly and forbiddingly, the eyes withdrawn to fix on something harmless and insensate that could not stare back at him. The skin rugs, the gilded chair, the Norman ancestors in the tapestry, with their conical helms and long hauberks. Isambard had felt the green glance leave him, but not to go far. He was learning already how to orientate himself by the slight movements other men made; even the light rustling of a sleeve had meaning.

'I'm thirsty, Harry. There's a pitcher there on the chest. Give me a drink.'

And so he did; quietly and neatly, like a well-trained page, he poured milk, and came and raised Isambard in one arm, while with the other hand he held the cup to his lips. For a moment the lord of Parfois lay against his enemy's shoulder, and felt under his cheek the strong, eager beating of the boy's heart, that hated him so faithfully and well but would not pay him less than his due.

'I thank you, Harry, that was kindly done.'

The supporting arm lowered him carefully to his pillow again as soon as he made to go, and withdrew from him without any intimation of relief or loathing. The eyes, those eyes whose changeable mid-sea colouring was belied by their aggressive steadiness, had come back to him; he felt them taking in with awe and wonder the details of his disfigurement, and the obliterating pads of linen like death-pennies on his eyes.

'True,' he said thoughtfully, 'I should have been the one who died, if we all had our deserts. The comfort of the wicked is that in this world we so seldom do. But I am sorry you have lost a friend. I would have spared him to you if I could.'

Would the boy stoop to ask what he must be longing to know? He had come a long way since the first inquisition in a cell below the Warden's Tower, when he had shut his frightened, obstinate young mouth and presented a stony front of silence; but he had come by his own stubborn ways, and he was not so greatly changed. Growth, after all, is not so much a matter of change as of ripening, and what alters most is the degree of clarity with which we see one another. Had I, thought Isambard, to lose my eyes in order to see him so clearly? He will not ask.

And he did not ask. John the Fletcher had come with a message from Benedetta, and the lord of Parfois had given him a reply to take back to her. But John had not taken it, and John was dead. That was all he knew. He had no means of knowing whether the message had to do with him or no, or what was to happen now; for the moment that was put aside. He had come here upon another errand; his trouble was that for the life of him he could not determine exactly what it was or how to set about it. All he knew was that it had brought him here, and more than half-unwilling, at that, and that he could spare no energy for anything else until he had fulfilled what it required of him.

'I am sorry, my lord,' said the low, dogged voice, picking its way none too graciously, 'that you have met with this misfortune. I am very sorry you are in pain.'

It cost him a deal of discomfort to get it out, but he did it; and by the great sigh he heaved, his heart was eased of an uncommon load when he was rid of it.

Isambard lay quiet, smiling his mangled smile into the timbers of the ceiling, where the dusk was beginning to gather. His long, emaciated hand, half-open on the sheet beside him, held the unexpected offering very gently, like a bird that had come to him of its own grace and could not with honour be caged, or held a moment longer than it chose to rest in his palm. But neither need he move or speak too soon, and frighten it away. He was still so long that the boy grew restive, and stole closer to discover if he had fallen asleep.

'Harry!' said the voice from the bed at length, very quietly.

'My lord?'

'Bathe my eyes before you go.'

Harry brought the small bowl of milk and herbal infusions from the chest, and with fearful fingers, holding his breath, lifted the pads from Isambard's eyes. The sight of the swollen lids, red-rimmed and raw, made him draw in his breath sharply, grieved for the ruin of what had surely been beauty. That, too, Isambard understood.

'Ah, that will mend,' he said, and lay submissive beneath the boy's careful ministrations. His touch was light and shy, and his steady, earnest breathing fanned Isambard's cheek as he bent close. At the end of it Isambard opened his eyes fully for the first time, and looked up into his face.

A pale blur, with vaguely discernible features, and an undefined shining of great eyes. No more than that. And then the light hurt and warned him, and he lay back and let his lids close upon that glimpse of his charmed bird. No dove, certainly, more a young gerfalcon, and a wild one at that. It was not to be expected that it would return to him often, or remain with him long. But if he refrained from closing his hand it might at least leave with him the last frond or two of its eyas-down when it soared.

CHAPTER FIVE

Parfois: *September* 1233

He came out of his fever on the fourth night with senses clear and cold, his mind like a new sword, his body so weak that when he tried to lift his hand from the bed it would not obey him. There was light in the room, a candle burning. He saw it only as a pale, diffused aureole about a white point, summoning shadows, separating them dark from pale; but he saw it. Shapes so vague as to be no solider than cloud yet served to identify for him the corners of his own bedchamber. Someone was asleep and snoring on a wooden chair beside the bed. It seemed death had no use for him yet. He turned back to the world without regret, but without illusions. It would be no easy world henceforth for him.

Men were moving shadows, things were fixed shadows. And sometimes the two became confused, and he found that shapes which had clustered so still between him and the light could move and disperse when he showed he was aware of them. He knew then that it behoved him to nurse and value the senses he had left, for he was going to need them; and he thanked God, with a gambler's satisfaction, that his hearing was sharp as a wildcat's even without any cultivation on his part, and could be polished to even rarer brilliance now that he knew the need. There were tendencies in the moving shadows that cried a warning plainly enough; hesitations to move at command, that silent clustering together in his presence, and that palpable attention of their eyes in unrelenting attendance on him. Everything had acquired an extreme significance, every aspect of human behaviour could enlighten him if he courted his opportunities.

The voices, of course, the voices were still grave, concerned, prompt, obsequious; they knew he still had his ears. But on the second day after his return to reason he began to observe that the page who was left to wait on him made no great haste to jump to his orders. His lord called for water, for he was still plagued with an inordinate thirst; and the boy, secure that his name would not be required of him and his face was a blur that might have belonged to any of the youngsters about the household, came in his own good time, and served indifferently and inattentively. Isambard let it go then, well aware that he could barely lift a hand, much less lay the boy flat as he deserved. But he made acute note of the cocky young voice, and knew he could pick it out again from a dozen not so far different. Give him six or seven days of convalescence, and the patience to bide his time, and the score should be paid, for the sake of all who might fall into the same error.

They let Harry in to him that afternoon. The head on the pillows was raised alertly at the sound of his step, the face turned towards him pricked and aware, like a pointing hound.

'Harry!' said Isambard with satisfaction, not questioning, confirming his own excellent intuition. 'Child, you come very timely,' he said, when they were alone and the door shut. 'Come here to me and lend me an arm to get out of this bed, for I'm sick to death of it.'

'My lord,' said Harry, appalled, and lending the arm rather to hold him where he was than to help him out of it, 'you'll kill yourself. Only two days since you were still in fever.'

'Ah! Have you asked after me, then, while I've been out of my wits?'

Harry had, daily, and daily been denied entry to the sickroom, until this day when Isambard's recovered senses and strongly asserted will made it politic to avoid the appearance of keeping him under too strait a guard. If he wanted the boy, let him have him.

'You cannot stand,' said Harry sternly, forbearing from answering the question. 'You should lie quiet for a week or

132

more before you put foot to ground.'

'But I cannot afford a week, Harry. In a week I shall be allowed to stand and go, with even Hilliard's blessing, and there will be a hundred pairs of eyes watching to see how poor a show I make of it. I intend they shall have good reason to think again. Can you be secret?' He laughed at the stiff silence that answered him. 'Then who better for my purpose? Give me a little of your patience and obstinacy – I know you have more than enough of that – and I shall be ready and able to run before they know I can walk.'

He braced one hand into the mattress, and clung to Harry's arm with the other, and swung his legs out of the bed. As long as Harry had known him he had carried no flesh but the hard, spare muscle and sinew that clothed his long bones so magnificently; now fever had wasted the half of that from him, and pitted neck and shoulders and trunk with blue hollows. But he had lived a rigorous, athlete's life, and the frame of strength and agility and grace was still there, ready and willing to make the assay.

'My body never yet was my master,' he said, wrapping his gown about him on the edge of the bed. 'Let's see if I can still make it do my bidding, before I begin on the bodies of others.'

The boy was standing back doubtfully, watching him. Now that the fires in his eyes had cooled, and the burns about his lips had fined down and dried into flat, brownish scars, he was not so greatly changed. The same brown stains flecked his forehead and cheek-bones, but in the bronze of his skin they were not offensive. Only the ravaged eyes, still inflamed and red about the rims and dulled and darkened within, the high lids distorted by swollen tissue, defaced his old splendour. The oblique smile came haltingly on a slightly misshapen mouth. The hands that fumbled at his gown were a hawk's talons without the dexterity, for he was still very weak and moved with the calculated deliberation of one who knows his own feebleness.

He had caught the quality of Harry's fixed silence. He looked up quickly, and the tilt of his head challenged.

'Are you pitying me, boy?' The voice still had a core of steel.

'No, my lord. Do you know of any reason why I should?'

'I know of every reason why you should not,' said Isambard grimly. 'Let me but see the light of pity in your eye and, by God, I'll take a whip to you, as mannish as you are.'

'When you can lift one,' said Harry tartly, bent on wiping out the word 'pity' from between them. 'You'd have trouble holding one at this moment. Do you want me to be your prop, or don't you?'

He lent his arm and his shoulder as they were needed, and flatly refused both when he thought they had driven the worn body to exhaustion. The first day it was no more than the assay of standing, and walking a few unsteady steps about the bed; but day by day Isambard drove his resigned frame to more strenuous efforts, until he was prowling the length and breadth of the room like a caged tiger. By the time Master Hilliard ceremoniously allowed him to rise from his bed he was ready to daunt them all by the manner of his return.

They had expected a wavering invalid to be half-led, half-carried into the sun, and propped in his cushioned chair, there to lie as helpless a prisoner as in his fever-bed, at the mercy of the arms that waited upon him. Isambard had himself carefully and elegantly dressed, and came forth from his room in his old splendour, treading the uneven timbered floor with confidence, and descending the staircase without leaning or stumbling. When Master Hilliard protested that he was mad to venture so far, Isambard laughed in his face. Who was to know that he saw only a blur of darkness against a steadily dimming light? It was impossible to tell from the appearance of his eyes whether he could see or no; by his movements they judged that he could. Even the young squire who went before and lent him a shoulder seemed to be used rather as a decoration than a prop.

He chose out at leisure the neglectful page to attend him to the mews and kennels, crooking a finger imperiously to summon him from among a dozen of his fellows; and who

134

was to know that he had selected him by his voice alone, locating by means of a quick and accurate ear one shadow among shadows? The boy allowed himself to wonder, and half in bravado and half in the complacent conviction that he could not be detected, fell a pace behind in their walk to the kennels, and amused his following friends with a rapid parody of his lord's large and arrogant gait. Isambard heard the infinitesimal ripple of suppressed laughter that followed him, and tracked it contentedly to its source. He was round like a greyhound, and by sheer good fortune took the youngster neatly enough by the forearm he flung up in alarm to protect his head; his hair would have done just as well. A twist brought him to his knees, bleating now like a scared lamb.

'You are very forward to entertain us, my friend,' said Isambard, smiling down at him grimly. 'You shall be given all possible scope. Let's hear if you can also sing.' And he delivered him to be whipped on the spot, and stood by to ensure that his order was carried out.

After that the pages were markedly more prompt and respectful, and there was need for only one more demonstration to restore the quality of the hush that had always accompanied him about his castle wards. When one of the kennel-masters mishandled a deerhound bitch, and answered sullenly on being called to account for it, Isambard took the occasion as it offered, and laid him flat with a blow of his bony fist that slit the man's cheek open. He struck as the fellow muttered, using the voice to guide the blow into a face he could barely see, and the effort he put into it all but dropped him over his victim. But these secrets he managed to preserve to himself alone, and not until he had returned in good order to his bedchamber and closed the door on them all did he acknowledge at last the failing of his flesh. He lay on the bed staring into the growing darkness that had nothing to do with the ending of the September day.

It was all very well striking out about him thus publicly once or twice, with a madman's luck, to demonstrate that he was still to be reckoned with. But how much time could he buy by these means? He dared not appear in hall, he could not eat with them, or ride, or ever again engage in sword-play, without betraying that he could no longer see anything more precise than light and shadow. All the more difficult of the small operations the human body performs daily with-out thought, such nothings as pouring wine or sealing a letter, he must keep out of sight behind his closed door, until such time as he could evolve some arduous technique for dissembling his disability as he performed them; and no matter how ingeniously he planned, no matter how assidu-ously he schooled ears and fingers to do duty for his ruined eyes, sooner or later some detail must betray him. He could hope for nothing else. The time was coming when even light and darkness would be one; he knew that by infallible signs.

I shall be a blind old man, he thought, standing eye to eye with himself in the darkness on which he could still con-jure pictures and colours from within, now all from without failed him. A blind, clumsy old man, fumbling his food and spilling his wine. I shall give orders, and they'll say yes to me very civilly for a time, but do nothing, secure that I cannot pursue them. And in a while they'll no longer trouble to answer or heed me. Today I've staved off certainty; they've drawn in their horns for a while. How long? A week? I doubt it.

Not long enough, then, for Benedetta to come to him and depart again with the gift he kept for her. He had refused to face that certainty until now, but he could fend it off no longer. It was time to set about clearing the ground about him, so that he might bring down no more people with him in his fall. What kind of protection would a blind man be to either the boy or the woman? Get them all away, all those who could be used to influence him, all those whom he could be used to harm. In the last battlefield let there be no cover anywhere to allow the enemy to approach undetected. Walter, when he returned from his errand, must be sent on another, a longer, one that would keep him well clear of the clash to come. Harry must go, and Benedetta must never come. These things settled, the innocent put out of reach, the

136

liabilities disposed of, he could set to work to fortify his position and delight in his last warfare.

'What are they saying of me now?' he asked, when Harry came in to see him that night.

'They say your friend the devil had lent you a new pair of legs and two more eyes,' said Harry, not without a certain note of grudging admiration.

'Do they so? Good! I'm glad I did not take my life in my hands on the staircase for nothing. But I doubt we're all going to find it a short-term loan.'

'And they do not say,' said Harry deliberately, 'but I know, that de Guichet sent off a courier with a letter yesterday, to the king's camp at Usk.'

There was so equivocal a note in his voice at this that Isambard drew himself sharply to attention, and controlled whatever reaction he might have shown to the news. The boy would have to be handled carefully. Already the straight stare of his eyes had grown uncomfortably close and searching.

'Ah, so you know that, do you? And how did you come to be let into the secret?'

He let his thin hands lie open and easy on the arms of his great chair, to have their tranquillity seen. It was not so difficult, after all, to deceive the outer world, for a time at least, by means of one carefully planned sortie; but Harry had paced him about the room here day after day, and had better opportunities to use his eyes and his wits.

'I came late from the tracing-house, and went to the stables in the dark to have a moment with Barbarossa before sleeping. Young Clifford was there saddling up, and that was queer enough at that hour, you'll allow. He had one strap of his saddle-roll broken, and he was in haste, so he borrowed one of mine. He said he'd return it as soon as he came back from Usk. And since he can hardly be going with a message to the earl of Pembroke inside Usk castle, his business must be with the king's host laying siege to it. He ran off to collect his dispatch, and thought no more of me. I waited to see him come again, and it was de Guichet who sped him from the doorway of the Warden's Tower. I saw him make a parchment secure in the breast of his cotte before he mounted. In the dark,' said Harry sombrely, 'it wasn't hard to lie close. I know Parfois very well by now.'

'You take a deal of interest in this letter,' said Isambard, placidly smiling. 'Shall I recite you the content?'

'No need, I can do it myself. Not word for word, but as near as makes no matter. "If you should be of a mind for it," it says, "the game is running well. The old wolf we held off from hunting has come by an injury, and is no more to be feared – being blind – "'

He broke off there, seeing the lean fingers clench and the starting bones of the face pale from bronze to pallid gold.

'Did you think I did not know?' he said, low-voiced and quivering. 'There was one night you all but put your hand into one of the candles, if I had not snatched it away, and you never knew. You can practise on them outside, knowing every stone of the wards as you do, but beware of letting any get too close to you. And even so, what will you do when you have your body in health again, and no excuse left to keep a boy under your hand to lean on, to count you down the stairs and show you by his own movements where you must turn?'

'Faith, child!' said Isambard, relaxing with a sigh, 'I have been wondering the same thing myself.'

All things combined to confirm him in his conviction. It was time, and more than time, to set his house in order. He sat back in the gilded chair, gathering his faculties calmly, as a provident general marshals his troops for a critical field.

'It's true, then?' said Harry, confounded. 'You cannot see at all?' In spite of his certainty he had almost hoped for a flat denial, even for some proof that he was mistaken.

'Between night and day I see a shade of difference.' Even that, if he had said all, grew daily less discernible. He put it by with a movement of his hand, turning his mind to what was left. Blind or seeing, he must dipose as best he might and fight out the day. If de Guichet had sent word to William yesterday, today he might well have suffered some doubts of

138

his wisdom; but would he on that account call the messenger back? It was not likely. The throw was made, and could not be withdrawn; they would stand to it, and watch him warily until the answer came. De Guichet would always be safe enough, never having committed himself publicly. As the mastery went, so would he go.

'You spoke of Usk,' said Isambard, frowning over his thoughts as though his long-sighted eyes still served him. 'Pembroke had it garrisoned and provisioned. You say the king has attacked there?'

Both sides had hitherto held off from irrevocable action, Henry probably from timidity and incompetence, the earl marshal out of his strong reluctance to put to the issue of battle what he held to be rather a matter for reform. No man had ever less ambition to be a rebel and a leader of rebels, but the times and his own sense of right had thrust him into it, and he would not deny.

'By what I hear, the king made up his mind to take Usk, by way of a demonstration, to bring the earl to heel. Before he laid siege to the castle he denounced his feudal obligations to the earl and all his confederates, and Pembroke has renounced his homage to King Henry in return, and so have Basset and Siward and all the rest.'

'Then this is no mere matter of punishing a rebellious vassal,' said Isambard, 'or taking an outlaw. It's war, open and honourable, between man and man. The king has disarmed himself of his own best weapon, but I see he could hardly take the first action without cutting the link. And Pembroke held off with such patience. Henry could always hesitate and change course, but he never knew how to sit and wait.'

'But he's had no success at Usk, or so they're saying. We heard today that he's thought better of the attempt, and sent envoys to the earl, suggesting a way to an honourable peace. If the earl will formally surrender Usk to him he's promised to restore it within fifteen days, and to give him safe conduct to come back to the council at the next meeting, where he shall have a proper examination of all his grievances, and

139

reform where reform's due.'

'Ah, that's my Henry!' said Isambard with a short crow of laughter. 'He would promise the world, if God would but save him his face. But when his face feels its dignity secure, the earl had better have a good lawyer to bind the pledges, and a hand on his hilt into the bargain. And has Richard taken him at his word?'

'My lord, we've heard no more.'

'He will. He can do no other, feeling as he feels. He may doubt the king's honesty, but he cannot let the offer go by. Now Henry could close this without discredit, and disarm his enemies, if he would but keep to terms. But I'd wager my soul that when fifteen days are come and gone he'll say no word about handing Pembroke his castle back. As for reform, we shall hear no more of that. You could never give him a penny out of magnanimity but he would jump to it you were a fool or afraid, and grasp at the whole mark. He's had his knuckles rapped more than once for it, but he never learns. And Richard Marshall,' said Isambard reflectively, 'is neither a fool nor afraid. Well, so it stands, does it? Within a month the whole march will be in on the king's side, and Wales cannot stay out. It will be a race for which first sets light to the heather. And a border castle cannot be left in suspect hands when the march is burning.'

He smiled, the old, wolfish smile, pricking up his head to the scent of the blown smoke, and his ears to the sounds of battle; but he shut his teeth upon the rest of his thoughts.

A border castle in an advanced position, such as Parfois, must be in the hands of a trusted castellan at such a time. War is war, and old established right must give way to need. In the king's name, in England's name, in the name of William's long hunger, blind Ralf Isambard, near his dotage and already compromised by his championship of Hubert de Burgh, that hapless prisoner in Devizes, might plausibly be displaced from authority and held in protective custody in his son's charge, and that without reproach to the best and most magnanimous of monarchs. Cautiously, of course. His honour was widely scattered, and discretion was necessary, for fear some garrisons of his elsewhere might feel it their duty to question his retirement. They might even ask that he be produced alive, which would do the royal credit no good, even if the demand could still be complied with. Scandal would be avoided if possible. But the exigencies of war cover a multitude of irregularities.

Did he believe that the king would lend himself to such a piece of business? A difficult question. The king would be very careful not to know of any proceedings which might actually be looked upon as criminal. His hands would cover his eyes from seeing evil, but it would be reasonable to assume that he would be peering through his fingers. If the worst came to the worst he could produce a revelation of treasons plotted against him, and a holy and righteous rage to prove that he was the injured party. Who could determine how much of what went on in that curious mind was self-deception?

'Harry? Are you still there?' It was so quiet in the bed-chamber that for a moment he thought himself alone.

'Here, my lord.'

First things first. Let William lean to des Rivaulx's ear, and des Rivaulx to the king's, and let them compound among them as they would; the next move here in Parfois was plain. He should have recognized it long since, on the day of John the Fletcher's death; he should never have sent Walter with the ring, after the way had been closed to him once with so marked and forbidding a sign. But his heart had refused to acknowledge what his mind must have known, even then, only too well, that he could not hope and must not seek ever to see Benedetta again.

'Harry, you have long desired to go home.'

The distrustful silence hung between them like a curtain, but blind eyes are not hampered by obstructions. He saw the young face quicken and lift, eyes watching him hungrily, alert for the trick behind the words.

'And so you shall,' he said with deliberation. 'You will make ready tonight. Put together your things – the tools also if you will, such of them as you can easily carry – and to-

141

morrow morning I will see to it that the gate is opened to you.' Horse and habit and all that is his, Benedetta had said. All that is his, and more than he came with.

'Go?' said Harry in a stunned whisper, somewhere on the distant side of the room.

'Go, child. You heard me very well. You know that I mean what I say. Go and prepare yourself, and never fear that I have any trick to play on you this time. No one will drag you back. You're free.'

There was silence for a long moment. He felt the leap and surge of the fierce young heart towards liberty, heard the frantic clapping of the half-extended wings for an instant, before they were hushed and stroked and muted back into stillness. The struggle that convulsed the boy, flesh and spirit, vibrated through Isambard's own body and left him shaken and amazed.

Blunt and loud: 'I won't go!' said Harry.

Fulfilled and joyful, what did he need now with eyes? What did he need with more years of life? They could give him nothing better or stranger than this. *Nunc dimittis*, he thought, lying mute in his sweet amazement and smiling into the dark. Lord, now lettest thou thy servant depart. In peace? I doubt it, he owned, and smiled still. What had he ever had to do with peace? But in enlargement and content.

So he, too, had felt the gathering insecurity, and feared it not for himself, but for the old, blind man suddenly vulnerable among fair-weather friends, who would turn on him as soon as the wind changed. How could a man abandon even his enemy in such a case? But how could he say as much to his enemy?

'I won't go,' repeated Harry, challenging the silence.

Not his most attractive voice, rather surly and stubborn, and unreasonably furious, like a child's utterance when he feels he has been driven into a false position by unfair means, and is discharging all the weight of his own self-reproach and pain upon his elders. A voice that must have earned him many a box on the ears in his childhood. But gently now, to the man, and not the child. The voice was a recoil and a defence; behind it the man could be reached, for the words were his, and the indignant heart from which they had risen was his. He would listen to reason. There was no need to fear a final refusal; was it too dear an indulgence to hold this one in his hands for a moment before he let it go from him?

'Yes, Harry, you'll go. Not at my command, but because you must. There are reasons enough.'

The boy had expected and dreaded astonishment and questions, and been ready to counter them with what might have been insolence but for its complications of bewilderment and distress. To be understood without the need for words was more vexing, in a way, than to be pressed for explanations. No one likes to be read like a book. Nevertheless, he heaved a great breath of relief at not having to account for his change of heart, he who had fought tooth and nail for the freedom he was now refusing.

'You have no choice, Harry,' said Isambard gently. 'There is something I have not told you. If you refuse to go, Madonna Benedetta will come here to Parfois to surrender herself in your place. If I cannot be sure of affording you protection any longer, how can I guarantee her protection?'

That brought the boy across the room in a rush of light steps, to crouch beside the arm of the chair and catch at the lean, long hand. 'Madonna Benedetta? Coming here? But how – What compact was this? And not a word to me! Never a word! Was *this* the message John brought you?' He was quivering with anger and dismay. 'How dared you? You had no right ... no right ... !'

'Neither had she, but she did it. She offered her own person in exchange for you, and I accepted the offer. Your John, God rest him, thought to get you out of my hands by a different way and make the bargain void, and it might have been well if he had succeeded, but he did not, and we must live with what we have. After he was dead I sent Walter in his place to take my ring and my pledge to her, never thinking how soon I might have cause to wish both back again.

143

I doubt he's thought it best to avoid Aber, and had to waste some time hunting for her, but by this he has surely done his errand. And if you do not go and halt her on the way, she will come to Parfois to be your ransom. And just at a time when I can no longer be sure of my power to hold her safe.' He closed his fingers with careful respect upon the boy's smooth, vital hand. 'And that's why you must go, since I cannot. You must ride and intercept her on the way, tell her both you and she are free of all debts and commitments to me, and take her safely home.'

'You could send someone else,' said Harry, distracted and trembling.

'No one else, not even the elders who knew her once, can be so sure as you of knowing her now. No one else can present her in his own person with the prize she's coming to purchase. And for the rest – consider my household, Harry. With Walter already out of it, whom would you trust with such an errand? No, you cannot evade your duty; it's you must go.'

Harry's head went down in a revulsion of helpless bewilderment, his forehead on the clasped hands, while he searched his heart wildly, in agony to single out what he ought to do from what he wanted to do. Out of hiding his muffled voice blurted desperately:

'But how can I leave you?'

No question now of dignity and reticence, and no sense of having compromised or lost them. Naked and simple the words came, and he said them, and was eased.

'You can because you must. And if you want a more selfish reason from me, because I can get along, saving your lordship's presence, better without you than with you. Walter will be here soon to supply a pair of eyes and an honest tongue for my use, and what more could you do if you stayed? The greatest aid you can furnish me is to take Benedetta out of danger. Never fear for me,' he said, himself marvelling at the serenity of his voice, 'I am an old campaigner; I can hold my own here on my own ground. Go and make all ready, and tomorrow, as soon as you've broken your fast, come here to me. I'll put you on your way myself.'

It was necessary. Who knew if the thought might not strike de Guichet that the boy had better be retained, that he might some day be a useful bargaining counter?

'Well, will you go?'

The smooth forehead stirred on his hand, the troubled face came up to him slowly; he felt the long, anxious stare of the sea-green eyes searching him through and through, and knew that he had won his way. He would go because he must. It was not necessary to find comfort for him; life would soon do that.

'I'll go,' said Harry.

They came to the gatehouse together as the long, level shafts of the dawn threaded it and felt their golden way into the outer ward. Isambard's left hand gestured, and the guards who had looked askance at the prisoner fell back obediently and let them pass.

They stepped on to the timbers of the bridge, and Barbarossa's hoofs sent their hollow echo reverberating along the rocky cleft below. Before them on its high plateau of grassland, fringed with trees along the edges of the escarpments on either side, the church of Parfois soared like a golden lance. The singing light fingered its way into every course of masonry framing the deep doorway and the great east window, and set the taut lines of the tower quivering like the strings of a harp.

Here, thought Isambard in his darkness, *he* came forth, that day. She had him by the hand, she loosed his fingers then and fell behind him. Something she cried into his ear as he looked up. I saw his face clearly, I can see it still, amazed and enchanted by the thing he had made. And then he fell. Here, just here, he fell, and she caught him in her arms and sank to the ground with him, and held him on her heart as he died. It took such a little time for him to die, hardly long enough for her to kiss him on the mouth. When we took him from her he was far out of our reach. We stripped him by the river. Naked and brown, he was like one of the country boys along Severnside who learn to swim as they learn to walk. Slender and wiry and young. And dead.

'My lord,' said Master Harry's son, watching the lofty hawk's face beside him, and feeling the lean hand grip tighter about his arm, 'is anything the matter?'

'Nothing, Harry. I was remembering something past. Old men do.' His voice was still sardonic when he chose to describe himself as old; after all its batterings his body could not believe that it had lost its youth.

There was a matter still between them of a death, and the ravishing of a grave. He thought they might yet come to speech about it, and if he would not have welcomed the reckoning at this last moment, he would not have shrunk from it. But Harry walked beside him and was silent, matching his easy, young-man's stride to the deliberate and careful steps of his companion, and nursing him away from any broken ground or stony places. Barbarossa sniffed the morning air and danced for joy.

Close to the tower now, close to the pale scar of the foundation, enclosed in its rising wall. They heard the voices of the masons, the scraping of shovels in mortar, the chink of hammers and chisels on stone. There were many people there, others of the household besides the workmen and the guard. De Guichet was there, talking to Master Edmund; Isambard heard his voice among the many voices, and smiled. He was waiting for one arriving rather than for a departure.

'When you meet her, be sure you say to her that there are no debts remaining. You know which way she is likely to come?'

'There's but one good and direct way from Aber, my lord.'

'Good! Then I can leave her safely in your hands. Are we yet at the guard point?'

146

'Fifty yards more, my lord.'

'Take me through, Harry, before you mount. I would have you off my boundary. What do you see in their faces?'

'I think they are still in awe of you. They go on with what they are doing, but with their eyes on us. The guards have moved back to leave your way open.'

He was still princely; he could still command dread. And they were still not sure, not quite sure, how the wind might veer.

'That's well. Are we through now?'

'Yes, my lord.'

'Then here we say our farewells.'

They halted, strangely irresolute now. Barbarossa pulled impatiently at Harry's wrist, wild to be off. He turned a moment to chide and soothe him.

'They are all watching us. Some have stopped work. I think it is only that they wonder.'

'Let them wonder. You mount and ride, and lose no time. God speed, and commend me to Madonna Benedetta.'

Harry turned to mount, and could not; looked over his shoulder and turned back, feeling his heart in him torn in two.

'My lord, I'm loath ='

'Arrogant imp,' said Isambard, 'do you think no one can make shift without you? Be off, I don't need you.'

The still splendid figure, alert, fastidiously shaven, carefully and richly dressed, had borne witness in every movement to the continued competence of his vision, until this last moment of leave-taking. Suddenly he wavered, made an abrupt step forward, and raised a hesitant hand, groping towards his parting prisoner in a blind and helpless gesture; and Harry, forgetting everything but that fumbling hand feeling for his face, caught it in his and guided it to his cheek. Its fellow came gently, of its own accord, and held him. The beautiful head stooped a little, the hawk face inclined, the hard, scarred lips saluted his cheek very lightly.

Silently, trembling, he submitted to the kiss of kinship;

147

and when he was released he reached impulsively and returned it, with a child's fervour and clumsiness.

'God be with you, my lord.'

Nothing more, not a word. Explanation was out of his reach, justification he did not need, understanding was somewhere within him, heart-deep, part of him now whether he would or no, and not to be questioned. He set his foot in the stirrup and mounted. Barbarossa stamped the ground gladly and stretched towards the valley in an unchecked canter, and the wind of their going, sharp with the morning coolness, stung where Isambard's kiss had rested.

They were gone. It was over. And now he could set his mind to what remained to be done, and fear, in the sense that he understood fear, was finished with. The game of life and death had still to be played, but the stakes were within his control now, and mattered no more than a game should matter. He stood listening until the soft thudding of the hoofs in the grassy ground had ebbed away into the valley. Then he turned, and took a step back towards the towers of the lower guard, and suddenly he was alone, without light or landmarks, in a featureless landscape of nightmare.

He listened for the hammers, but the hammers had stopped; for the voices, but the voices were silent. Uphill he must go; but he felt carefully about him with a stretched toe, and could not determine how the slope lay. He had lost his guide, and made no provision to replace him; but there was surely more in this silence than their covert interest in his movements and caprices. The quality of their stares crowded and burdened him. Sweat broke in his palms. What had he done? Something revealing, something irrevocable, that betrayed the weakness of his position. For they knew he was helpless. They knew he was blind.

Then he understood. Every eye had been on him when he lifted his hand tentatively towards Harry's face. But for that he might have kept up his deception even now, called to Master Edmund, made some pretext to get him to his side so that he might make use of him on the first stage of the

148

return journey, and borrow a man from him for the rest. It was too late now; they knew. There would be no more pretending. Harry had taken the hand as it reached sadly astray, and laid it to his cheek. Did I not say, he thought ruefully, that he'd be the death of me yet?

So now he had the choice of fumbling his way back dangerously and ludicrously alone, or commanding help openly, and accepting their knowledge and his own loss. He was aware of many watchers, none moved, many gratified, not one anxious to help him. Even when he called peremptorily for a shoulder to lean on, the stillness and the silence held. He knew his loneliness.

'Master Edmund! Where is Master Edmund? Bid him here to me, some of you. Move!'

Slowly, grudgingly, they stirred. Only one creature, somewhere there in the foundations of the tower, dropped something out of his arm with a flat wooden clap against the stone of the rising wall, and came in a shamed run to take him by the arm. Something new was revealed to him in the touch. Never in his life until now had he been a target for compassion. It needed some adjustment to welcome it, even in his situation, yet he did it in the measure of the first step they took together. Whoever this fellow might be, he had a right to his enlarging impulse; only a mean heart could grudge it to him.

'Here, my lord, this way.' The hand turned him and put him on the smoothest of the roadway. 'Lean on me. Is it back to your apartments you would go?'

A kind voice, young but not very young, and one that would have been timorous in addressing the lord of Parfois in any other circumstances. The careful steps that attended Isambard's long strides were those of a small man, the arm on which he leaned his hand was thin. The eyes that were only just being born in him drew him a picture from these contacts, of a young fellow of about thirty-four or five, somewhat below medium height, and of modest and gentle appearance and mild attainments. Not a mason, the muscular development was not there, the fingers had not that kind

149

of dexterity that went with tools. The sleeve was rough home-spun, but the wrist was smooth.

'Friend,' said Isambard, using new forms of address in new situations, and tasting the lessons of his old age as sharply and acutely as those of his youth, 'I think I should know you. Have you been in my service long?'

'Nearly twenty years, my lord. Take care here, the ground is stony.'

'You are one of those engaged on the tower, are you not? As I think, a clerk.'

'Yes, my lord.'

Twenty years a clerk about the building-works of Parfois made him but a boy when Master Harry Talvace fell to the arrow of God and of John the Fletcher. Here, on this spot, where the morning sun lay bright along the open grassland before the bridge. There had been a boy then in the tracing-house, one who ran faithfully and adoringly at his heels, cleaned parchments for him, dwelt on his every word and stroke like a worshipper, and wept himself half-blind at his fall. The small, transmitted lightning of Master Harry's passionate kindness quivered, muted, in the hand that guided Master Harry's destroyer back to his refuge.

'I know you now,' said Isambard. 'Your name, as I recall, is Simon. You were his clerk.'

'I was, my lord.'

How was it that he knew, without the need for thought or question, who 'he' must be? He answered readily, with no note of wonder at the length of this cast. Harry is as alive to him as to me, thought Isambard, astonished, and as timeless.

'We are at the bridge, my lord. Step a little high.'

Master Edmund had done nothing to advance him. He was jealous always of those Harry most relied on, Isambard reflected. And he had brief thoughts, as they crossed the outer ward, of repairing that minor injustice; till he recalled at his own door, with honesty and certainty, that his favour was hardly likely to advance any man again, unless it was into an early grave.

150

From the leads of the tower roof, in the old days, he had been able to see the blue hills of central Wales rearing to westward, across the wide green valley laced with silver; and Pool upstream, and Strata Marcella down, had balanced each other in the sunlight, grey stone against grey stone. Even in his blindness something of the enlargement of freedom came to him there. The air blew clean across from the lofty peat-bogs and the shallow heron-pools in the uplands, and brought scents of heather and withering autumn grass, its seeds ripened and shed.

Somewhere beyond those dim, remembered shapes of heath and cloud Benedetta and Harry rode homeward now together without haste. Walter on his return journey had not encountered Harry, for Walter had come by way of Shrewsbury, to gather the latest news of King Henry's devious proceedings at Usk; but surely by now the woman and the boy must be nearing Aber. His heart was delivered of them.

'She took the ring from me,' Walter had faithfully reported what he did not understand, 'and I think she was glad, until I told her what befell her man. She was quiet a long time, but she did not weep or rail. She said that she took that guilt upon her, that she should have opened her heart to him. And she said that there would be a time to talk of it.'

Nothing more. The rest she had kept for her coming, when she had made, as she said, provision for the old man who dwelt beside her; and now he would never hear it. There might have been a time to talk of all things that lay unfinished between them, but now there never would, never in this dear world.

So much the better. She was safe, she had her darling again; and as for him, the house of his mind was swept clean and the fortress of his loneliness well provided. Walter was dismissed to Fleace, on the pretext that his master meant to follow him there shortly; and Simon the clerk was gone with him, recommended to service under Humphrey Paunton's mason at work on the new hall there. One more inno-

cent from under his feet, clear of the stray shots that cared
little where they fell. Parfois in the days to come would be
no place for gentle creatures who took pity on their enemies
grown old and blind, and led them by the hand out of harm's
way.

He turned from his dark contemplation of Wales when
the wind grew chill. The upper reaches of the tower staircase
were narrow and worn; one of the pages usually led him up
there, and waited within call until he chose to come down.
But on this evening of late September he called, and no page
came.

He waited and called again, less patiently. He listened,
and there was no young foot stirring, no voice answering;
but there were other sounds, rising with a slow, spiral splendour out of the wards below. A ceremonious clashing of
hoofs in procession, a murmur of voices quick with excitement and eagerness; all distant, all belonging to the lower
world, and filtered through the golden acres of air. Some
company riding in. The young men still rode, still hawked
and hunted; every day the outer ward and the stable-yard
were busy with riders. But this had a different sound, alien
and bright.

He waited to see if they would bring him word, but no
word came. He was neither surprised nor dismayed, for he
had expected nothing. And after a while, satisfied that his
attendant had deserted him to run and stare with the rest of
the household in the outer ward, he felt his way along the
merlons to the doorway, and began to descend alone. Step
by step, with due caution on the tapering treads, it took him
a long time to negotiate the upper flights. It did not matter.
He had plenty of time.

Between the thick walls he was closed in from the world,
and there was no sound but the sounds of his own body, his
feet treading slowly and carefully from worn stair to stair,
his long, even breathing, the steady, strong beat of his heart
thudding at the cage of his bony breast. At every arrow-slit
in the turns of the well a current of cool, sweet air blew over
him, and at every brief landing the darkness seemed heavier.

152

He no longer saw either shapes or shades; all was one darkness.

He reached the level of his own apartments, and stood for a moment by the stair-head, listening with reared head and stretched ears. No movement within the tower, no voices. From without, heard more faintly here, a certain hum and bustle that had still a note of excitement in it. But somewhere here, close to him, he felt rather than heard the even rise and fall of breathing. Not his own: that rhythm he knew intimately by now. Somewhere in a room aside from him, but with the door open between. And so still. And by its very evenness and quietness, whoever breathed and waited there was aware of him.

He felt his way along the wall, and reached across to the doorway of his own great chamber. The door stood half open; he had closed it with his own hand when he left it, an hour earlier. He pushed it fully open and went in, without concealment and striding easily, for here he knew every knot in the timbers, and every irregularity in the oak of the floorboards. At leisure he took his stand in the centre of the room, and turned his imperious face, that quenched lantern of splendid bone, slowly to left and right, and fastened after a moment on the direction in which he felt the palpable presence. There he fixed and held, utterly calm and sure of himself, and faintly smiling.

Someone was sitting in his great chair, an act of usurpation that marked, at least, the end of a pretence. His smile deepened at that. He took his time about considering identities. A large, self-confident breath, a sense of bulk, someone broad-set and well-fleshed; but uneasy under the blind stare, for he stirred a little in the cushions, and then, in a movement which startled Isambard into astonished laughter, got to his feet. He thought he had him then; taking his lord's chair in the first place and quitting it now chimed so well with his nature, and were so revealing.

'De Guichet?' he said, disappointed and disdainful.

'No,' said a voice out of the darkness before him, soft, smiling and deliberate, 'not de Guichet.'

153

'Ah, is it you? Fair, sweet son,' said Isambard in a large sigh of understanding and fulfilment, 'what has kept you so long? I've been looking for you these ten days.'

CHAPTER SIX

Aber: *October* 1233

Saint Clydog came out of the long dream unwillingly, to a grey sky hanging low over Moel Wnion and a distant, desolate crying of the sea, an empty hut, a quenched hearth, an unpeopled heart, and an agitated young man crouched before him in the deep grass, holding his knees in big, supple, golden-brown hands and staring up into his face with great urgent eyes that he had seen somewhere before, in another countenance. A desperate voice battered insistently at his reluctant senses with a name, coaxing, pleading, bullying, cajoling, dragging him back to a world he desired to know no longer. He tried to shut up his ears and seal his spirit, but the hands held him cruelly, and the voice like the hilt of a dagger pounded at the closed doors, and would not leave him to his quietness.

'Where is Madonna Benedetta? Listen to me! Help me! I must find her. Where is Madonna Benedetta?'

The old man opened his eyes fully, and with infinite pain dragged himself back into the fragile confines of his body, that little cage in which the great bird fluttered feebly with cramped wings and bursting heart. He remembered this face: this was the boy who had beckoned her away.

'She is gone,' he said, shrinking in the grip of the young hands that did not know how strong they were.

'I *see*, I *know* she is gone.' The coarse blanket was folded on the narrow brychan, the fire-stone was cold, the arched window to southward stared blind. 'When did she go? How is it I have not met her along the way?'

Harry knelt in the grass, holding the saint's aged knees in his palms, staring up into the face that was no more than a drift of draggled grey down from a hedgerow of thistles, lit

155

by two remote and dim blue eyes.

'Dear saint, help me! I must find her, I have a message to deliver.'

'She is gone to Parfois,' said Saint Clydog, the old voice suddenly clear and aware. 'There was a squire who came and brought her an answer to her message. She begged me a boy to care for me and keep me, and then she went from me on her journey.'

'To Parfois? But I've come from Parfois. At every grange and hospice on the way I've inquired for her, and never any news. She has not passed that road. I thought to find her still here.' He leaned and took the frail little hands that lay light as moths in the old man's lap. 'Did she ride alone? Surely she took some escort with her from Aber? The prince would never let her –'

He halted there, sure as soon as he posed the question that no one could have known better than Benedetta what the prince would and would not let her do. To have her come down out of her chosen solitude would be like having the sun turn back towards dawn from the zenith. Her every move would have been questioned earnestly.

'She did not go near Aber,' he said, loudly and bitterly, enraged with his own stupidity. 'Oh, sweet saint, tell me quickly, which way did she go? Who attended her?'

In Aber they could not even be aware yet that she was strayed from her place.

'She went down by the hill road into Bangor,' said Saint Clydog, staring above the boy's head as though he saw her now taking that lonely path over the shoulder of the mountain. 'She asked Bishop Martin for a boy to attend on me, and for a horse and a mounted manservant for herself, to bring her as far as Parfois. And I did not see her again. Only the boy came up to me. He's there below now at the brook, fishing. A good boy, but young and strange. I was used to John the Fletcher,' he said wistfully.

'Then she took the road straight from Bangor?' It would mean that from Dolgynwal on she would be travelling by the

156

same road on which he had made such haste. If she had been a day earlier, or he a day later, they would surely have met. 'When did she leave here?' he questioned, shaking fiercely at the rough brown sleeve. 'How many days since?'

'Three days – or was it four? It rained when she was gone. Two days were rainy, and then the sun came for a little while, and that was yesterday. Four days ago.'

'And your boy – when did he come?'

'Towards nightfall, on the day after she left me. A good boy. Quiet,' said Saint Clydog, dropping the feeble tears of old age down his tangled beard unawares. 'There's no peace where there are women. They must be for ever coming and going. I always knew she would not live out her life here.'

Harry was up out of the grass like a rising bird. Give her one night's rest in Bangor before she rode, and she could be only three days advanced on the journey. Past Dolgynwal by now, surely, while he rode up here in his ignorance still watching for her on the direct road. She could still be overtaken. He turned to reach for Barbarossa's bridle, and then, remembering his manners, plunged as impulsively back again to plump to his knees before the saint and ask his blessing.

'Sir, pray for me! That I find her in time!'

The wrinkled hand touched his head, and rested a moment like a dry leaf caught in the tangle of his hair.

'In God's time, or in yours?' said Saint Clydog sadly.

He rode down the steep cleft of the valley beside the stream, and the great enclosed shape of the prince's maenol came into sight below him, backed into the fissure of the hills and commanding the narrow strip of marshland and meadow above the sands. The long, dark line of the encircling wall and rampart folded hall and stables and living quarters, kitchen and kennels and mews, the low tower of the royal apartments on its broad undercroft, and the timber keep on its towering motte. Outside the wall the village sprawled, clinging to shelter, and the little river bound the maenol in a silver ribbon before it flowed down through the level marshes to the sea. His heart leaped and clamoured in his breast, frantic to be there.

He could have turned Barbarossa, and ridden straight back along the way he had come; but he had taken thought in time that he needed help with this hunt, and more men on fresher horses would have a better chance of success. The first thing he must do, before he rode again, was to pour out the whole story into Llewelyn's ears. He need fear no long explanations there, no checks of sheer incomprehension; his foster-father's quick senses leaped into understanding as naturally as trees lean to the light. He need only cry out what was needful, and questions could wait for an ampler time.

Past the mill the road opened out and grew less steep, and he spurred eagerly, and came at a canter into the postern gate. The offered challenge fell away from him before a cry of recognition and joy. He leaned to reach a hand to old friends as he rode by them, and to gasp out his haste. The dark gateway in the tall timber wall gulped him and gave him back to the light of day within, as he reined to a standstill in the courtyard before the hall.

A woman at the well knew him, and dropped her pitcher to run and cry the news. Men came running, men he had wrestled and climbed and played with from childhood, surrounding him, hoisting him bodily out of the saddle, crying questions, fondling him, passing him boisterously from hand to hand. He fought them off, panting.

'The prince – first I must speak with the prince. I must! Don't keep me!' Somewhere in his heart a frantic child, in tears of excitement and joy, was howling rather for his mother, but that must wait.

He had set off at a run for the steps of the hall, but they lifted voices and hands to turn him towards Llewelyn's private apartments, and ran on his heels to bring him there with acclaim, until he outran them on the wings of his eagerness and burst in at the door of the prince's tower alone. Up the great staircase in four striding leaps, like a deerhound, and the heavy door of the private audience-room was hurled back to the wall before his rush, and he was in Llewelyn's presence.

The three men at the table, heads close and faces grave and intent, looked up as one man, startled and wary. The stranger's hand went to his hilt with formidable rapidity but admirable smoothness. Ednyfed Fychan came to his feet, frowning, and opened his lips to challenge the unmannerly intruder. Llewelyn, who sat with his back to the door, turned a scowl of impatience and displeasure; but the next moment the blaze of knowledge flamed in his face. He let out a great bellow of: 'Harry!' The chair, whirled aside to give him passage, span jarring back against the wall. He leaped to meet the boy's impetuous rush, arms spread to take him to his heart.

Harry ran and flung himself at the prince's feet, and caught the great right hand down to his breast, kissing it fervently, laying his forehead for an instant against Llewelyn's knees before he was caught by the arms and hoisted exuberantly to his feet.

'Harry, is it you? Is it you indeed?'

Long arms strained him to a broad, brocaded breast; he felt the massive, impetuous beat of the prince's heart pulse through his body, shaking him to the marrow of his bones. Bearded lips kissed his cheek and his brow, and he was held off to be devoured by far-sighted black eyes blazing with laughter and delight. A hard palm under his unshaven chin turned up his face to be read and re-read.

'Stand to be seen, boy, give me my fill. Why, you're taller by inches than Owen, I'll swear, and pressing David close.' He was round upon the seneschal with shining eyes. 'Run, Ednyfed, send for my lady, have her bring Gilleis with her – tell them Harry's come home safe and sound. And David, and Owen – and Adam Boteler if he's to be found. Hurry!' And upon the stranger, who had withdrawn courteously into the shadows, and stood watching them with a slight, grave, uncomprehending smile:

'You'll pardon us; it's not every day I regain a son. This is my foster-child, Harry Talvace, who has been prisoner this

159

long time to Ralf Isambard at Parfois. It's nearly two years since we've set eyes on him, and never a word or a sign that we could hope to see him burst in like this – as loud and unruly as ever,' said Llewelyn, and thumped Harry heartily on the back. 'Make your reverence, boy, to Alan Delahaye. He is come to us as envoy from the earl of Pembroke.'

Harry made his bow and his excuses, still further excited and confused by this mention of the earl marshal. What could Pembroke want to discuss with the prince of Aberffraw but the issue of peace and war?

'I beg you'll forgive so rude an interruption, sir. I would not have ventured to burst in unbidden, but there's a matter that can't wait. My Lord, may I speak?'

'You may, you must,' said Llewelyn. 'I'm waiting to hear. How is it we have you again? Are you free in very truth this time? Have you broken out of hold?'

'From Parfois,' said Delahaye dryly, 'I think he'd be the first.'

'I did not break out.' Seven times in all he had made the attempt, there was nothing any Englishman could teach him about the impregnability of Parfois. 'He set me free. But – '

'What, are there still buts? What has he devised this time to your hurt? If this wind holds, it's I shall be paying off the account with him.'

'My lord, it's not as you suppose. But I'm charged with an errand I could not do yet, and until it's done I'm not free. Madonna Benedetta – she's gone from her place, and I must find her.'

'Madonna Benedetta, gone from her place? What's this? An errand? *His* errand,' said Llewelyn, falling upon the word like a hawk upon its prey. 'And to her!' He drew the boy with him back to his chair, set him on a footstool at his feet, and kept fast hold of him by the hands. 'Tell me!'

Harry took breath and poured out the whole of it short and bare into his lap. The prince's great, vital hands held him, and never started or tightened.

Before the tale was done the prince's message had brought

160

them all running to confirm with their own eyes that Harry was back among them, to touch him for proof and hold fast after touching. Gilleis came flying with skirts kilted up like a wild girl, and flung herself upon him in a rush of happy, incredulous tears. He opened his arms to her without pausing in his tale, and Llewelyn surrendered him without relaxing for a moment the intensity of his attention. Gilleis knelt beside her son, kissed his breathless mouth once between the tumbling words, and kept her arms fast about him to the end. Owen came, glowing with the news, and David, flushed and bright with joy. Adam Boteler came, and leaned to kiss his stepson gently on the head. The princess came, and the boy, distracted, would have risen and knelt to her, but she reached a hand to quiet him and hold him where he was, and touched for present salutation the preoccupied lips that brushed a kiss upon her fingertips between the syllables of Benedetta's name.

'I was at fault; I made too great haste, and thought too little. If I'd taken the road more easily I should surely have met her on the way. You see I must go back, I can't rest till I've found her and brought her home. Oh, Mother, you'll give me leave for a few days more –'

Gilleis closed his lips with her palm and hushed him. She knew already, by the height and the breadth of him, and the golden-brown down of his chin and the deep voice, and by the look of his eyes even when he smiled at her thus through dazed tears, shaken to the heart by the warmth of his welcome home, that she must give him leave lifelong if she wanted to keep him now. The years she had lost there was no replacing. Even the years restored might all too soon be forfeit to another woman, but let that be faced when it came. He was free, he was his own man, and for her heart's quiet no less than for his, Benedetta must be regained.

'Child, do you think there's anything I could grudge her? Go with my blessing. If I could outride you after her, I would.'

'But let me go in your place,' offered Owen, seeing the weariness not far behind the brilliance of Harry's eyes.

'You've taken no rest. Have you slept at all since you left Parfois?'

'Let him be,' said Llewelyn briskly, wise in his young men, 'this charge is his, not yours. Do you go with David, and choose him six good men who know the holy woman, and mount them well. Best send two by way of Bangor, Hal, to follow her traces the road she went, and take four over the hill track with you to meet the road at Dolgynwal. If you get word she's passed there, well and good. But if not, let two ride ahead fast with you, and two turn back to meet their fellows from Bangor, till they do hear certain news of her. You shall have my writ to take whatever mounts or men or aids you need as far as the border. There, go make your choice from the stables, and what else you need or want before you go, never spare to ask or take. God helping, we'll not lose Benedetta.'

'A good lad,' said Llewelyn, still gazing thoughtfully after them when the door was shut between. 'Take him faults and all, as good a lad as ever stepped.'

'One of the king's best allies on your borders,' said Delahaye from his place in the shadows, 'has troubles enough of his own, it seems. If you do choose to move south and lift the weight from the earl's flank, my lord, you need not fear Parfois, that's clear.'

'Fear of Parfois would not trouble me. I have a vow registered in heaven concerning Parfois, in God's and my good time to take and destroy it for the sake of Talvace – the father and the son. And I see nothing here to loose me from that oath. Let the son be freed, yet the sire's dead, and his grave dishonoured. And yet – blinded!' he said, and shook his head over it, frowning. 'I would have had him with all his powers at their best.'

'You need not disturb him unless you choose. It's enough for us,' said Delahaye, 'that he should be out of the reckoning, and it seems this poor wretch who was killed has taken care of that. The earl would rather have you pin down Brecon for him while he keeps his hands free to clear the valley of the Usk. But should you choose indeed to pursue your vow, coming in upon our side at least gives you the opportunity.'

'You do not believe,' said Llewelyn, 'that it can be done?'

His eyes kindled golden, like a hawk's, his head pricked up loftily to stare with joy upon the sweet temptation of the almost impossible. But he put it by, shaking the lure out of his vision. There were other considerations. If he went to war for the last time – surely the last time, for the latest years of his life must be given all to consolidating the kingdom he had carved out for his son – it would be for graver reasons than the satisfying of a boyish lust in his own heart. Something might yet be won and added to David's inheritance, his position as neighbour to England established yet more firmly, his native right more unmistakably demonstrated. The English had a marked liking and value for precedents and points of law and custom; it was for that tradition that Pembroke was fighting, whatever the personal wrongs that had launched this unexpected war. For that and for a standard of integrity in the relationships between men and government, so firmly fixed and well respected that it should be impossible for a weathercock king to disregard it.

And there lay the final and compelling reason for saying yes to Pembroke's proposal of alliance, beyond all the reasons of interest: Pembroke was in the right and Henry was in the wrong. Whatever the minor rights and wrongs of who struck first or who suffered deprivation first, seeing the whole great quarrel large, Pembroke was in the right.

'God disposes, my lord,' said Delahaye, smiling. 'I would not say there is any fortress that *cannot* be taken.'

Llewelyn had moved so far from the impregnability of Parfois that it cost him an effort and a little wonder to get back to it.

'I doubt it will never be put to the issue,' he said, a shade regretful still. 'Please God, Harry will bring back Madonna Benedetta safe and well, and I shall have no stake within the wall there, to draw me to the assay. God who disposes must dispose of me and my vow, if I do not keep it. An archer

163

with a handful of quicklime can be as effective as an angel with a flaming sword, I doubt.' He turned resolutely from this unprofitable harrowing. 'This warning that reached the earl on his way south to the council, and turned him back into Gwent – do you hold it certain it was true? Would the king have impeached him? He had given him guarantees, so recent that no one can have forgotten them.'

'He gave de Burgh guarantees, an oath sealed on the relic of Bromholm, not a month before he felled him like a tree. And whoever sent the warning spoke no more than the truth about the king's intentions at Usk. The appointed time is well past, and he has made no move to give the castle back. That, too, he guaranteed. A good earnest for all his other promises.'

'I grant you. And Usk,' said Llewelyn with a glittering smile, 'for all the king could not take it, is not impregnable.'

'By this, I think, Turbeville is out of it, and the earl has his own again. He wearied of waiting for Henry to keep his word. But the true measure of the rottenness of the king's credit,' said Delahaye fiercely, 'is that such a warning could be received by any honourable man and not *dis*believed. It may not in every case be true, but in no case dare a man discount it, for all too evidently it *could* be true. To what has the crown come, if this must be said of it?'

A man is not necessarily a better advocate because he believes passionately in the cause he must argue; but his faith or his close alliance with Richard Marshall had lent Delahaye a conviction that rang more gratefully than eloquence in Llewelyn's ears. There was another test he could set beside the first, and the contrast was marked. If Pembroke had made him a promise, without the sanction of the rood of Bromholm or any other relic, he would have rested absolutely secure in its fulfilment. If one had come riding after him with a warning that Pembroke meant to betray him in Pembroke's own house, he would have laughed and ridden on without a qualm. The test of any man's honesty is whether you are willing to stake your life on it. Who would do that on King Henry's?

There was still time to reconsider. If he held with them he held with them to the end; no separate terms, no separate peace. How if the entire march came in with its full weight on the king's side? How if he brought in more and more foreign mercenaries like the Count de Guisnes and his Flemings? Des Rivaulx had seen to it that all the streams of revenue were channelled securely into his hands; as long as he lasted Henry could afford to buy troops abroad. He was well financed, he was making a strong bid for an established rule of his own, free of the council and loosed from custom and tradition. And he would deal with his enemies without mercy if he did prevail.

The time to think of the end was now, before he began. Not his own life and his own fortunes at stake now, but David's princedom, the dream of Wales. If he held with them now he held with them to the end, and prevailed or foundered with them. So be it! And now, he thought, smiling and content with his cast, let us give our minds to the details, and see to it that we prevail, and not founder.

'It will take me a little time to get my army into the field,' he said deliberately, 'but not so long as it will take Henry to bring in the lords of the march. By the end of the month I can be ready to cover your lord's flank from all assault from Shropshire and Herefordshire, without laying my own lands open.' He spread his hands upon the table, pushing back his chair, happy and committed and at the edge of action.

'You may tell the earl of Pembroke my answer is: Yes. Before October is out I will declare for him, and take Gwynedd to war.'

'My lord,' said Delahaye, burning up like a furze fire, 'I was sure of you.'

It remained only to ensure that they should command success. Llewelyn stared into the coming weeks, brilliant-eyed, measuring the musters of Corbett and Lacy and Fitz-Alan on his borders. But not Parfois. Parfois held, if Harry had the tale right – and Harry was shrewd enough, and had had every opportunity to assess the possibilities for himself

– the seeds of its own civil war. If Ralf Isambard held his own, Henry would never call him into service, for Henry, an ill judge of men, did not trust him. If he let his governance slip through his fingers. . . .

'Blinded!' said Llewelyn, brought up short again upon the inconceivable image of darkness. 'God knows at the worst I never wished him that!'

The small, chill wind of the evening over the shoulder of Moel Wnion brought with it into the grassy hollow the salt breath and the melancholy crying of the ebbing tide along Lavan sands. Far across the strait all the little bells of all the oratories on Ynys Lanog of the saints made a tiny, stammering chime, the faint recollection of a long-past dream of bells.

Saint Clydog was in the very doorway when he heard them, and for a moment he stayed with his foot across the threshold, uncertain whether they were calling him forward or back. They had a sweetness like the first intimation of bliss, but very far away; they had a sadness like the last convulsion of remembered sorrow. He peered forward into a darkness pulsing with the promise of light, but his eyes had still too much earth in them, and he could not see into the brightness beyond. He looked over his shoulder into the twilit hollow, but his vision was hazy already with the as yet unrealised image of light, and the shapes of the world withdrew from him.

But after all, there was no longer any reason to stay. The shapes of the world were the shapes of emptiness and loss. No light in the stone hut, no foot on the door-sill, no voice at dawn. No more to be said here, no more to be done, no more truant boys for whom he must wait. No need, no need to have waited for Harry.

The sea mourned, the gathering night shivered, cold and loneliness and sorrow stood silent at his back. And the angel that attended his sleeping and his waking drew him on through the doorway, reassuring him gently that the woman would not be far behind him. He looked back no more towards the desolation where she had been. He went on, deaf to the voices that entreated him to return, untouched by the hands that clung to him, free of all the prayers, troubled no more by the burden of gifts and vigils and visions. He entered at the doorway of the dark, stepping over the door-sill of his yet unmade grave, and time closed behind him so softly that no one ever knew the moment when the latch slid into place.

His boy, coming up from the hut an hour later to lead him to bed, found only the little huddle of bird-bones discarded in the grass.

CHAPTER SEVEN

Parfois: *October to November* 1233

At Dolgynwal they picked up her tracks, and held them strongly for a great part of the way, riding hard and drawing lavishly on Llewelyn's writ for remounts wherever their beasts laboured and there were fresh horses to be had. At Meifod she was but a matter of hours ahead, and Harry took heart to believe he would overtake her after all. Why had she pressed so? He would not have believed a woman could have kept her lead of him across Wales, and he riding night and day without sleep but what he snatched on the wing. His heart accused him that she made such haste for his sake, and he drove himself the harder.

And then, at Strata Marcella, they found no word of her. Could they have overridden her somewhere between, while she rested in some cottage? Two of his six Harry sent questing back, to make casts right and left from the road; two he ordered ahead with all speed to make straight for the ramp of Parfois and keep close watch there on all who approached the lower guard; and he himself with the remaining two turned south for Castell Coch beyond Pool, in case she had chosen the southern rather than the northern ford for her crossing of Severn. Wild with self-accusations, hugging to himself the blame for her speed and ardour and devotion as well as his own tardiness, Harry came into Castell Coch at the drop of night, reeling in the saddle; and yes, she had been there, but no, she was there no longer. She would not sleep the night over, she rode again in the late evening, not long before sunset, barely an hour past.

Harry turned his horse and rode for the ford of Pool. Severn was hardly higher than its summer level yet, they plashed through it and threaded the silver pools in the water-meadows beyond; and as soon as the ground was firm under their feet Harry was spurring into a gallop again. Up the green road from the river to the shoulder of the Long Mountain, and uphill again on the ramp, and one of his own men started out of the trees and waved him to a halt.

For all their haste they had come late. She was ahead of them still, and inside Parfois.

'Fair, sweet son,' said Isambard, sighing, 'you waste your time and mine. Not that I complain of that. My time's long enough, in all conscience, I can spare you a few hours and no grudges. But if you hope to get what you want out of me, you won't do it by these means. I told you from the first, I'll give you nothing – what you want from me you must take. Asking won't do it. Think, my heart, if I signed and sealed your delivery I should be depriving myself of these daily consolations, your sweet company, your filial solicitude. Even on one unchanging subject, I love to hear your voice.'

'There are more ways than one of asking a question. As you may yet find, my beloved father. Your grandsire provided a very handsome array of persuasions, there under the Warden's Tower, and I may yet be put to the necessity of using them.'

'I think not. If you had dared you would have used them long ago. Not that they would have gained you anything, that I promise you. No, if you have spared to break my bones or flay my flesh off them, it's for the same reason that you've not thrust me into some hole to dwindle into a foul and noisome old man, or set to to starve me into reason. It's because you may at any moment have to produce me before the world, whole and sound and not past recognition. If Paunton or d'Enville or some other of my castellans doesn't force you to show me, some travelling envoy of King Henry well may. And the one would be as awkward for you as the other, if I were not kept utterly presentable every hour of every day.'

'You do well to threaten me with King Henry,' said

William, grinning. 'It's well seen which of us two has his favour. I have his authority to hold and garrison Parfois for him against the Welsh, in spite of your head. Does that look as if he'll stir for you?'

'Not for me, William, not for me – but for himself he'll stir in no uncertain fashion, you'll find. Oh, I grant you Henry would hardly be displeased if you rough-handled me a little. But he would certainly be *embarrassed* if you were put to the necessity of producing me on a hurdle because a few of my bones were out of joint. He's committed to you, William, since he's accredited you his castellan here. Better not commit him to too much, or too irrevocably.' He smoothed long fingers round his well-shaven jaw and yawned, and sat smiling aggravatingly towards his son's chair. 'Drag him into murder when he's only expressly authorised robbery, and you'll see what a tiger the lamb can be in his own defence. You still don't know him as I do, William. He'll hound you to the day of your death if you compromise him.'

'That might not be necessary. There are ways of accounting for injuries. A fall – blind men do sometimes venture alone and fall,' the smiling voice mused, encouraged.

The echoes in this small, bare upper room of the tower were still unfamiliar to Isambard's ears, after the ampler air down below, in the apartments he had for so long made his own. It was like William to possess himself of those particular rooms, out of all the many he could have chosen, but it was not all vanity or spite, either. They commanded this solitary stair, and the well-guarded chamber above. No one had access here but William's leave.

'And dislocate wrists and ankles, or crush a few fingers on the way? No, you're no such fool. A whisper of scandal would be enough, and the king would take his arm from you and leave you to pay the score alone. And you know it. Besides, that is not what you want. You want title and right, so clear that no one can point at you. The king can give you command of my castle, in the name of England's safety, but title to my honour he cannot give you. While I live only I can

170

give you that. Only I!' he said with finality and content, and laughed to hear the violent rustling of silk as William wrenched himself out of his chair and began to pace the room. The blind face followed his prowlings, amused and mischievous. 'And I will not,' said Isambard.

'Will you not, my beloved father? I swear you shall yet. And be thankful to do it. You shall sign and seal away your rights to me, living, ware, knowing well what you do. I offered you easy terms, honourable retirement to Erington or Mormesnil or wherever you would, a proper household and all that you could need. I take that back.' The pacing feet halted abruptly. A hand caught at the old man's wrist and shook it fiercely. He felt his son's heavy shadow leaning over him. 'Now you shall sign your goods and gear and lands and men over to me on my terms, and do what living you may afterwards on my bounty. I'll have your seal and your hand on the deed, no matter what it may cost you in torment or me in trouble. You hear me?'

But he knew he would not. To threaten was easy, but there was too much truth by half in what the old man had said. Henry might wish him dead, but for his own protection would surely turn and rend whoever killed him; Henry might relish the idea of putting to a little salutary pain the man who had rated him publicly before his court, but he would be the first to exclaim in horror over the deed and set the hounds on the doer if ever the facts came to light. How else could he ward off the shame and danger of being implicated? There had never been any relying on him if the day went awry, and there would be none now.

Isambard put off the displeasing grip from him with a strong turn of his wrist, and wiped the touch of the hand from his flesh.

'I hear the boast,' he said disdainfully. 'Now let me see you make it good if you can. Here I am. Force me!'

How many days now had he been defying the same threat? He had lost count of time in his darkness, and the servants who scrupulously dressed and groomed and shaved him, and provided him with food and drink and all his

171

needs, had their orders not to give anything that need not be given. A word of news, a message from anyone without, a weapon – these he had never asked for, knowing they would not be granted. When had he ever begged favours of any man? He could hold his own here as he was, naked of friends. Better so. Whatever they practised must be practised upon him. So the deadlock held fast. He could not prevent William from establishing dominion over Parfois, William could not get from him the concession that would give his forcible dispossession the sanction of right. He had signed nothing, sealed nothing. In the keep of his own solitary spirit he held Parfois still.

Someone was at the door, the light double knock de Guichet used. Isambard was the first to hear it, and sat with held breath to trap and decipher the sounds that alone communicated with his darkened being now. They could not know how acutely trained his ear was becoming, or they would have taken even their whispers out of the room.

'My lord, Blount says he has news for you, something important –'

'Not now. Let him wait.'

'My lord, it bears on – ' That was never ended, unless the significant silence ended it. A glance thrown in his direction, a brow lifting. He braced his fingers along the arms of his chair, nerves at stretch. It bears on me; it bears on this issue between us. By what forgotten postern were they attempting entry now?

The door closed, and they were outside it. He was out of his chair like a cat, and across the room, left hand spread to confirm where the table stood and guide him safely past it, right hand flattened before him to find the panels of the door. He laid his ear to the wood, and listened, but they had taken the precaution of moving well away from his prison, and all he heard was the slight stir of his guard shifting his weight from foot to foot resignedly outside the door. He strained his senses beyond, catching at any sound, any word. There was a murmur at no great distance, but too low to have meaning, until suddenly William's voice rose from monotone, loud in anger:

'Fool, what do you know of it? You were hardly born. You could do your worst and he'd laugh. In God's name, what worse could you do than he did himself?'

And Thomas – always Thomas, busy Thomas, ambitious Thomas! Thank God at least for his high, girl's voice, that grew shrill in fright or indignation, and carried so much more clearly than de Guichet's deep tones. Thomas was both frightened and indignant now, and piping like a scared and ruffled bird.

'My lord, I tell you I was there, I saw his face.' Hopeful, too, and vehement, certain of himself whoever doubted him. 'If that was hate – ' He was overridden then, and hushed, but he cried a moment later: 'At least put it to the test!' And a silence, and a stillness, that needed no interpreting. Put it to the test – whatever it might be, why not? Whatever it might be, they had nothing else.

They were coming back. The guard laid hand to the latch of the door, fingered the heavy key, and that was warning enough. Isambard felt his way back to his chair, and composed himself with a care that was partly for his own conviction as well as theirs. Nobody knew better than he how much the tensions of the body could betray.

He was ready when they came. The click of the wooden latch, the massy, low creak of the heavy door swinging, footsteps entering. How many? All three by the varying treads he counted. Young Thomas had his reward, he was suffered to creep in here on his new master's heels to feast his eyes on the impotence of the old one. That was a large grace, but if his snare proved effective, whatever it might be, there was no alternative to trusting him hereafter; and if not, well, no doubt he could be intimidated or disposed of. It would pay William not to underestimate Thomas, thought Isambard, and smiled a little grimly, remembering Harry's warning. To his enemy, dear God! All the doctors of all the schools might find matter for a lifetime's disputation, trying to discover how the very ground of a man's warfare can revolve under his feet and leave him keeping his

173

enemy's back against the whole world; but Harry went where his confident heart drove him, and did what it urged him to do, and his wisdom, like his simplicity, was far out of the philosophers' reach. Isambard fingered a spot in the hollow of his lean right cheek, and was slow to realize how the quality of his smile had changed. It did not matter. With the windows of the eyes shuttered there are not so many ways left, and none so dangerous, by which a man can betray himself.

'We wasted our time, it seems, arguing ways and means,' said William's voice, softened, calculated, smiling. Do him justice, if he was unsure of his weapon he gave no sign of it; he moved in leisurely and easy, like a master. 'There's a guest arrived will alter your mind for you without any effort on my part. Your guest, my dear father. Do you not remember inviting her? A certain lady who once knew you too well for her comfort, and thought it better to refuge in Wales. Ah, I see you do remember!'

He saw nothing, for there was nothing to see. Not a muscle of the bronze mask had moved until Isambard allowed his arched, arrogant brows to signal polite question and nothing more.

'It's not like you, William, to talk in riddles. Come to the meat, and let me at least stand on the same ground with you. I expect no guest. I invited none.'

'My lord,' said Thomas eagerly, 'it was in the church, and every word I overheard. He sent word for her to come in place of Harry Talvace, and the ring passed as his token to her. He must have sent it by another messenger after her man was killed.'

By another messenger! So they did not know, and he was so far blessed and justified in knowing it was not from Walter they had this cast. Busy Thomas in the porch there, with his ear at the door, storing up every crumb that might some day be used to choke his beloved lord. That accounted for their information, and eased his heart into the hope that information was all they had. Given a sharp eye to detect what the sight of her ring and the mention of her name had

174

meant to him, this trick was simple enough. 'I tell you I was there, I saw his face. If that was hate – ' And William, who had occasionally sat sulking at the same table with Benedetta, and grudged her his father's gifts, William who knew how it had ended: 'Fool, what do you know? You were hardly born. What worse could you do than he did himself?'

He acknowledged that thrust for truth, but he breathed again. Almost certainly this was a trick. He need not give an inch. There was no guest arrived. How could there be? Harry had met her by the way, and taken her safely home.

'She brought you your token again,' said William, smooth as honey, and took his father's hand and opened it on his knee. Something small and hard was dropped into the palm, and involuntarily his fingers closed upon it, and with a burning convulsion of agony knew it. The facets of the ruby bit deep, like fangs. How? Walter had delivered it; how had it come here again? Was there ever a way but the one way he could not bear to consider? And if she was here, how best manipulate that ambivalent relationship of love and hate so that they should think their calculations mistaken and their lever ineffective?

'Ah, that!' he said, hands under control again now, turning the ring thoughtfully in his palm and threading it back upon his finger. 'I'd forgotten. Small revenges have not much weight now. The score I had against her was hardly worth settling, after all. I turned Harry loose in the end without any ransom. What message did she send with this? Her forgiveness? As I remember her, she would always have the last word.'

He laughed. It was not difficult, the blank, wary hush seemed to him so ludicrous, and their revulsions of doubt made so marked a heaviness upon the air. The ring would not go easily over his knuckle; he turned it indifferently, and drawing it off again, span it gently into the middle of the table.

'My joints are old and swollen, and by reversion it's yours in the end. I brought it from Acre in the Crusade – the stone is good. Wear it if it fits. Or give it to Thomas for

175

his wages, if you think his tale worth it, but for my part I think he'd be overpaid.'

They stared upon him all three, narrowly, doubtfully and long, even Thomas shaken.

'Fool,' said William, turning a black stare upon the boy, 'did I not tell you this would never move him?'

'My lord, he's lying.' The girlish voice rose high with apprehension; it was not rubies he could expect if his invention proved useless now. 'I saw his face, I heard his voice then, I *know* he'd sweat for her. Whatever happened between them once, whatever she did to him or he to her, she has him by the heart still.'

'It can still be put to the trial,' said de Guichet, low and rapidly, for his master's ear alone, but Isambard caught the words, all the more terrible because they were not meant for him, and by that token must be true. No question, then, but she was here and in their hands? Or had that whisper been meant to be overheard? Was that too great a subtlety to be attributed to de Guichet?

'True,' said William, calmed, 'we can easily put your indifference to the proof, my dear father. If you can't be marked, there's no such ban on touching her. How if we have you down with us to the cellars of the Warden's Tower, and teach the lady how to ask you for your signature and seal? Then we might discover in what regard you do hold her.'

'I had thought you knew,' said Isambard, sighing and yawning. 'Many curious things have been said of me, but never, I think, that I had the habit of tossing my friends into the Severn.'

'Then if you're still of the same mind we might pass an hour or two very pleasantly for you. You have not your eyes, it's true, but you'll hear well enough, we'll see to that. And we'll keep the deed at hand,' said William tenderly, 'in case you're moved to sign it of your own good will, out of charity even towards a woman you hate.'

And he would do it? Why not, wanting his way as he wanted it? She was in his hands, he could make use of her, and in the turmoil of civil war who was ever to question the act close enough to bring it home to him? Perhaps by now he even knew he would not have to proceed far.

Isambard sat silent for a moment, revolving behind his calm, closed face the courses open to him; and it seemed to him that his outer defences were already lost from the moment that Benedetta entered at the gates. Could he buy more than a precarious safety for her even by surrendering his barony? He doubted it. If they found her effective, all the more surely they would not let her go as long as they needed a hold upon him; and as long as they held her he could be made to do anything they wished. They did not yet know that, but he knew it, it was one of the facts with which he had to deal. He smiled, acknowledging it. Give him yet a small measure more of life, and he might learn to go with his heart as impetuously as Harry, and question it and reason about it as little.

Two things only he could do. First, satisfy himself beyond doubt that they had her in their power; and second, give what was necessary to protect her if he could not deliver her. Give his honour into his son's hands, signed and sealed. Promise them his own submission and good behaviour as long as they used her well and gave him earnest of it.

'I do not believe,' he said deliberately, 'that Madonna Benedetta is here at all. If she is, confront me with her.'

'Ah, no! Not that, my dear father. I have too high a respect for your wit to let you within speaking distance of her.'

'Dear God, you have enough curbs on me, I should have thought. What could I do by speaking with her?'

'That I never quite know, and there's the rub with you. With your leave, I'll take no risks of any secrets passing under my nose. And forgive the crudity, but to show her to you from a window is hardly possible now.'

'Then bring me where I can hear you speak with her, and I'll be content with that.'

'Why not?' said de Guichet, after a moment of considering silence. 'She's down in the great chamber below. Let us

177

bring him to the head of the stairway, and he'll hear her voice plain enough, and she'll be none the wiser. Go down and greet her, and leave the door open between. Let him have his proof.'

They brought in his guards to pin him by the arms before he so much as rose from his chair, they had still such a wary respect for his strength and cunning. He went docilely where they led him, stepping hesitantly down the spiral stone stair, feeling with anxious toes for the wider part of the treads, leaning on his warders; it was well to appear more, not less, helpless than he really was. Thomas tripped lightly ahead of him, elated now and sure of his reward.

By the stone balustrade at the head of the lower flight, outside the door of what had once been his own bedchamber, they halted their prisoner, and one of the guards with indifferent kindness took his groping hands and guided them to the rail. He heard William descend the last steps without haste, heard the door of the great room below open. In his memory he saw the faded tapestries within drinking and dulling the light from the narrow loopholes, and the heavy, carved chairs tall and spectral in the shadowy corners. And standing in the middle of the room, facing the doorway, waiting for the man she would not see, Benedetta.

In that moment he saw her clearly, splendidly large and generous of movement and regal in stillness, with breadth and valour in everything she did or thought or said, a woman, a tower, a world.

'Madam,' said William's voice below him, echoing faintly hollow from within the lofty room, 'you are most welcome back to Parfois.'

She said: 'I thank you,' and it was enough. Her voice, unmistakable even after so long of absence, not changed, not dimmed at all. 'I came at your father's wish. I did not think to see you here. Is he still so sick?'

'Not dangerously,' said William, surely with a smile not far behind his eyes, if she had known how to read it. 'Did his courier tell you what befell him? He has lost the sight of his eyes.'

178

'He told me it might well be so,' she said, low-voiced. 'May I not see him?'

'Not yet, I regret. He is not well enough yet to be visited, and I am here as the king's castellan in his place. But I will have an apartment made ready for you, and if you will be patient and wait a little while, he will surely mend.'

A moment of silence; no irresolution in it, only thought. Then the clear voice said with deliberation: 'Yet he was master of himself, and sent me a plain message. And that was the day this injury was done him.'

'He has. been in fever since then,' said William, a shade too quickly and easily. 'As soon as he is fit you shall see him, and welcome.'

'And you are come from his bedside now?' she said, so softly, so dryly, that there was no mistaking the irony. 'I am glad he has so devoted a son to take his burdens from him.'

She did not trust, she did not believe. She had forgotten nothing and lost nothing, she could still look through a man and leave him naked to his own self-knowledge. 'He made a bargain with me,' she said. 'I hope you will honour it for him. He promised me that if I would come to Parfois to take his place, he would release Harry Talvace. Ask him, he will tell you. Ask him, and send the boy home.'

Isambard's hands tightened on the stone. So she did not know. Somewhere along the way Harry and she had passed unknown, by what accident or chance he could not guess, and she who had come to set the boy free found even his captor captive. What must her anxiety be now for the child she had carried in her arms, new-born, to deliver to Llewelyn at Shrewsbury all those years ago? And he would not tell her! He would keep that, too, in store, in the armoury of his invisible weapons, for use later at need.

'That we can surely discuss tomorrow. You are tired now, and a day or two more is nothing lost. Tomorrow we may be able to talk to my father about the boy.'

'Harry is well?' she said, sharp and fierce with dread.

'He is very well.'

'May I see him?'

179

'Later, when you have rested.'

And was she to be content with that, sleep on that, ask and ask day after day and still be held off and tormented with perhaps, and later, and tomorrow, until evasions added up to certainty of harm? One thing at least could be saved for her, her peace of mind and heart over the child. Isambard calculated instants and words, and the length of time it would take to shift a hand from his arm to his mouth. How many words had he for the phrasing of what might be his last communication with her? He might be adding to her danger by a shade, but what was lost there could be regained when he conceded his seal and consented to strip himself bare; and in the meantime she could sleep serenely, and thank God that Harry was out of the battle.

He leaned over the stone balustrade, and suddenly flung his arms wide, thrusting his guards off-balance; and in a great voice he cried down the well of the staircase:

'Harry's safe. I sent him –'

So far, and one of the clutching hands found his mouth. He wrenched aside and freed his lips again for a moment.

' – sent him to meet –'

No more then. They dragged him back by both arms, a hard forearm in a cloth sleeve was clamped over his mouth. De Guichet had him by the hair, wrenching his head back. He heard Benedetta cry: 'Ralf!' and knew that at least she had heard him. He heard running footsteps below, the slam of the door closing. Then he was down on his back on the flagstones, and they were on top of him, and with what breath he had left he was laughing, even with his mouth choked with a fold of his own surcoat. Someone struck him in the face, so puny and spiteful a blow that he thought it must have come from Thomas, and hardly even grudged him his morsel of satisfaction.

They dragged him bodily back up the staircase, and they were not gentle. They flung him down in his own chair, and shut the door, trembling, on him and on themselves, cursing him low-voiced and viciously.

He wiped a trickle of blood from the corner of his mouth,

and shook his surcoat into order. By the time he had his breath mastered enough for speech William was in at the door and stooping over him. The air shook and grew hot with his rage, but he kept it in. All he said, in the suppressed, breathy voice of extreme forbearance, was: 'Do you think that was wise?'

'Not wise,' owned Isambard, still fingering blood away from his lip, 'but at least honest. I'm ready to study wisdom now if you make it worth my while. Where have you lodged her?'

'Where you'll hear no more of her,' said William, breathing hard.

'Ah, but I shall. Or you'll get nothing from me. This much I'll promise you, not to try to speak to her or call her attention again, if you for your part will put me in the way of assuring myself, now and then, that she's alive and well and not molested. Bring me where I can hear her speak but once a week, and that's enough for me.'

'And is it you who can afford to lay down terms?'

'I think,' he said, 'I can. If I am to give over to you my title in all I have, then I must have somewhat in exchange from you, and your oath to keep it.'

He heard his son draw deep, satisfied breath, sure now of the mastery, sure of the value of his hostage. 'Is not my word enough for you?' he said, with hypocritical indignation.

'Fair, sweet son,' said Isambard gently, 'no. I would not stake a dog's life on your word, since you ask me. I must have it on oath that you will use Madonna Benedetta well, keep her as she should be kept, and give her a measure of freedom – ah, content you, it can stop short of the place where I am, have I not promised you to let her alone?' He did not even ask for her liberation; he knew it would not, could not be granted, not yet, not until his abdication of his rights was published and accepted, perhaps not until he was safely, demonstrably, respectably dead.

'Swear to what I shall ask of you concerning her,' he said

181

deliberately, 'and you may bring on your deed when you will. I'll sign it, and deliver you my great seal.'

Harry would have ridden in after her, but for the hollow doubt that opened in his heart like a wound, and held him back to wait for morning. If all was as he had left it within there, there was nothing to prevent him from following her and bringing her away with him; but he knew, by the desperation of his own ride after her, that he did not believe he would find the order in Parfois unchanged.

He lay curled under the bushes in his cloak through the dark hours, sleeping for a few minutes now and then, starting awake again to harrow over old ground yet once more, and reproach himself for every moment lost on that ride; and at first light he roused himself to climb up through the bushes and reconnoitre the lower guard. The men there were strangers to him; even their officer he had never seen before, he who had lived the greater part of four years of his life in the castle, and learned to know every man in the garrison. He kept watch all the morning through, and it was past noon when he saw the bright cortège weaving its way merrily down between the trees, and dropped into thicker cover to see them go by.

Three falconers, two of them known to him but the third a stranger, knights and squires and pages, faces he knew now, the court of Parfois dancing attendance on its lord, and in very ceremonious state indeed. In their midst, the stem and centre of their brightness, rode the man he had last seen by torchlight, mounting in the outer ward after kissing his father a dutiful farewell.

Large and confident in proprietorship, arching his neck in swinging stares about his domain and smiling to see its excellence, William Isambard rode out to hawk on the crest of the Long Mountain. And at his elbow Thomas Blount cantered assiduous and devoted, feeding his master with smiles and sallies. Thomas, who never expanded his leaves but to the rising sun. In their glory, the one and the other of them, men in possession.

182

So there was no rushing back into Parfois, to make, if his fears were justified, one more hostage, one more sword to be held at the old man's throat. That would not help or deliver Madonna Benedetta; it would simply deprive her of one ally who might yet be of use to her if he kept his freedom of action. There was no salve to his conscience in an empty and contemptible heroism, which would only serve to place in greater danger the very people he desired to protect.

Had William put his father from his place? Or was he moving cautiously, content as yet to be his father's proxy, now the old man could no longer be active about his own affairs? He rode out attended like a conqueror, but the hangers-on would be courting him as their effective lord in either case. Dared he proceed so far and so fast as to depose his father? What Harry needed first was certainty. If he could not go in and out and listen to the whispers inside Parfois, there were those who could. There were men in the villages who had kinsfolk in the castle; and if he did not know where to find them and how to reach their confidence, he knew those who did.

He sent his men back to Castell Coch, there to rest and wait for him, and went alone along the riverside path he remembered so well. With the small green paddock barely in sight between the trees, and the faint smell of wood-smoke from the hearth just tickling his nostrils, he halted and stood silent on the path; for Aelis was there in the yard, raking out the ashes of the fire from under her clay oven at the end of baking.

Such a weight of fondness gathered about his heart at sight of her that he felt himself braced and magnified to carry it, a man endowed and burdened with the world. Her hair, heavy gold, hung over her shoulder in a thick braid. She had grown tall and slender, and the shape of her, as she stooped to her task with long, smooth, faintly weary movements, was the shape of a woman, daunting and wonderful. Her face, pensively inclined, had a mysterious air of sadness. At once humbly and vaingloriously he added that to the load of

183

his own guilt. What comfort and joy had she ever had of him? He had brought her nothing but trouble and pain and labour since the day she and her father had first taken him in.

He wanted to call to her, and he was afraid and ashamed, for some reason he himself could not understand, to disturb the delicate concentration with which she was working. As though he expected her to turn to him at the first word, as though she must drop whatever she was doing, and run to wait on his concerns. He knew he was about to pour out the sum of his trouble and tiredness into her lap for comfort, when he would rather have been bringing her some better gift, something to please her, something to shed reflected light upon her, and not exact attentions for him. He came always demanding, even if he was too proud or too small-hearted to do it openly; and there was such a thirst and hunger in him to give to her.

She heard a twig snap beneath the horse's tread, and rose and stood tall and ready before the gate, head reared, eyes wide, fronting the gap in the trees where the rider must appear. The horse was from Meifod, and unknown to her; she waited, intent and still, to get a closer view of the man. Green light and greener shadow between the leaves veiled him from her recognition a moment, and then she knew. By what motion of his tired body in the saddle, by what tilt of his head or trick of his carriage, who knows? He was still a dappled shadow-man on a pied horse, thirty yards away from her along the narrow ride; but she knew.

She let fall the forgotten scraper out of her hand, she seemed to stretch her head upward for a moment and grow taller, as though she would strain free of the tall grass of time that had hidden him from her. Then such a blaze of silent joy flamed in her face that he could not believe he was the source of it, and looked beyond himself for some better cause implied in him, her sisterly kindness pitying the prisoner and radiant at his release, her selfless pleasure in his bettered fortunes. No one, not even his mother, had looked at him like that, or hung so still and rapt in joy, a joy that must be for him, since it could not be of him. Why should anyone be so purely glad of Harry Talvace?

As always when he was at his sorest and haughtiest, praise undid him. The magnificat of her eyes delighting in him cut the ground from under his feet, and set him trembling in a passion of humility. He tumbled from the saddle, clumsy with haste and weariness, and ran and dropped at her feet like a shot bird. She had sprung to meet him, but he dropped through her arms, catching at the slight brown hands and drawing them down against his cheek, pressing her open palms to his forehead and eyelids.

'Oh, Aelis! Oh, Aelis!' he said, his voice no more than a quick, fluttering warmth in the palm of her hand.

'Harry, is it you? Is it truth this time? Are you free?'

She took her hands from him only to stroke and fondle him in a rapture of tenderness, putting back the tangle of brown hair from his forehead with a maternal gesture of the hand that had been an urchin's so short a while ago.

'Not yet. Not quite free. There's something I had to do, and I've failed badly, and there's all to put right – '

'But you need not go back?' She lifted his face to her by the chin to look into his eyes, her voice quick and jealous in alarm. 'Are you only loosed to go running off to the war, like that last time? Oh, why did you never tell me, that time? I waited and waited, and never a word. You wouldn't do that to me again? You'd tell me, if you had to go back into Parfois?'

'I'd tell you. I would tell you. It's not like that. I'm loosed, but I'm not free.' He had so much of his own to tell that the sense of what she had just told him penetrated his senses but slowly, and the sting came with a sudden shock of excitement and ardour, hoisting him from his knees with a leap. 'Running off to the war, you said? Is it come, then? Is it war already?'

'So they were saying at Castell Coch this noon. The miller was across with flour, and he brought back word. They're saying your prince has declared for the earl marshal, and taken his muster south to Builth. Is it true, do you think?

Could it be true?'

'Yes,' he said, momentarily caught away from her, staring over her head eagerly into the uncertainties of the future. If the prince was in the field, then his foster-son had an army at his back. 'Yes, it could well be true,' he said, quivering, and caught too late the still, woman's sadness in her eyes, already steeled to new waiting without complaint. The princess had given her fair warning. *If we want them at all we must take them as they are.*

'You'd best come in,' she said with determination, 'and tell me now what it is you're at. Father's away at Forden, but he'll be home in an hour or so, and happy to see you whole and free again. Can you bide overnight at least? And if there's anything you need from us before you go –'

'Ah, no!' he said, suddenly flooded with the molten weight of his tenderness, as though his heart had burst. 'I'll not leave you yet. Not yet! I need your help to know what I must know, but more than that I need from you, my dove, my dear.'

He took her face between his hands and turned it up to him softly, and between his palms she began to flush and tremble. He kissed over the soft curve of her cheek from brow to chin, kissed her grave eyelids closed, smoothed with his lips the golden arches of her brows.

'If I must go again, it's only to come back the sooner. However far I must go, however far, I'll surely come back. I love –' he said, whispering his way down her cheek, and having arrived thus inarticulate at her mouth, fastened there like a famishing man, and tasting her tears, closed astonished lids upon his own.

At the light touch on his shoulder he started out of a dream of pursuit and loss, instantly wide-awake like a hound, ears pricked and nostrils quivering to the scent of a stranger in the room; his hand was at his dagger hilt and a knee braced under him to rise before Aelis could close her fingers round his wrist and soothe him into stillness.

'Hush, now! Here's no harm. But there's news for you.'

The light of a candle-end glimmered by the hearth, and cast wavering shadows among the smoky beams of the ceiling. Robert was up and making fast the door softly on the thick darkness of a murky November midnight; and in a huddle of rugs over the slow fire damped down for the night a man lay steaming and shivering, one naked arm stretched out from his coverings to the cup Aelis held to him. His teeth chattered against the rim as he drank. Beard and hair drooped lank and wet. The rags he had stripped off oozed a slow pool of water in the rough boards of the floor. Wild eyes looked up at Harry across the rim of the cup, ready with hostility, sharp with fear.

'Be easy,' said Robert, low and quickly to them both, 'there's none here but friends.'

'What is it? What happened?'

'He's from Leighton. He came down the river, like your father once, but alive. One of three taken in Isambard's private chase last evening, and won free before they could get him into hold, but they broke an arm for him before he took to the river. Here, lend me an arm of yours to hold him while I set the bone.'

Harry went down on his knees and raised the chilled body to lie in his lap. It was not the first such injury Robert had handled, and not by many a one the first runaway he had hidden and put across the Severn by night.

'One of his foresters struck at me with his staff when I ran,' said the fugitive, through teeth clamped fast to stop their chattering. 'But for that I'd have been across the river without the need of a boat. I could make no headway across the current with only one arm to steady me. All I could do was go down fast with it, and crawl ashore when I was out of their reach and sight.'

'They'll be hunting him,' said Harry, and lifted a flaring green stare of alarm to Robert's face.

'No, they think me drowned. I lay low in the bushes until I heard them draw off.' It was near to frost outside; he might well have got his death that way in escaping the river.

187

'Safe enough here for a day,' said Robert, large hands busy and gentle at the distorted forearm, as brown and sinewy as his own. 'Hold fast now! And Aelis, the linen band here.'

She had been tearing and rolling it in the edge of the candlelight; she came to Harry's side and held the roll ready. Faintly they heard the bone grate. The huddled body jerked once in Harry's arms, as the man turned his head and clenched his teeth in the fold of the rug that wrapped him; but in a moment the grip relaxed again, and he bore the rest of it without stir or murmur.

'Tomorrow night we'll put you over into Wales,' said Robert, making firm the first smooth turn of the linen about the cased forearm. 'He's had his belly-full of the lordship of Parfois, Harry. Ask him, he knows. It was strangers, not Shropshire men, who took them with the venison.'

'Strangers?' repeated Harry sharply, and leaped ahead into understanding. 'William's men!'

'William's men, and laying claim to be the foresters of Parfois. And ready to stand to it, too.'

'They brought us into Leighton,' said the poacher, his head rolling back wearily into Harry's shoulder, 'and Wilfrid's wife came running with the rest and saw us, and had the good wit to run for the reeve. And he came and argued for us, that they had no right to clap us into Parfois's prison when they had no authority from the old lord. The chase is his, he says, not his son's, and without we see his order and seal to back you, we'll not let you take them. We'll send to the justice, he says, and if any man wills to charge them he must do it according to law. And the village was standing by watching all, four to every man of theirs, so they had need to mind how they handled it. They claimed the lord William had the king's authority as castellan of Parfois, but old Harald, God bless him, wouldn't have it make any difference; he said only the lord of the honour could have us taken into private custody. Then they laid claim to that right, too, saying the lord Ralf had ceded his honour to his son. And Harald said bluntly he'd never believe it unless he

188

had the proof of it under the old lord's signature and seal. Till then, he said, he'd hold us, and deliver us when there was due warrant shown. He could do no more: we had the two beasts we'd taken slung on poles between us when they caught us, there was no denying them. It took a bold man to go as far as he went, but of late we've been left in peace in the woods, and we took in measure, and spared to tempt our luck too hard, and he fairly believed this was no more than a presumption by the son's men, taking vantage of the father's infirmity. And hold us he did, and they went off threatening.'

'But they came again,' said Harry with certainty, shifting a little to give the injured man more ease. His eyes flashed to where Aelis stood, and found her watching him with a face wary and regretful. She knew the ending already.

'In the late evening, and de Guichet the seneschal with them. And brought a parchment with him, and would have Harald read it out to all the village. And then they took us, and nobody could prevent without turning it into a hanging matter, and God knows we never wanted that. But I thought on the cells under Parfois, and how a man could rot there, and I cut and ran when we passed through the copse, and would have got over the river well enough but for this chance blow.'

'Then your reeve had his proof? He can read? He read the parchment himself, you say?' Why was he clutching at even the last doubt, when he already knew, in his heart, both the end and the means? They had seen her value, then, and turned her to calculated use. How else could they have extorted concessions from Isambard? Had they threatened his own safety he would have laughed in their faces.

'That he can, and better than many a clerk. If he could have found a grain of justification for it he'd have had somebody ride to the justice. No, there's no gainsaying this. He read it aloud as he was told, with de Guichet standing over him, and showed the hand and the seal for all to recognise.. It was no lie. The old wolf's done what I never thought he'd do, crippled or no – delivered over all his lands to his son

– freely, he wrote, of his own will and desire. Signed everything he has over to the lord William with his own hand, and put his great seal to it, and lain down somewhere in a warm corner of his hall like an old, blind hound, to die.'

CHAPTER EIGHT

Brecon, Aber, Parfois: *Early December* 1233

At Builth he had thought to find Llewelyn, but the prince had moved south, and was laying siege to the castle and town of Brecon, and penning close within its walls the great garrison the king had looked to use as reserves for his harried companies. The border stood to arms, but as yet hung in a sultry and uneasy stillness. But already Basset and Siward had swooped upon Devizes to pluck de Burgh out of hold, and spirited him across the Severn estuary to the earl marshal's castle of Striguil, while Earl Richard himself blazed like a bush-fire through Gwent. Abergavenny had fallen to him, and Newport and Monmouth; he had raided the king's camp in the chilly dawn of a November day, and driven him headlong out of Grosmont. John of Monmouth was hard put to it to remuster the royal armies, and had them standing off now warily while the earl marshal consolidated his gains and reprovisioned his castles. And the winter had come down early on the hills, but could not quench the fire.

Over Mynydd Eppynt the snow lay thinly, a lace veil over the mountain's faded, wintry hair; but the falls were not yet deep enough nor the wind bleak enough to drive Harry into the valley ways. He took the upland road at the best speed he could make; and before twilight he saw from the crest overhanging the Usk the dull glow of fires and the hanging pall of smoke above the town of Brecon.

Smoke wreathed the black, gnawed shape of the castle, stark against the palpitating gleam of fires burning out in the town below. Smoke clung like a gauze scarf, faintly rippling in the wind, about the thick grey tower and fortress walls of the priory church. Harry's eyes travelled the long, lofty line

of its great roof, and found it whole, and was glad, and then
half-ashamed of his pleasure in the survival of stone when
he looked beyond at the reeking ruins of the homes of men.
All that the people of Brecon had built up again since the
last destruction lay blackened and razed now by the soiled
wintry waters of the river, a desolation, de-peopled but for
the dead. Huddled and cramped within the castle wards, the
survivors hoarded their food and water, and waited for the
relief King Henry's Flemish mercenaries must surely be
bringing from Gloucester. But day after day they kept watch
from the walls, and never a sign of the banners or the lances
bright above the snowy hills.

In the sullen dusk the fires glowed and faded, smouldered
and spat into spasmodic bursts of flame as the fallen timbers
settled. And on the hill-slopes above the bank of Honddu,
drawn tight round the stubborn castle, the contravallation
and circumvallation of Llewelyn's camp stood black against
the snow, and the gaunt dark shapes of mangon and tre-
buchet still battered fitfully at the scarred walls. No need to
press the assault too closely, he had them sealed in from all
help, and the countryside scoured clean of provisions; and
he believed no more than they now did in the king's will to
relieve them. He could hold them immobilised at his
pleasure without loss of men, while Earl Richard swept his
way through the valleys of Usk and Wye, and carried all
before him.

The riders from Builth were sharply challenged at the
borders of the camp, for they came at a gallop with their
cloaks drawn up about their chins and capuchons low over
their brows against the thin, driving snow. Harry slid from
the saddle, stiff with weariness, and asked after the prince;
and on that the sentry knew him and hailed him gladly, and
he was passed eagerly from friend to friend through the
circling single street of this circumscribed town, congested
with stores and arms and cattle and horses, to Llewelyn's
pavilion.

From the murk and the gathering dark he stumbled into a
close, pungent warmth, and from the low, rug-strewn bry-

chan both his foster-brothers shouted his name and rose to close with him gladly. He put them off almost roughly, though his eyes acknowledged and warmed to them. He threw himself on his knees at Llewelyn's feet, and kissed the hand that reached to lift him.

'Harry, you're welcome to my heart! You've kept us waiting long for your news.'

Harry lifted a travel-stained face; from heavy lids swollen and bruised with wakefulness the green eyes stared appalled, suddenly confronted with the impossibility of communicating what he himself had experienced without understanding. Llewelyn caught the confused light of bewilderment and despair and appeal, and leaned and kissed him heartily.

'How have you fared?'

The constriction of helplessness that had settled like frost on Harry's tongue melted, and the words came bursting out of him without concealment or calculation.

'My lord, badly. I've let her slip through my hands. My lord, we made what haste we could, but Madonna Benedetta kept her lead of us. She's in Parfois, for all we could do.' That had the unpleasant ring of self-excuse, and he had no will to soften his own guilt by the least shade. 'I am to blame,' he said, fending off sympathy fiercely.

'The rate you set out from Aber,' said David warmly, 'if she outrode you she must have ridden like a lover to his wedding.'

'I did press hard,' owned Harry, shaking. 'I thought I did. We missed her by no more than an hour, but we missed her, and what I did may have been well meant, but it was not enough. And that's not the worst. I would have gone in openly and asked for her, and he would have let me bring her away with me, but the time for that was gone by, too. They were strangers at the lower guard when we came there. We drew off and kept watch on the gates, and in the morning we saw William Isambard riding out with his falconers and his knights about him, like a prince. All those who most fawned on the father have turned to court the son. We saw it, and had the taste then of what had happened, but we could not be sure. I waited to have it all before I brought you word.'

He had wanted to heal with his own energy and devotion what he conceived he had done amiss, to recover single-handed what he had lost. He's ridden his beasts almost to foundering, and taken no rests himself along the way, thought Llewelyn. Whoever comforts him, for all that, he'll fight off like an enemy.

'We sent men into the villages, but they knew no more than we did, and were waiting and wondering like us. I thought to get word by a fellow Aelis found for me, who goes in and out carting away rubble from the old tower. I bade him find out Langholme with a message, but he brought back word Langholme was gone, sent away somewhere on his lord's errand and never returned. Walter would never have left him willingly. And if he sent him away, I well know why. He would not have one of us near who might be made to suffer for his sake. If he still had his way there, he would have sent Madonna Benedetta home again out of Parfois, with an escort to bear her company and keep her safe on the road. I knew in my heart then that all was wrong within there. But then came this man by night, a poacher taken with two comrades in the act, in Isambard's own chase. And then we had certainty.'

He drew breath to tell the whole of that tale, and cut it short enough.

'It was the reeve himself who read it out to them, and he knew both the seal and the hand. The king's writ making him castellan would never have served. But this was Isambard's own act and deed. And Madonna Benedetta is the instrument they've used to get their will of him! It's for her protection he's sealed away his honour to his son, and while William holds her he can make his father do whatever he will.'

'This is a very strange showing,' said Owen, frowning dubiously over the puzzle. 'Saving your presence, Harry, you've changed your tune. I thought he proposed harm to her himself. So we all thought. The old scores were never settled. From all we knew of him and all we heard from you, she had no need to expect better of him than another humiliation and death. Granted he relented of his worst intent, since he sent you off to meet her and turn her back. But do you tell us now he's beggared himself to keep her from harm?'

'Only God knows, my lord,' said Harry passionately, clinging with wild green eyes to Llewelyn's face, 'if ever he willed to do her hurt, when he took her at her word and bade her come. But *I* know he would die now to keep her safe from hurt at William's hands. And if William does not know it yet, it will go hard but he'll learn it soon, and make ill use of it, too. Beggared himself for her – yes, so I swear he has. And I dread he's a close-guarded prisoner for her. And if there's aught more they want of him, they'll make use of her again to bring him to heel.'

'If he's signed away his all,' said David reasonably, 'what more is there to be pressed out of him? What are the family quarrels of the Isambards to us? It seems to me we might very well deal directly with this new lord of Parfois, and strike a bargain with him for Madonna Benedetta. He can spare her now; she's served her turn. Why should he want to keep her longer?'

'No!' Harry held his aching head between his hands, for it was so heavy now with the warmth and the fumes of the low brazier that he could scarcely carry it upright. 'If we sent to ransom her he'd wonder and fear how much we knew of his dealings already, and how much she might be able to tell. Do you think he'd hesitate to do murder, if he thought his treason was to come out?'

'Ah, you're dreaming, lad!' David flung an arm round his shoulders and shook him rallyingly. 'Whatever he feared from her telling, he'd fear far more to do her to death after the prince of Aberffraw had claimed her for his own. He'd never dare touch her.'

'Not her! *Him!*' Harry threw off the affectionate arm furiously. 'How long do you think *he* would live,' he cried, quaking with anger and distress and despair, 'if they had cause to fear too close questioning over him? A move from us, a visitor due from the king, an old friend passing out of turn and asking to see him, any one might be his death. I'm feared, I'm feared it will be soon! There are those in other castles of his who won't believe too easily in his giving up his honour. Signature, seal and all, they'll want his word for it face to face that he gave it of his own free will. While he's alive there'll be no peace for William. And it wants but a worn tread on a stair – a blind man's not so hard to kill.'

They stared upon him great-eyed with astonishment, the hurtful words of wonder and doubt ready on their lips. They loved him, and meant him no hurt, but what did they know of Parfois? What did they know of the long, strange, testing companionship, that had shaped and sharpened and whetted him without his knowledge, and brought him about in his own tracks to confront once again, as if for the first time, his ancient enemy? How could he hope for understanding, he who understood nothing of what had befallen him? He went where his heart drove him, and trusted it to know its way. What else could he do?

'The boy's right!' said Llewelyn roundly, head reared, eyes beginning to shine with the reflected light from action contemplated. He reached a hand to clap Harry about the shoulders and draw him close to his side. 'At the first move from us touching their hostage, Isambard's life would not be worth an hour's purchase. But I can do better than that. William Isambard holds that march for the king, does he? Let's prove his fitness for his command.'

The two young men were gazing at him with as much consternation and as little comprehension as was in the looks they turned upon Harry; and Harry himself had lifted heavy eyes to search his face with scarcely less bewilderment, but with a reviving gleam of hope and ardour that warmed his heart.

'Owen, go and find Madoc. Bid him come to me in half an hour, and bring his captains, for tomorrow I'll have him move from Brecon. I think we have held this garrison penned long enough; they have work to do here will keep them from under Earl Richard's feet a few weeks yet. There's one way at least, the only one, I can approach Parfois now and not be suspect, and that's in arms.'

He turned his glittering glance upon his son, met his wondering eyes, and smiled. 'David, go with him. Leave us a little while alone.'

They went, faithfully and readily, but they did not understand. They recognised and welcomed his intent, but the reasoning that moved him to it was beyond their grasp.

'Never trouble for them,' said Llewelyn, when they were gone. 'What you don't tell they'll come to know in God's good time. They're young yet, they look for reason and order in all things. But they love you too well to question. Lean on them, whatever your need, and they'll not let you fall.'

'My lord,' said the boy, trembling, 'I know it.'

But what was he to say of the prince, who spanned the gulf of incomprehension at one stride, and took the very burden of wondering and agonising from him? He slid to the ground beside Llewelyn's chair, and laid his head with a great, shuddering sigh of gratitude upon the prince's knees, clinging to him in silence; and after a moment dry sobs began to quake through him, softly and without distress.

Llewelyn smoothed a hand over the shock of brown hair, and held him so. 'I know! I know! What you did was not enough, but neither could I have done better. No man can go through his life without some day falling short. You must learn to live with yourself failures and all. As princes do. As I do.' The bowed head made a brief, violent motion of denial, and he soothed and held it between his long palms gently, smiling a little ruefully into his own memories.

'As *he* does,' said Llewelyn softly, and stirred to the long, answering sigh of deliverance and peace. 'Do you think he would find any fault with you for failing?'

There was never any need to tell him anything, with that way he had of leaping into the heart of whatever creature he loved, and feling in his own spirit the surges and stresses that contested the sealed being of his tongue-tied child. And yet once that clairvoyance of love had failed him, and cost them all a year of desolation. Harry, too, remembered.

'If you've read it aright, Harry, *she* will be safe enough. If they still need her as a hostage for his quiescence, they'll take very good care of her. And even if she's served her turn, they have nothing to gain by harming her, and no reason to wish her harm. And for him – I tell you this, Harry, if no one leaps too soon to question William's title and right or meddle with his scerets, then he'll be very loathe to put his father out of the world yet. You need not fear that mishap on the stairs. It would come far too abruptly on the publishing of the deed, and raise doubts in too many minds. King Henry has no use for compromised men about him, there'd be neither office nor countenance for William once the world began to whisper against him. No, he'll rather let some weeks or months go by, if he safely can, That he desires this death I don't deny. Like you, I see it plain. But with a measure of discretion, for fear he should bring on himself the very notice he desires to avoid. And not yet! Not yet!'

'My lord!' said Harry, clinging to him fervently as to a rock in a stormy sea. 'Everything I see so changed. He never hurt me, nor let others. Nor broke his word to me.' His voice came muffled and dazed out of the folds of the prince's gown, proffering glimpses of the truth as his groping fingers found them. 'He struck de Guichet once. For me. When I would have despaired, he forbade me. When I was down, he pricked me up again. And yet – and yet he –'

'And yet he ripped your father out of his grave,' said Llewelyn, laying before him gently the thing he could not say.

Abruptly, briefly and passionately the boy wept. It was the one thing he could not see changed, and the one thing he could not bear.

'Child, child,' said Llewelyn, soothing him with rough, warm caresses as he would have fondled a much-loved hound, 'do you think you're the only one groping? We're all

198

in the dark together. Wait until God please to clear the sky. You can, you have time.'

'Oh, my lord, I'm so astray! I understand nothing!'

'Let it bide, Harry, let it bide. You have time. But time is what William shall not have. For we'll be under his walls before he dreams, and he shall have more to think about than his stolen inheritance. We'll not ask for our holy woman again; we'll not offer a price, we'll give them no warning that we know or care aught about my lord Isambard, you and I. We'll go in arms and take castle and prisoners and usurper and all. And you with your own hands, Harry, shall give back to Isambard first his liberty and, after, all that is his. Will that content you?'

Wonderful, inscrutable, appropriate, he thought, looking down at the young, heavy head upon his knees, are the dispensations of God. To this has he brought down our revenges, Harry, yours and mine. I vowed to take and destroy Parfois for your sake, and so, by God, I may, but not as I looked to encompass it when the vow was made. And how many promises have you not made in your heart to that young father of yours to have Isambard's life for his? Never thinking how strangely you would be moved to dispose of it when at last you held it in your hands, giving it back thus freely, and with it a morsel of your own heart turned traitor. Traitor as the world's usage measures, but I think you have as good a guide in your breast as any the world can provide you. Neither do I question. God knows what he is about.

Harry had made no answer, unless it was due answer that his clinging hands slipped down gently into the skirts of Llewelyn's gown, and his body softened and sighed eloquently against Llewelyn's knees. Vindicated, reassured, accepted, abetted, he had let himself fall unresisting into the arms of the prodigious sleep that had been waiting and reaching for him ever since he rode from Parfois. He confided utterly. He was content.

Llewelyn leaned and gathered the boy into his arms, as roughly and affectionately as long ago he would have hoisted the child worn-out with play and plumped him down

199

in his bed, secure that nothing short of a thunderclap could awaken him. 'The length of you, boy!' he said, hefting him bodily from the ground and tumbling him on the brychan. 'Could you not bear to let him outdo you even in inches?'

Harry stretched out with a vast sigh of pure pleasure, and burrowed his cheek into the rugs. The distant warmth of the voice reached him, and he drew it down with him, smiling, into the bottomless well of his sleep; in a moment he put up an arm to cover his face from the light, and shuddered once from head to foot, and then was blissfully still.

'You may well!' said Llewelyn, pulling the covers over him. 'There was never one of my own led me the dances you have. God knows, child,' he said, looking down with a shadowed smile upon the long, rapturous heave and fall of Harry's sleeping breath, 'whether we can save him for you. But in the name of God we'll try.'

He sat down beside the bed to ponder the enterprise laid so confidingly in his hands. Man proposes, man performs; but God turns the very ground on which he stands, and leads him to a consummation he never foresaw. He rides to destroy his enemy, and arrives to deliver him. Well, so be it. God knows what he is about.

And for the practical problems, they were not in dispute. The assault of Parfois, captains and engineers would say with one voice, is an impossibility. Good, thought Llewelyn, roused and restless, brooding above the sprawled limbs and eased, trusting face of the boy, that's agreed. Now let's see how best to set about it.

'There!' said Gilleis between laughter and exasperation, appealing to the princess over her son's shoulder. 'What did I tell you? He brings me my son back for an hour, only to take away my husband as well. What are we to do with these men?'

'More to the point,' said Joan with her rueful smile, 'what are we to do without them? We lack them more often than we have them. You and I, Gilleis, will pack up and ride after them to Castell Coch for Christmas. If we keep it here it's

200

plain we shall keep it alone.'

'If it were not for Benedetta,' vowed Gilleis, 'I would not lend you Adam. He's a master-mason, not a soldier. But for her – if you asked me for the blood out of my veins, what could I do but bare my arm for the knife? Oh, Harry, if you could but remember that ride we made together into Shrewsbury, when you were no more than two or three weeks old. She in Robert's clothes, and you asleep in her arms as sound as in your own bed, you trusted her so – and well you might. Oh, Harry,' she said, drawing him to her heart again, 'bring her off safely!'

Having him again, even thus changed and grown, so much more his own, so much less hers, she had shaken off years of her age, and glowed and flushed like a wild girl, her great black eyes radiant. He felt himself her elder, and loved her the more for it.

'Mother, we'll do what we can. The prince says she'll surely be safe in Parfois for a while, and trust me, he's moving fast to her rescue. The vanguard were away in the night, before ever I awoke. Madoc and his men will be over Severn by now, above and below Parfois, and the prince with his main army has abandoned Brecon to join them.'

He saw again the shell of the razed town smoking, the battered walls of the castle stained and reeking. The Welsh must have had more than half of their force on the march before the garrison realised that their long ordeal was over, and ventured to put forth cautious foraging parties into the ashes of the town. And little enough they would find there, and little enough in the countryside for miles around. There would be no pursuit from Brecon, no recovering sortie to harry the rear-guard. The defenders would have just enough strength left to hunt their food, but none to spare for their enemies.

'What men can do we'll do,' he said. 'And we need Adam for our engineer. It was the prince thought of it, and sent me here to fetch him. He knows rock, and he knows Parfois, says the prince, and what there is to be known about quarrying he knows as well as any man. If we can't get up there to them, he says, we'll bring them down to us, castle and all. Men who wanted building-stone, he says, have brought down mountainsides before now, and turned bigger crags than Parfois into caverns, and why should not we do as much for Madonna Benedetta? So you see, Mother, you can't grudge him to us. Four years, says the prince to me, you've surely been trying your best to gnaw your way out; if there's a weak place from within you'll lay your finger on it, and if there's a means of probing it from without, Adam will show us the way. Put your heads together on your ride, he says, and cross Severn with a handful of ideas ready, or I'll put you to slaving in the camp kitchens, he says, as no use for better.'

'And rightly, too,' said Gilleis warmly, hugging him to a heart bursting with pride and pain and happiness. 'There, of course he'll come for her, with all his heart he'll come. Run and find your father and tell him, child, he's up at the sheep-folds.'

Harry embraced her briefly and was off like a grey-hound.

'Father, foster-brother,' said Gilleis, looking after him fondly as the door swung crashing to. 'Dear God, I hardly know which of them I'm talking to nowadays!'

They crossed Severn by the ford at Pool, in the bitter frost of a dark dawn. From the early snow and the first thaw the water was high, and had covered every hollow of the low meadows, and later frost, night after night hardening and day after day scarcely yielding even at noon, had turned every pool into sheet-ice. The main course of the river was treacherous black fringe ice for some yards on either bank, and ran brown and dark and turgid in the centre, bringing down broken floes with it from the hills to make their passage hazardous. In midstream the horses lost their footing and had to swim, and getting them back on to the shore was dangerous work, for the ice crumbled under them wherever they tried it, and left them floundering against the jagged edges, breast-high to a barrier of knives. Harry had to dismount precariously on to the black surface and prospect for a sheltered place where a spit of land jutted into the flood; and there they coaxed their labouring beasts on to shallower and sounder ice that brought them slithering and snorting to the bank at last.

Barbarossa allowed himself to be led, quivering, along the tongue of solid land, and was all but safe in the deep, snowy grass when he shied violently at a gleam of colour that slashed at his eyes out of the water. Harry had much ado to quiet him and get him past it, and no leisure to wonder or stare until that was done. But when they looked to see what had startled him they drew breath almost as sharply as the frightened beast.

Under the ice the crimson gold of Isambard's livery shone from a dinted shield, and a face stared up at them with wide-open eyes, long, greying hair tangled over a broken brow. What light there was in that early hour lay burning in the colours, and found points of brightness in the shoulder of a chain-mail hauberk. They beheld the first of Parfois's dead; and looking about them now with eyes alerted for the signs, they traced the running course of the brief battle at the ford.

Here a helmet, there a broken sword, frozen into the shallows of Severn. Drifted close under the bank where the currents had dug out a deep pool, four more bodies, all English; if there had been Welsh dead, the Welsh had carried them away for burial, but these lay untended. An unstrung bow, half-buried in snow, tripped them as they stepped into the long grass. Broken arrows, a bloody shred of a white surcoat, stiff as steel, the stains bleached to a faded rose-colour. Last, in the edge of the forest, contorted among bushes, a thick, muscular body arched over the stump of a sword as he had crawled and frozen and died; they turned him face-to-the-light, and he turned all of one piece like a stone grotesque for a gargoyle, and showed them the bushy beard and hard countenance of old Nicholas Stury, the master-of-arms.

Harry looked long at him, and a small gaping emptiness of

dismay opened within his heart and began to ache like a wound. This was nothing new; he had seen dead men before, even some of his own killing, and never wasted overmuch thought on them. Why should the sight of a known face trouble him now as soon as he stepped on to English ground? A man for whom he had had no love or even liking, a surly old bully who had enjoyed battering his more timid pupils at exercise, and taken it sourly against the grain if anyone bested him: what need was there to weep for Stury? And yet they had brushed shoulders daily in the orderly routine of Parfois for a matter of nearly four years, and had some part, however grudgingly, in each other's life; and a man whose comings and goings you have shared for so long is flesh to you, and blood, and quirks and moods and all, closer than a stranger whether you will or no. Harry signed the stone-cold forehead with a cross, and turned to the path and left him so.

'One that you knew?' said Adam from the saddle, watching the boy's fixed face and sombre eyes.

'Yes,' said Harry shortly, and offered nothing more.

'Was he good to you?' asked Adam, assaying a guess wide of the mark.

'No. Nor to any other that ever I noticed. But he was alive, and doubtless he liked living no less than the kindly men do – in his own fashion.' He put old Nicholas by with a shrug, and mounted and crossed the ribbon of meadow towards the woods. There would be more of them, no question; he had better get used to the thought.

The murk of cloud hung so low and thick that now they were on the English shore they could not see the Welsh, and the shape of the Long Mountain over them was only a purple-black gloom of trees receding into mist. But now their pricked nostrils quivered to the heavy stench that hung over the forest, and they knew that half at least of the obscurity that clouded the world was not mist, but smoke. Iron frost could keep the corpses from stinking, but could not quiet the acrid fumes of fire. Under the fresh snow they began to tread charred brushwood, and the trees stood here and there as mere blackened stumps with the broken remnants of branches. The underbrush was burned away in many places, thorn and bramble and bracken and all, and the beasts had fled the desolation. Only a few birds, returning, hopped and pecked in the snow, the first creatures to take fright, the first to take heart, the frailest and the most resilient of the forest's children.

They passed a burned cottage, the stumps of the walls standing stark out of the snow; and huddled close to it, powdered over by the last fall, the cottager lay with the broken shaft of a Welsh arrow upright in his back. That gave them fair warning what to expect when they came to the hamlet below Leighton: a wilderness of blackened shells of houses, empty byres, a dead dog or two, and one luckless villager who had stood to and defended his winter store instead of taking to his heels. The rest were either huddled inside Parfois before the invaders, or fled into the distant reaches of the forest with the beasts, to live or starve as best they could. Every grain of corn, every cow, every fowl, had been swept up to swell the commissariat of Llewelyn's camp; and the first outpost of the Welsh army challenged them here, and gave them word of the prince.

He had drawn up his engines of war and the main body of his army to feign a frontal attack upon the ramp of Parfois, and keep the garrison in a heat of dread for their lower guard, while his mountaineers prospected the rock on which the castle itself stood. Contravallation and circumvallation had been drawn tightly round the single approach, and there in the siege town they would find the prince's headquarters; but all round Parfois from river back to river again was strung the loose, mobile line of Welsh strong-points, sealing the castle off from the world. No one could get in to them, nor could they break out; if they had twenty posterns to bring them like conies out of the sandstone, they would still find themselves with the strangling cord of enemy troops, and have to fight their way through.

'We've not left a pig or a chicken or a handful of corn that could help to feed them,' said the sentry, grinning. 'They never had time to shift their stores, we were on them too fast. If we can't dig them out we can starve them out.'

'And the people? What's become of them?' asked Harry, staring upon the naked ruins that had once been homes.

'They ran, most of them. Some into the castle, to make more mouths to feed, some into the woods. And some crossed us, like fools, and we had to kill them.'

Who better could he have expected? This was war, and it was he who had launched it. Efficient war, war with a deadly purpose, no longer a game of strategy. He had leaped gladly to welcome it when the prince proposed this assault in arms, seeing in it the fulfilment of his own obligations and the deliverance of his own soul. But it was these who had to pay for it. He had seen Cardigan surrender, he had seen Brecon burn, but there he had come lightly and gone lightly, playing the game as it came, and only occasionally troubled at heart by the revelation of life and death; he had come and gone a child and a stranger. Here he was a man and a neighbour, and every death bereaved him in his new manhood.

He stared appalled at the ravished granaries and plundered byres. Here in these villages, Adam had once told him, his father had helped to bring in the harvest when too many of the menfolk were pressed for King John's levies; he had argued the rights of these same cottagers and franklins and villeins sturdily against their lord, felt for their wrongs, sealed into stone for ever his affirmation of their humanity. The son came now to empty the barns and slaughter the cattle, and pin the farmer to his own door-sill with steel. And he could not withdraw. He was committed, he above all: all this coil had arisen for his sake.

'And those in the forest?' he asked, his heart sickening within him for fear. She would be safe, surely! Surely! If David forgot, David who had seen her but once, Owen would see to it that she and her father came unscathed out of it, and bring them to a place of shelter as he had promised. Yet he could not avoid the burden by laying it on Owen. The responsibility was his; he should have foreseen what war and siege must mean, the assarts in ruins, the forest in flames.

'Gone to some holes best known to themselves,' said the sentry, heaving a careless shoulder. 'There were some living wild that would burrow with the foxes rather than run to Parfois for cover, and some that likely would have run there if they could, but never had the chance. We were over the river before they knew. We got their beasts, they had no time to move them. If they lived as light as us they'd be quicker on the wing.'

Harry wheeled Barbarossa and was off again in an agony of dread; and when Adam without question stretched to match his pace, he turned to search his face with one wild glance, and found little wonder there, and much compunction.

'I should have warned you,' said Adam, as they checked where the path grew steep.

'I should have known. How else could Parfois be sealed and taken? Oh, Adam,' he said, 'I begin to know that I was born English.'

'No help for it now, lad,' said Adam with grim gentleness. 'We go through with it.' He thought in his heart, are you come to that already? Well, Harry would love you the more for it. 'There's Benedetta to win,' he said, and shut his mouth in time upon Isambard's name.

'I don't forget. It's I began this, and I'll see it to its end.'

He wanted to ease his heart by speaking of Aelis, but he could not, even to Adam who knew her, who had slept in Robert's house and broken bread of her baking. His mouth dried up with fear on the shape of her name, and he spurred uphill towards the casual, muffled thunder of the trebuchets. Where they wanted cover they had left the trees alone, and only the daylong ponderous duel between mangon and arblast had spattered the branches with shot and littered the snow with splintered boughs. Harry and Adam were in the outer lines before they knew, and the palisades rose about them and drew them into the narrow siege town, swarming with men and beasts; and there was Owen hailing them gladly from a lean-to under the wall.

Harry came plunging from the saddle to meet him. He heard not a word of what Owen began to say to him.

'Where's Aelis?' he demanded, as blunt as a blow.

'God knows, Harry!' said Owen honestly, the brightness of welcome struck from his face. 'And God knows I'm sorry to have no better an answer to make. It fell out not as we'd planned, and I missed my chance. I've had men out searching – '

'But you should have made provision,' shouted Harry, shaking him furiously between his hands. 'You promised! Could I be with the vanguard as well as on my way to Aber? I thought you would ride for her the minute you crossed Severn. I thought you'd have her and her father safe in Castell Coch before you loosed your men. Dear God, what have you let them do?'

'But I was not with the vanguard, either, no more than you were. Could I know how it would fall out? They had orders to wait and cover the ford until I overtook them there, but by pure chance they ran full tilt into a company of troops from Parfois, on the Welsh bank after a runaway villein, and bore them back through the water in a running fight. With the secret out, what could Madoc do but drive hard ashore and set to work? When I came through the ford next day the forest was burning and the villages were black.'

'And you did not stir for her,' panted Harry. 'You let her be hunted into the earth like a vixen – you never thought of her – '

He took his hands from his foster-brother to knot them in anguish and unbelief, they burned with such a dismaying lust to batter hard at Owen's anxious face. Owen caught the clenched and welded fists to him indignantly, and flung an arm about the boy and held him still.

'God's truth, Harry, I did think of her, and ride for her, too, the minute I had grace to go. But it was done by then. The cottage was ash, and the cow was slaughtered – What would you have? They had to work fast, and what was there to set Robert's assart apart from all the rest?'

That truth went into Harry like a wound; for indeed how was his loss and grief different from any other man's? The wife of that dead cottager below there had as good a right to her sorrow as he to his. For every death someone suffered this very fury of protest and pain that convulsed him now.

'And they were gone? And did you even look for them?'

'What do you think I am, Hal? For two days and more I had men out searching, and the assart is watched still in case they come back. There were traces, we tried to follow them – '

'They didn't go into Parfois? But they wouldn't, they knew – '

'No, into the forest. Both, I swear it, Hal, I saw the tracks. But there was fresh snow that night, and they were covered deep, and we lost them. Sooth, I'm sorry! I'd give this hand to get them safe back.'

'What good's that?' said Harry roughly, and put him off with stiff movements to arm's length, and so got free of him. He stood back from them, his face grey like the soiled snow, 'Where is the prince? I must get leave of him. I must go to her.'

'Go to her? Dear God, boy, where will you go? They may well be in Shrewsbury by now.'

Did he believe it? Harry did not. The Welsh were on both flanks of the Long Mountain, and who would venture to try and thread their lines now, once having tasted the fire?

'Where is the prince?' he repeated fiercely; and hard on the answer he turned, spinning on his heel, and lunged away from them.

'Wait, I'll come with you,' cried Owen, shaken and grieving.

'Let him be,' said Adam. 'Do you think I would not go? He'll have neither you nor me.'

'No!' He turned to wave them back furiously. 'I want no one; I'll go alone.'

There was no time to soften that rejection, let them think what they would. Hunted and bereft and afraid, Aelis would never show herself now but to him, and the more surely if he

209

came empty-handed and alone. He ran from them, and burst breathless and tense into Llewelyn's presence, and bent the knee to him, the words he needed ready on his lips, and pared to the bone.

'My lord, I've done my errand, Adam is here. And here I deliver you my lady's letters. And now, my lord, give me leave yet to go and look for Robert and Aelis, who housed and helped me when I was lone here. They've taken to the woods from us, and their home's burned. Give me leave till I find and bring them to shelter, as they sheltered me.'

He lifted his head, and looked into the bright falcon's eyes that stared upon him unastonished, ware and wise from the heart; to one out of reach of surprise there was nothing that could not be said.

'My lord, this is no light prayer,' said Harry, desperately grave. 'From my soul I love her, and I mean to make her my wife.'

The fence of the paddock was down, the garden a waste of snow, the assart deserted. Of the little house only the charred and blackened crucks leaned like broken teeth. Owen's two watchmen had split Aelis's clay oven apart to make a hearth, and were feeding their fire with the remains of her chicken-coops.

'Day and night, watch and watch about here,' they grumbled, 'and never a sign of life. We're wasting our time here. They won't come back.'

So Harry thought, too, while these two remained. 'Get back to your fellows,' he said, 'and leave the place solitary.'

'That's more than my skin's worth,' objected the elder of the two, eyeing him sharply, 'if Owen ap Ivor comes to hear of it. He gave us plain orders to stay and keep watch here.'

'No matter for that. Go and report to him that Talvace released you from that order, and I'll be your warrant he'll find no fault with you. And dout your fire before you go, and take away all with you. If there's anyone to see, let them know the watch is withdrawn.'

On that assurance they doused the glow in the shattered

oven, nothing loath, and took their remaining stores and made off cheerfully back towards their camp; and Harry was left to the desolation where Aelis had been.

No use calling her now, she would not come. If she lived, if she still lurked somewhere in these violated woods, she would have to be hunted and taken like a wild creature. The first time, he thought in the anguish of his heart, they waited without fear when the Welshmen came, knowing it must be I who brought them, and thinking no harm; and the steel was out and the arrow fitted and the torch at the roof before they knew what was happening to them. Maybe she saw her cow driven off, and the first chicken's neck wrung, before she could believe in fear. Maybe Robert roared at them to let be, and stood in their way; maybe he was bleeding when he ran for his life at last. And she – No, why should they come near us again willingly, after such a treason? Not even to me! Least of all to me, if she did not love me, poor Aelis! I am the cause of this. God forgive me, and help me to make amends.

And where would they run, schooled at last to terror? Not towards the ridge of the Long Mountain, for there lay Parfois, and there they would be trapped between the devil and the deep. These particular fugitives had as good reason to fight shy of Parfois as to run from the Welsh. Not along the used pathways that clung to the level ground below the ridge, for there mounted men could go freely, and they would soon be ridden down. No, towards the river they must have gone, to lie clear of both armies in the precarious fringe of land that neither coveted. There at least they might hope to make their way round the whole terrible contention, if it cost them days and nights of labour to do it, or at the ford at Buttington they might make shift to cross the river and find shelter in Strata Marcella, where the good brothers would not ask a destitute man his parentage before they took him in.

The thick woodland along the riverside, where no paths were, had escaped the fire. He left Barbarossa tethered, and took to the underbrush, and with fearful patience hunted her

211

downstream along the shore. Twice he saw bodies lying tangled in the frozen weed where they had drifted, and walled in with the thickening ice, and clawed his way down to them with his heart in his throat; but they were none of his, and he breathed again and pressed doggedly on. He would not go back without her.

The mill had not escaped them: it was emptied and stripped and fired, and the miller lay hacked and dead in his own frozen pool. But they had not waited to see the destruction completed, and a contrary wind had spared the undercroft and left it a whole roof. Harry searched the ruins eagerly, for this was the first shelter that had offered; but nothing living stirred in the wreckage, and across yards of black ice the boat lay motionless, islanded and helpless in the grip of the frost.

He searched hour after hour while the day slipped by him without consciousness of hunger or thirst or cold or weariness; downstream to Buttington and beyond, until his own heart warned him he had spent that hope, and must needs turn and look elsewhere. Nevertheless, on the way upstream he kept to the river fringes as before, sure of his reasoning; even in panic and confusion Robert would know what he did, and keep to the riverside, where alone they might hope to escape pursuit and avoid chance encounters. Chilled in body and spirit, still he held obstinately to his hunting. And in the last of the light, with the murky winter dusk heavy on his eyes, he came again within sight of the mill, and that from a tongue of land downstream and thickly wooded, where the fire had not reached, and he himself could move unseen.

He halted and froze there, staring. From the boat a slight dark figure crept out over the ice towards the mill. Stooped and limping she went, like a sick child, like a cripple, she so straight and wild and light; but he knew her by the instant convulsion of pain that rent his heart and dragged the desperate tears to his eyes, and by the joy beyond the agony, that started him whispering thanks and vows to God silently within his trembling lips.

She lived, she moved, he would take her and tame her again however she fought, hold her in his hands from escaping him, fold her in his arms tightly from doing herself an injury in her terror, until the touch of him moved and melted her even against her will, and she listened to him and grew quiet, too weary to fear any more, too spent to fight any more; until his words and his caresses touched her understanding and stroked her erected feathers to rest, and her heart and her body knew him and turned to him. Even against her will!

He stole forward with aching care through the trees, lost her before she came to land, hurried with dread scalding his heels, and found her again as she climbed from the ice to the shore. Step by wincing step he closed in upon her, in fear of the snapping of a twig or the stirring of a branch that could betray him. He came to the sagging fence that hemmed the small garden of the mill.

Why had he not examined that plot as carefully as the mill itself on his way downstream? He could not have missed the strange signs of human occupation then, and he would have known she was there, hiding from him, hiding from every terrible touch of man, who had done to her such infamous things. She thought herself alone now in the shelter of the dropping night, and she had crept from her place of refuge to continue her work. Shaking and half-blind, he saw that she had brought a mattock from the miller's store, and was trying to break the iron ground with it. How long had she laboured at it already, to have hollowed out that pitiful, shallow trench that showed black in the smooth undulations of the snow?

She had rags of sacking bound round her feet and hands, and only the tatters of a sack about her shoulders over her coarse gown; she must have run without even a cloak. Her long hair hung tangled on her neck, coiled carelessly out of her way. Her face he could not see, partly for the dusk and partly for the shadow of her hair. He stole from cover at her back, climbed over the wooden pales, and closed like a hunting cat.

213

For all his caution, she heard him. She sprang round and away from him, sudden and silent, and heaved up the mattock to strike at his head. He caught the flare of wild eyes, enormous in a pinched and pallid face, and could not tell if she knew him, or if she had any senses left in her to recall him. The face was rigid and blank, a broken fragment of the ice from the river, the eyes blue flames of fear and horror. He leaped in beneath the blow, and the stock of the mattock bruised and numbed his shoulder. The fingers that grasped at her closed on the hem of the sacking cloak, and she wrenched herself away from him and left it in his hand, and, flinging down her weapon, ran from him madly like a wounded deer towards the shelter of the trees.

He was after her instantly, and even desperation could not help her to outrun him. At the garden pale he caught her by a fistful of her gown and her hair, and at the lamentable cry she gave the breath knotted and sobbed in his throat in an answering whimper of pain, but he could not and would not let her go. She turned and sank her teeth into his wrist, and down they came together into the snow. She fell with hardly more substance than a leaf, so slight and light under him, her struggling arms so thin, that all his being flooded with an inconsolable torrent of grief and horror and shame. But there was no help for it; he lay upon her with all his weight, pinning her down until she tired, struggling with her until he held her helpless, only her poor head weaving in agony from side to side to evade even his glance, as though that, too, had power to hurt and kill.

He eased his grip of her a little, feeling her body grow still under him, and in a flash she had freed one arm, and her nails tore furrows down his cheek. He caught and pinned her wrist and let his weight lie on her, not daring to risk so much again. Even his head he laid hard against hers, cheek to cheek, his brow upon the snow, to hold her still. She heaved and panted in long, quivering breaths, and the feel of her thinness and coldness and hate passed into him in convulsions of desire and anguish, until the ache of his body after her was almost more than he could bear.

214

'Aelis! Aelis!'

He had hardly voice to speak her name, but he whispered it brokenly over and over into her ear. There was no tremor of knowledge, no softening, no acknowledgement in the rigid body under him. Yet she knew what he did not, that he was weeping, in great gulping sobs that shattered the syllables of her name. Through the thin chink of her human astonishment wonder came in, and pity hesitated on its heels, shy to follow. The quality of her stillness changed. When he dared to lift his head and look at her again the great eyes, fixed and dilated with shock, held a small, awakening flame of doubt and thought that heartened him to believe the mind and the soul were still alive in her.

'Aelis, don't you know me? Harry? Don't fight me, don't run. I came to find you, to take you with me. Aelis, my love, my little heart, don't be afraid of me –'

Not yet. It meant nothing to her yet but a faint and not unpleasant sound that for once did not threaten her. There would be a long time to wait before she came back to him, but at least she had cast the first glance over her shoulder.

He took one hand from her at last, still with terrible caution, unloosed the chain of his cloak and dropped it over her. Shifting his weight carefully, he snatched her up in one arm before she was aware, pinning both her arms above the elbow, and rolled the cloak round her, twisting the folds close so that she could not fight him. She started and struggled in returning panic, but that effort was soon spent. The sensation of warmth reached and confounded her; for the first time she felt that there might be kindness in the hands that wrapped her, and the arms that held her prisoner.

He had her now, she was helpless. He raised her into his arms, and carried her into the undercroft of the mill. There was the remains of a bolt of dry hay in the corner; he sat down with her there and made a nest for her, and hushed and soothed her; but he did not cease to hold her fast in his arms, for fear she should break from him and escape him again.

'I came as soon as I could, as soon as I knew. No one will

hurt you now. I'll take care of you. I'll take you away to a safe place. I'll take you to my mother – '

Over and over he told her all his heart, over and over he stroked and gentled her. She softened a little in his arms, the frozen pallor of her face eased. He laid his lips to her forehead, and she trembled and turned her eyes upon him in wonder and longing, remembering caresses. Then he kissed her slowly and gently, brow and cheek and throat, and at last her mouth; and it awoke under his touch, and stirred and quickened to him, fastening hungrily with a great sigh.

His body was quiet enough now, heavy and selfless with tenderness; he could wait his time. He held her fast until the exhaustion of wonder went over her like a wave of the sea, and she fell asleep in his arms. After that he waited a long time, until he could be sure she would not lightly awake, and then he laid her down and lapped her close in the hay, and went out noiselessly from the hut. The door was broken-hinged but heavy; he barred it upon her, and knew that she could not move it. There were things he had to do.

First he crept out over the ice, the rising moon showing him where the boat lay. An old canvas was stretched over the thwarts, a fold of it turned back as she had left it. And he found what he had known in his heart he would find. Robert was there, stiff and stark where he had died, his wounds in breast and arm crusted through the bandages she had torn from her shift. Her cloak was here, too, tenderly laid over her father's body. Half-naked to the bitter cold, she had set herself to the long labour of hacking out a grave for her dead in the frozen earth. That at least he could spare her. Robert had a son now, too late to help him living, but at least in time to bury him, dead.

Harry knelt on the ice and said a prayer for the departed soul; and suddenly the burden of his responsibilities and the load of his guilt overwhelmed him for a moment, and a burst of tears shook him as the wind shakes an aspen tree. But it was brief enough, and left him whole and calm. He rose and went back to the shore, and made his way as fast

216

as he could to the place where he had left Barbarossa tethered. He brought him, eager and uneasy and indignant, back to the mill, and into the shelter where Aelis still slept. There was bread and meat and wine in his saddle-bags, and the horse's great body would be their fire against the cold of the night.

She lay as he had left her. He put his hands upon her, there being now no light by which to see her; and she did not stir. But when he loosed the folds of the cloak and crept in beside her and wrapped it closely round them both, she stretched and sighed; and as he took her in his arms and drew her close to share his warmth with her, she turned to him confidingly in her sleep, and nestled against his heart.

All night he lay wakeful and held her in his arms. And in the morning she opened her bruised eyes, washed by sleep to the clean, virgin blue of cornflowers, and said: 'Harry!' doubtfully and wistfully, as though she had dreamed of him.

'I'm here,' he said, taut and tremulous with hope, and kissed her on the cheek, the gentle, reassuring kiss he would have offered to a child.

She threw her arms about his neck suddenly, and strained him to her with all her strength. The barrier of loneliness that had held back her tears broke, and the torrent of her grief spent itself gratefully on his breast.

He fed and nursed her, kindled fires to warm her, held her in his arms by night, and by day hollowed out for bitter penance Robert's iron grave. By the second evening, when he had made a sledge of boughs and drawn the swathed body ashore over the ice for burial, she rose and came out to him of her own will, her face pale and sombre but wonderfully calm, and helped him to lay her father in his grave. She prayed with him, and her grief was a human grief, and bearable, and her tears came softly, not for an inconceivable horror, but for a comprehensible sorrow, no longer past healing.

On the third day they left the mill, and crossed the ford

at Pool. There was no difficulty now; from shore to shore the river was frozen over. Harry muffled Barbarossa's hoofs in bindings of rag, and led him across without danger.

They came into the gates of Castell Coch about noon, and there were other travellers arrived but a quarter of an hour before them, and busy unloading in the courtyard. Harry saw the bright blazonings of Gwynedd, counted the array of grooms and squire and chamberlains, and knew that the princess had kept her word and come early to the borders, to keep Christmas close to her lord. He was eased and glad, for now he could confide Aelis to the safest of all safe-keeping; but he was constrained and uneasy, too, for some new and quite unexpected instinct quickened in him at a touch, warning him that it is not so simple to tell your mother that you have become a man and a lover without giving her warning or asking her leave.

Gilleis, coming out from the princess's apartment to see Joan's personal baggage carried in, halted on the steps of the hall at sight of the chestnut horse pacing in with his double burden. She forgot her errand, forgot the annoyances of travel and the relief of arrival. All she saw was that sturdy, well-set young man, a stranger with sombre, resolute eyes, and a stubble three days old and yellow as ducklings on his chin, holding the slender girl before him in his arms as though she were a chalice of gold from which he feared to spill one drop of nectar. She watched him dismount, taking his arm so softly and reluctantly from about the swathed figure, and her exasperation flared at seeing him ride without a cloak in such weather, and chilled with more than fore-boding as she realised that indeed he had had a cloak, but the girl was wearing it. And pale and thin and soiled as she was, she wore it like the purple, and leaned to Harry, as he raised his arms to lift her down, with the naked, confiding worship kings seldom inspire. For that Gilleis warmed to her, even in her pain.

Her time was come upon her too soon. He was not yet nineteen, and for four years she had lacked him, and now to lose him to gold hair and a wild and innocent face, and

218

eyes like cornflowers in an unreaped field!

He set the girl on her feet with delicate care, as though the earth might bruise her. He gave his bridle to a groom, and turned towards the hall with his arm clasped close about his companion's shoulders. And then he saw his mother standing, and knew that he was seen.

Gilleis marshalled her powers and her love, and went down to meet and embrace him.

'Mother,' he said, 'I'm thankful you're come. Here's one I should be glad to confide to your care, one who befriended me, and is orphaned through me. This is Aelis, Robert's daughter, of whom you've heard tell from me. We're newly come from burying her father.'

He took her in his arm again, for she had hung back from intruding upon their greeting; he brought her forward with a high colour and a grave face.

'Mother, this is my bride I'm bringing to you. Take her and keep her safe for me till I come. But for you and me she has no one and nothing in the world now.'

His voice was careful and proud and even, but Gilleis saw the child who was gone look out of his eyes for a moment, between defiance and appeal, before the young man fronted her again with his high, imperious stare. God bless the boy, she thought, saved by the irresistible laughter that moved her always at the ingenuous solemnities of men, does he think I had ambitions to match him with some little Welsh princess with a couple of cantrefs in her pocket? Or did God teach him the cunning to come at me this way, knowing I could never give him up with a good grace but to some poor creature who had nothing besides? If it must come, what's left me to do but embrace it? Better give him freely than have him wrested from me.

She looked at the girl, and saw the dark rings under her eyes, the pallor of her cold cheeks, the poverty of her dress. So young and so lonely, without possessions, without kin, who could grudge her that close clasp of hands by which she clung to the world, and hope, and the promise of happiness?

'And where should you take her,' said Gilleis roundly,

219

'if not to me?' And she took Aelis from him, took her to her heart and kissed her warmly. 'Child, you're dearly welcome. God knows I'm sorry for your loss, but I'm glad of my own gain.' God record the lie to me for merit and not for sin, she thought, and teach me to make truth of it. 'Come in with me,' she said. 'Come in from the cold, both of you, and warm yourselves at the fire, for you look perished with this frost. Come in to the princess and tell her your news; she'll be happy for you.'

He said no to that, already light with relief and straining back anxiously towards his duty. But her reward was with her, for he hugged and kissed her again with the exuberance of joy, over his trouble and riding smoothly now. Like all the men, she thought, a sunny soul when you get your way; and she laughed at herself and him, and the old delight was still fresh and untarnished. What had ailed him to doubt, or her to fear? Had his father asked any man's leave when he chose her to wife? And had she forgotten the boldness of her own courses, when she set her heart on Harry Talvace of all men, and so staked her life that it should win her him or lose her all?

'I can't stay, Mother, I must go back, there's work waiting for me. I know Parfois from within; they need me there. Only take care of her, and I'm happy. And love her, Mother,' he said in a pleading whisper into her ear, 'for *I* love her dearly.'

'And who should take better care of her than her mother?' said Gilleis, hugging him back with good will. 'And who should love her more? There, then, if you must go you can be easy about us here. We shall do very pleasantly together, pulling you to pieces till you come again. There are things I can teach her about you! There, child, be off if you must. Kiss her and trust her to me.'

He kissed her, and took his cloak and went, content for his womenfolk and off like an arrow to the burrowers under Parfois, busy probing the rock for every fault and fissure where heat or frost or iron could bite.

They looked after him in a brief and perilous silence, and

when he was gone they looked at each other for the first time narrowly and deeply.

'Madam,' said Aelis, measuring what might well prove to be a formidable opponent, 'I will be obedient to you, and grateful, and learn of you how best to serve him. But I tell you now, I will not give him up.'

Who would have thought at first glance that she had so high a heart in her? Gilleis studied her long and thoughtfully, saw beyond the pallor of cold and privation and grief the resolution and composure of the clear face, the deep spark in the eyes that looked back at her so straightly, marked how the flower of a mouth nevertheless fashioned and finished every word, and cut it free with the cleanness of a sword. She knew what she had said, and what she had said she meant; the challenge was there to be accepted or let lie, *she* would not change. She gave honest warning, without bitterness or malice; but if she had to fight for him, she would give no quarter.

'For I think,' said Aelis with deliberation, blue eyes as bright and daunting as swords, 'I am not what you would have chosen for him.'

'Girl,' said Gilleis with a sudden blazing smile, 'as God sees me, I begin to think you *are!*'

CHAPTER NINE

Parfois: *December* 1233

In the night, in the deceptive silence of the motionless frost, Parfois lay as still and untouched as the very stars overhead. It was bright in the great hall, even pinched as they were now for candles; and sparing as they had to be with food and ale and wine for their swollen garrison, yet they did well enough. On the roof of the Lady's Tower William Isambard paced out his nightly vigil, watching the glimmerings of fires distant under the mountain, the tiny links of the chain that bound him close within his own guard, and yet left him in such apparent peace. The very waiting was heavy to bear; three times he had tried to lift it by well-armed sorties in strength, but the burden of his losses had taught him to forbear such costly relief. He kept his lower guard by main force, the battered tower there reinforced by a hurried three-fold barrier reared from Master Edmund's building-stone, and manned by half the garrison. If the ramp was taken they could bring up their engines to the plateau of the church, and assault the castle itself at close quarters; but as long as it held Parfois was impregnable, its capture an impossibility. And here he beheld it beneath him, intact and orderly and quiet, inviolate, inviolable.

Down under their feet, like conies, like moles, the Welsh pecked tirelessly at the rock on which their fortress stood, gnawing it inchmeal away from under them. But where was the sense in that? What could they hope to do like that? As well set out to drain the river with ladles.

It maddened him when the old master-mason insisted daily on reporting his perpetual obsession, or when de Guichet, following him here at night, thought fit to refer to the same derisory activity. Did it matter that they broke their fool teeth chipping away the earth? Every man knew the Welsh could climb, every man acknowledged they could scale the cliff and thread the gully that severed the rock of Parfois from the rock of the church. What then? They could get no engines up there, there were no practicable posts even for their archers; and even if they could have climbed to the very foot of the wall itself, they could bring up no ladders to it. Let them burrow!

'My lord, Master Edmund says he still hears them. Under the gate-towers, but most clearly under the outer armoury and the tracing-house. He swears they are mining there under us.'

'Let them! What good can it do them? The one bolt-hole that could have been dangerous we've stopped with stones, and the doors within are guarded. If my fool father had not made use of it for his tricks we need not have sacrificed even that; they'd never have found it from without if the boy had not known it already. And there are no more such posterns.'

'No, my lord. But there are crevices and shallow caves. And the prince of Aberffraw has his masons, too, who know how to quarry rock as well as Master Edmund does.'

'And do you think they can tunnel a way into Parfois? In how many years? Let them burrow! Pick them off when you can, and leave troubling me with them.'

There were archers stationed perpetually on top of the gate-towers and the walk between them, and on every gallery of the wall on that side. Occasionally an incautious clansman showed himself clear of the cliff, and paid for it, but of late they had learned to lie close, and the overhang gave them generous shelter. Once at least, when the Welsh had brought up by night a larger party than usual, and were detected, the defenders had tipped oil down into the gully and thrown torches after it, and lit a flare that drove several men screaming in flames from cover, to be executed at leisure by the bowmen on the wall. But they were quick to learn. They hugged the cliff now, and came singly and in silence, and perhaps they had enlarged their holes enough to lie clear of

223

the range of fire. But what of it? Let them grope busily in the dark until they grew as blind as the old man himself. What harm could they do there?

'As you will, my lord. We do what can be done. The boy, my lord, is also a mason, you'll recall; he learned under Master Edmund –'

'Leave that, I said. Is there more to tell?'

'Not new, my lord. The old lord, your father, has asked again if he may walk in the inner ward, mornings. I said I would ask you. He's sickly with being mewed up so long, after the life he's lived. You might think well to let him out to the air now and then.' The brief, meaning look he lifted to William's face added: ' – if you still want to keep him.'

That brought an assuaged smile. It was an acknowledgement of the reversal if that demon of arrogance had been brought to ask favours.

'Let him, then, so he's watched carefully. No one is likely to mind him now. No need to attend him, if he wills to walk let him do it as best he may, but watch that he keeps to the inner ward. The woman's safe in the outer ward, she cannot come to him. Does she ever ask for him?'

'No, my lord, she asks for nothing.'

She asked for nothing. She seemed not to be a prisoner; she moved through her days in quietness, perception and thought, untroubled in the centre of the stillness at the heart of the whirlwind. Sometimes they almost feared her. The wide-set eyes took in with so daunting a tranquillity and so precise an intelligence the detail of other people's madness, while she moved immune. If death came for her, she would examine it with as large a calm, and go with it as readily. The holy woman of Aber, the Venetian courtesan, the adventuress who had come back to Parfois as a prize of war from the Crusades – she had seen and experienced so much that she was out of reach of astonishment. She was of small relevance now. With this warfare on his hands he would have been glad to be rid of her if he could, but she was there, and no help for it; and she might yet be needed, she was the

224

only goad that could move the old man if he turned obstinate again.

'See he keeps from her.'

'He will, my lord, he pledged it.'

'Do you see to it, I said. I trust neither him nor her. With whom does she spend her time?'

With no one. Or with everyone. She would return words readily, yet she had no need of any man's company.

'Sometimes with the women, or the musicians. She plays and sings; they say, well. And the fellow from Reichenau, rogue as he may be, he has some learning – she talks of books with him.'

That was one more guest they would willingly have done without, the spoiled monk with his glib tongue and his knowing eyes, who had come south from Chester with his pack and his stories, to peddle a dubious fragment of the rood of Saint Peter to the old man. Ralf Isambard had been known in his day as a collector of such relics, and a witty tongue could get board and largesse out of him even if the merchandise was suspect. Straight from the Holy Land, the fellow said, fresh from shipboard and still pale from sickness after a winter crossing from France. And to Parfois he came, and in Parfois he was penned perforce now until the Welsh should withdraw; and mightily he complained of his ill luck, in falling unawares into such a wasp's nest the minute he set foot in England after years.

'I could never abide these scholarly women. The devil made them. But my father's taste was always for the devil's creations, for all his crusading piety.' He swung abruptly towards the tower stair. 'What's that? Who comes? Did I not tell you to keep them from me at this hour?'

'My lord, they know your wishes, there's not one would dare – '

The footsteps on the stone treads, mounting at speed, echoed hollowly out of the dark doorway.

' – without good need,' said de Guichet, and went in haste to meet the intruder.

One of the chamberlains came bursting breathlessly out

of the narrow shaft of the stairs, stumbled at the lintel, and made haste to humble himself before William's frowning face.

'My lord, pardon! This is too urgent to keep. The well — the great well, the one in the outer ward — '

'Fool, do I need telling where my wells are? What of it? What's amiss?'

There were two wells within the walls, one, the older and for some years inadequate to their needs, in the deepest heart of the inner ward, the second and newer in the outer ward, not far from the gate-towers; and on this richer supply the garrison chiefly depended.

'My lord, it's dry!'

'Dry? Fool, how can it run dry? When did it even sink before?' Purpling, William gripped the man by the shoulder and swung him round to the light of the half-moon. 'Are you drunk, to run with such a folly? Who told you this?'

'My lord, the scullions who went to draw water there brought the word to the master-butler, and he to me. But I did not take it on trust, I went to put it to the test myself. My lord, it's all too true. We lowered and lowered and got nothing, and never touched water until we touched rock alongside. There's but a puddle at the bottom of the shaft. Come and see, my lord, you'll find it as I've said.'

But his lord had already dropped him and swooped through the doorway like a plunging hawk, and was descending the stairs in great circling leaps.

The blind man in his sealed and guarded room heard the clamour go by, and turned his head with ears pricked to catch the few words that flew within earshot as they passed. He was quick to connect as to hear; sometimes his perception made even his guards afraid. He had but to catch the word 'well' and the hubbub and agitation in the voices, and he knew. In his darkness he could reason at leisure, without the need to run and confirm. He thought of that ponderous household of more than a thousand souls, the measure of their cups suddenly dwindled to thimbles, the length of their resistance shrunken to the depth of the inner well.

There had been trouble enough even in peaceful dry summers until they sank the second well.

Who was it had shrugged off the industrious burrowings of the Welshmen so lightly and contemptuously, calling them conies and moles? His bellowings rang loud and frantic now as he cursed them. What could they do, indeed! They had shown him what they could do. They could plot with exact care the position of the well; they had those among them who knew it to a yard. They could send their patient craftsmen up into the gully, and set them to work under the shelter of the overhanging gate-towers, quarrying away at the rock, prising with steel crows at every fault and every fissure that led them inwards towards the shaft, until they hammered their way through, and the first thin spurt of water told them they had tapped the spring. Easy work then to enlarge the leak until it could drain the lifeblood of Parfois, and send it trickling away in a new stream down the gully, to fall in a series of silver strings over the cliff, and make its way to the brook and the river below.

Doubtless when daylight came they would be able to see for themselves, from the gate-towers, Severn's new tributary threading the rocks below them, far out of reach of their thirst. The flow might even be strong enough to keep it from freezing for a night or two, until the first pressure was spent and only the steady feed of the spring remained.

'Well done, Harry!' said Isambard, laughing into the dark. 'From one mole to another, well burrowed!'

It was three days after the piercing of the well when the renegade monk of Reichenau, pressed into service carrying timber to repair the barricades at the lower guard, fell twice under his load, and complained of pain and sickness. They pricked him to his feet again at lance-point, sure that he was play-acting to escape from his labours, for he shunned work as the devil shuns holy water. But when at last the party returned across the bridge into Parfois, he reached the rim of the empty well and leaned there hunched over fearful cramps, and in a moment he straightened up and fell on his

227

face, stiffly as a log falls, and rebounded and rolled like a log, his mouth open and running spittle into the frozen snow.

A page, young and innocent enough to feel pity, ran to tend him, but one of the men-at-arms caught the boy back by the arm.

'Let be! Don't touch him! Who knows what ails him?'

Others who had hesitated stepped hurriedly back at that, staring uneasily upon the fallen man, who stirred feebly and groaned, the breath heavy and loud between his parted lips. He spread his arms, and those nearest shrank from him. A faint stain of blood marked the snow beside his mouth.

Madonna Benedetta came out from the doorway of the Warden's Tower, crossed the ward with her long, vehement step, and went on her knees beside the sick man. To her no one said: 'Let be!' No one reached to hold her back. Prisoner as she was, her actions were her own.

'Paulinus!'

He had the name of one of the sweetest singers of the antique world, though she thought he had bestowed it upon himself and not got it from his parents in baptism. And indeed he had a certain graceless sweetness still about him, for all his rogueries, and a touch of the true freshet in his voice sometimes that clearly caught even himself unawares. She touched his shoulder, and he turned and opened his eyes. Within the circlet of his sometime tonsure the hair grew greyer and thinner, an old man's ragged hair. His face bore the marks of his life; if he had run from his cloister and turned *vagus*, the world had battered him enough for it.

'Paulinus, what is it? Where's your hurt?'

He rolled his head against her sleeve, and could not speak.

'Some of you help me with him,' she said, looking round upon the starers with authority. 'We must get him to his bed.'

They gazed at her warily, and with small, furtive movements inched not forward but back. One said: 'Do we know what ails him? Best leave him alone. You may be the next, mistress.' And they shifted and murmured uneasily.

228

There was nothing to be got from them, and if he lay here in the frost he would surely die; she had no time to wonder or persuade. She lifted him sturdily, her hands beneath his armpits, and stooping, drew his arm round her neck and held him about the body.

'Can you rise? Lean on me, and try. It's not so far, and I'll help you. You mustn't stay here.'

He did his best. Labouring he came to his knees, and got one foot under him. His face was dark, as though the blood thickened purple beneath the skin. He groaned and wrenched at his throat and breast, dragging open his gown as if he could not breathe; and plainly they saw then how his flesh was mottled with crimson stains. Over his chest and climbing his neck the angry blotches erupted and swelled, and he clawed at them and drew blood.

The crowd reeled backwards, and broke into a confusion of cries and warnings. She had not realised until then how many they were, all round her, all staring upon her, and others gathering on the run from every quarter, until de Guichet himself came striding to see what this excitement could be. He was thrusting his way through towards them when first somebody whispered:

'Plague!'

It was a spark to tinder; it flared in an instant, and was taken up on all sides in a mad outcry, hardly a word now, only a bellowing of beasts. De Guichet broke through upon them roaring, and recoiled faster than he came at sight of the mottled body and marred face. Hands clutched at him, protesting and imploring.

'Plague! He's brought the plague from overseas. God pity us all, plague's among us!'

'This is not plague,' cried Benedetta stoutly, keeping her hold of Paulinus as he swayed at her side. 'Plague I know, plague I've seen, and this is none. Let me get him within, and ask your own physician.'

They screamed no to that. Bad enough he should be even within the walls, but he must not be lodged among them like a whole man.

'Nor her, neither,' shrilled one of the women. 'She's held him, she's handled him, she's as foul as he. God help us all if she's let run loose among us.'

'Put them out,' voices began to cry, shrill and hard, scarcely human in their terror. 'Out of Parfois! We won't have them within the walls. Drive them out!'

'This is not plague,' Benedetta cried into the wind. 'His death will be on you if you cast him out. He'll die of cold, not of plague, and God will require his life of you.'

They shouted her down. She saw all round her a fantastic dance of terrified faces, she was battered by the shrieking of frenzied voices. The sick man's head lolled on her shoulder. She held him upright, standing off his frightened enemies with her broad brow and blazing eyes; but she saw death walking towards him, and the shadow touched herself no less than him. She turned her head quickly, searching for one face, one, that kept its wits and its humanity, and offered her an ally to whom she might appeal; but the demon of panic, more contagious than plague, had stricken them all into the grotesque anonymity of masks.

'My lord,' said de Guichet's voice behind her, shaking and appalled, 'plague – we're harbouring plague among us.'

She turned, and saw William Isambard. Doubtless he had heard the turmoil and come in anger to know the reason, with raised voice and noise enough, if there had not been too hideous a clamour already for him to make himself heard. When he struck out about him with his fists, after his ready fashion, then they knew who roared at their backs, and broke apart and gave him place; and so brought him headlong to the front, face to face with Paulinus and still ignorant of what waited for him. She turned in time to see him recoil with a leap that sent the nearest babblers reeling. She saw his face in the instant of recognition, stricken white and motionless in its grimace of displeasure, the eyes fallen blank as glass, empty lanterns until fear found a colour and a spark to kindle them again.

At that she smiled, and he saw the smile. She, with her arm about the pestilence and death's hand heavy on her

shoulder, still had heart to laugh at him. Anger came back
to habit with his fear. But what did it matter? He had no
power at all, he went where he must, where circumstances
thrust him. There was no help in him.

'How came this? How long has he been so?'

'God knows, my lord! He must have brought the contagion with him from shipboard. Only now he fell, and we
saw – '

They crowded close about their master, those who dared
clutching at his sleeves in demand and entreaty.

'My lord, save us! Cast them out before they poison us
all!'

'My lord, for mercy's sake!'

'Look at her! His mark's on her now, no one can make her
clean again. Drive them both out quickly – drive out the
plague from among us, or we're all lost like her.'

'My lord,' said de Guichet, quaking, 'what's to be done
with them? If this is indeed plague – '

They clamoured that it was, that it would flare through
Parfois, shut in as it was and short of water and food, like
a flame through dry grass, and make of the castle a grave-
yard. William bellowed for silence, and shut the nearest
bleating mouth with his fist.

'Hold your fool tongues! Do you suppose I want pestilence
in my house? Have I less to lose than you? Whether this is
plague or no, I dare not harbour it. We'll have them out of
here in short order.'

'The man will die,' said Benedetta, 'if you put him out in
the cold. In God's name give him at least a shelter where I
can tend him. A hut outside the walls, where we cannot
breathe contagion on you, anything, so he has a roof over
him.'

'He shall have a roof over him, and space enough,' said
William, and the cold, frightened eyes that had learned to
hate her when she laughed took some comfort now when she
stooped to beg, even though she did it as one having rights.
'De Guichet, take them and shut them into the church.
Fasten the doors on them. All the doors. Nail up the lower

windows, make them secure.'

'Yes, my lord.'

'On your head be it if they break out. Get them hence, get them out of the wards, I care not how. You have men enough.'

He drew back thankfully, his eyes still on the woman and her groaning burden. She saw him shudder with the same dread and revulsion that had made monsters of the men of Parfois, men no worse than most of their kind when they were not mortally afraid. He drew his furred gown about him and put a fastidious distance between himself and the contagion of misery, but he did not leave the scene, he waited apart to see his orders carried out. He had not only a life to lose like any other man, but a garrison at war to safeguard and preserve, and his castle and his lordship depended on keeping them not only from disease but also from the panic fear of disease. In her heart she did not blame him overmuch; and though she had opened her lips to entreat him once again she did not do it. For the baying of the pack he would not have heard; but if he had heard he would not have heeded.

'Hold up, my heart,' she said into the ear of the rogue monk, and braced her shoulder under his, 'for the good name of all scholars.'

His eyes rolled wide and stared upon her, and the sharp mind was still there, raging within the failing body. The contortion of his mouth she knew for a wry smile, the kind fortune had chiefly drawn from him all his life long, and very fitting for a salute to his death.

'Where you go, I go, too,' she said. 'Even a cold welcome's warmer, shared.'

Why should the unwilled cruelty of fear blaze so readily into the hot frenzy of hatred? The men-at-arms had run for lances, and for all their terror came almost with glee, levelling the steel. Benedetta turned about to put her body between them and the sick man, baring her teeth at the foremost like a hound on guard.

'Are you men? Keep off! Touch him, and by God I'll

breathe plague down your throats though I must claw my way up your lances to reach you. Spit me, and you must shift my carcass with your own hands, plague and all. Let us alone and we'll quit your company as fast as we can. Use your goads on us and I'll make you bury us.'

For all their din they heard that, and wavered. The lances hovered, even touched her breast. She gave back not at all she even leaned a little forward, as best she might for the weight that hung upon her shoulder, and pressed her body to the points, staring the too eager herdsmen in the face with wide and blazing eyes; and the steel shrank from her touch, and left her ungrazed. Him they would have pricked along, had he been alone, for by no other means could they have driven him out of their gates. And if he had died on the way they would have transfixed him and dropped man and lances into the gully to breed among the Welshmen. But she was a different matter. With her aid he might make shift to walk to his tomb, and spare them the need of touching him even at a lance's length. And there was no denying she had shocked them into second thoughts about driving her too far. Who could tell? She might be holy, after all, as the Welsh held her. The lightning of God might do her bidding. They brandished their weapons all round her as she addressed herself to the melancholy journey out of Parfois, but they held off from drawing blood, however they howled and threatened.

Paulinus moved with dragging feet at her side, heaving harsh breaths that rattled in his throat. As best he might, he walked; and when he was forced to halt for a moment, she wound both arms about him and held him upright against her breast, eyes flaring warnings over his shoulder, until he was ready to drag himself yet a few yards towards his death. Slow and lame and bitter was the journey, with the hunt for ever snapping at their heels and the din of frantic voices shrill and cruel in their ears. All Parfois ran shrieking after them, followed them streaming across the drawbridge, hemmed them into the narrow path that led straight to the church. Even the men from the guard-posts that ringed the

233

plateau left their stations and came panting with excitement, to stare and question and add their voices to the babel.

So they brought them to the west door, and drove them within. She turned then to look from face to face, and with quiet eyes and still voice she said: 'For charity give us at least food and water.'

Water? They had but one inadequate well now to keep a thousand souls alive, why waste a drop on two already condemned to death? Food? Who knew how long they might have to hold out yet? They could spare nothing.

The door swung to and closed upon her face. All round Master Harry's church the men of Parfois seethed, making fast doors. They ran with timbers and nails and hammers, sealing the world within from the world without, closing the tomb.

Young Thomas Blount came back from the entombment and leaned to his lord's ear in the shelter of the merlons on the wall.

'My lord,' he said, soft and content and fat with his own cleverness, 'it's done. They're penned so fast they'll never break out.'

'That's well,' said William, and for all he kept his eyes on the deceptive stillness below in the river valley, he listened yet. There was more news than that in the voice.

'And, my lord – ' The boy's fair head leaned closer to whisper: ' – they're three, not two, within there.'

William turned his head then for a moment, to cast one steel-bright glance into the gleeful face. The archers manning the wall moved at no great distance; he eyed them thoughtfully and questioned from motionless lips: 'The third?'

'My lord, when the alarm began the old blind man was at his exercise. Those who were watching the archway forgot him and ran with the rest, and he heard and followed. I saw him hanging on the edge of the crowd, he'd know who it was we had at the end of the lances, and where they were bound. I did not see him or think of him again till we were circling the church. I was first round to the south door, and I saw what no other saw.' Smiling, sure of his ground, he dropped the words softly into the waiting ear that inclined to him. 'He's gone to her. I saw him enter. He's sealed up in the church with the plague-carriers.'

A moment of silence, while William's bearded face kept its stony calm; then a sharp gleam of interest and gratification showed for an instant in his eyes. Low-voiced, he asked:

'You are sure?'

'Sure, my lord.'

'And no one else marked him?'

'No one, my lord. They had no eyes for anything but the business they were about.'

No one. No one but clever Thomas, who had such sharp eyes, and knew so well how to make use of what they saw to ingratiate himself with his master.

'And you've said no word to any but me?'

'No, my lord, I swear it.'

'No need, boy, no need. Your word is enough. So this is private between us two. And we've seen nothing – eh, Thomas?'

'Nothing, my lord. When they venture at last to come and confess they've lost their charge I shall be trembling with them.'

'That's my own Thomas! I shan't forget your devotion.'

'My lord, I serve as I can.'

'And you shall not lack your reward. Come to me tonight, to the tower, and you shall have present earnest of my favour. Come privately and early, before de Guichet reports to me. I would not have him made privy to what you and I know.'

'Trust me, my lord! Two who have seen nothing is better reckoning than three.

And there went a happy man, secure in his duty well done and his lord's gratitude well earned. What better could one wish him than to keep that high content of heart to his life's end?

The hand that pointed down towards the Welsh fires in the valley, the same hand that had bestowed the lavish gift on him only a few moments since, scooped suddenly along the rim of the embrasure between the merlons, where the white of the latest fall lay thick, and flew to clamp like steel over his face, filling mouth and nostrils with frozen snow. The arm that had leaned so flatteringly upon his shoulders dropped to grip him about the thighs and heave him from his feet. He had no time even to claw at the stone as he was hoisted over it. He fell without so much as a cry, choking on startling coldness. He fell with the words of commendation and affection still quick in his ears.

William leaned over and looked down into the dark, faintly silvered with starlight before the rise of the moon. He stroked his sleeves into order, and listened for the impact below, but it was long in coming and dull and muffled when it came; he doubted if it would reach any other ears. He smoothed out at leisure the long tracks of his fingers in the snow, modelling the edge to its old sharp ridge, filed by the wind. The Lady's Tower stood sheer above the cliff; only the Welsh, far below there where the cover of bushes and trees began, were likely to stumble on the remains of Thomas Blount, and wonder how he had been ushered out of the world. A pity about the clasp, he need not have been so over-generous. Some tribesman would be swaggering with gold fasteners to his tattered cloak within the week.

A pity, but no matter. And now let any other charge me that I knew and connived at my father's self-murder. I am clean. The obstinate old fool refused to die an open, blameless death becoming his age; this was his own choice. Who am I to cross my father's wishes? Am I his seneschal, that I should break in on his devotions? Am I his confessor, that I should stand between him and his mistress? Did I give any orders concerning him, except to enlarge his liberty? Was I there when he hid himself in the church? All Parfois knows I was not. I have seen nothing, I know nothing.

And one, Thomas, one is better than two.

He was pacing the leads of the tower, heavy and preoccupied and alone as was his blameless habit at this hour, when de Guichet came up to make his nightly report.

Benedetta came in from the west porch dragging wearily, cramped with the ache of half-carrying the dying man; but when she stepped within and the praying hands of the nave arched over her she was drawn erect, and opened her lips and drank her fill of the inexhaustible radiance of the air within that space.

Beneath the altar the singing children on the great stone frontal filled their sturdy young lungs, and lifted to the light rapt, delightful faces and earnest, bawling mouths round as rosy apples. Above them the great lancets soared like launched arrows. The length of the nave the fluted pillars burgeoned into the wonderful, coiling, clustering, living leaves, the leaves of the holy tree, the tree of hope, the tree of affirmation, the tree of love. Out of their quivering tension of energy the ribs of the roof sprang, arched to contain the great charged space that was the shape of beauty and prayer; and at the roof-rib they met, and the glowing bosses that bound them were like notes of music, cries of joy, the inaudible sound of the warmth of hands clasping.

The hammers had ceased their wood-pecking chorus at the outer doors, the grave-diggers were gone; softer sounds could come in to her now, a hungry calling of birds, cold and plaintive, a snatch of drunken song from one of the outposts along the escarpment, the slow, hesitant steps of a man, leather feeling its way upon stone.

She raised her head intently then, for that sound was close and strange, and before her, not behind. Paulinus could not have passed her, she would have known; nor did she believe that he would ever walk thus steadily and firmly again. But there was no other man; there could be none. She waited, and the steps resumed, halted again, waited as with breath held to match her waiting.

And then she saw him. He had come from the south porch, and stood so matched with one of the slender, springing uprights of the rood-screen that until he stirred she could not find him. Tall, lean to emaciation, sombre in browns, gold at his belt and his breast, the ageless body still erect as a larch, the head still wonderful, shapely, proud. Not even age could spoil those immortal shapes of bone, or deface the immaculate fit of the cap of iron-grey hair over the lofty skull. The face, fleshless and still, quested upon the air blindly, straining after her. It had a terrible and admirable patience, that sat strangely in its humility and simplicity upon those arrogant and splendid features. He was not marred, but for the darkening of the deep eyes, torches burned out and blackened to charcoal under the high bronze brow.

'My lord?'

The vault took her low voice and filled every corner with it, as though the stone spoke.

He turned his blind, searching stare instantly upon her. She saw the face full; she saw the quenched eyes find her, she saw the long lips smile.

'My lady!' He loosed his hold upon the screen, and with reared head and intent face came towards her; but still at some little distance he halted and waited again of courtesy, lest he should seem to lay claim to her, who had no claim now upon anything in the world that was not given out of charity.

'My lord, what are you doing here?'

'My lady, listening to your voice and praising God. And, as I think, dying.'

The same voice, the old voice, but of its own will it had relinquished command and turned within, to the argument of the soul. Not in penitence: she had seen penitents, and this was none. But the breaking of age he accepted for experience and profit with as sincere a passion as the making of youth, and that which was strange and new to him, even humiliation and death, he took and examined with whole-hearted curiosity, and never drew back. Penitents recoil; he went forward, and what he let fall by the way was sloughed because he outgrew it, and not because he repented of it.

'Praise be to God, you cannot send me away. Touch me,'

he said, smiling, 'breathe on me, give me your contagion.'

'Why have you thrown your life away?' she said, sharp with protest and reproach. 'Were not two of us enough?'

'I have not thrown it away. I'll keep it as best I may, as long as I may. I have only laid it where God may take it if he will; and if he spare, I'll take it up gladly and carry it yet a mile or two more. Will you not take my hand, Benedetta?'

At the sound of her name in his mouth she started, as if someone long absent had called her; and she laid her hand in his because she could not leave it lying thus patient and empty in air. But at the closing of his long, lean fingers she achieved again the visitation of peace.

He had chosen to die with her; that she knew. And blind though he might be, this at least he had done with open eyes. No man would bring them food or water now, no one would open the doors to them. Parfois could not be starved out fast enough to save them, nor did she believe it could yet be taken by storm. And what she knew, he knew better, for he was Parfois, the blood and the life of it, whoever had wrested it from him.

'This is the only place,' he said, 'large enough to contain me upright, and provide me breath enough to fill my body. Don't grudge me this escape, I've been in strait keeping long enough. Moreover, you have a sick man to care for, and good need of one like me, who carries his own plagues and fears no other. Where have you left him?'

'In the porch. I could not get him farther. I came to see what provision I could make for him.'

'We have a world,' said Isambard, turning his blind gaze at large about his last barony. 'We have the house of the archangels, and the forests of heaven. Chapels enough to choose from for his death-bed and your bower, privacy at need, and a place of meeting, the most beautiful in England. Praise God, in my day I made good endowments, whether for piety or pride God best knows, but we have the benefit of it now. There's a chest full of vestments and altar-cloths and draperies. Come, take what you need for his bed, and choose where you'll have it laid, and I'll carry him there. Is it plague?' He loosed her hand, he moved before her with assurance in his own best kingdom, and looked back with a crooked smile when she was slow to answer. 'To God and me it's all one. I do but ask.'

'I think,' she said, following him, 'he brought some fluctuating fever with him from the east, and has some aggravation of it now from a poison in his food. But it's enough. For I think he will die.'

'So shall we all, bond and free,' said Isambard. 'There's nothing there for grieving. But at least let him die covered and warm. It will be bitter cold here by night.'

He brought her to the great, carved chest that held the trappings of the altar, with the assurance of one who knew every worn place in every stone about this church of his. He lifted the lid, and turned the eternal questioning of his blind face upon her.

'Take what you will.'

She did not hesitate to fill her arms. 'He's plagued by thirst. He was groaning for water.'

'We have water,' he said instantly. 'There's water in the stoups, at least the walls keep out the frost. Better, we have wine. There's wine in the sacristy. Pity indeed we have no food. But if he'll die the more gently drunk than sober, in God's name, why not? I think the mercy of heaven would not hold it against him that his last act of contrition was a little thick on the tongue. Come, see where you'll have him laid, and I'll bring him there. I lack nothing but eyes. Hands I have, make use of them how you will.'

And so she did, moving side by side with him in dreamlike simplicity about the business of living and dying. Together they piled a broad bed of tapestries and brocades and embroideries in the small chantry chapel to southward of the high altar, walled round every way from draughts, where their shared warmth could at least temper the bitter cold. Together they carried Paulinus of Reichenau and laid him there, and wrapped him in such velvets as had never before touched that worn and venturesome skin of his. Together they took chalices of wine and candles from the sacristy, and bore them to their sanctuary against the falling night. He fumbled flint and steel doggedly in his hands, but she took them from him, and herself blew upon the spark that caught the tinder, and fanned it into a small, quick flame. It went to her heart that he should think of light for them, he who had no further need of light.

'There's a cresset-stone in the choir yonder, and another within the west door, but I doubt if there's oil beyond what's left in them. They keep the oil outside. The smaller I could bring here into the corner. It would give warmth as well as light.'

He brought it, dragging it after him upon a length of velvet, for fear it should scratch or crack Master Harry's tiles. It had thirteen cups, and was carved between them with a deep-cut tracery of vine-leaves.

'His making,' said Isambard, smoothing his fingertips gently along the coiling stems, 'like all here. All we have is twice-borrowed, once from God, like our lives from the beginning, and once from him. Shall we light it? Lend me your eyes, I am not to be trusted with fire.'

'If this is all we have,' she said practically, 'we might do well to spare it for a worse time. We shall be here long enough.'

He turned his questing face a little, as though he looked upon the sick man, who lay open-eyed and shivering and mute in his princely wrappings. The rattle of his breath and the burning of his flesh spoke eloquently even to one without eyes.

'We shall. But his time, as I think, is short. Keep it, then, until his need is at its sharpest.' He measured the oil in the shallow round cups with a fastidious fingertip, and wiped away the smoky smear upon scarlet and gold embroideries. 'There's little enough we can do for him, but we can spare him a death in the dark.' He smiled, feeling her sharp and rueful glance upon him. '*I* shall not need it, that's true enough. What's darkness to me? I habit with darkness, I have no fear of it. I have no fear, Benedetta,' he said, soft-voiced and still, 'of anything except that I may yet awaken in some other place, without you, and know that this was something I dreamed in my captivity.'

'It is no dream,' she said, her voice shaken and low. 'I am here, and you I know by sight and touch to be very man. And I think we shall not be divided now, for good or ill, as long as we live.'

'You comfort me,' he said.

Where were they now, the years that had set them apart body and mind and spirit, the tensions and the terrors, the spites and the revenges? Where were they gone, the irrevocable memories of wrong and grief, the love unpaid, the injuries unrequited? They moved in tranquillity about the furnishing of their last household and the cherishing of their last guest, and felt no need to speak of the past; mutually forgiven, if this was forgiveness that looked back now and felt no sting, with nothing asked or answered, nothing atoned for.

They were far beyond any such needs, spent into quietness, all hatreds and distresses burned out. And all loves, too? God knew! Love has so many faces.

Paulinus of Reichenau lay for two days and two nights in high fever, while the flesh steamed and pared away from his shaking bones, and the two who nursed him watched over him without pause and held him swathed in his covers. On the third day the fever ebbed before the near approach of death, and he opened his eyes wonderingly upon the strange paradise of his cell. The slender stone pillars of the chapel arched above him into a vault like a double star. He was wrapped in velvets and silks, purple and gold and rich blue like colours for a king. Candles burned beside him on tall candlesticks of iron, and in the corner the cresset-stone sent up its thirteen small, straight flames out of the last inch of oil. The faint smell of smoke touched nostrils that knew nothing of the stench of his own sweat and sickness, and set them quivering. On one side the woman sat cradling his hand in hers. On the other an unknown man with the lofty and far-looking face of death gazed down at him with hooded eyes that had no radiance; but the austere counten-ance was calm and did not threaten. Nevertheless, he was afraid.

He whispered his need, and the woman leaned to listen close, for his voice was no more than a thread, frayed almost away to silence.

'A priest – I'm heavy with this load.'

'Here's no priest,' said Benedetta, 'only God. Speak to me, and never fear. He has sharper ears than mine.'

With all the strength of his clinging to her hand, it seemed to her she nursed only the claw of a dead bird. Close to the final silence he found a voice that had more substance than his dwindling body.

'I have not been a great sinner – only a persevering one – I studied hard to improve.'

He saw her smile, and was appeased. However sorry a creature man may be, he should think shame to think shame of what his maker made. Himself to the end, he made his wry confession word by word as his strength served, and drew it out long.

'Even this rood of mine – a fake, but a good fake – my own work. To tell truth, it was a morsel of a wine-cask from Angers. My lord Isambard – would never have known the difference. All these lordlings are fools –'

The man who stood brooding beside him put back his head and laughed aloud, like a boon companion over a tavern tale, like a pleased child at the fall of a pompous knight into the kennel on a muddy day. If death could laugh like that, what was there to fear? Startled and warmed, Paulinus essayed to echo the laugh, and choked on it feebly. She lifted him, and he died on her arm, as easily as snuffing out the last candle.

'He's gone,' she said, and she was glad, for he was not made for hard dying.

They said the prayers for him together; and then with one of the giant iron candle-spikes for a crow Isambard opened the two-year-old grave of old Father Hubert in the choir, and there beside the chaplain of Parfois they laid the renegade monk and peddler of relics, and there buried him.

'I doubt if the old man would relish the company,' said Isambard, straightening flushed and breathless from the lowering of the stone, 'but if he will not give him a night's shelter in his house he's no Christian. God rest him! To die laughing is no bad death!'

And then they were alone.

'What is it?' asked Benedetta, waking in the night to the long, low rumbling echoes of rock shifting and falling.

'Nothing to fright us. Only the Welsh moles gnawing away the foundations from under Parfois.' He drew the covers up more closely round her, and stroked back the coils of heavy hair from her thin and fallen cheek. 'Many more such bites, and they'll bring down the walls. The weight of the gate-towers could well be their downfall. And there the gully is shallowest. If the gate-house falls, the wall is breached and they have a ladder to reach it by.'

'What if they bring down towers and rock on themselves?' she whispered, aghast.

'For shame, my heart! Can you not trust Adam Boteler to know his business? How many years did he quarry stone for me in Bryn, and did you ever hear of his losing a man that way?'

She turned her mind back with wonder and effort to the stresses convulsing the outer world, where armies clashed and princes still contended. 'Can they speed so? Is it possible to take Parfois this way?'

'Rankly impossible. But so it was to breach and drain the well, and they did it. Who knows if they will confound prophecy a second time?' The faintly-drawn breath that warmed his throat was even and calm, her body tranquil in his arms, but for fear she should fall back into the torment of hope he said with careful gentleness: 'It cannot come in time to deliver us, my heart. We must not trust in it.'

'I am content,' she said. 'I look for no deliverance.'

Did she even desire it now? She looked into her heart, and could find there no desires at all, except, perhaps, the impossible longing to see the boy again. Yet they had tried to deliver themselves, day after day, as creatures in duty bound to live if they could, she the eyes and he the hands probing every cranny of their prison; but every door was sealed and every lower window securely barred, and there was no way out. The search had helped them during the worst days, when they were still strong and hunger was at its sharpest, courteously to conceal from each other the gnawings of the wolves within. The pack had drawn off now, sated, leaving behind the dullest of aches, and a languor that told them their days were beginning to draw in. By night they lay clenched fast in each other's arms, with the mutual chaste kindness of their bodies staying each other between the hours of shallow and dream-filled sleep.

'Forgive me,' said Isambard, 'for bringing you to this. God knows you owed me no second death.'

'I came of my own will,' she said. 'There is nothing to forgive. It was I asked you to open your doors to me again, you did but grant my asking. More than my asking! I never ventured to suppose I should be taken back even into your bed.'

The wry mouth pressed against her hair shook for a moment with a tremor of laughter, as brief as it was silent. 'Ah, Benedetta! Ah, Benedetta! I never dared to hope you would come. Girl, I meant to give him to you freely. I would have brought him, all unsuspecting, to meet you at the gate. You need not even have crossed my threshold, unless you pleased to do me so much honour of your own grace.'

'I do believe it. All the same, I think I should have come in. And delivered you the price I offered for him, whether you would or no.'

'Because you are of the boy's mind, and would not be beholden to me?' he asked ruefully. 'Or because I was old and threatened and blind, and you pitied me?'

'Pitied you? No, I was never so far out in my reckoning as that. Rather because I was ageing and secure and barren without you. And because I had it in my heart that it was time, and that you were come to the same crossroad where

245

I stood. I could not get it out of my mind that there was still something you and I had to set about doing together, before the tale of our days was made up. I did not know it was dying. But liefer with you than with any,' she said, speaking her mind with the old large and resolute generosity.

She had always a princely way with words. He would have borrowed that for his tombstone, he thought, if there had been a mason by to cut it for him. Liefer with you than with any! Living, dying, my best and dearest, in heaven or hell or where you will, liefer with you than with any!

'Benedetta!'

'My lord?'

'Hear me a word or two, here in the night, and be as blind to me while I speak as I am to you. I have yet somewhat on my heart.'

'I am listening,' she said. 'I am blind.'

'You have never asked me,' said Isambard, his voice level and low beside her in the dark, 'what I did with him when I snatched him out of his grave.'

She lay still, her breath held for an instant; it came so suddenly and softly upon her, like the drawing of a curtain from between her and the light. Thus she had lain, roused and wakeful, with Harry in her arms, and death waiting its hour without impatience at the door. Time had completed another immeasurable circle, and restored the lost balance of love.

'I know what you did with him,' she said simply. 'He is where he should be. He is here with us, under the altar.'

A deep sigh ebbed out of him; the clasp of his hands softened. He did not ask how she knew. In this marvellous eloquence of silence and stillness where was the need? At every breath they drew in knowledge and reassurance until all questions fell away like shadows from the brightness.

'I opened the tomb alone,' he said after a long, charmed while of quietness, 'with these hands. It was to have been mine, but I ceded it to him as having the better right. With one of his own iron crows I raised the stone, and mighty

246

surprised I was to see how much thought and engineering must go to the act if one man takes it on himself alone. In these arms I lifted him down to his true place, and gave him cloth of gold to lie in, and covered him to his rest.'

She felt the passion that quickened in the stillness of his long hands, as though in this moment they embraced not her wasted and withering flesh, but Harry's young, slender, stubborn bones.

'I know it was your wish,' said Isambard with bitter compunction, 'that the hands of love should some day lay him there. For that at least forgive me.'

'No need,' said Benedetta. 'I am content.'

His fingertips moved softly over her face, lingering on her lips. 'You are smiling,' he said, marvelling.

'Would you rather I wept?' she said. 'I could weep.'

'Ah, no! When did I ever see you weep? You laughed when you struck me down and went to him. You laughed when you were dragged to your death for him.'

'I wept when they dragged me back to life.'

'It may well be. Life without him was no such wonderful matter. God knows, girl, whether I more grudged you to him or him to you. Since he died I never could take pleasure in any man's death. I never shed blood but it was his blood, never hanged even the meanest felon but it was Harry's neck they roped. I never came to the point of distraining on a tenant or flogging a villein but I heard him out-arguing me, and drew in my hand. If I forgot how his face looked, it confronted me endlessly here, and if I forgot the pleasure and excitement he had in other men, I saw it again in the stones of this house, and there was no escape from it. He has been a contagion in my blood, he who could not leave hewing and carving even when he was dead. Many a time have I cursed him for it and struggled to be rid of him, but I never could.

'And I knew I had destroyed him. And for all I could feel no guilt, I knew I had robbed the world and maimed myself. Against his life taken I had nothing to set but my own. And if it was forfeit I willed to pay it, but I had no clarity in me to judge, and no heart to surrender cravenly what might not be due, even though I had no joy in it. But as I might I offered it where God might take it at will, and never shut my hand on it to snatch it back. And time and again he let it lie. And this is strange, Benedetta, that as often as I offered it to be taken I valued and wanted it the more. Dead, Harry taught me how to love life, and I learned hard. The dearer it grew to me, the greater agony it cost me, still to expose it, but I would not withdraw. So it may be I have paid, take it all in all, somewhat of my debts.'

In the momentary silence the fabric of the church and the rock beneath it quivered to another slow, rumbling fall, and they held their breath and listened until it was spent.

'Benedetta!' he felt with searching fingers along her cheek as the tremor stilled, and touched eyelids still fast closed; but the lashes were wet. 'Ah, my heart, not for me! Why?'

'Go on,' she said, her voice no more than a breath caught and held gently in the palm of his hand. 'You had yet more to say to me.'

'To you or to God. But God knows it all before I speak. And now I see that there is little enough of me you do not know.' Nevertheless he resumed softly, with long pauses, as though the crowding memories caught him away even from her into wonder and forgetfulness.

'And then the boy came. Here in this place he appeared before me suddenly, the mould and pattern of his sire. I could not let him go. I had to find out if the same mettle was there, if I was living this agony to no purpose, if God was fooling me. I never struck him but once, when he willed to throw his own life away so he could take mine – and he fifteen years old, and all this dear world his for the taking, and to value it so little! But in his heart I think he was glad even to take my blows, and know by the sting he was well alive. I never had to teach him so again, but in my fashion I used him hard. Sometimes I rapped him harder than I knew, but always he rang true. I knocked him, and he knocked me as best he could, but never could I tame him. And at the end of it the wheel came round full, for like his father before him he staked his own liberty and life to stand by a threatened child that was nothing to him. And this time – oh, Benedetta, conceive it! – this time I was the child! I gave him his liberty, I bade him go. And he would not! Out of care for me, out of fear for me, because I was blind and open to my enemies, he would not leave me.'

The long night was passing, the first faint glimmer of shape and proportion gathered and grew over their heads. Before there was vision there was form, the enlargement of peace, the impress of tranquillity. In a while the tension of the vaulting would spring into their consciousness; she would see it, and he through his hands and his body and his blood would feel and remember what she saw, and share her delight. The detail would come later, the light carving it afresh with every dawn.

'Now I have lived a miracle, I know how softly and naturally they come forth upon the world. I was Harry's against my will, and Harry is mine against his will. Not a small part of what he knows I have taught him. What he is, in part I have made him. I am in his blood as his father has been in mine. And please God, to as faithful an ending. For of all the good I have to bequeath, God be my witness, I have made him the heir. And only God knows,' said Isambard, smiling in his assuaged repose of joy, 'how I have prized and loved him.'

She opened her eyes upon the noon light, and reflected sunshine quivering in the vault of the nave. The angels in the bosses cried aloud to God, arching their golden wings.

She lay in the soiled wealth of brocades and silks, her face a wisp of whiteness drawn over staring cheek-bones, and a great, rapt shining of eyes, her body a little armful of bones, the skeleton shining through the skin. The heaven of light leaned to her, tremulous as gossamer, durable as stone. No, more lasting than that, long as memory, durable as love.

For the achievement was not in the stone, though the stone had burst into flower under his hands. If the shell that holds this shape of splendour were broken and lost, she said in her heart, marvelling, yet this miracle would be here for ever, because he once conceived it and made it live. As the soul outwears the body, his work will outwear the stone. Eyes that have once seen it see all things differently thereafter, having learned the measure of wholeness. And what we have learned we surely transmit to others, and what we have received of revelation somehow we give again, in a perpetual laying on of hands. Shatter this church, and still in some secret measure Harry will have changed the world.

Most marvellous of all it was, to her audacious spirit, to see that perfection is not the end of energy, nor peace the end of venturing. Both are beginnings, and not of stagnation or weariness, but of some inconceivable ardour of passion that draws out the powers to their highest, and lengthens the longings of the heart beyond the last limitation of knowledge. They acknowledge no limitation; they are prolonged to infinity; time has no meaning for them, now is forever, here is everywhere. Go nowhere, make no more effort, wait, here all things come to you, enter into you, are one with you.

Her mind lay clear and still like a pool of mountain water in her wasted and enfeebled body, reflecting the vibrant changes of the light. Often she dreamed of water since the stoups had run dry, for all their austere husbandry, and left them only a dwindling drop of wine to keep off thirst. She moved now only when she must; she slept often, and dreamed much. She knew the brevity of her powers, and hoarded them for the efforts that must be made. The effort of re-coiling and pinning her great burden of hair exhausted her, speech hung heavy as lead, her garments had the weight of the world. She refuged in stillness, and her spirit lay open to wonder. Wait, go nowhere, here all things come to you and are one with you.

She put out a shrunken hand and felt for Isambard beside her, her eyes still dazzled with the heaven of ecstatic light that drew her upwards into the vault. No quick, careful hand came to meet her touch. She looked round then, the contours of earthly things shaking into clarity again about her, the tracery of the chantry, the cresset-stone, long ago darkened, the sultry, rich colourings of the bed, here in shadow. Isambard was gone from beside her. How long had she lacked him? For time she had no memory; she knew only that this must be the height of the day, but of what day only God knew.

She lay listening, and there were sounds that quickened a chord somewhere in her heart, and touched some instant recollection of solemnity and pity. The grating of metal against stone, a long, heaving breath that halted on intense silence, a gusty panting that ebbed in a groan of effort and relief. A pause, and again the probing and prising under the stone, and this time by an inch it slid from its place, she heard stone and stone engage. She understood then. He had left her sleeping, and gone to open a grave for her.

He cannot, alone, she thought, dismayed, and caught at the slender, springing pillars of the chantry to drag herself upright. He'll break bones and heart, and die.

Clasping and embracing her way from pillar to pillar, she brought herself out of the chapel into the choir, and instinctively turned her eyes to the spot where old Father Hubert's tomb sheltered his unexpected guest from Reichenau. Where else should he look for a resting-place for her? The stone was hardly settled yet, and could be turned back against the solid wood of the stalls without overmuch risk of breakage. But the corner was empty and still, the stone undisturbed. Higher, towards the altar, inch by inch another stone was levered carefully from its place. She heard the deep gasps of effort fetched up from a labouring heart, the long pauses between, while he gathered his body for one more assault. And without sight, his fingers painfully and patiently and perilously serving him for eyes! Her own eyes filled and dazzled for him, she who never wept. She groped her way towards him, holding by the stalls, and at the steps of the presbytery her meagre tears dried and left her vision clear, and she saw him.

The brief, chill sunlight, bright and hard as ice, poured

251

through the lancets of the east window and spilled jewels upon the paving of the floor. In the cascade of green and gold and scarlet Isambard lay face-down over his improvised tools, heaving exhausted breaths into his body. He had broken two of the heavy candle-spikes, and torn and rasped his own fingers to the already starting bone; but he had done what he had set out to do.

Under the high altar, under the great frontal with its singing children, the centre stone was levered aside upon its fellows, and the shimmering stars and lozenges of light fell glittering like winter flowers into the stone-lined pit of Harry Talvace's grave.

Her body failed her at the steps, and brought her to her knees; and on her knees she dragged herself to his side across the bright waste. For the pounding of blood in his ears he did not hear her come; he lay panting, his spread hand dangling a drop of blood over the rim of the tomb, his brow against the stone. Only when she laid her hand on him did he raise his head and show her the bright, fierce ruin of his beauty, the faded, ambiguous mask of devil and angel yellow as brass, the quenched eyes mute under their lofty, fleshless lids, all the petrified splendour of death, yet with life and passion blazing through it to the end.

'And will you send me back,' she said, touching his dusty brow with feeble fingers like the stems of withered flowers, 'to be his bedfellow again?'

'Where else?' he said. 'Where else should I lay you? If you go before, make my peace – make my peace!'

He laid his head in her lap and wound his skeleton arms about her, and so lay still. She cradled the rough grey crown of hair in her hands, and over his shoulders she looked into the grave. It was not so deep, she saw the stone lining bone-dry in the withering cold, and the sheen of the cloth of gold almost untarnished. She saw the slender little bones outlined in that glowing shroud, the quiet head that showed through its princely veil the soft, muted form of a sleeping face. She thought of the cell beneath Parfois, and the dark, dear head heavy on her breast all the night through.

252

She took Isambard's head between her wasted hands and lifted his face to her, and kissed him on the brow.

'You wanted his heart once,' she said. 'Put in your hand and take it. He would not grudge it to you now.'

CHAPTER TEN

Parfois: *December* 1233 *to January* 1234

For three days the fire burned in the rock beneath Parfois. They heard from the walk between the gate-towers, in the quiet of the night, the busy, muffled crackling of brushwood and branches, and the rushing and roaring of wind as the flames devoured the air; and by day, though these sounds were buried and lost beneath the ordinary commotion of life under siege, they had other signs to keep the prodigy in mind. For on the first morning, before the dawn had even a flush of colour to brighten it, one of the guard had run bellowing to his officer that smoke was belching from the empty well-shaft, that hell was boiling beneath Parfois, and the day of judgement upon them. They burst in upon William Isambard with the same wild story, and he cursed them for fools, but he ran to see. Adam's chimney fumed to the leaden sky, spitting hot air aloft in a column of blackness, and the crackling of flaming thorn from deep within the rock terrified them with threats of demons. By night there was a faint glow over the shaft, to redouble their uneasiness. Argue and reason as he might, William could not reassure his garrison that these were natural portents; and when he had shut himself in his own bedchamber with his thoughts he himself found small comfort there.

The sharp, withering wind in the funnel of the ravine served Llewelyn well, and kept the fire ablaze at intense heat longer than Adam had dared to hope. On the second night Parfois shook to the sudden, rumbling falls in the heart of the rock. Only then did they begin to understand what was happening to their stronghold. The earth under their feet quaked. In dread they moved about their labours on the threatened ground, trying to keep their very weight from falling too heavily, lowering their voices for fear the shock of a cry might set the walls tumbling. Smoke rolled along the gully and hid the valley from them. The frozen brook flowed again, but daily now it changed its course as the gradual landslips settled, and nightly the frost climbed again to silence a few more feet of water, as the fire burned down and the rock cooled.

On the fourth night the frost came into its own, gripping with ferocity where the fire had already ravaged. It was the twenty-second of December, and the hardest night of the winter. Towards morning all Parfois leaped from its bed in terror to the grinding roar of rock and masonry collapsing together, as the cliff-face split like thunder beneath the gate-house, and the western tower, the foundations ripped away from under it, burst from base to roof, and crashed forty feet into the gully. The eastern tower still stood, the bridge lurching drunkenly from one chain; but the walls had sagged out of true, and cracked in jagged lightning slashes, and beneath them the smoking dust of the fall parted on the wind to disclose great slabs of rock hanging percariously, ready to shift at a touch.

William drew out the survivors, and beat and cursed his shocked garrison to work rigging a new bridge, reinforcing the lower guard, and manning the breach with every creature they had who could bear arms, feverishly expectant that Llewelyn would press his assault while they were in con-fusion. But whatever the temptations, Adam knew better than that, and Llewelyn was wise enough to be schooled in a business which was new to him. The rock was hardly cold yet; there would be fresh falls before the day was out, and to set men to scaling that quaking, choking mass before it had had at least a day to settle was to invite their deaths. So William had his day's grace, and time to think over the impregnability of his Parfois.

He gnawed his knuckles on his tower, feeling the lofty mass vibrate beneath him still. It was time to admit the doubt that had never been real until now. The wall was breached, the well pierced, his garrison shaken to the heart.

255

He stared into a morrow as bleak as the frozen valley below. If Parfois should hold he might yet carry all with him, secure his honour in the teeth of Humphrey Paunton's distrust – what was his error there, what had made the old fool at Fleace bristle and demand sureties? – discover the third body in the plague-church with loud and convincing innocence and grief, bury him publicly and honourably, and have the king's blessing still, and the king's protecting shadow to justify him. With Henry's commisssion instructing him, with England's borders to lose or save, that dispossession could hardly be questioned. And how could he know, when the old dotard slipped his collar and vanished during the alarm, where he had chosen to hide himself? How could he seek him beyond the walls of Parfois, when he was close beset here, with a tight Welsh cordon drawn round him? Had he not believed him fallen from the rock in his blindness, and grieved for him as dead? He had taken enough pains to establish the image of his filial anxiety. Could he have known that he was in the church? No one could accuse him, he had seen to that. No, if Parfois held, if he remained profitable to the king and kept his castle, all things would march yet.

But here he was, brought up newly and coldly against the knowledge that Parfois could fall.

And then? If Llewelyn captured Parfois, if Llewelyn opened the sealed church, what then? He would raise such an outcry over the body of Ralf Isambard that no counter-eloquence would ever be able quite to silence the first scream of parricide. The nice presentation of the case William had ready at his finger-ends would be shattered from the beginning, his cause lost before ever it was heard. The very suspicion would be enough to undo him. The old man had known well enough what he was talking about when he had said that Henry would take away his arm and leave his servant to pay the score alone at the first breath of scandal. There would be no future for the man at whom the prince of Aberffraw had flung the accusation of parricide. He heard his father's voice still, infuriatingly confident and amused, saying: 'He'll hound you to the day of your death if you compromise him.'

The resolution hardened within him that the bodies in the church must never be found, never at least in their own recognizable shapes. Could he have the doors unsealed and the dead secretly buried? No, the garrison would break if he added the renewed dread of plague to the terrors they already suffered.

But since the Welsh had made use of fire, why should he not borrow from them, and credit them with the invention? There was woodwork enough within the church; in this frost it should blaze no less merrily than Llewelyn's underground furnace. There was oil in store there close beside it, oil for the cressets and the lamps. The wind was westerly and keen. Two or three men, chosen for their thick heads, could do the work for him well enough from the western windows, without entering, and believe they were purging the last threat of plague. And let Llewelyn make what he would of the charred, unrecognisable bones.

Before dawn on Christmas Eve Llewelyn's camp, roused and in arms in readiness for the assault, looked up at maimed Parfois to see a new, tall tongue of flame soar on the wind, and unfurl into a long, streaming banner fringed with smoke. They straightened and stared; Llewelyn came out from his pavilion in haste at the alarm, and Harry, half-armed, ran with a cry of desolation and fury to clutch at Adam's arm.

'The church! Adam, they've fired the church!'

Like a torch, like a beacon, Master Harry's noble tower sprang upon the murky dawn, filled with angry light, and from its highest windows the wavering banneroles of flame streamed westwards upon a veering wind like long red-gold hair.

On that Christmas Eve they took Parfois.

The three-pronged attack had been planned with precision, but it was put into action some hours before the time

257

intended, and in fierce haste. Llewelyn with something less than one-third of his total forces developed at last the frontal attack so long expected, and with no preliminary dawn battering by his engines of war the ranks of his knights drove hard at the tower and barricades of the lower guard. David with his companies had climbed into the mouth of the gully from the east during the hours of darkness, and turned loose his best archers to find for themselves niches in the rock from which they could command the jagged breach in the wall above, and pick off any defenders who exposed themselves there; for the greatest danger to the assault party would be the insecurity of their ground, the shifting mass that could all too easily be set rolling again by one boulder thrust over the edge. The rest of David's men lay close in what cover they could find, ready to press home a second wave of attack as soon as their comrades from the west had made the ascent. These, the main body of the assault, held off until the alarm on the ramp had drawn reinforcements tumbling in haste over the improvised bridge to fend off Llewelyn's repeated and damaging charges, and the clamour from among the trees had reached the steady, savage music of a pitched battle. Then Owen loosed them, and they broke cover and swarmed upwards into the gully of torn and tumbled rock.

Harry was the first to reach the treacherous fringes of the fall, and he set foot on the shifting rubble of rock without hesitation, and pressed on against the steep slope towards the breach in the wall. The defenders above were chary of approaching the edge of the fall too closely for fear of its rottenness, and from their more withdrawn stations their marksmanship was none too accurate. He was in greater danger from the quaking ladder of rock he climbed than from the enemy above. Twice he set foot on a hold that gave under him and brought him down, and once he started a terrifying slide, and would have gone down with it to grind his bones in the jostling rocks below if someone labouring close at his elbow had not snatched him aside and clung over him grimly by head and hands and splayed feet until the dust subsided and the quaking surface stilled.

'Gently, now, gently!' said Adam's voice in his ear. 'Keep your father's son alive, boy, and let the church wait.'

He wondered then, with the corner of his mind he could spare for the exercise, what Adam was doing there so opportunely at his elbow, Adam who was engineer rather than soldier, and had no business to be storming the breach with the men-at-arms. But he had no time for more than a quick glance and a breathless word, and then he was up and climbing again like a squirrel.

If de Guichet's men in the ward above them had not feared to venture close to the rim they might, with some losses to themselves, have stood off greater numbers than Owen brought against them, for they had but to start the nearest stones rolling, and they could have swept the Welshmen down like pebbles in a torrent. But their spirits were shaken and low, the hard earth of the outer ward was ripped apart by cracks that widened perceptibly at every shock, and they had but to set foot on this crazed surface to feel it quake beneath them. Not until Harry and the foremost of his fellows were groping for foot- and hand-holds to clamber over the crumbling rim did the defenders discard one terror under pressure from a greater, and the boldest leaped to slash at the spead hands and undefended heads that heaved over the edge into their vision, and prise loose the boulders and blocks of masonry that hung balanced on the edge of the fall.

They had left it late. The archers below, who had been waiting for them with fevered restraint, loosed gladly at every target that stood clear, and it was a rolling body, not a stone, that started the first slide. Harry missed his footing and slid a yard or two on his face, lunged upward again to see one of the blocks of hewn stone from the gate-tower rocking above him, and glimpsed de Guichet himself leaning with braced shoulder to dislodge it. For an instant they stared upon each other eye to eye through the grilles of their closed visors, and death hesitated between them. Then one of David's archers loosed without haste from a niche in the

opposite wall of the gully, and de Guichet dropped and lay
embracing his missile, one slack hand dangling. A little dust
trickled from the pressure of his wrist and ran harmlessly
down the slope like a puff of wind. The stone swung gently,
and kept its place.

Harry breathed ease after his instant of honest terror, and
scrambled aside to give the obstacle a wide berth, shouting
a warning to those below. They had not all been so fortun-
ate: he heard the clatter and roar of rocks descending, away
to his right, and prayed for David's men.

He was up now, he was over the edge in a flurry of running dust. Thick as fog it hung everywhere on the air of the
bright morning, dust and smoke and the stench of burning.
The fire had split the rock, the frost was pulverising it. The
taste of sandstone was in his throat as he launched himself
across the few yards of shattered ground and into the ranks
of Parfois. Close on his heels, as his sword engaged, the men
of Gwynedd came pouring, to keep his flanks and lend
their weight to his, to drive forward clear of the dangerous
ground, guarding at their backs an arena where their
fellows might arrive without danger.

Once the firm ground was won, Parfois was won. After
that it was but a matter of fighting forward until resistance
broke, and of never giving back a step before the desperate
rallies that sought to sweep them over the edge.

David's men came after, and more easily and carefully,
being delivered now from the most immediate peril. The
archers in the gully changed ground, and plunged across the
ravine to seek cover on the inward side, whence they could
rake the plateau of the church, or at least pick off anyone
foolish enough to expose himself near the edge. The defenders upon the walls and the towers were hampered by the close
engagement in the ward below them, where friend and foe
hung locked inextricably together, and arrows might strike
the one as indifferently as the other. Before noon it was
grown into a matter of sheer weight against weight. Buckler
to buckler, breast to breast, the Welsh thrust their way outward from the breach like ripples spreading over a pond

from a tossed pebble. They held the outer ward, and could take their time about clearing the towers. The archway to the inner ward was blocked against them stubbornly for a while, until they broke their way into the Warden's Tower and, swarming out along the wall, set their archers to raking the ground within from every angle. They drove in the gate, and they were through.

They parted company then, secure of their holding, and Owen pressed forward to clear the inner ward, while David detached half his force to turn back over the bridge, and take in the rear the companies that were still resisting Llewelyn's advance. But that battle had already broken out of the trees to the open ground of the plateau, and it needed only the alarm of David's coming to end it. The remnant of Parfois broke and ran, or dropped their weapons and surrendered themselves to any enemy who would hold his hand long enough to accept them. The castle was lost, no late heroism could retrive it now.

Harry was through the archway into the inner ward among the first, and driving hand to hand towards the Lady's Tower. Swept into the arms of the enemy, they fought across the ward in a confused mass, locked so close that they shortened their swords and used their arms like wrestlers. The confused blazonings of Parfois, the colours of knighthood and the dun of men-at-arms, danced before Harry's dazzled eyes. He thrust off strongly from the mailed shoulder that was flung against his breast, and made room before him for his blade; and the man he had thrust away caught the flash of the steel and swung instinctively, headdown, to lunge beneath the stroke. His visor and a long strip of his mail gorget were ripped away; there was blood smearing his cheek. Harry stared into the face of William Isambard.

They bristled like dogs, and in an instant they were at each other like dogs. Harry lost sight of the turmoil around him, his vision drawing in to the single struggle. They were but two left in the world and none other by, only objects that hemmed and cramped their field, frustrating the man's

261

longer reach and hampering the boy's more passionate speed and lightness.

This was a formidable swordsman, and no play, but deadly earnest; why had his heart failed in him for a moment, and let in the swinging blade so close to his hip? The build of his opponent, the long movements, the balance of the strokes that stood him off, all knocked at his senses with a familiarity that was like physical pain. This rapid recoil he knew, and the darting stroke that came out of it so unexpectedly, and the lightning lunge beneath the half-successful parry. But he knew the answers to them also. They had learned from the same master; they would see who had been the more apt and devoted pupil.

That early slash that had caused him one instant of wavering for the father's sake had drawn blood for the son. The sleeve of his banded mail hauberk had exposed his stretched wrist, and his glove was full of blood, his hilt slippery. Faces swam at him for a moment out of the press, bodies closed and hampered him, struggling movements impeded his sword arm. He shook off all, and clung with fixed, fierce eyes and darting, weaving point to his opponent. And when he felt the congestion of struggle reel away from his back he gave place by one rapid step, like one daunted or tiring. His enemy followed close, a blazing glance taking fire from the omen. Harry thrust tentatively for William's left side, and William beat off the stroke and swung suddenly with all his weight.

Harry sprang in beneath the blow, locked hilt under hilt to hold off the blade from his face, and wrenched sword and man onward together over his braced thigh. No time here, no space for the measured swing with which Isambard had once disarmed him. Instead he flung himself with all his strength upon his reeling enemy and brought him to the ground among the stamping feet, and with the weight of his body held down the arm that had not relinquished the sword. His own blade he had dropped to free his hands. His dagger was out before William could heave him off, the point pricked beneath the ear from which the covering mail was ripped away.

'Where are they?' he panted furiously. 'What have you done with them? Where is Madonna Benedetta?'

A knee heaved beneath him, driving at his belly, but the weight of William's own harness hampered him. Harry leaned on the steel hard enough to feel the flesh shrink from it.

'Where is she? And your father? Speak, or I'll kill you! If you've harmed them – '

Through his teeth William spat: 'Find them!' and hissed and moaned at the thrust of the knife-point. It bit and held; the close green glare of the eyes never wavered.

'By God, I will know! You *shall* tell me! *Where?*'

'In the church!'

The words were prised in a snarling moan from drawn-back lips tight with rage and hate. Folly, folly to have admitted to any knowledge at all! And why the truth? But the boy had death in his voice and eyes, he meant killing or knowing, and the flesh cries to live.

'The church!' said Harry, jerking upright on a horrified breath, and saw flames start again before his eyes. He let go of the stretched throat, he took his weight from the still able and treacherous arms, forgetting everything but the dread that drove him. He set foot to ground and was up in one spring, turning from his prisoner without another word or thought for him, turning to tear his way out of the press and run for the glowing shell of his father's church.

A hand lunged and took him about the ankle, bringing him down heavily and knocking the breath out of him. He rolled instinctively upon the dagger, keeping it out of reach with his own body until he could free his arm. He let the vengeful hands find his throat rather than let the dagger go, and half-blind, half-choked, he felt with clawing fingers for William's neck, and struck beneath the angle of the jaw, driving the steel home deep. Not consciously aiming to kill now, or even to wound, only to break free by the most certain way, and go to find his own.

Blood gushed streaming over his hand and arm, the body

locked with his jerked and heaved in one immense convulsion, and the hands that gripped his throat relaxed and fell away harmlessly, twitching on the ground. Still gasping, still with darkened eyes, he tore himself free and battered his way loose from the press, and ran wildly through the archway into the outer ward. There arms caught at him and held him, and for a moment he fought to break away, until he knew Adam's voice and raised great, frantic eyes to stare into his face.

'The church! They're in the church!'

'They? Who?' said Adam, springing to meet the word.

'Benedetta – and Isambard – I made him tell me – '

Then they were running together, and Harry was weeping, and did not know it, and would not have cared if he had known. Llewelyn's companies were just crossing the bridge into Parfois, gradually and cautiously for fear of putting too great a strain upon the timbers. Harry ran headlong across in the teeth of the careful riders, and caught at the prince's rein.

'My lord, my lord, he's killed them – the church – They were in the church – '

He could not speak for the labouring of his bruised throat. It was Adam who cried the news in a fashion they could understand. Llewelyn was out of the saddle with a spring, and shouting his orders before the words were off Adam's lips; and with swords and axes, with whatever tools they could find, they rushed to hack away the barricades that sealed the doors of the church.

The fire had died down while they fought, the veering wind turning back the flames to westward. The windows of the nave were out, threads of lead from the cames streaked the stonework, smoke blackened it; within, the charred remnants of beams still glowed. There the heat beat them back when they had the door stripped and essayed to enter, but they saw sky yawning at them where a part of the vault had fallen. The tower was a cooling shell, windowless, roofless. The fire must have reached the choir before its impetus slackened as the wind changed. But when they circled the

264

smoking hulk to the east end they saw the great lancets of the altar window intact, the stonework almost unstained; and the small door of the sacristy was whole and unmarked.

'Open here,' said Llewelyn, and Harry was the first to drive a chisel under the timbers and begin to prise out the long nails. Streaked with grime and stone-dust and blood he wrenched away the last obstacle, and finding the door locked and the key absent, went to work on it with an axe until he burst the lock and was flung forward into the sacristy.

The roof of the presbytery was blackened, and the air still quivered with heat, but not beyond what they could bear. They stripped off their helms and entered, hushed and fearful. Faint fronds of smoke coiled in the vault, and the smell of burning rolled over them from the choir, where the charred stalls were still outlined with a few glowing embers of the heat that had devoured them. But the flagged surface of the presbytery floor let them walk its stones unscorched, and the altar with its angelic choir stood immaculate and beautiful. Beneath it the yawning rectangle of darkness drew their eyes. In wonder and dread they approached, and fearfully they looked into the open grave.

In the bottom of the well of stone Benedetta lay upon velvet, her long hair like quenched fire about her head, a gold-embroidered altar-cloth over her like a coverlet. Her hands were thin and tranquil upon the bright, coiling flowers, her face was a shape of ivory skin drawn taut over the pure pattern of its gallant bones. Someone had carefully closed and weighted the great arched eyelids and composed with love and reverence the emaciated body. Her they knew, every man among them; they knew her even though she was no more than the half of the woman they had known.

But the golden shape that lay beside her, that had been lifted and moved to make room for her, who knew that? Man or woman? So slight, no taller than she, and she had not been tall. So long dead, for on the cloth of gold was traced faintly the fragile shape of the bones within. Buried with so much honour, like a prince or a cardinal, but with something humble and strange at his feet – a mason's mallet, a chisel, a fine punch, the common tools of the craft.

And black athwart their brightness, sudden and terrible as a descending angel, a long, dark shape plunged head-down between the two, his brow pressed into the crook of a golden arm, his wide sleeves spread like wings over the honoured sleepers. Long arms embraced them, binding all three together. On the gaunt fingers that folded them even in death with such an intensity of passion, the rings hung slack, dangling between swollen joints. Too weak to climb out of the grave when his work was done, thus he had fallen and thus he had died. The hands still agonised, clasping those two whom he had buried; but against the cleft heart in the golden shroud the old, proud head rested as gently as in sleep.

Not fire nor frost nor summer nor winter would ever again have any power to trouble those three, or set them at enmity.

The boy stood motionless and mute at the foot of the grave, his lashes low on his cheeks, staring in wonder and dread at the measure of his loss and the magnitude of his gain. He was still for so long that they began to fear for him, but no one ventured to touch him. Under the grime of dust and sweat and tears his pallor was extreme, but so was the calm that had come upon him. When he looked up it was to meet the prince's grave, considerate eyes, bent upon him from a courteous distance.

'You have close kin here,' said Llewelyn gently. 'Closer to you than to any.'

'Yes,' said Harry in a whisper. Was he speaking of one only, or of two of them? Or of all? For he had always been quick to follow the wanderings of his children's hearts, even when they themselves were lost.

'It is for you to order all things here as you would have them. We will so dispose as you see fit.'

The young head came up quickly then to devour the prince's face in a hungry green stare. He opened his lips to answer, and fell trembling.

'My lord, with respect – there's one in Castell Coch has a

better right. I would have her see,' he said, low-voiced, 'what we have seen.'

'That's well thought of, and like a dutiful son. Adam,' said Llewelyn, 'ride to Castell Coch and ask Mistress Gilleis if she will come to us here. Tell her there's a matter on which we wait to hear her pleasure. Say that by the grace of God we have found Master Harry's body.'

Gilleis came before the light was gone, pale and silent by Adam's side.

The chaos of the battle yet lingered below Parfois, the dead lay where they had fallen; but the prince was in William Isambard's lavish apartments by then, and William was in the chapel, on a trestle before the altar, washed and cleansed of the blood Harry had let him, with the death-pennies on his eyes. Gilleis passed by the battered tower of the lower guard without a glance, and picked her way through the litter of cast and broken harness and cast and broken bodies on the ramp. She saw nothing of all this. Her eyes looked inward, looked back. In life or in death, Harry's face had never been so clear to her as it was now. The old hates, the old loves rose in her bitterly like contending tides.

On the plateau Llewelyn was waiting, and young Harry came to her stirrup to lift her down. The sea-green eyes, the grave embrace went to her heart like wounds; since he had got that fierce, earnest, man's face on him there was no question whose son he was, body and spirit. He kissed her hand, and then her cheek, and brought her on his arm into the shell of the church of Parfois; and Adam fell back and let them go first and alone.

At the grave-side even Harry disengaged himself and stood apart from her. She looked into the stone pit, and drew breath deeply once as though she checked what might have been a cry; and then for a long time she was silent and still and pale, her eyes lowered to the two bright shapes, and the spread arms that covered them like a cross.

She saw the torchlight quiver upon the golden shroud, as though the dear bones it wrapped stirred for a moment to the

267

recollection of life, and would have risen to her. She saw the lean dark arm embracing his body, and the hand, the same hand that had swathed him in his royal winding-sheet, seemed to close its wasted fingers more jealously and tenderly upon his arm. All the agony, all the hate and the loving, the wrongs and the revenges, came down softly into this little space at the end.

She looked up at last, and across the open grave she saw her son's face, pale with passion, watching her. A long stride nearer the fullness of his inheritance than yesterday, and wanting something of her, and willing himself not to let his longing show in his eyes, for fear she should give for his sake what for her own she would have denied. Oh, Harry, she thought, show me what I am to do! I'm torn so many ways. But he would not. This she must resolve alone.

Nevertheless, the possessive pain that clamoured behind her still face fell shamed to silence as she gazed at him. The true impress, the single legacy, and hers, to give if not to keep. She had but to give him freely, and she could not lose or want for him. And was she, then, so poor that she could not give a little sleeping-space in Harry's ground to these who had good need of rest?

Must there still be banishment, and dividing, and ravishing of graves?

'Cover them over!' said Gilleis, and saw the warm flush of joy quicken in Harry's cheek, and the wild gratitude of love in his eyes.

'Cover them over. Let them rest.'

At the last moment, when the men of the rear-guard were stamping their chilled feet in the snow at the head of the ramp, and David was calling impatiently back to him from the bridge, he took his foot from the stirrup again and turned back to the tracing-house.

Half the ground of the outer ward was crazed with cracks now, and daily the small, unregarded crumbs of sandstone slid away softly into the ravine. It was high time to be gone. Another yard of the curtain wall had slithered away in the night; come the spring, Parfois would be given over to the crows.

High time to leave, and they were the last to go. The women had set off on their journey back to Aber on the fourth day of Christmas, with Adam to bear them company on the way, and the baggage trains of booty from Parfois trailing after them half a mile along the snow. Harry had ridden as far as the ford with them, to see them safe across, and kissed Aelis before them all at parting, to seal his rights in her. To tell the truth, he stood in some jealous awe of her now, she had grown so dangerously aware of her womanhood since she put up her hair beneath a wimple and took to wearing his mother's gowns. They were close and confident, those two, they tended to catch each other's eye and smile over him when they thought he was not attending – or, more daunting by far, when they knew very well he was. He would have to mind his interests with them, or they would compound together to have the whip hand of him.

Two days after the departure of the princess and her retinue, the disarmed garrison had marched out of Parfois, with what they stood in, their personal goods, and a sparing allowance of stores. The best of their horses and hawks and hounds, and all their military gear, were forfeit to the conquerors, but they were happy enough to be allowed to take their lives and their freedom in their hands, and pledge their word to stand no more in arms against Llewelyn. Some had gone to Fleace, with courteous letters from the prince of Aberffraw to Humphrey Paunton, acquainting him with the manner of the death and burial of his lord, so that in due course the news might be laid in proper form before King Henry. Some had set out for Erington, on the border of Herefordshire. Isambard's wide and scattered honour fell now to his elder son Gilles, in Normandy, if the king saw fit to grant his title, but after the trouble Richard Marshall had cost him he would be chary of admitting another Norman-bred magnate and vassal of the king of France to such a position of power in England. Let them fight it out how they would, Ralf Isambard slept no less soundly.

And yet a great line was passing here, and he, Harry Talvace, had lopped the last branch from that formidable tree. The pomp of the world seemed empty and ephemeral enough in depopulated Parfois after the garrison was gone.

And after the vanquished, the victors. They left on the eve of the New Year, the prince and all his captains, hot towards Breidden in arms, leaving David to bring the rearguard after. The whole border lay open to them for plunder, for on the day after Christmas the earl marshal had beaten John of Monmouth out and out in a pitched battle, close to the town from which he took his name, and there was no royal army active in the field now to stand between the king's enemies and the king's quaking subjects along the march.

'Leave the lad Herefordshire,' Llewelyn had said largely when the dispatches reached him, 'he's earned it. We'll go north and east and have the heart out of Shropshire. Rising nineteen years since Benedetta came galloping after me to the gates of Shrewsbury, Harry, and brought me you for my pains. I have a fancy to knock at their doors again, even if it cost me another such penance.'

And he had ridden blithely but purposefully to his reiving; and God help the villagers under the Breidden, and the uneasy burghers of Shrewsbury, for war was a killing thing. It had killed Parfois. Even if Gilles came, even if he essayed to rebuild this shattered fortress, the venture could not prosper. The rock was riven and the heart was still. The man was dead who had been the spirit of Parfois, dead and buried beneath the altar of his own church with his love and his love's love, with his dark deeds and his bright; that book let God decipher, none other had the right. His arch-enemy had had masses said over him, and his most irreconcilable prisoner had prayed passionately peace to his soul.

And now they were going, the last companies, David's clansmen eager and fierce after their prey, David himself not loath, for he had a border to consolidate, and to force acknowledgement of it with terror now was to hold it the more firmly hereafter. The last hoofbeats had left the hollow-ringing field of the bridge, and hushed in the snow of the plateau. Only Harry Talvace still lingered, the last to leave the shaken ground of his four-year captivity.

The silence fell about him like a muffling cloak, curtaining him from the world. The early, angry light of a January morning, shot with slanting red gleams of sun from beneath hanging cloud, edged the merlons of the wall with scarlet. The door of the Warden's Tower, the ports of armoury and mews and stables, stood open upon emptiness. No one moving, no voice where there had been so many voices, not even a dog left to bring life back to mind; only he, Harry Talvace, crossing the seamed and rotting ground softly, with breath hushed in awe of the silence, pushing open the dragging door of the tracing-house across a cracked, uneven floor, standing on the threshold of the forsaken room and staring round him upon the long tracing-tables where Master Harry had pieced out his ambitious plans, and the bench where he had marshalled punches and chisels to hand and sketched out his ideas in stone. The fruit of his labour they had defaced with fire, but they could not destroy it.

Harry stood and gazed, and the room was full of echoes, quick and piercing in his heart: 'Not his match! Have you not the heart in you to be anything but best? How many are his match?' And how significantly now, how poignantly: 'The dispensations of God are always just. We get the sons we deserve.' Why had he so often failed to hear or understand the things that were said to him?

Recollection drew for him the outline of the erect and fleshless shoulders, the poised head, the shadowed, oblique smile against the window, and quickened the voice again to the old tormenting sweetness. Here he had first been offered his father's tools, and the fragmentary stones he had left behind him at his untimely death. Here he had been schooled hard to work ungoaded under provocation, and learned even that lesson at last. And if the work he had done could not match, would never match, his father's achievement, had he not the heart in him to be anything but best? They should see that he had, that he knew how to

271

serve humbly and faithfully where he deserved.

Looking back now in amazement at those four years he could not feel that he had been unhappy; and that was strange enough, after all his agonizing. But stranger far it was to look calmly upon the long fretting and scheming and struggling after liberty, and be unable now to recapture the sense of having been a prisoner.

He crossed the room silently to the bench he had been allowed to use as his own; and there in the corner, thrust back against the wall, was the sketch Master Harry had made in stone for the last head he ever set in the triforium of the church of Parfois. Harry had taken it to be a final self-portrait. But Isambard had known better: 'This is no signature at the end, but a prophecy at the beginning. Do you not know yourself?'

He had not known himself, but he had believed; even then, even then, with his will or against his will, he had trusted Isambard to know truth and tell him truth. He did not know himself even now, the head still daunted, bewildered, excited him with its promise and its clarity; but still he believed. There was yet some way to go, but he had set his feet on the road to that identity, and he would reach it all in good time.

Strangely wonderful he had thought himself, fondling the planes of that young head, strangely wonderful, and a terrible responsibility. He closed his hands upon it again, and the same passionate pride and humility gathered molten about his heart.

He took the large cloth in which Master Edmund had been wont to roll his parchments, and wrapped the head in it hastily, sure that David would be losing patience by now and sending someone back for him. The bundle was small but heavy; they'd think him mad for loading Barbarossa with twenty extra pounds, when they had some hard riding to do. No matter, he would not leave it here.

He cast one last quick glance about the room, knowing he might never see it again, and then he went out with his precious prize under his arm, and drew the door to after him; and there was Owen just lighting down beside Barbarossa, and tossing the reins on his horse's neck.

'The devil, Harry, what ails you to be mooning here still? What were you at? David's off without us.'

'We'll overtake him,' said Harry, stowing his unwieldy bundle hastily away in the saddle-bag, where it hung heavily and clumsily, and Barbarossa shifted indignantly at the heft of it. 'I just thought of something I'd liefer not leave here.'

'Stir then, man, and let's be after them. We'll be well out of here,' said Owen, eyes roving the derelict stones that sagged towards the ravine. 'Come the thaw, half this headland will crumble away. I'd sooner not be too close to Parfois then.'

Harry mounted and spurred for the narrow timbers of the bridge, delivered now of his need to look back. The past was resolved, the future he had swinging at his saddle-bow. As soon as they were off the bridge and trotting across the plateau towards the trees Owen drew alongside, and leaned to prod curiously at the bundle.

'What is it you've got there?' He clapped a hand to the bag and exclaimed at the weight, punched it and cursed tenderly over his bruised fist. 'Dear heaven, what have you loaded the poor beast with? Stone? What can you want with such a lump? There's stone everywhere, must you carry it with you on the march?'

'It's a design of my father's,' said Harry placatingly, giving the husk and keeping the heart of his own counsel. 'I thought some day I might manage to copy it.'

EPILOGUE

Parfois: *July* 1234

After six months he rode that way again.

They were retracing their steps from the great meeting at Myddle, from the signing of the triumphant peace that had crowned Llewelyn's achievement and set the seal on his life-work. Richard Marshall's war was lost and won, and his brief, splendid and tempestuous life, strange for a man who had desired only order and justice, had ended in the hour of his victory. A greater prelate than Winchester, and a better, had put Winchester from power; a sounder order than even the efficient des Rivaulx could impose had dispensed with des Rivaulx's expert services. England, by and large, had its dour and sensible will; and Wales had the confirmation of all its conquests, peace within its borders, respect without. No wonder David took his retinue home to Aber in high spirits.

They rode by way of Knockin. From Parfois to the very walls of Shrewsbury they had burned and killed and plundered, and nowhere with greater slaughter than here, about the ditches of this battered castle. That had happened in January; and now in July half the fields lay untilled for want of men to do the work, and the women laboured desolately into the dark to raise a little food for their children. Meeting the eyes of the widows of Knockin, Harry was not proud of himself. Well, he had learned hard, perhaps, but he had learned throughly; he knew now what it was in him to do.

A whole chapter of a chronicle had been written in the march since that January campaign. So well had it run, so securely had they established themselves as masters of the border, that Earl Richard had felt his position in Wales to be safe, and taken himself off to Ireland, to retrieve the castles the king's men had purloined from him in Leinster. He had left Hubert de Burgh with Basset and Siward in command at Striguil, and sailed for Leinster early in February. And that same month Edmund of Abingdon, treasurer of Salisbury, had received the royal confirmation of his election to the vacant archbishopric of Canterbury, and attended the great council.

What did Henry think now of his new saint? Had he given him his voice willingly, or sullenly and grudgingly for want of the courage to resist? For Edmund Rich had begun his primacy, before ever he was installed, by leading the bishops in a demand for the dismissal of Henry's hated ministers, and a return to the rule of law and charter. Henry had wriggled and quibbled and pleaded for time; but they had carried their point in principle, and sent the bishops of Lichfield and Rochester to the border at once, to sound out Llewelyn with a view to conciliation and peace. They had found no difficulty there: he was willing and ready, since it seemed the chief point at issue was as good as conceded. After the necessary to-ing and fro-ing over terms they had agreed upon a truce at the end of March, and arranged to meet and effect a permanent settlement on the second of May.

Armed with such a tactical success, fortified by this manifest forbearance and good will on the part of a prince who might very well have exploited his advantage by holding out for steeper terms, Archbishop Edmund had come to the April council with all the bishops of the province of Canterbury solidly at his back, but for the lone wolf Winchester whom they were bent on pulling down. Henry could no longer protect his favourites without risking injury to himself, and he never went so far or so fast that he could not stop short of that. Rumour said he had taken Winchester and des Rivaulx and Segrave into monastic retirement with him for a while after the February council, sure sign, by token of his usage of de Burgh, that they could look for nothing good from him once it became advisable in his own interest to abandon them. However that might be, he had announced their dismissal when the bishops pressed him, and promised reform, a return to the constitution, all that was demanded of him. Not knowing then, for no one in England yet knew, that his enemy was already on his death-bed.

For Earl Richard had allowed himself to be persuaded to a meeting with the king's men on the meads of Kildare on the first day of April, and somehow, no one knew how or by what hand, he had been set upon with swords and fatally wounded. Treachery, some said, and involving the highest. Others put it down to a flare of temper when the argument ran high, for Richard would have his castles back, and there were those who had no mind to let go what they had taken. However it was, Richard Marshall was carried from the Curragh to a bed he never left again, and after two weeks he was dead. Dead with victory and reform and honour in his grasp, that fine, high-minded man who had never willed to make war on his king.

The news had come like a thunderclap in England, shaking men to the hearts, and not least King Henry himself. Had he truly lent his countenance secretly to the earl's murder? Or had des Roches and his close companions taken the act upon themselves, and brought the suspicion of complicity unjustly upon the king? Whatever the truth of it, he had made frantic haste to cover and deliver himself by turning like a tiger upon his ministers. Until then it had seemed that they might be allowed to withdraw without undue disgrace, but now for a time they tasted what they had visited upon de Burgh, hunted from place to place, denounced and proscribed, until the bishops who had brought about their downfall stood between them and their sovereign frantic with his own righteousness, and lent them a hand to rise. Commissions sat to hear complaints against them, investigators searched out every detail of their conduct in office, and checked every penny they had handled. De Burgh had his revenge.

Howbeit, the earl marshal was dead. And Llewelyn, when he heard the news, had declined to proceed with the May meeting. He was gone who should have been the negotiator for the English confederacy; until all his adherents should receive satisfactory terms of peace Llewelyn would accept none. And the protection he extended to them in this act had been effective enough to hasten a general conciliation. May had seen Gilbert, the new earl marshal, granted safe-conducts for himself and his brothers, for de Burgh and Basset and Siward and all the other confederates, to come to the council at Gloucester under the archbishop's protection and seek the king's grace. Pardoned, their outlawry declared illegal, their lands restored, themselves admitted again to favour, some even to office, they had good cause to be thankful for so formidable and faithful an ally as the prince of Aberffraw.

'He would have laughed himself sore,' said Harry suddenly, concluding aloud the sequence of thought he had been following in silence, 'could he have seen how it all ended.'

'He?' said David absently, and flashed an inquiring glance at his young foster-brother, only to snatch it back again in haste as he recollected who 'he' must be. 'What, with de Burgh admitted to the council again, and Winchester and des Rivaulx down where they kicked de Burgh? And the prince my father riding to the rescue of his oldest enemy, and keeping his vow to take and destroy his Parfois none the less – yes, a man might find a kind of laughter there, I suppose, if he had the heart. And I always heard he was de Burgh's man.'

'He had the heart,' said Harry roundly. 'And he was his own man, and no other's.'

'But the cream of the joke,' said Owen, 'is that if this French Isambard you speak of does come to claim his English honour, Parfois is one castle he must do without. By the terms of the agreement he can't rebuild.'

And that was true: Parfois had its death-wound from them. The agreement Llewelyn had signed at Myddle, with the archbishop himself in attendance, had as its ground adherence to the state of things at the outbreak of Earl Richard's war. Every party kept what he had in his possession then, however recently conquered; Builth and Cardigan remained in the hold of the princes of Gwynedd, and that was no mean gain. But no new castles were to be built, no ruined ones restored. Good-bye, Parfois! And most appropriate, perhaps, that it should not outlive Ralf Isambard.

For two years only that truce was sealed; but by consent it could be renewed year by year thereafter; and who would venture to try and take Builth or Cardigan from between the paws of the lion now? Llewelyn had shown England once for all who was master along the march as long as he lived, and done all man could to ensure that David should be regarded with the same awe and respect thereafter. Under the castle of Myddle, among the bright pavilions spread on the summer meads, they had seen the apotheosis of Gwynedd, and surely, surely, the true conception of a princedom of Wales. It remained only to bring it safely to birth, and that was for the statesmen, not the soldiers.

'My lord – ' said Harry, clearing his throat gruffly upon the declaration he had been nursing ever since they left Myddle; and flushed and hesitated at the stilted sound of this address, when there was no one within earshot but the three of them.

'My lord!' David mocked him gaily and gently. He was happy in the summer and the fair weather, and their triumphant achievement, and even in his ceremonial finery, and the pleasure of riding light, without the cumbrous casings of steel. He was in no mood to be grave, but with all his heart he could be kind.

'I've had it on my mind,' said Harry, his solemnity unshaken, 'to speak to you about my future, now that we have peace and, God willing, hope to have it for years to come. Your inheritance is secure now. If ever you should need to call me to you again, you know I'll come with all my heart. But while you're not in need, I ask you to let me from your side to my own craft.'

He could not say outright the thing that most troubled him, the dismay he felt at the price even of this victory, the burned villages, the scattered corpses, the slaughtered cattle, the fields unploughed that should have been golden, the earth desolate that should have been yielding generously. Born English and raised Welsh, his heart and mind fought on both sides. How could he shed Welsh blood or English, and not feel himself bleed? But there was more to it even than that. The denial of life, the frustration of fruitfulness, affronted the deepest instinct in him. He could not be a breaker, it was against his bent.

'Your own craft?' said David, astonished and laughing. 'The times I've heard Adam trying to drive you to your tools, when you were a lad in Aber, and you slipping away the minute his back was turned to run to the tilting. And as apt as you were at it, too! What's come to you suddenly?'

'It's not so sudden. That was long ago, and I've been working with Isambard's master-mason in Parfois since then. And I've seen my father's work. That's enough to set a man off after him. I could not ask to leave you while this war was on our hands. But I've seen now what I want. A career in arms is very well,' said Harry sturdily, 'but I can't find my satisfaction this way. I'm a stonemason, like my father before me, and that's what I mean to be. If you'll give me your good word?'

'My good word you have, whatever you choose to do, Hal, surely you know it. And Adam will be happy to have you broken to harness at last. And yet it's a pity,' said David regretfully. 'You quit yourself so well at Parfois. You should have heard how the prince commended you when you were not by. Have you told him what you intend?'

'Yes, my lord, before we rode. He said I must broach it to you. And he said I should do whatever I must for my heart's content, and so long as I did it with my might I had his blessing. But you're my prince and my brother, and I'd fain have yours, too.'

'Could I refuse it to you?' said David heartily. 'You do as your heart needs, and never fret. Good swordsmanship's never wasted, even on a stonemason.'

'Then hear me one more request.' He had paled a little with the intensity of his desire. 'May I ride south, where the roads meet, and go down to Parfois? I'll not linger, I promise you. I want only to see it this once more. Before you reach Oswestry I'll be with you again.'

Owen opened his lips to offer to go with him, and closed them again with the offer still unmade. He knew when Harry willed to be alone. So at the crossroads at Knockin they parted, Harry riding south towards Breidden, and his brothers north towards Oswestry, with their retinue behind them. The mason rode unattended, and that was fitting, too. Adam had said long ago that it was time he faced his own estate.

This was the countryside they had torn to pieces on their way to Shrewsbury, and the wreckage still stood stark to challenge him wherever he turned his eyes. In the villages they had crept back to the ruin of their homes, those who survived, they had even built themselves brush hovels to tide them through the kinder summer, and were building hard at better shelters against the winter to come. So much destruction, so much suffering, so much waste, all affronts to the passion of affirmation he felt within him, the urge he had towards life, and joy, and creation, and fulfilment. Let there be no more such campaigns! Let them keep these houses, and reclaim these wasted fields! Let them get new sons, and win the derelict earth to bear again! The doggedness with which they had taken up the threads of living was itself a reassurance. They were men, they could not be downed so easily.

He crossed the river at Buttington, a summer river now green with weed, white with floating crowfoot, smiling and drowsy. He came along the riverside path by the mill, he passed the ruined assart, the cords of his memory knotting into a momentary congestion of pain. He rode beneath the cliff of Parfois, and there on a sudden the path was stopped. Rock and masonry together blocked his way. He took to the woods close beside the water, and made his way laboriously round the obstacle, the lie of the land still hiding the heights from him. Only when he reached the green slopes beneath the path that climbed to the ramp could he look up for the crenellated crests of wall and tower against the sky, and see the light filtering through the ravine that separated castle from church.

His heart turned and cried in him, torn between grief and exaltation, so sudden and violent was the vision he had of the passing of the world's power and glory. The mighty of the march were fallen indeed. The ravine showed no lance of light transfixing its shadowy spaces; the sudden thaws and rotting snows of February had crumbled away the misused rock from under the wall until the shattered ground could no longer hold up the vast weight it bore, and yard by yard, stone by stone, the curtain wall had cracked and slid and heeled away, silting down into the ravine to fill up the shallower place beneath the bridge, and gradually spreading to shed fringes of rubble and rock from either end down the cliffs below. The bridge had slid with the rest, but only to settle harmlessly, uselessly, a few feet below its old level. A man could walk up the ramp now and cross into Parfois without need of bridges. Into what was left of Parfois!

And the destruction could not end there, for between the subsiding bulk above and the overburdened foundations below the rock would have no rest. The balance and tension that held up all had been disrupted, and the ruin they had begun could not be halted. Time and weather would fret stone from stone, seeds would settle among the lurching staircases and cracking floors, and grow to saplings, bursting the walls apart. Young oaks would grow and root in Isambard's great chamber, and ravens nest in the jagged bones of the King's Tower. Fifty years, and Parfois would be no more than a name clinging to a desolation, a levelled place where once there had been a great rock and a great house.

The Warden's Tower was down, and had flung its huge head clean across the gully in dying, and buried its stone forehead deep in the grassy level of the plateau. The tracing-house was down, with all that had clung close to this southern expanse of the curtain wall. The constant shocks had even shaken away the edges of the plateau, there were torn-out trees lying among the rubble below. For the thick summer leafage on those that remained he could not see even

281

the tower of the church from where he stood. In dread and awe, with the silence and the desolation closing cold about his heart, he turned Barbarossa and began to mount the path.

At the sharp bend where the ramp began he saw, and for a moment could not persuade his doubting brain that he had really seen, the cart-tracks driven deep into the soft grass of summer. Why should there be traffic of carts here now, with no hungry household to feed and supply? Someone cutting and carrying away wood? He saw no great sign of timber's having been carried; there were usually axe-chips or dust to be found where the reivers had been. Brushings for firing? In the middle of summer? No one could be so forward and provident in these bereaved villages, where every surviving man's labour was claimed over and over for the mere necessities of the day. Yet the ruts in the bruised grass climbed with him. They were not new, they had worn through the turf in places and bared the soil and the stone. Carts heavily laden; and he guessed now with what merchandise. It was not wind and weather and frost and thaw only that had helped to bring down the walls of Parfois.

The solitary tower of the lower guard, battered to the ground during the siege, lay in a litter of rubble and mortar in the grass grown tall and seeding whitely beside the path. Very slight, those few scattered piles of stone, to be the remains of such a massive strongpoint. The outline of the new tower was lost in the growth of brambles and vetches. The worked stone of the barricades, dressed for building, had vanished clean.

He came to the crest of the ramp, where the trees fell away, and halted with breath caught hard in his throat to stop a cry. The Warden's Tower had flung its hard skull far in dying. The gutted tower of the church had received that impact at its roots, and fallen westward upon the vault of the nave, crushing it. The shaft of gold, the stem of the holy tree, was broken. All that tapering, soaring subtlety of beauty, fluted with quivering tensions of light and shadow, withdrawing stage by stage in charmed proportion and

282

drawing the eyes and the heart after it – all lost, all defaced for ever, past recovery now. The great vault fallen with the tower, the west window, with its harp-strings of deep mould-ing in which the light played such threnodies, standing stark over a chaos of shattered stone.

He dropped from the saddle in frantic haste, as though his hands dreamed for a moment that rescue was possible. He clambered through the beautiful ecstatic arches of the nave, touching and fondling and near to weeping, but that the dismay that opened within his heart was like a well of darkness, too deep and awful for tears. He flung himself on his knees at the foot of Master Harry's grave, above which the vault of the presbytery still soared undamaged, and the nine several images of Owen in childhood still inclined their seraphic heads over their psalters and instruments, and sang and played to the glory of God.

But to what end? To what end, if this was all? The prayer he had begun died in his throat, sticking fast to choking.

It takes, then, so short a time for castles and churches to fall to ruin, once men have withdrawn from them. How much of his father's master-work had the carts carried away already? If his eyes had been open he would have seen the manifest traces. Castle and church together they were helping to bring down, and steadily pilfering stone from both. Every village within ten miles must be privy to the quiet dismemberment. Everything they had had they had lost in the winter campaign, burned and razed and slaughtered; and here for the carting was a vast supply of ready-cut stone to their hands, to build new homes, sheep-folds, yards, byres, barns, all that they needed. When they had used what lay on the ground, they would bring down the rest after it. With no Isambard in Parfois, who was to re-strain them? It would take time to complete the undoing, but given ten years, or twenty, they would have erased all. All dissipated, all lost, all his father's work, passed clean out of mind as though it had never been. Is creation no more durable than destruction, after all? Is this the end, not only of the breakers, but of the makers, too? Then to what end is any effort or any passion?

He came back to Barbarossa with a set and stony face, bleak as winter in the rich, soft sunlight. He mounted and turned from the church of Parfois with averted face, and rode down the ramp without looking back. Did it alter the value of the work, that men destroyed it? Was it less valid because it was unrecognised and misused? But was there *nothing* remaining? Not one echo after such music?

He had no wish to return by the same way, to see again the desolation above him against the sky. He turned instead towards Leighton, to cross the river by the ford at Pool, and take the road north for Oswestry after his brothers.

Now that he was ready to see them, his eyes began to pick out everywhere the stolen bones of Parfois. Threading the village, he saw them built, massy and incongruous, into the rising walls of new cottages. Master Harry's stone from the quarry in Bryn was unmistakable with the sun on it, waking the soft gold that slept within the clear, warm grey. Here and there he caught that gleam, and the jealous ache in his heart gnawed afresh at every reminder; until at the end of the village he was suddenly brought up short by a small shock of wonder, and stood at gaze, his resolute despair for the first time a little shaken.

The smith of Leighton had crowned the yard-posts of his toft with two small capitals; the crudely-built but not ill-proportioned pillars burst at the top into twin clusters of radiant, living leaves, the same that had held up the vault of Isambard's chantry chapel. And was it after all so absolute a violation? If he had not seen in them something that took him by the heart, would he have carted them all this way and gone to the labour to set them up there, where they had no function but to delight?

He rode on, slowly and thoughtfully, questioning his own heart no less than their actions. The byre-wall of the farm beyond was crested with the moulded stones of the string-courses from the tower; and there at the gate they had set up a segment of a clustered pillar to seal the end of the wall. Wasted? Desecrated? Lost? What Parfois had lost someone

284

humbler had found.

Harry's heart revived, mistrustfully yet, and against his will; his love was sore in him, and he grudged them their scattered morsels of what should have been whole and all men's, and was hot against them for the disintegration with which, however unwittingly and under whatever pressure, they had leagued themselves. The poor ravished stones shone in the sun, golden as fallen ears of grain. He came down towards the river bank still at odds with his own doubt, though the youth in him ached with its willingness to be comforted.

The beds of osiers, just beginning to redden, flushed along the edge of the river below the ford. There was a tumble-down hut there where a weaver plied his craft; white, peeled wands lay piled to hand in the grass, and the frame of a coracle was pegged down to the ground beside them, half the light shell of basketry already filled in. Through the doorless opening half-turned away from the river he could see the stacked osiers within, and five or six long, narrow eel-grigs shining with newness; but the sound that pricked his ears came strangely from such a workshop.

Busy and absorbed and content, the steady tap-tapping of metal and stone. What need had they of hammers in an osier-weaver's hut? They prided themselves on securing whatever must be secured with withies. For pure curiosity, and because that diligent pecking caught so intimately at his own tender memory, Harry lighted down from Barbarossa's back, and slipped soundlessly into the hut.

A lean, wild boy, not more than eleven or twelve years old, was bending engrossed over something he had propped upon a rough wooden block in the light from the vacant window. His shock-head was stooped over it lovingly; for the neglected coracle he cared not at all.

When Harry's foot stirred the osiers the boy gave a whimper of fright, and span round with an arm thrown up to protect his head. The hand had a flat, heavy pebble in it; its fellow grasped a long iron nail.

'Easy, easy!' said Harry mildly. 'I'm neither the devil

nor your master, I mean you no harm.'

A pinched brown face peered up at him distrustfully from under the fell of dark hair. The child was used to blows, and expected them from every quarter, but his sharp eyes had more than fear in them, a desperate and devoted bravery. He kept his wiry little body between Harry and whatever it was he cherished there in his private place; and he kept his hold on the strange objects which were clearly not meant to serve him as weapons.

'What have you there?' said Harry, roused and curious.

'It's mine.' The boy spread his arms defensively, a spark kindling in his dark eyes. 'I brought it here myself. It's not stealing. If they can take them, why shouldn't I?'

Harry put down a hand and moved him gently aside by the shoulder; and at the touch a brighter boldness eased the boy's face, and he stood calmly, no longer trying to hide his treasure. Those he had need to fight shy of had another way of handling him. He resented being watched and interrupted, but he had nothing to fear, and if he made no show of concern the interloper would go away the sooner.

A block of Master Harry's yellow stone – with those puny arms, how had the child ever conveyed it here? – stood upon the uneven stump of a tree. The others had spent their fondness on carved stones, this child on one yet to be carved. Stone and nail were for mallet and punch. Who had even taught him the manner of tool he needed, or how to set about the shaping of such an intractable material? The small, grimy hands made the best of their clumsy instruments, held them with conviction and passion. And propped on the stacked osiers beneath which, most likely, he hid all these things from his elders and natural enemies, was a broken fragment of one of the corbels from the south aisle, a curving branch, a countryman's sly head, the muzzle of a braced hound pointing game.

He had begun by copying it, crudely but vividly; and then on the tilt of the poacher's cautious face the sculptor's ambitious hand had itched, his imagination had taken fire. The man who had crouched still burst out of the bushes, the hound leaped. Botched, clumsy but alive, they broke cover to course the quarry, and there was glee in them, and devilment, even though they had the scrawled drawing of a child. With a stone and a nail, dear heaven! And no one belonging to him, likely, no one within a mile of him, who would not clout him for it and toss the rubbish into the river if they caught him at it. But he had found something he would not easily let go. His fierce face spoke for him, his charged eyes and purposeful hand. He had discovered a well of fire within himself, he would not let it be quenched.

'Who showed you,' said Harry, 'how to do this?'

'Nobody. I tried. I looked at that one, and tried.'

'And had you seen such before?'

'Not like these! Have you been there? There are faces there! Alive, like my mother. I never saw such. I couldn't take them, but I found this in the grass under the wall, and hid it. Would you think there could be trees, and animals, and men in the stone?'

'There can be anything in the stone,' said Harry. 'All the creatures of God. Who knows it better than you? Two of them you've loosed there that never had life before.'

'I wanted to make such things myself,' said the boy. 'I'll make more yet,' he said, 'and better,' and set his dour young face like stone.

'If you want it enough, you'll make them. Creatures as alive as your mother, and churches like that great church.' And, by God, thought Harry, drinking deeply of a wellspring of revelation and gratitude and joy, he well might, he has the passion in him, and he has a true eye and a daring hand. 'God prosper the work to you,' he said, and turned back into the sunshine with a lightening heart.

The child watched him mount and ride, burning eyes remotely gratified but still aloof and self-sufficient. Had Harry carried any tools about him, he would have given them to him gladly, but he was in his finery and had nothing to give, and indeed this single and possessed heart needed nothing from him, not even encouragement. Where he was going, there he would go, and nothing would halt him or turn him

287

back. A torch lit from one spark of that communicable fire scattered now so widely, a green shoot from the fallen scarlet seed of Master Harry's blood and life and passion, the indestructible seed with which all this countryside was sown.

And he only the first fruits of the harvest.

Harry tightened his knees upon Barbarossa's glossy barrel, and plashed forward into the shallows of the ford. Swimming in midstream, the filigree rafts of water-crowfoot dimpled and swayed as he passed, and all the small white flowers shivered on their delicate stems. The sun upon his face warmed him through to the heart; and deep within him he felt the dead stirring, all those dead of whose sowing he was the living harvest.

The thought did not daunt him, his spirit rose to it, truculent and gleeful. In Aber Aelis was waiting for him, and the tools of his chosen craft, a good craft, his father's craft, worth any man's while.

Placid and green the Welsh shore invîted him. Behind him the small, stubborn, constant bell had resumed its indomitable chiming.